Praise for
THE TALES OF NEDAO
by Ru Emerson ...

"A fascinating addition to the genre's ranks."
— Dragon Magazine

TO THE HAUNTED MOUNTAINS

"Refreshing ... a believable world!" —OtherRealms

"Ru Emerson has a deft and confident knowledge of both the geography of her world, and the more subtle inner terrain of her characters' emotions."
— Megan Lindholm, author of The Reindeer People

IN THE CAVES OF EXILE

"There is sorcery, bravery, evil, love and hatred ... Action-packed from the very first page!" —Rave Reviews

"Ru Emerson has a talent for tight plotting and strong characterization."
— Charles de Lint, author of Jack, The Giant-Killer

ON THE SEAS OF DESTINY

"Each of her books opens new territory for me, and takes me down unexpected trails ... I specially set aside one weekend to read On the Seas of Destiny because I knew I wouldn't be able to set it aside, and I was not disappointed!" —Mercedes Lackey, author of The Heralds of Valdemar series

"Emerson's distinct and refreshing style easily earmarks her as an author to watch—and read!"
— Jennifer Roberson, author of the Cheysuli series

Ace Books by Ru Emerson

THE PRINCESS OF FLAMES
SPELL BOUND

The *Tales of Nedao* Trilogy

TO THE HAUNTED MOUNTAINS
IN THE CAVES OF EXILE
ON THE SEAS OF DESTINY

The *Night-Threads* Trilogy

THE CALLING OF THE THREE

RU EMERSON
NIGHT-THREADS

BOOK ONE:
THE CALLING OF THE THREE

ACE BOOKS, NEW YORK

This book is an Ace original edition,
and has never been previously published.

THE CALLING OF THE THREE

An Ace Book / published by arrangement with
the author

PRINTING HISTORY
Ace edition / October 1990

ISBN: 0-441-58085-8

Ace Books are published by The Berkley Publishing Group,
200 Madison Avenue, New York, New York 10016.
The name ''ACE'' and the ''A'' logo
are trademarks belonging to Charter Communications, Inc.

PRINTED IN THE UNITED STATES OF AMERICA

10 9 8 7 6 5 4 3 2 1

FOR DOUG

And to Bob, with ''fond'' memories of 4:00 A.M., Selectrics, scissors and tape

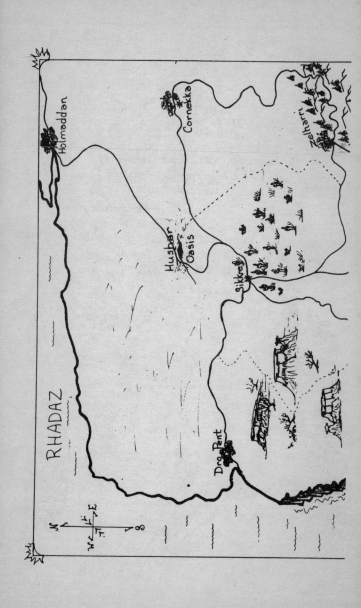

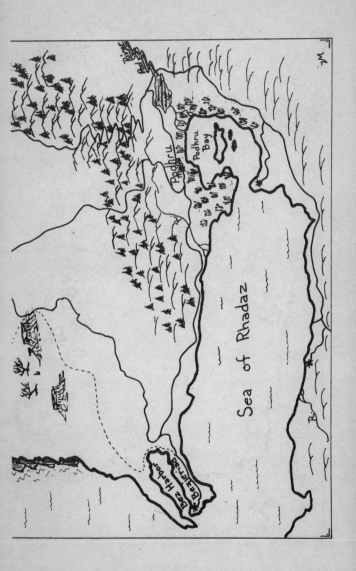

i

⚞

AMONG the lands east of the Herdyun Sea, the greatest in size is Rhadaz; so vast the distances between its borders that a man astride the swiftest mare could not cross from the coastal marshes of Dro Pent to the mountain-locked dells of Fahlia in the southeast in fewer than six days. So vast and unwieldy Rhadaz, with all its varied lands and peoples, that the great-great-great-grandfather of the present Emperor, Shesseran IX, divided Rhadaz into nine Duchies and gave control of these smaller kingdoms to his nine nearest friends, who founded the Nine Households from which the Dukedoms all descend to this day. Shesseran IX of course continued to take his taxes and such other levies of goods and men as necessary; the Dukes were accountable to him for following Rhadazi customs, for keeping the fests and holy days, for maintaining the standards set by the Emperor. But Shesseran left actual governing in the hands of his friends. He sent no special auditors, observers or spies to watch openly or in secret. He kept strict control thereafter of only his own massive estates and the surrounding game preserves composing the Duchy of Andar Perigha—and, of course, his capital city and chief port, Podhru.

Shesseran IX was widely criticized for having entrusted so much of Rhadaz to mere friends and not kindred—but he was a shrewd man and knew not only who was most loyal to him, but how to secure that loyalty: All Rhadaz prospered under the Duchy system, from the merchants of Sikkre to the Zelharri woodcrafters, even to the meanest herders and nomad tribes of outermost Dro Pent and Holmaddan and Genna.

In Shesseran XI's time, the Duchies were reconfirmed to the descendants of the original nine friends, and the inheritance con-

firmed bloodline. The Emperor preserved his right to interfere
in the internal workings of those Duchies but the grandson of
Shesseran IX interfered even less in Duchy business than had
his grandsire. He had, after all, more than enough matters to
occupy his time and talents just managing his estates and preserves. And Podhru had become the richest and greatest trading
port anywhere on the eastern seaboard.

Shesseran XIV—Shesseran the Golden—inherited wealth and
power greater than that of all his forebears together. More importantly, he had his forefathers' shrewd understanding of trade
and the increasingly complex politics inherent to the Herdyun
Sea trade routes, and the patience to deal with them.

It is held that Shesseran XIV made only two serious errors in
judgment during his long reign, and those were near its end,
when ill health and age began to increasingly influence his decisions. He had turned recently to religion, spending increasing
amounts of time and vast sums of money on festivals and galas
for Podhru's motley blend of gods—perhaps hoping they could
cure his ills on earth, or possibly to ensure his welcome beyond
it. He left negotiations for trading pacts to his advisors so he
would have more time for the artists, poets and musicians who
cluttered his court; for celebrations and plays. He no longer
hunted, but pursued a lifelong interest in the breeding of game
and the tame herds on his estates. This left little time for anything outside Andar Perigha, but then, Shesseran the Golden
cared for little outside his city, his household and his preserves,
particularly so long as everything outside that world functioned
quietly and well.

He maintained the trust of his many-times great-grandfather
in his Dukes, but with less cause. The men who ruled the nine
little kingdoms no longer held immediate gratitude to the Emperor for what had so long been theirs, and their primary concerns were their own well-being, their own households and
families, their own pockets. And there was not one of them who
did not know how great the cause would need to be for Shesseran to interfere in Duchy matters.

The Emperor's second error was held to be his relaxation of
the five-hundred-year-old prohibition against Hell-Light and its
Light-Shaping Triads. Shesseran had not intentionally permitted
the return of Shapers, even though it had been so many years
since the rise of Hell-Light and the resulting civil war. Somehow, Shapers had been included among other priests when the

bill was presented to the Emperor, listing religions and cults that would no longer be actively persecuted.

It seemed unnecessary to fret over Hell-Light, after so many hundreds of years: Shapers were few, Triads extremely rare. But several major trading families and at least two nobles breathed relieved sighs that they would no longer need to hide household magicians who touched on Hell-Light. Certain nobles, however, kept Triads and prudently kept them still secret. One never knew, after all.

It is also held that Shesseran the Golden suffered only three reversals of luck in his fortune-blessed reign. The first was the invasion of Podhru Harbor by Lasanach raiders and the simultaneous attack on distant, northern Dro Pent that cut its trade lines with the Gyn Hort nomads; the second, that two Lasanachi died suddenly and woundless within Dro Pent walls. The plague they carried decimated six-tenths of the townspeople. Worse still: Even after the Empiric Navy and a rough fleet of Bezjerian cargo ships routed the Lasanachi, the Gyn Hort were no longer on terms of trust with Dro Pent, a link not repaired for nearly a generation.

The third event was not as readily linked to the Emperor, not until long after. In the year 770, nineteen years before the invasion of Podhru Harbor and fifty leagues due north in the deepest forests of Zelharri, Duke Amarni's horse went suddenly wild during a hunt and threw his master. The Duke fell full into a previously undiscovered pool of Hell-Light and wasted away over the next four days. When he died the pool was visible day or night and Amarni was no longer even recognizable as a man. He was survived by his widow Lizelle and their two young children, the nera-Duke Aletto and the sin-Duchess Lialla, and mourned by all his Duchy. That number included his younger brother Jadek, who had ridden to the hunt with him, had pulled him from the Hell-Light without consideration of the personal risk. He had remained by his brother's bed most of the Duke's last days and appeared at the funeral in deepest mourning. His escort of fifty armsmen also wore mourning bands.

Once Duke Amarni was sealed in his stone cairn, however, young Lord Jadek showed no signs of returning to the lands granted the Duke's younger son, nor of sending his armsmen away. Two days after the funeral, he announced his betrothal to the Duchess Lizelle—to help her, he said earnestly, with the enormous tasks of governing the Duchy until Aletto should come of age.

Like his brother, Jadek was handsome, easygoing, comfortable with other nobles and his householdmen alike. Unlike his
brother, Jadek was not greatly loved, though few people could
find any reason why they did not like him. A set to his mouth,
or the flat way his eyes fixed on them, perhaps.

The betrothal raised heavy suspicion of Jadek's motives and
rumor was rife throughout Zelharri. But there was no specific
wrong thing to point to. Lizelle herself had appeared with him:
pale, quiet and clad in deep red mourning. But she made no
protest at any time, then or after the wedding, which Jadek held
at the beginning of Gourding-Month, a mere nine days later.

Suspicion remained high thereafter, though most common men
and women had the wit to voice such suspicions in whispers, if
at all. Particularly when it became clear that men who spoke
louder now and again vanished. And men who had served Duke
Amarni—his closest friends and highest-ranked householdmen—
left Duke's Fort. Most of those left the Duchy entirely. Merchant
families complained of new competition or restructured taxes
and fees, and moved away—many to neighboring Sikkre with its
sprawling market at the center of four trade-roads; others to
coastal Bezjeriad, which increasingly rivaled the Emperor's port
city for traffic.

Emperor Shesseran knew within hours of Amarni's death, and
of Jadek's actions after, for Zelharri bordered the northern edge
of his Andar Perighan estates. But so long as Jadek paid the
Duchy's semiannual taxes and sent the proper number of arms-
trained men on request, he did nothing. And Jadek, knowing
the Emperor would not interfere without greater cause than a
dreadful accident and a hasty marriage, was much too clever to
make any overt move to supplant nera-Duke Aletto.

After all, he knew there was no need while Aletto was still a
green boy and so barred from ruling. Until the nera-Duke passed
his twenty-fifth birthday, Jadek was for all practical purposes
Duke. Even after that date passed, there had been excuses, ways
to keep wealth and power, ways that did not involve a frontal
attack. Particularly if one took into account all factors, including
Aletto's physical condition.

There was also Lizelle, of course; she had been still young,
and she had already borne healthy children. There could have
been an heir for Jadek—a boy who would not be next in the
succession but would have a foot in the door. Unfortunately for
Jadek, Lizelle irritatingly never quickened.

And so, Jadek waited, and planned, until the Spring of the

Emperor's Blossom-Month Fest—Fifth Month, Sixth Day of the year 789. The numbers would not fall in such a pattern again for more than a hundred years and a full moon-season of secular and religious festivals were being set. While Shesseran XIV was so deeply involved in planning and rehearsing the Fest, the man who had taken his brother's wife and her right of interim rule moved to consolidate the rest of the Duchy. *His* Duchy.

I

SIN-DUCHESS Lialla had eaten bread spread with a sweetened apple mash in the small courtyard, rather than face a midday meal at the family table. It wasn't enough food and she would be hungry again by late afternoon, but that was small price to pay for avoiding her uncle and the general unpleasantness between him and her mother, the undercurrents to conversation. Not that hiding had helped this particular afternoon, not entirely. She pulled the black scarf higher on the back of her neck, shivered as she left the sunny little garden and hurried along the shadowed walkway. It ran like a hall between the public and private portions of Duke's Fort; chill wind flowed its length winter and summer.

She turned left at the third opening, crossed a darkened and empty room. A narrow staircase built into the thick stone wall, seldom used except by herself and her mother's woman—the Night-Thread Wielder Merrida—was illuminated by a finger of daylight from somewhere high above. She climbed carefully; the steps did not have a uniform rise and they were all just enough too tall that it was impossible to adjust to them. They passed by the second floor without egress and came out in the middle of an equally small room on the third and uppermost floor of the family apartments.

There were no windows in this chamber, no lamps. A small fire was kept burning in the grate near the door, giving just enough illumination for the young woman to find her way across. Merrida's doing, that fire. A servant of her own saw to it, saw that it was never allowed to die out entirely. Merrida's books—ancient clay tablets, some of them, or rolled hide, pulped reed or wood—were hidden in this room, hidden behind a maze of

Thread that kept the chamber beneath Jadek's notice. He passed it at least once a day, on his way from his and Lizelle's apartments to the lower halls. He hadn't paid it the least heed in years.

Lialla scrubbed the back of her hand across her lips. The apples had been mealy-soft and too sweet before the cooks mashed and honeyed them; the mess on her bread had left her mouth feeling coated, her lips and fingers sticky even though she'd dipped them in the fountain before coming away.

Her palms were damp, but that had nothing to do with the food. Jadek had sent her a summons, sending one of his men to her small, sunny sanctum. One of his grubby, hulking men, all creaking smelly leather and cold steel blades. He'd watched her with black, intent eyes; his fingers had actually tried to touch hers when she took the folded paper from him. She wouldn't go back to that patio again, not soon—not alone. Not with that to remember it by.

The message itself was courteously phrased, but an order all the same: "I would speak with you on the subject of your future, Daughter. If it is not inconvenient, your mother and I will be in my accounting room at third hour." *Not inconvenient,* Lialla thought as she slipped past the heavy door and hurried down the hall to her small suite—two rooms and a privy. *And if I said it was, what would he do then?* She wasn't certain she wanted the answer to that question. Jadek had never actually used force against her. But his voice could flay her; he knew every least insecurity and played upon it. She'd cringed under his voice for years. And violence—she knew he was capable of it; he'd let her see how capable more than once, against servants, or commons. People who couldn't hit back. People like herself.

It didn't matter, though, that last. His voice would be enough. If she didn't come, she wouldn't hear the end of it for days.

The halls were empty at this hour. Servants would be eating or airing curtains and bedding on this first warm day in so many; they'd welcome the opportunity to stay outdoors as long as possible. Lizelle seldom left her private rooms unless Jadek required her presence at a formal dinner or at council. Merrida often slept at this hour. And Aletto—gods. Lialla slipped into her rooms and pressed the door shut behind her. Aletto was nearly as much a recluse of late as their mother.

Perhaps more, and with more cause. Three years past the time to claim his rights! Jadek gave such smooth excuses to postpone the ceremony, Aletto couldn't counter him, and Lialla knew how that angered and frustrated him. Besides, his limp was more pronounced during the damp spring months; with nothing else to occupy his time, he had begun hiding behind his door, drinking until both the physical pain and the emotional were temporarily dulled.

Lialla slid the bar across her door from habit. It had been there as long as she could remember; she'd only begun to use it the past year or so. Jadek's armsmen, some of them, walked the halls of the family apartments. And Jadek himself—now and again he stopped on his way to Lizelle, to tap on her door. To talk, he said, or to ask a question. . . . She didn't think anything certain; she didn't let herself go so far as that. She set the bar in place whenever she was in her rooms.

It was warmer here. Sun pooled on the floor by her bed, and with the windows closed the room was rather stuffy. But when she pushed one ajar, a chill breeze blew across her face and the backs of her hands; she shivered, and shut it again.

It was a nice room, all light wood and whitewash, low-ceilinged enough to be easily warmed in winter. The glass was truly ancient, thick and bubbled in places; it gave her a headache to look out for long across the main courtyard, the horsebarns, the outer curtain of the fort. There was little to see out there, anyway; a few of Jadek's men on the walls of the curtain, one or two in the yard and now and again a horse.

Horse. She sighed. She wasn't permitted to ride in winter or bad weather. Even now that it had turned nice, Jadek hadn't issued new orders. If he was in a decent mood, perhaps she'd ask him this afternoon. Winter and its close confinement left her cross; inaction made her feel loggy, bloated and soft.

Her bedding was faded with age, the carpets frayed and patched. Jadek would doubtless have given her better if she'd asked. She didn't care enough to bother. Her clothing was in no better shape, but she cared even less for her appearance. There had been no suitors in three years, none she'd accept before that. Men like her father were rare, men like Jadek all too common, from what she'd seen. She wouldn't grow old early like her mother, a faint look of drawn suffering pinching her cheeks, her eyes all wary, sidelong looks. She had more important things to do with her life.

Jadek had made no objection at all to her summary rejection of applicants for her hand; Lialla suspected he would rather keep her dowry to himself. But she couldn't leave: She was all Aletto had to keep him from drinking himself to death, even though her influence over him was almost nonexistent nowadays. It was still greater than Lizelle's. Her mother hardly bothered any more.

But that was another thing: Lizelle needed her, too. She couldn't just abandon her mother. Lizelle had Merrida, of course: Merrida had been with her forever.

And that, of course, was a thing at least as important as any other: Merrida. Merrida had taught Lizelle to Wield, and Lialla suspected it was Night-Thread magic that kept Jadek sonless. She herself was a black-sashed initiate, Merrida's pupil. One day she'd be a full-fledged Wielder, and then—oh, then! Jadek would learn, he'd pay for everything, and she'd—

She turned that thought off. Merrida had warned her never to plan such things in advance. "Vengeance is better when you don't try to work it out too long beforehand—for the satisfaction as much as for the spell. But it's foolish to let such thoughts fill you: They interfere with other things, and Jadek may have his own ways of knowing them. Better, isn't it, to catch him unaware?"

"As if he doesn't know how deeply I loathe him," Lialla mumbled bitterly. She turned her back on the sun and dug into the chest where her clothes were stored.

An initiate Wielder traditionally wore plain black. Lialla had two changes of such blacks, the baggy trous worn over knee-length leggins and bound at the ankle with thin, charcoal gray cord only slightly paler than the rusty and faded black. A thin, body-hugging, sleeved and high-necked shirt of tight, smooth weave tucked into the trous; a sleeveless, shapeless overshirt was caught at the hips with a wide sash. Her sash was black, Merrida's pale lemon yellow. Her mother's, kept in Merrida's firelit room with the blacks she hadn't worn since her husband's death, was deep orange. There were two ranks above Merrida's, but according to the old woman, no one in all Rhadaz had wrapped his blacks or her blacks in either silver or white since Hell-Light was confined to pools and the Triads unmade or driven into hiding.

It was a practical garb for riding, walking, some sort of strenuous activity, or long hours in the dark and chill of the night, manipulating Threads. It was not designed to be attractive, bundling the body into shapelessness as it did, and black did not suit Lialla. It muffled the red in her dark brown hair and made her look sallow, too thin, and alarmingly young. Lialla was unaware of that, and would not have cared if she knew. She tucked

Jadek's message in her sash, shoved her feet into short black boots, and went down to see what Jadek wanted.

ALETTO'S door was closed; a small stack of used dishes sat beside it, next to a bowl of congealing soup. Small flies hovered in a cloud over a dish of sliced fruit. Lialla closed her eyes briefly, hesitated, brought her fist up. After a moment, she let it fall to her side, stepped back and went on down the hall.

THE man who opened the door to her was middle-aged and broad-shouldered. Grizzled brown hair ringed a sunburned and freckled pate. He was unfamiliar to her; his livery was similar to that worn by Jadek's personal servants, vaguely unsettling. He stepped aside, let her in, pulled the door to behind her and remained beside it. Lialla cast him another glance, sidelong from under her lashes. A red silhouette of a hunting dog on the sleeve. *Carolan*. Carolan was at Duke's Fort.

She kept her face utterly still as she stepped into the spacious room that had been her father's library, and that Jadek called his accounting room. She saw her mother first, a too-slender figure seated near tall, mullioned windows that cast bars of shadow across her pale blue skirts. Behind her mother's chair, Merrida stood, so still she might have been part of the fabric of curtains or the chair; she wore black, but not Wielder black. Merrida's eyes held hers briefly; her fingers shifted along the side of the chair, index fingers overlapping for the least instant, then slipping back out of sight. Lizelle's hands were neatly folded in her lap, thumbs joined.

Caution. Danger. They were warning her. Lialla knew that much already, though. One cause for it sat at the long table, polished wood stretching to either side of him. Jadek had scarcely aged at all in the years he'd held Duke's Fort: Even with full sun on his face, there were no lines save faint ones around his eyes; his dark hair was as thick as ever, and only a few pale hairs marred it. He was clean-shaven, though, and had been since his mustache began coming in a mix of red and silver. His smile was still wide, and he had all his teeth. The smile went no higher than his teeth; his eyes were very pale blue, ringed with darker blue, and as chilly as a hunting bird's. Lialla inclined her head in a dutiful child's greeting, then waited for him to speak first.

She would not let herself look at the man who stood behind Jadek's chair: Carolan, Jadek's disgusting, horrible cousin, was smiling the way he no doubt had practiced before a mirror, and trying to catch her eye.

"Daughter, thank you for coming." Jadek's prepared little speech brought her eyes up to his face. He was going to be particularly slow at coming to his point this afternoon, she could tell already. And the point was already dreadfully clear, with Carolan in his best and least soiled garb—pale lavender velvet, an ocean of purple edged in gold thread; a broad, sequined sash crossed one shoulder and came back across his enormous belly. Carolan, whose exploits among the paid women of Sikkre's markets had even reached her carefully sheltered ears.

It took what seemed hours: Lialla managed somehow not to fidget when Jadek spoke of her age, her station, her rank. She bit the corners of her mouth not to either interrupt or shout with laughter when Jadek began to list Carolan's virtues—a long list of very invented virtues. Her uncle's color was becoming high; try to speak now and he'd lose his temper. As she now stood, she couldn't see her mother without turning her head, but she could almost touch Lizelle's tension.

But Jadek was finishing up his speech. "And so, my cousin Carolan has come to me, to ask your hand. What say you, daughter?"

Lialla drew a deep breath, cast a swift glance at the smirking creature behind the chair. "I thank him for the honor. But I must decline it." Carolan stirred and would have spoken; Jadek held up a hand.

"It's an honorable offer, Lialla," he said reasonably. "You are at an age where you will not receive many more of them."

"I do not wish to marry. My thanks for your concern and for your cousin's request, but no." Silence. She drew another deep breath and used it to steady her voice. "It is my right."

Jadek leaned back in his chair and crossed his legs. "Not if the succession is in question. And it may be. Your mother and I have no children of my blood—"

"But Aletto—!" The words were out, her voice sounding high and frightened. She bit her lip, swallowed the rest. Jadek gazed at her with that lack of expression that knotted her stomach. His eyes had gone even colder.

"Aletto has not—has not been well for some time, as you know. And his infirmity may well preclude him from the succession."

"But he's not really ill, you know that! Not any more! He's only—"

"Are you contradicting me, Lialla?" Silence. Then Jadek slammed both palms on the table with a crack that echoed. Lialla flinched; Jadek's voice was suddenly a bellow, hammering into her. "How dare you interrupt me? How dare you gainsay me? When did your brother last leave his rooms?"

Aletto—he'd put Aletto's rights aside entirely! Fear vanished; Lialla's temper flared. "I always knew you'd steal his birthright! You couldn't wait to take Mother after Father died, couldn't wait to take Duke's Fort for your own, and you won't give it up now, will you?"

Jadek caught hold of her sleeve and yanked her across the table, off her feet; his free hand cracked across her face. The room blurred, and she blinked tears aside furiously. "Aletto is a drunk and a cripple," Jadek said flatly. "Is that what you want me to say? Should I let your father's Duchy—my brother's birthright, you wretched girl!—fall to ruin at the hands of an incompetent, limping, winebibber?" *Because you made him a drunk,* she thought defiantly, but the words wouldn't come. Her knees were trembling so much that he must have felt the tremor through the hand that gripped her elbow. "Well, Lialla?" Jadek's voice rang through her; he brought his hand up again and she shrank away from him. He lowered it, gazed at her in silence for some moments, then let go of her arm and resumed his seat.

"You shouldn't anger me like that, Lialla. It grieves me to hurt you." She kept her eyes on the floor before her feet and tried to keep tears behind her eyelids. He'd never hit her before; and to strike her in front of her mother, her tutor—in front of Carolan. "I know your intentions and your desires, Lialla." Jadek offered her a smile; his eyes were still cold. Lialla glanced at him, away again. "These aren't the best of times for them. And it's not natural, what you want. Magic," he said, and laughed a little. "It's not safe, dabbling in the unknown. Something terrible might happen to you. Besides, rumor has it the Emperor may again restrict such things, once his Festival is past, and he has time to devote to the matter." *Not Night-Thread magic,* Lialla thought dully.

"I don't say," Jadek went on quietly, "that Aletto might not take his rightful place and rule for his full years. I hope that he will; I love the boy as much as I love you, Lialla. But if anything happens to him, there is no immediate heir but you—that is to say, of course, a son of yours." Silence. He was waiting for her to speak; she still couldn't trust her voice. Merrida, her mother—she could see them from under her lashes. They might as well have been statues. No help at all, not from them. *You could say something!* she thought miserably. Jadek was still speaking; she'd missed a few words. "You've turned down Dahven in Sikkre—he's wild, admittedly, but still a proper mate for a noblewoman. You refused both the heir and his younger brother in Bezjeriad. Of course, the heir has no interests at all save that curious Holmaddian religion and they say he's gone quite gaunt from all the fasting. And there were rumors about the brother and other young men—well, but that's all beside the point." Silence again, and this time he was watching her, visibly waiting. Growing angry at her stubborn refusal to speak.

"Rhadazi women are allowed to choose not to marry," she said finally; her voice was low and flat, utterly expressionless. She sounded sullen to her own ears, and that wasn't good; Jadek wouldn't want to hear that.

"Rhadazi common women are permitted choice," Jadek corrected her gently. "Duke's daughters are allowed that right only when there is no succession difficulty. Even your own father, Lialla, would have been quite angry if you'd chosen a common soldier or a stableboy for your husband. I'm sure he'd never have approved your playing with magic, and he'd never have let you substitute it for a husband and children."

She shook her head. "I can't—I need time to decide."

"No. You have had years, more time than you should have been permitted. My cousin Carolan has made you an honorable offer, and he is waiting for an answer."

"But I already told you I can't—"

Jadek rose; Lialla took an involuntary step back from the table. Her uncle's face was flushed, his lips compressed into a tight line. "That was an unacceptable answer, Lialla." His eyes, all pupil, fixed on hers. "I suggest you try again. Right now." She opened her mouth, closed it again as no sound came. Jadek's eyes terrified her, but she was more afraid to look away from him.

A heavy blow on the door pulled his black glance away from her. Carolan's man reached for the latch and the door slammed back, knocking him sideways into the wall. He sat on the floor, abruptly, clutching his nose and moaning.

Jadek's eyes narrowed; Carolan's chubby mouth sagged. Lialla slid sideways along the table, four steps and out of her uncle's reach, before she turned. Aletto stood in the open doorway, braced against the jamb. He clutched a sword awkwardly in his right hand, the knob of his walking stick in the left.

Jadek recovered first. "Nephew. What are you doing here?
You were not asked!"

Aletto tried to laugh; what came out was a snort. "Doing
here? S'— That's good, Uncle!"

Jadek blinked, then smiled. "You don't look well at all."

"You mean I'm drunk," Aletto snapped. "P'raps. I've had
wine. Then I heard 'bout this. Disgusting." He shifted against
the doorway, waved his stick to take in the room.

"Heard. How did you hear, Aletto?"

"None 'f your business. Got m' sources, Uncle. Li?"

She swallowed past a terribly dry throat. "Aletto?"

"You're all right?" he demanded. She nodded. "Didn't agree
to—t' anything, did you?" She shook her head. "Good. Don't."

"It isn't your concern," Jadek said flatly.

"Liar!" Aletto roared, silencing him. "S'— It's my sister!
My dukedom!" He rubbed the back of his sword hand over his
eyes, swayed back and forth the least bit. Lizelle shifted in her
chair. Aletto glanced at her; his mouth twisted and he looked
away. "Uncle, my sister won't marry that—that—" He shook
his head to try and clear it, edged himself a little more upright
on the door frame. "I w—won't have it."

Lialla gripped the table behind her back lest she sag at the
knees, and caught both lips between her teeth. She wasn't certain if she'd laugh or cry, just now, only that she wouldn't stop
if she once started. Then Aletto pushed himself away from the
door, and came into the light, into the open . . . and there was
nothing amusing at all in watching Aletto walk.

Marsh fever: It struck the young, mostly boys just at puberty,
and most of those it killed. Those boys it didn't kill, it maimed;
there was no cure, no way to avert it, and Merrida's magic had
been only partly successful. She'd saved his life; he had use of
his eyes and his ears, his wits intact. But his heart sometimes kept an erratic pattern all its own, there was no feeling in
the toes of his left foot and entirely too much feeling in the rest
of his leg. His left shoulder was too high, and particularly when
he was tired his head inclined toward it. The right side of his
face—once easily as handsome as his father's—was scarred,
partly dead.

He could walk more or less normally at times, but this wasn't
one of them. Wild with fury and addled with drink, he lurched
across the room, virgin steel held out to the side, high and well
away from his body.

She wanted to close her eyes; she didn't dare, knowing he'd

see and take it for pity. His eyes gleamed as Carolan took one involuntary step back.

Jadek didn't move, and after that first startled glance, he hadn't so much as looked at the sword. "You're being a fool, Aletto. Your sister and my cousin will make a good marriage; it will take some of the pressure from you to find a wife."

"What, one who'd have me?"

"I didn't say that."

"You've never had to! It's in your eyes, all the time!" Aletto shouted as he came up against the table.

"They needn't leave, of course," Jadek went on. "They can remain here at the fort, if you wish. We'll provide them a proper suite." Aletto tried to balance himself against the table's edge and bring the sword up for a broadside stroke. The blade hissed through the air well away from Jadek or Carolan and cut into the side of the table. Aletto swore wildly and yanked it free, nearly sending himself to the floor.

"You'd bed my sister with that?" Aletto glared across the table, over Jadek's shoulder.

"He's my cousin, he's noble—"

"He's a pig," Aletto snarled. He got no further. Jadek lunged, caught hold of the nera-Duke's wrist and squeezed. The sword clattered to the floor; Jadek shifted his grip to Aletto's ear and brought their faces close together.

"You will apologize to Carolan for that remark," he began, but got no further. Aletto's walking stick caught him a stunning blow across the shoulder. Lialla screamed; Jadek released Aletto so suddenly that his nephew fell heavily, striking the side of his face on the table's edge. Before he could recover, Jadek had thrown himself across the table, caught up Aletto's stick and brought it down across his back. Lialla caught at his arm as he raised it for another blow; he shook her off with no effort at all and Carolan's hands—unexpected muscle under the softness—gripped her shoulders and pulled her away. His breath was warm and herbed against her ear.

"He sought this, beloved; leave be." Lialla twisted against his grip but subsided at once when his breathing quickened and he leaned into her. Aletto swore as the stick cracked down again, then screamed when the fourth blow broke it in half. He went limp in Jadek's hold, hair falling across his face.

There were other men in the room suddenly; it was full of men in Jadek's livery. Lialla blinked to clear her vision; Carolan had her in such a tight grip she couldn't even wipe her eyes.

Jadek stood between her and her brother, blocking her view entirely. Two household men came at his gesture and picked the nera-Duke up. Jadek dropped both pieces of the walking stick on Aletto's chest, handed the sword to another man. ''Put this back in his rooms.''

''Do you want him locked in, sir?''

''Of course not,'' Jadek said gravely. ''He's the Duke's heir.'' He watched the procession leave the room, then turned to his cousin and Lialla. ''Lialla, you look distressed. Go to your rooms, stay there until your nerves are eased. Until you can give sensible thought to the matters we spoke of earlier.'' He laid gentle fingers against her bruised cheek; she somehow managed not to wince away from his touch. ''Go and rest. Tonight—no, tonight's impossible. We'll dine together here, tomorrow at mid-day, just the three of us.''

''Tomorrow,'' she whispered. And Jadek stood aside as one of his householdmen held the door for her.

Her arms felt the pressure of Carolan's fingers long after he let go of her. Somehow she avoided the kiss Carolan would have put on her cheek, or her shoulder, but not the one he placed on her palm; somehow she escaped the room without setting Jadek's anger off once more. She walked two long halls and three flights of stairs to her rooms, alone and unaided, and could never after remember which way she'd gone, or whom she had passed.

She retained just enough wit to bar the door behind her before the tears came.

2

JENNIFER glanced up as a telephone rang—one of the partners' private lines, far down the hall where the larger and more luxurious offices were. The service took care of calls on the regular lines at this time of night. After fifteen echoing rings, it finally went quiet again. Jennifer smothered a yawn against the back of her hand, let her glasses slide down her nose and rubbed tired eyes before she went back to the piles of books, documents, files and yellow pads that buried the top of her desk. Somewhere behind a stack of California Appellate reports, her desk radio was playing Mahler.

It was late; hours after the secretaries and the receptionist had left; hours after the cleaners had roared down the hall with the vacuum, banging trash cans, talking loud Spanish over a boom box playing Latino hits. At this end of the hall, offices were small, strictly functional. Hers was sparsely furnished: old maple desk; credenza of the same wood but a slightly different style; two brown chairs for the odd client who saw her instead of the partners she worked under. The only new piece of furniture was her high-backed brown leather chair; she'd bought that at an outlet, Christmas present to herself. The nick in the wooden grip didn't show, once she'd rubbed oil stain into it. A few framed items, a shelf holding a spill of blooming ivy geranium and half a dozen books completed it.

From the windows of her seventeenth-floor office, the lights on the roof of the parking garage below were mustard-colored pools, picking out an occasional still-parked Toyota or Ford sedan. The Mercedeses and BMWs weren't parked on the roof, and they'd be gone by this hour of a Thursday night, anyway. There wasn't much else to see out that window at night—another building blocked most of her view. But she kept the curtains open, smiled briefly and tiredly at the drawn woman reflected on the glass before she turned back to her research. A year and a half ago, there hadn't been windows; there had only been a closet-sized cubby shared with another law clerk and mounds of current files, boxes of closed cases, a computer terminal and numberless yellow pads and blue stick medium-point pens.

She stifled another yawn, rubbed the back of her neck where the muscles had gone hard and tight hours before, finally gave it up and shoved herself onto her feet. There might still be coffee in the pot; if not, she'd make some.

The day felt like it had gone on for weeks; the particular facet of eminent domain she was researching was duller than tax law. But there was nothing for it but to wade on through, finish. A senior partner needed his answer by Monday morning. Friday, actually; his client's deposition was Monday at ten.

The coffee pot wasn't quite empty but the stuff in the bottom resembled molasses; she sniffed, grimaced and poured it out. While water trickled through fresh grounds, she leaned against the counter, stretching out her back, her neck, the backs of her legs. "I did this better when I was twenty-five," she mumbled to the pot. It spat the last of its water through the filter, emitted a series of obscene noises. She rinsed her cup and refilled it, sipped gingerly. Not great; but hot and drinkable anyway. At least caffeine didn't give her the shakes, just kept her awake like it was supposed to. She topped off the cup and went back down the empty hall.

Someone in the back corner was running the ancient draft printer; James Neally and his secretary staying late, finishing yet another draft of a trial brief for the four partners involved in the case to pick apart, no doubt. James spent more late-night and early-morning hours here than she did. As she turned into her office, she heard voices, words indistinguishable over the rattle of the old daisy wheel. James, coat in hand, came by moments later.

"Hi. Thought Mandy and I had the place to ourselves."

"You were leaving her alone?" The partners frowned on that, particularly after dark. And James was ordinarily good about walking Mandy to her car at night.

"In the office. She's finishing section seven; I'm off for some racquetball. I come back, we look it over, I walk her out. And probably spend the rest of the night tearing it apart so she can start over tomorrow, poor girl. But what're you doing here alone at this ungodly hour?''

Jennifer smiled. ''The rule's for secretaries; good ones are less expendable than mere law clerks and associates.''

''Because there are so many of you,'' James chided. ''So how about coming over to the club with me?'' And as she began shaking her head, he continued, ''Just across the street. I know you keep your gym bag in your trunk; you can borrow a racquet. You need a break, Jen.'' He looked over her shoulder at the mess spilled across the desk. ''That's Charlie's crap, isn't it? The boundary dispute? It shouldn't take *you* long to finish up; you're pushing a tired brain, girl. Give it a break, why don't you?''

''Yeah, I know. Next time, all right?''

''Look, Jennifer—'' He sighed, gave her a gentle shove, jerked his head toward her office and followed her in, closing the door behind him. ''You look like hell tonight, you know that?''

''Thanks.''

''You know what I mean. Look, there's nothing wrong with sticking with the game plan here. You don't need to prove how good you are to anyone.''

She shook her head. ''It's not that. I don't think it is. It's just—what I want. Partner in three years, Jimmy.''

He flopped into one of the client chairs. Jennifer moved her stack of books aside, turned the radio down a notch and began fiddling with the tuning. He looked at the windows, past the framed law degree, let his eyes rest briefly on the matted poster of Ayers Rock in Australia, before turning his attention to the enlarged snapshot of a woman and a boy—Jennifer's older sister Robyn and her nephew, her only family. There was no resemblance between the faded, overweight blonde in the picture and the woman sitting behind the desk. Jennifer was tall and rangy, all cheekbones and dark brown hair. The wide-set hazel eyes under the glasses belied the intelligence behind them; he had suspected for years she wore glasses rather than contact lenses because people wouldn't take her seriously otherwise. Some people—like certain senior (male) partners, older (male) judges, opposing (older, male) counsel. Anyone who worked with her like he did, any other associate or law clerk at Heydrich & Harrison knew better.

There was no sign of the driven determination that was Jennifer's in the photograph of Robyn and her son Christopher. And the contrast between Chris and either woman was ludicrous.

Robyn, with her long, straight, center-parted hair, looked like a refugee from a revival of *Hair*, Jennifer like a model for the cover of a magazine for executive women. Chris, with his shaggy hair, black jeans, that leather jacket—Chris might have come straight from an MTV video.

The two in the picture didn't explain Jennifer to him; and Jennifer, though she'd worked with her since their first summer clerking for this firm, hadn't ever given him much clue to her drive. Just now, she was playing with a ball-point, doodling on the edge of a yellow pad covered with notes, clearly waiting for him to go so she could get back to work. The radio was playing something sloshy and orchestral. "No one makes partner here in under five years," he said finally. Jennifer's generous mouth quirked in what might have been a dubious grin or a grimace; she shrugged. "All right, Steve did it in three and a half. But not your way, remember? He brought in a pharmaceutical company and an office furniture chain; they've kept Heydrich & Harrison in petty cash for years."

"I know that."

"You might know it, but I don't think you've taken it to heart. It's not just the hard work. And all this grunt work—five years of this nonstop, you'll look like a drudge and your brains'll turn to pudding."

Jennifer stirred indignantly and set the pen down. "That's not nice, James. Or even true. It's part of the game, we all do it. Besides, what am I supposed to do the next time Harrison comes by with a research project—Just Say No?"

James laughed and settled his body a little lower in the chair, crossing navy blue trousered legs under the edge of her desk. "Don't be silly. Besides, you can't ask *me* that. I'm Steve's camel, remember? The guy who carries the briefcase and pulls the baggage cart when we go into court. Of course we all do it; sometimes you even get lucky and get landed by a firm like this one where the partners still resemble humans. But even the honchos over at Gimmel and Charles don't insist their grunts work nonstop, barring the odd emergency."

"I know someone over there myself; everything's an emergency." Jennifer laughed, shook her head. "Look, it's not that bad; we work differently, that's all. And as for looks—what's the big deal? This isn't the Ford Agency, is it?"

"You start looking like death warmed over and you can kiss court time goodbye."

"Nonsense."

"All right, that's only an ugly clerk-room rumor. All the same, you can't afford to wear yourself down like this. You want to burn out?"

"I won't."

"Harrison's last secretary probably said that once. The one who left him last year? Sold french fries at Burger King for six months. I think she's pushing cosmetics or see-through undies at house parties now."

"I remember Cindy. I'm not like that."

"You need contacts," James said bluntly. "I'm putting in the hours myself, I'm pulling down points, it all counts, after all. Look." He sat up and leaned forward, planted his elbows on two yellow pads. "Why do you think I joined the health club across the street? And the one over in Santa Monica? Because—of—the—contacts." His fingers tapped her desk, emphasizing the words. "I'm just telling you. Bring in an Iranian condo developer, get a big-name actor. Bring in money, prestige or perks."

"Just like that."

He sighed. "You're in a sour mood tonight, aren't you? That's the gravy that gets you partner early."

In spite of her rising irritation, Jennifer laughed. "James, I'd like to strangle you sometimes. You sound like a used-car salesman."

"How do you think I put myself through law school?"

"Cute. I'm not going to pick my friends because they might get me somewhere here. I'm not a damned ambulance chaser."

"Well, neither am I," he growled. The chair rocked as he pushed to his feet; he steadied it, bent down and retrieved a pencil from the floor and tossed it onto the desk. "I am, however, a realist." He shoved his jacket sleeve back, glanced at his watch. "I'm late, gotta go." He paused in the doorway. "Look, I wouldn't have brought it up at all, except that frankly, girl, you look like hell lately. You can't make partner if you kill yourself before Christmas, all right? And if you think you have to prove how good you are to anyone else—well, you don't." He was gone, out the door and down the hall before she could say anything.

Jennifer scowled at his back, brought her attention back down to the case she'd left half-read. She shook her head and sighed tiredly as he yanked the outer door closed behind him, turned up her radio, turned over a blank sheet on the top yellow pad and began writing.

* * *

HOURS later, the coffee pot was empty, her eyes dry and itchy,
her throat rough from dictating. Two tapes, her notes, opposing
counsel's latest pleadings and the case file made a daunting heap
on her secretary's desk, ready for her to start the memo; the last
page of a yellow pad, still attached to the cardboard back, leaned
against the pile, on it a red felt scrawl: "Jan, Harrison needs
this ASAP. Hope it makes sense, JAC." She rubbed her eyes,
resettled her glasses and focused on her watch. Ugh. It wasn't
late any more, it was early.

The night air was damp and smelled faintly of fog; a street
cleaner rattled past. No other traffic on Century Park East; the
last movies must have let out an hour or more earlier. The chill
revived her a little; she left windows down just a slit to keep her
awake as she drove down Avenue of the Stars, out Pico toward
the beach.

Her apartment—in Santa Monica, but nearly a mile from the
ocean—was dark and what seemed abnormally quiet; Chris had
spent most of the summer and early fall with her but when Robyn's latest boyfriend finally moved out a week before, he went
back home. Jennifer turned on lights, turned the stereo on low—
without Chris around, she didn't have to adjust the volume or
the station—and stared into the refrigerator.

She didn't really feel hungry, but not eating would be a mistake. She dragged out a Coke, cottage cheese and a small can
of peaches, carried them into the living room and ate at the
coffee table. Imagine leaving Coke in the fridge and finding it
still there, she thought. Chris drove her crazy sometimes; at the
moment, she rather missed him.

"Friday already," she told the bathroom mirror as she brushed
her teeth. A rather long Friday, from the look of it, but Charles
Harrison was taking her and her secretary Jan to lunch, as
partner-style thanks for the rush research and the typing. She'd
taken lunch all week at her desk, eating whatever Jan could
forage in the nearby sandwich shops for both of them.

And she was safe counting on the weekend: Barring total disaster, no one at Heydrich & Harrison Law Corp. worked Saturday or Sunday. She glanced at her watch again, considered,
finally shrugged and punched the first button on her auto-dialer.
The phone at Robyn's rang only four times before Chris picked
it up.

"Hi, kid. Aren't you supposed to be in bed at this hour?"

"Aunt Jen? Hiya. Why should I be?"

"Beats me. School?" He was in his senior year, in a high school in Robyn's neighborhood where some of the sophomores scared Jennifer half silly.

"No classes tomorrow, teacher conference."

"Good planning on your part."

"Hey. I try."

"Your mother still up?"

"Asleep," he said briefly. *Passed out*, his tone of voice said.

"Oh. We still on for Saturday?"

"You bet." More enthusiasm this time. "Devil's Punchbowl, though, not Vasquez Rocks. Too many city types out there."

Jennifer laughed. "Sure, country boy. What did Robyn say?"

"Said she'd do a picnic, chicken and stuff."

"Swell." Jennifer didn't take this any more seriously than Chris did; experience was that Robyn's intentions were good but a bottle of wine usually got between her and the intentions. There were places on the way to pick up food, plenty of fruit and vegetable stands on the other side of the mountains. "What do you think, if we leave your place about ten?"

"Sounds fine." Robyn wouldn't be conscious any earlier, probably. "Say—what're you still doing up, Aunt Jen? Don't you work any more?"

"No one likes a smart-assed kid," Jennifer told him sternly, but she was smiling, and he knew it. Chris was still chuckling as he hung up.

She was tired; glassy-eyed tired. Sleep evaded her. The apartment was stuffy, her window air conditioner only partly effective, and the noise it made was irritating. The sheets were new, the dye not yet softened by time and washing, and they scraped against her legs. Yellow paper, blue-lined, danced before her eyes; case names echoed in her thoughts. A theme from the Mahler symphony repeated itself. She tossed and turned, finally got up and found her aspirin bottle, dumped three into her hand and swallowed them. They left an unpleasant taste in her mouth, and she doubted they'd be very effective.

There *was* another bottle in the cabinet, a prescription bottle of small blue tablets; they'd put her to sleep, all right. God knew the same stuff, stronger dosage, had been effective for Robyn for years. Jennifer had opened the bottle a dozen times the past year and recapped it each time, still full.

When she climbed back into bed, the office was gone, pushed aside by another mental treadmill: Robyn. Poor, weak Robyn; poor addictive-personality elder sister. *I'm not that way*, Jennifer

told herself. But it was because of Robyn that she couldn't make
herself take the pills.

Guilt, fear, concern, worry—there wasn't an end to it, there
never had been. She barely recalled first grade or anything before it, back when there'd been a real family. Except her parents
fighting, constantly fighting, and then the divorce. She'd been
such an object of pity and curiosity; divorce in a small Wyoming
town in the early sixties had caused a major sensation. Ostensibly it started when Marion Cray began talking to the Watchtower
people but rumor on that had gone both ways—that George had
driven her to it, that she'd driven him to file for the separation
when she cut herself off from former friends, her old church,
everything not Adventist.

And George—he had only filed for separation when Marion
threatened to take their daughters with her. Mill Junction people
had been relieved when the judge gave him custody. Marion had
gone away by then, the sensation died down for a while. But
George hadn't known what to do with his six- and fifteen-year-
old daughters, now that he had them.

"Wasn't particularly interested," Jennifer told the ceiling in
a near-soundless whisper. It still hurt. He'd only cared that *she*
didn't win, and he couldn't bear to look bad in front of his co-
workers at the mine, or his drinking buddies. Jennifer and Robyn
had been shipped off to a second cousin and his wife in Southern
California as soon as the ink was dry on the final decree.

Jennifer had been lost, bewildered by a world where city
stretched on all sides of them, where the other girls judged her
by her clothes and who she knew, who or what her parents were.
A girl from a one-room grade school in Mill Junction, Wyoming, couldn't possibly fit in a Sherman Oaks school where
three kids in her class had TV actors for parents and others were
picked up in Cadillacs and Lincolns. She'd have been lost even
if she'd had money for constantly changing fads. And their new
guardians—Aunt Betty, Uncle Hal were almost old enough to be
Jennifer's grandparents, childless. They didn't understand things
like that, even if they could have afforded them.

The checks from their father had stopped after the first year;
Jennifer hadn't seen or heard from him except for a Christmas
card a few years ago. He'd put a return address on it, but she'd
dumped the envelope without writing it down. Her mother might
never have existed, for all anyone had heard of her over the past
twenty or so years.

Junior high was better; Jennifer had made some friends by

then, and she'd discovered music. She still owned the cello she'd played in the high school orchestra. Now she played only for herself, and between work and family she hadn't taken it out in nearly a year.

She'd wanted it, badly, in high school: seeing herself acting, or playing—cello with the symphony, singing with a rock group on the Strip, it didn't matter. Common sense and a grim determination not to stay poor any longer than she could help it forced the dream aside. She went into pre-law and then to law school.

That had been—she didn't like to think what it had been. The grades to get her in. Tuition. She'd lived on campus, in the communal house for girls who couldn't afford dorm fees and hadn't the pull to make a sorority; she'd worked a full-time night job for three years, took in typing, worked weekends in the school cafeteria. Those years were a blur, little ever standing out. Law school wasn't any easier, but at least summer clerking for Heydrich & Harrison paid well enough to fund most of her next year's classes, and—her second year—for the decent haircut, the makeup, the two good dresses and the sharp red suit that put her above the poverty-stricken, dowdy clerk bracket. Suddenly, there was an offer of a job, the Bar was behind her, there was nowhere to go but up.

Professionally, anyway.

Personally—there wasn't any personally. Lying under the scratchy sheet, listening to the clunk of her air conditioner, to someone's dog barking down the block in response to a motorcycle revving from stop sign to stop sign, she thought about this briefly. Shook her head as the rumble of the bike faded. It didn't matter—correction, it *shouldn't* matter. Any more than Jimmy's remarks, which still rankled.

"If it doesn't matter—if you don't need to prove anything to anybody, then why are you still chewing on it, Cray?'' she asked the ceiling.

Personally—it really didn't matter. She hadn't dated much in high school and there hadn't been much time for guys in college. In law school now and then she'd go off with one crowd or another for pizza and beer, or half a dozen of them would congregate outside the library. There'd been a few movies with a classmate, a couple of dances. Since coming into the firm, she'd taken in a few movies with James, played tennis with him once or twice—when? Maybe a year ago, he'd thrown over tennis for racquetball about then.

James was nice, but not her type; she didn't think she was his type, either. And dipping the pen in company ink wasn't a good idea. She sighed, turned over and stared at the far wall, at the hot blue-white pattern the street light made through her closed blinds. There'd be someone; she wasn't in a particular hurry and now wasn't a good time to start a relationship anyway.

Was she trying to prove something? To herself, that she wouldn't become another Robyn? To her father or her mother, that she could succeed without them? "Sounds like one of Jan's magazines; pop psychiatry in two columns, cure all your problems," she growled, and rolled onto her other side.

She worried about the wrong things, in that case. She had little in common with her father, that she remembered. Nothing with her mother. She couldn't become another Robyn; they had things in common, but they weren't really alike. One of them had firm control of her life and where it was going. The other— "God. Poor Robyn."

Poor old Robyn. She loved her sister, everything notwithstanding; she always had loved Robyn. Robyn was sweet, kind, caring. But when the partners had suggested she invite Robyn to the Christmas party this last winter, and to the celebration when they won the Mayer case in April, she'd found an excuse both times and not mentioned either to her sister. Was she ashamed of Robyn?

Frankly, brutally, she knew the answer had to be yes. At least, in certain company. There wasn't any polish to Robyn; she looked like an aging hippy or a redneck compared to all those varnished attorneys' wives, of course, but then, Robyn *was* an aging hippy, and not apologetic for what she'd done; Jennifer respected her for at least having the courage of her convictions. But she could almost hear the whispered comments behind both their backs, the jokes . . . And Robyn wasn't safe to take places, sometimes. Her language, her interests, the things she stood up for could get embarrassing, and she got even louder and more plain-spoken when she drank. Robyn drunk: Jennifer had nightmares about Robyn, a Heydrich & Harrison party, and booze. "Fifteen years from now, here you are, senior partner, brilliant advocate, trial lawyer—hell, why not?—the next F. Lee Bailey, and still finding reasons why your sister can't come to the office parties," she mumbled. "Oh, hell." She rolled onto her stomach and pounded the side of the mattress, hard.

It wasn't fair. God knew, she loved Birdy, but— "But. I did it, *by* myself, no one helped me, I came out all right. I didn't go to hell in a handbasket and use Daddy for an excuse. And I don't see why I should have to choose between my new life and my family, either.''

By 1966, Robyn was hanging out weekends on Sunset Strip or up on Hollywood Boulevard. Then afternoons and evenings after school. When Aunt Betty rather timidly protested, Robyn threw a fit, quit school and moved out, staying wherever she could find a place for her sleeping bag. Or with any guy who'd take her in. Her phone calls came less and less frequently, then stopped. She wouldn't come out to the house in Sherman Oaks any more. Aunt Betty didn't help; she wouldn't even try to get Robyn back, just said she was over sixteen and responsible for herself now.

Robyn moved in with a guy named John somewhere along the line; Jennifer remembered being old enough to go off by herself and she'd taken the bus down to Hollywood once or twice. But she was scared and appalled by the casual atmosphere and the number of people actually living in the grubby apartment; the constant, thick smoke made her dizzy and ill. And it didn't seem to matter to Robyn if she came or not; Robyn was distant, usually stoned, often hallucinating, sometimes simply drunk. John tried to corner her when Robyn wasn't around, or his friends did. The last time she went there, someone followed her down the hall and out to the bus stop, left only when she flagged down a cop. She quit visiting. John had no phone; now it was three or four months between Robyn's calls.

When Jennifer was in high school, Robyn simply vanished. She showed up for Jennifer's graduation, though: too thin, dressed in torn jeans, a mirrored T-shirt, and ugly, flat sandals, with skinny little Chris in tow and one of her husbands—Karl, Jennifer thought. They'd both been pretty odd, Robyn's eyes didn't track, and she couldn't finish her sentences. Only her affection for Chris reassured Jennifer. Even then, the boy seemed to be parenting Robyn rather than the other way around.

Chris dated from her stay on a commune in Arizona—the members had shared everything, and Robyn had no idea which of the men was the boy's father. She was happy there, and left only when the group decided to go entirely macrobiotic and ban alcohol, pills and psychedelics. She moved back to Los Angeles.

By the time Jennifer was at Berkeley, she got letters from Robyn—a few sentences, badly spelled and in handwriting worse than any lawyer's, on cheap lined tablet paper. Or postcards from Chris. Now and again Robyn called when something went "sideways," as she called it. Things often did. She was untrained and uneducated, and unwilling to deal with the main-stream—the "straight world." She went instead from relief program to relief program, from disastrous boyfriend to even more disastrous boyfriend. There were two more husbands in there somewhere; Jennifer no longer tried to remember who, or when.

Robyn quit dropping acid the second summer Jennifer clerked in L.A., but only after a bad trip and a week in County General; she quit smoking weed but increased her cigarette intake. She managed to get herself off the prescription pills she'd gotten hooked on after one of her live-in boyfriends put her in the hospital with a concussion and a broken arm. Jennifer had a suspicion she'd quit taking those only because Chris read her the riot act—but now she was drinking again.

Nothing changed. Jennifer sighed miserably, rolled over, sat up and stared at the bedroom door. Her stomach was beginning to hurt. But it wasn't all bad, she assured herself. Robyn at least no longer took illegal stuff—partly out of concern for Chris. She'd always been a good mother, even when things were tight; none of her various men had ever laid a hand on the boy. And according to Chris, Robyn had kicked Arnold out herself, when he started leaning on her.

Jennifer groaned as she looked at her clock. Damn James, nice, helpful James, it was *his* fault. She ordinarily kept all this "Family from Hell" business decently closeted. He'd unwittingly pushed all the right buttons to bring it out.

Damn Birdy, for that matter. If Robyn wanted to ruin her own life, fine; she'd been trying long enough. Most of her original crowd had long since vanished or died. But it wasn't right; it was hard on everyone around her. It still amazed Jennifer how well Chris was turning out. Profiting by his mother's example, probably.

Damn herself for that matter, Jennifer thought sourly. Worrying about things at this hour, particularly things she couldn't change. "Why not worry about whether you can stop the next earthquake?" she demanded of her pillow. After all, Heydrich & Harrison wouldn't dump her if—oh, God, if Robyn got caught in the midst of a big drug bust, or got drunk at an office party, or buttonholed Mrs. Harrison, with her fur coats, about seal hunts. Someone might suggest on the quiet that Robyn not accompany her to office functions any more, that would be about all. But a midnight fantod like that hanging over her head wasn't doing her stomach any good, or her concentration. Any more

than the aspirin were. She reset her alarm for an extra hour—
Jan wouldn't have any hard copy for her until nine anyway—lay
back, resolutely closed her eyes and began running a Bach cello
sonata through her mind. It took time, but somewhere during
the third movement, she fell asleep.

3

IT was nearly dark. Lialla had slipped into the hall long enough to light two candles from one of the lamps and then barred the door securely behind her. There was enough water left from the morning to bathe her face. Her cheekbone protested the least touch. She let the air dry it and avoided her mirror. It wasn't the first bruise Jadek had put on her, just the first physical, visible one. She'd never seen him in such a rage before.

What had set him off? Or had it been deliberately planned, to send her cowering into Carolan's pudgy grasp? She couldn't think about that, not about any of it. The mere thought of Jadek's furious face was enough to set her shivering uncontrollably.

The woman who took care of her rooms hadn't come to light the fire yet; she wondered dully if Jadek had forbidden it. Shrugged finally. Myssa was under Lizelle's direction, Jadek never bothered with any of the household servants if he could help it, let alone the women. And there was no reason for him to forbid her her woman. He must think her cowed by what he'd done to Aletto if not to her.

"Aletto. Oh, *gods*." Her hands were trembling again. That had been pure rage, no pretense at all once Aletto had dared to hit him. It threatened to make her ill. Was it somehow her fault? If she'd done something differently—anything save swear to horrid Carolan, because Aletto would never have given way if she had done that; he wouldn't have believed it. But if she'd kept her tongue civil, not angered Jadek so before Aletto came at him! Her mind scurried in an endless circle. She shook her head to clear it and only succeeded in making it ache.

Aletto. Three years her senior, and one of the very first things she could remember was when he'd named himself her champion, like a hero in the tales his tutors told him. Even now he tried to hold to the vow made in the dark hours after their father's death. "Whatever threatens, sister, I'll protect you." Such grand words, contrasting ludicrously with his piping boy's voice.

If she'd followed that wild urge to laugh, so many years ago, his feelings would have been hurt, but this afternoon might never have happened. Not if Aletto hadn't felt responsible for her. Not if she hadn't let him.

She stood, paced between bed and windows, then windows and door. The hall was silent, deserted; her windows reflected torchlight from the courtyard and the outer walls. She crossed the room, yanked the bar aside, pulled the door wide and hurried down the hall.

The empty pile of crockery was gone from beside Aletto's door; so was the soup. A wooden tray covered with a blue cloth stood on a small bench in place of the mess, a straight-sided, tall stone jug of water next to it. Lialla hesitated, glanced nervously up and down the hall, tapped on the door.

Silence. She swallowed dread and the sensation that someone stood just beyond the light, well down the hallway, watching. Jadek, or one of his householdmen, someone who'd report her out of her rooms. Jadek hadn't forbidden her to come here, but that wouldn't stop him from punishing her for it if the mood took him. She knocked harder, hissed, "Aletto, it's me!" against the wood.

Silence again. Then Aletto's muffled voice. "Li? Go away."

"No." Silence. She lifted the latch and tried the door; he'd braced it from inside. "Aletto, there's food and water out here, let me in."

"No."

She closed her eyes briefly, marshalled pain and fear-scattered thoughts. "Shall I stand out here until Jadek finds me? I'm not leaving until I see you."

He muttered something; probably as well she couldn't hear it, she thought. But she heard him moving about, heard something scrape across the floor. Lialla picked up the tray and jug and slipped into the darkened room as her brother pushed the door closed. He turned and walked slowly and carefully across the room, back into shadow. His limp was not obvious, but he moved stiffly.

"You have what you wanted," he said neutrally.

Lialla set the tray on the long table next to an empty wineskin and a pile of books. Aletto made a faint, protesting noise as she lit another candle from the guttering puddle of wax near the door and lit his silver reading lanterns with it. He let his eyes close and eased himself slowly down onto the corner of his bed. His shoulders sagged.

Lialla bit back a cry as harsh light struck his face. The right side was swollen and purple; his eye was turning black from where he'd hit the edge of the table. He managed the least smile, all left-sided, but his eyes were dark and brooding. "You haven't seen the best of it yet. I haven't, either; I'm afraid to look."

"Is any—" She drew a deep breath and forced the tremor from her voice. "Is anything broken?" Aletto's thin shirt hung on his lean frame. The front was smudged and grubby from the floor of Jadek's accounting room.

"I don't know. Never broke anything before; I haven't anything for comparison." He sighed, and his shoulders sagged further. The almost smile vanished. "You're here. You might as well look."

Lialla steeled herself, took both lanterns and went behind him. The once cream-colored fabric of his shirt was torn in two places, snagged in others, spotted and streaked with his blood. "That's got to come off."

"I know. I couldn't; when I finally tried, my arms won't move over my head. But I didn't want to send for anyone."

"No. Wait." She felt in her pocket, found the sewing bag with its small gold scissors. "There's no saving the shirt. I'm sorry, I know you like it."

"I did." In his place, she wouldn't have worn it again anyway, she realized. Not after today. He sat very still while she snipped. She wanted to weep when she finally set the ruined fabric aside. Four long, black welts ran across his back. He hissed when she touched them, swore when she ran light fingers across his ribs.

"Aletto, something might be broken. You can't leave it. Let me get Merrida; she can do a better job than I—"

"No," he said flatly.

"I know you don't like her, but she can help."

"Oh, yes?" Aletto said, even more flatly. Lialla sighed and left it. Aletto and Merrida had never liked each other, not since she'd failed to completely heal the marsh-sickness that left him permanently lamed. He sat in tight-lipped silence while she bathed his back. "You take care of it, Lialla; that's enough for me. For now."

"All right. I have some oil in my rooms. I can get it."

There was hesitation in her voice; he caught it and the reason for it. "Jadek's gone until midmorning, remember? There's a hunt tonight on Carolan's lands."

That was what he had meant earlier; tonight was impossible. "I didn't know. Don't move." He hadn't moved when she came back; he didn't so much as twitch when she smeared fragrant oil into his bruised skin, protested only a little when she cut the loose shirt into strips and bound his lower ribs with it. "You'll sleep on your stomach tonight," she said.

He nodded, winced and let himself down onto the mattress, pulling cushions under his chest and stomach. "I think I'll start now. Your hands hurt more than my stick did." He stared at the wall behind his bed. "Of course, I had a skin of wine in me then, and I was angry. It's harder to feel anything when you're drunk and mad."

"I'll try and remember that." Lialla pulled a stool around to the head of his bed, dragged the tray and the jug down to the end of the desk and tossed the cloth aside. It had covered flat bread, strong cheese, more mealy apples. Peasant food for the nera-Duke, she thought, while Jadek dines with his cousin Carolan on game birds in honey sauces. She was briefly furious, but that passed. At least there was food. She poured water into his cup, smeared cheese over a corner of the bread and tore it loose for him. It was cold and tough.

Aletto took it, sniffed and made a face. "Lialla. You can't marry Carolan." He touched the back of her hand as she let her eyes close.

"I—" She shook her head angrily. "I—oh, Aletto, damn! How can Jadek do this to me? Carolan, of all men! He's fifty, he's enormous and soft and stupid—he thinks of nothing but hunting!" She bunched her hands into fists, crushing black fabric between her fingers. "To think I turned Dahven down because I thought *him* unsuitable!"

"Dahven *is* unsuitable; he's crazy. He only thinks of ale houses and women, he must have bastards all over Sikkre's market by now. And I wouldn't be surprised if the Thukar disowns him in favor of his younger brothers, the twins are much more suited to following the old man; you wouldn't have even had Sikkre for consolation, if you'd wed Dahven—in my opinion. But you underestimated our uncle and stepfather, Lialla." Aletto tore at the tough bread with his teeth, chewed vigorously and washed the bite down with most of the water.

"Again."

"Don't look so awful about it; I'm no better than you. I never

suspected this trick with Carolan, and I—well. Never mind that.''
He looked up at her. ''Is that a shadow or dirt on your face, or
did he strike you?''

She shook her head and fought the urge to pull her face back
into shadow. Ashamed—but it was Jadek who should be
ashamed, hitting a woman so much smaller than he and with no
recourse against him. ''I wish you hadn't hit him.''

''I'm not sorry.'' Aletto closed his eyes; his mouth was a thin,
grim line on the overly narrow face. ''Because even with what
he did, I learned something. I'm not a child any more, Lialla.
Jadek isn't a man three times my size; he's better muscled and
he's trained to fight—the way he wouldn't let me be trained,''
he added bitterly. ''My leg, you know, my weakness.'' He
brooded on this momentarily, held up a hand when Lialla tried
to speak. ''He's no larger than I am, and I hurt him.'' He smiled,
a most unpleasant smile. ''I was drunk; I don't think I'd have
done it otherwise—and worried about you, of course. I do remember that much. But he's not a god, he's not someone to
cringe away from. Never again, Lialla.''

''Aletto, don't—''

''Oh, I don't intend to challenge him directly, I'm not quite
so lost to sense as that!'' he assured her. ''But Carolan—we can't
simply let him go on with this, Lialla. It'll mean my death,
Mother's—very likely yours, I can't say.''

''Don't,'' Lialla protested.

''Shh, listen. Mother won't give Jadek heirs. I'm twenty-eight
now, three years past majority. He's found excuses for postpon-
ing the succession ceremony for three years now, but he can't
put me aside for good and all without greater cause than he now
has: I'm a cripple, I drink to excess, but a Duke isn't called on
to be an army captain, and what he drinks is his own business.
Emperor Shesseran will eventually want better reasons than that
for Jadek's continued grip on Father's title and lands.

''But Jadek is no fool, as you and I know. He wanted eldest's
rights from the first and now that he has them, he won't give
them up. Whether he somehow engineered Father's death—'' He
shrugged, winced and closed his eyes briefly, then rolled cautiously and stiffly onto one side. ''This''—a gesture took in his
weak left leg—''wasn't any accident.'' Lialla stared at him,
shocked into silence. ''I can't prove that, either, but I think he
brought in marsh fever, in hopes I would die of it or be left so
hopelessly mad or crippled he would be free to take Zelharri.
And there have been one or two near accidents recently. Again,

nothing provable, but that's so like Jadek, isn't it? And how convenient for him to be able to say I had attempted too much on a maimed leg and fallen to my death. I nearly did last moon-season, on the kitchen stairs.

"Nothing since that, however. And I can see why now. If Carolan begets a son on you—"

"Don't." Lialla's agonized whisper momentarily silenced him; he gripped her fingers then and went relentlessly on.

"When you have a son, Jadek will be able to dispose of me. Carolan is no matter, he carries too much weight for a man of his years, he wheezes at the least effort. A young wife could be the death of him with no comment but a snicker here and there. Who'd lay *that* to our uncle's door? And then, there'd be no one to sit upon the Duke's Chair save your son, and no one to serve in his place but Jadek. It wouldn't be his son, but I doubt he cares what happens to the succession after him. He only wants to keep what he's had since Father's death." He ate the rest of his bread absently. "Is there more water?" Lialla spilled more on his carpets than went in the cup. Aletto was too distracted to notice. "You can't marry Carolan. So you can't stay here any longer."

She shook her head so fiercely hair flew wildly, whipping across her brother's face. He winced and drew back. "Aletto, I can't leave!"

"Oh, yes, you can! Unless you want me dead soon and yourself and Mother not long after! Do you think you can light candles with old Merrida and hold him off? That hasn't done much good, has it? Not lately, anyway!" He paused. Lialla looked at him, temporarily unable to speak. Aletto touched the back of her hand. "Here in Duke's Fort, you're as good as buried; no one outside knows what's going on inside. Isn't that so? But if you went to the Emperor and petitioned him for your rights—"

Lialla shook her head again, silencing him. "No. That's no answer. Shesseran's so deep in his Festival of Numbers, he's no time to listen and no interest in anything else. And why should the Emperor care what man my guardian thinks a fit mate for me? Jadek's arguments would carry more weight than mine, Aletto, and he'd see they reached Court before I could. And what he said today—" She sighed. "I *would* have to give way to his choice if the succession were in danger."

"Lialla, listen to me, will you? For the first time in months, I'm reasonably sober and I'm thinking. It's not easy, so bear with me, will you? All right, maybe not Shesseran, maybe you have to get access to someone else—one of Father's old allies. Someone who can present a petition to the Emperor, maybe for both of us.''

Silence. Aletto eased back down onto his stomach; Lialla stared across his shoulders. ''Mother might know someone—she certainly wasn't any use herself today,'' Lialla said, and the bitterness in her voice surprised her. ''But why Merrida didn't even *try*!''

Aletto shifted, swore as pain flared across his back. ''Oh, for—the woman is a *servant*, Lialla! I think you forget that all too often; I swear she orders you about as though your stations were reversed! But she's a servant, a member of the lower class, and you know the law! I'm sure she doesn't forget it around Jadek! Cross him in look, word or deed—Jadek would cut her throat. And Mother—what do you expect? She didn't even protest when Jadek married her!'' He sighed; after an uncomfortable little silence, he went on. ''Think about what he's done to us both, and ask yourself what she must go through, sleeping in his bed all these years?'' Lialla shook her head. ''I've watched him, Lialla. I know how his mind works, or I'm starting to. Think about why Mother was there today.''

Lialla closed her eyes. ''Not to give consent, or to back him. So he could show me that there's nothing Mother can do to oppose his choice.''

''Smart girl,'' Aletto said dryly. ''So, there's only one way out. You've got to cut and run for it, Lialla.''

She stirred. ''I will. If you'll go with me.'' The words were out almost before she realized what she'd intended to say. When she looked up, Aletto was staring at her in wide-eyed surprise.

''It's my dukedom, my inheritance. I won't abandon it,'' he said indignantly.

''You won't be abandoning it! But it certainly isn't yours now, is it? You can't take it from him if he has Carolan and''—she swallowed hard—''and Carolan's get to hold over us both. But you should shift the balance.''

''Not by leaving. Talk sense.''

''I *am* talking sense! I could find someone to petition the Emperor for you—why couldn't you petition him yourself? Or find that someone? Gyrdan is in Sikkre, they say. He was Father's right-hand man, but he left as soon as Jadek announced himself, and most of his men went with him. Gyr would support you, I'm sure of it.'' She waited. Aletto was gazing into the room, across her shoulder. He reluctantly shook his head.

"A good thought, if you had a whole man to seek his fortune in Sikkre."

Lialla gripped his forearm angrily. "You aren't as weak or useless as all that!"

"Let me be honest about this; we'll need honesty. I walk with a stick; I don't ride well and I cannot fight at all, since my uncle in his concern for my health forbade me horses, sword training or anything like it."

"You can learn, then," Lialla said flatly. Her eyes were darkly furious. "By rights I should have learned to properly sit a horse myself, to use a throwing spear; I should know simple wrestling throws. It's law. Jadek found reasons against my learning, too. But I can ride; I taught myself. If there's a way, I'll learn the rest." Aletto's face was unreadable. "You have the one thing that counts: Father's blood. The rest can come, if you want it badly enough. But Gyrdan will back you, because of Father."

Aletto looked at her dubiously. "A fight for what's rightfully mine, though—"

"There won't be a fight. The Emperor would take your side if it came to a battle, and Jadek knows it. Civil war is the one thing Shesseran would never allow. You need only return from Sikkre with enough of Father's men to prove your point, and to outnumber Jadek."

"There's a flaw in your logic. There must be." But Aletto smiled. "I suppose there are flaws in mine as well. There's no right choice, no simple one." The smile faded; he closed his eyes, mumbled to himself. "He'll want an answer before long. Has he said when?"

Dread temporarily submerged rose to twist her stomach once more. "Tomorrow, midday. A meal for the three of us, alone."

"Then say yes." Aletto laid a hand across his sister's lips when she began protesting and shook his head. "Say it only, you can deny it once you're away. Say your consent was forced. But consent for now; let Jadek choose the day, be agreeable, say yes to whatever he wants. Tomorrow night, late, we'll go. The two of us." He let his hand fall; Lialla looked at him with apprehensive eyes, finally nodded. Aletto took hold of her hands and squeezed the fingers. "I'll keep you safe, I swear it. Whatever happens."

"I know you will." There was nothing else she could say. He staggered to his feet and let her out, shut the door. She heard the chair slide across the floor to thump into the door moments later.

Lialla walked back down to her room, but stopped just short of her door. Merrida. If she and Aletto were to escape Duke's Fort and reach Sikkre safely, they'd need all the aid they could get. And Lialla had spoken from a half-formed plan she hadn't even known was there until the words came out. Merrida would have ideas of her own; Merrida would know what to do.

BACK down the deserted hallway, past Aletto's closed door. The room with the stairs was dark, the fire sunk to faint embers under thick ash. Thread, invisible and unworkable during daylight hours, crossed and recrossed the chamber, there for those who could see and touch—and use. "Merrida?" she whispered. No answer. But the thread which bore the old woman's feel/scent was directly overhead and when Lialla drew it down to her it reverberated under her fingers, sensation traveling from one to the other and back. "Merrida, I know you're here."

"Shhh!" The sibilant hissed through her, carrying a mix of fear and anger. Thread slipped from her fingers as she felt the tug on its other end, and Merrida was suddenly and simply there, in the middle of the chamber. Silver thread surrounded her like a lacework ball and ran out in all directions across the floor, briefly and brilliantly lit. "Hold still and be quiet!" Merrida stood still, eyes screwed tightly shut, mouth twisted in concentration, ample chin cushioned on her breast. Thread shifted, becoming again momentarily visible; tendrils split and redivided, snaking across the floor or floating from the upper curve of the ball to surround the younger woman. Merrida brought her head up and her hands together, working them as though she shaped dough into a sphere. The safety encircled them both and the silver light faded once more, leaving them in near total darkness.

Lialla was just as glad for that; Merrida's face had visibly aged since the last time she'd seen the woman, and her eyes bore sign of something that would have been panic had the eyes been anyone else's. It shook her, badly. Merrida never showed fear, seldom even showed concern unless it was for her Lizelle.

But when Lialla's eyes adjusted to the dark, the haggard look was gone, leaving her uncertain whether it had been a trick of the light or if she'd imagined it.

"We're leaving," she said abruptly. "Aletto and I. Tomorrow."

Merrida nodded. "I know."

So calm, so knowing—Lialla felt an unreasoning fury. "I'm not a first-day novice or a goat broker, to be stunned by your marvels, Merrida! I know that you know, and I know *how* you know, and I'm not particularly impressed! This is real!'' She fetched her breath with a little gasp, shut her mouth in a hard line to prevent any further words spilling out, turned away. Merrida waited her out. ''I'm sorry.''

''I know that, too. And I'm glad you realize the gravity of your situation. It *is* real.'' Silence. ''I would advise, girl, that you work harder to stifle that temper; it does your Wielding no good and it loses you allies.'' Silence. ''And it gets you into trouble—but you know that also, don't you? Come here.'' Merrida's fingers slid lightly across her cheekbone and jaw; Lialla winced and would have pulled back but Merrida had her hair in a tight grip. ''Pay close attention; the boy was worse hit than you but you'll have to do this for him, if you can.''

''I can't heal,'' Lialla mumbled defiantly. It irritated her that Merrida never called Aletto by name.

''You can ease the pain and swelling in a damaged face; simply do exactly as I am doing for you. It is an exercise learned by rote and nothing more. Thus.'' The fingers of her left hand traced a wavy path over skin, the right clutched the air before Lialla's face. She felt Thread pulling, tugging uncomfortably at her skin and the hair over her temples, then a sensation under her skin, as though a knot unraveled. ''Take hold, *feel* which ones I have. The boy won't let me touch him. His back—that will simply have to be borne.'' Lialla drew a relieved breath and let her eyes close as the pain went out like a guttered candle. Merrida's fingers gripped her shoulder, hard. ''Pay heed, I am not finished. There—no, not those, the pale yellow—*that*!''

''I can't—wait. I have it.'' Thread resolved itself under her fingers.

Merrida folded her arms across her chest and leaned back against the wall. ''Are you able to talk sensibly now?'' Lialla ran a cautious hand across her face, nodded. The bruise might never have been there. ''I hope that you are, and ready to listen as well. Jadek has become impatient, he's caught in a bind of time with the boy's twenty-fifth birthday years gone and his own early dreams failing to set fruit. Your plan to leave and seek out help is the most sense you've shown. It's a pity it took Jadek's fist to knock it into you.''

''I don't—''

''No.'' Merrida overrode her sourly. ''You do not. A young woman of sense would have wed by now, a husband with the status of a Dahven of Sikkre would have helped her remove the

Duke's power from Jadek's grasp, over time. If you'd had children by now, that would have done more. Instead"—Merrida compressed her lips into a thin line—"you not only avoid marriage but you goad your uncle into a rage when he not surprisingly acts as he did today and seeks to betroth you to his cousin."

Lialla spun away on her heel, blazingly furious; it was several moments before she could control her voice and her trembling jaw to reply. "I never intended to marry. You know that."

Merrida laughed. "Why not? Your mother did."

"Mother never planned to Wield—"

"Your mother reached Orange Sash; it's an honorable level and skilled. You can hope for Orange, Lialla, but you're deceiving yourself to want more. I know what you see in yourself, but I tell you that you do not have the concentration, the talent, the memory, the skills necessary. There's no shame in Orange, or Yellow—even in Blue, which will be yours by your brother's next birthday if you both live and retain your wits." Silence. Merrida's stare dug into Lialla's back; Lialla chewed at her thumb and ignored the prickling between her shoulder blades. "There has been no White in three hundred years, no Silver since the wars when Hell-Light was confined. The skill for either level is beyond me, I admit it; it is well beyond you." More silence. "It's another reason you must go, though. Jadek does not approve of Wielders."

"But you—"

"I do nothing that will permit him to see me; your mother does less than I and spends more effort covering what Wielding she does. He considers us dabblers and so harmless. But there is something you don't know, girl: Jadek is Shaping Light." Lialla whirled around to stare at her.

"He can't be!"

"No?" The old woman chuckled mirthlessly. "He has done so, off and on, for a number of years now. But this past moon-season, he's done more: He has a Triad." Lialla clapped a hand over her mouth and shook her head. "I tell you he has. Oh—not here, not in Duke's Fort. Shesseran has removed the restrictions on Light, by default rather than intent, but Jadek is sensibly quiet about his forays into Shaping, and his Triad. I smell them on him when he comes home after an absence."

"Carolan—Oh, gods, Carolan is sheltering them, then," Lialla whispered, and the whisper shook.

"I suspect it. I will not attempt to prove it, since by my inaction they do not know I know." She shifted herself away

from the wall and suddenly became all brisk business. "He'll
return to the fort tomorrow; he'll want your answer for his
cousin. You'll consent, of course; if possible you'll do it without
formally swearing, and you'll ask a full moon-season, thirty-two
days, to prepare. He'll not expect you to agree to such a short
time; that will work to your advantage in escaping. If you formally swear, it will take Carolan's death to free you, even if the
swearing was under duress. Do you understand that?"

Lialla nodded. "If Jadek insists, though—"

"Then you'll swear if you must; they must both think you
broken and compliant, and Carolan will then have to die." She
turned to stare into the fire, squatted heavily and stirred the
ashes, added a bundle of twigs and a scoop of charcoal to them.
The wood flared up, lighting her face from beneath, accenting
long lines running from her nose to the corners of her mouth,
down into her chin. She looked immeasurably old and tough,
but when she glanced up her eyes were dark with worry. "You'll
need aid."

"There's no one here Aletto will trust, save Mother, and she's
no use!" Lialla bit her lower lip and forced herself to silence.

"Hush, girl," Merrida said sternly. "She's been more use
these years than you know! But not all bruises are as visible as
yours, and the worst are not physical."

Lialla buried her face in her hands, ran them back through her
hair, dislodging pins and two fine ties. "I'm sorry. I just—"

"It was no easier for her, today, watching, than it was for
you being watched," Merrida snapped. "A lesser woman might
have slain herself years ago and left you entirely to Jadek's
whims."

"I know."

"Never mind. There's no go with here; your brother is right
in that. I haven't used a sending spell in all too many years, but
I still remember how; I'll find men to aid you. Somewhere—
let's see, the shallow cave a half-league from the road that leads
to Sikkre—not the main caravan route, the north herdsman's trail;
you know it?"

"There's a stream that crosses the road four times, a pool of
Hell-Light to the south of that, a dell that curves north?" Merrida nodded. "You and Mother took me there as a girl, before"—she drew a deep breath and expelled it hard—"before
Father died. Several times."

"Berrying. You remember well. The cave is another forty

paces up the dell, through a tight copse to the left side; it's not sealed against Light or any such thing, but it *is* safeguarded. Like this room. I'll send whatever aid I can draw through there, you stay until it comes. Your brother's no swordsman and you've no training in women's weapons."

"No."

"At least you realize your liabilities. Good. If the chance presents itself, seek out that training; you're not physically strong enough now, but you can become strong. Persuade your brother to whatever training you can.

"Avoid the Thukar of Sikkre. He has a Light Shaper among his household magicians but no Wielder; he sizes men and women and situations in terms of coin."

"Dahven?"

"The son? I don't know. That's for you to decide. There are men of your father's in Sikkre; you may need help in finding them." Merrida stood stiffly and clasped Lialla's shoulders between her hands. She shook the younger woman slightly. "I won't come to you or speak to you tomorrow, so this is farewell for a time. You have brains and skill; mind you use both. Your brother will need all the aid you can give him." Lialla nodded and swallowed dread. "I'll go out as soon as I dare tomorrow evening before you and he leave—you'll wait until the dead hour to do that, if you're wise. If I don't deceive myself, if I can still draw down outside aid; it'll reach you by dawn. Don't tell your brother how it came or he'll reject it!" Lialla nodded. "Arms-men, if I can, of course; a full armed guard if possible. But," she sighed, "it isn't always my choice. An outside drawing often takes life of its own and when the magic chooses—be aware of that; accept whatever comes to you."

"I'll—I'll try," Lialla said. Merrida laughed and kissed her on both cheeks.

"At least you're honest about it! Go now."

Lialla hesitated. "The kitchens—we'll need food."

"Food, blankets, at least one horse, proper clothing. Stay away from the kitchens and the stables; Jadek will have men watching for you to attempt escape tonight. I'll deal with the former and your brother can take care of the horses tomorrow; the man who has brought him information all this past winter is trustworthy. Besides, it will make the boy feel of use." Merrida hesitated, turned Lialla around and shoved her gently toward the door. "Remember that, too: Jadek has all but destroyed the boy's faith in himself. You'll need to let him rebuild it, if he can. If he's to rule in Zelharri when he returns.''

''I—understand. Merrida, thank you.''

''Don't thank me tonight; wait until it's certain I've done anything to be thanked for. Go; both of us in this place wear on my safeguards.''

4

It was dully warm in the central L.A. Basin, slightly foggy on the west side of the freeway, nearer the beach. Smoggy in the Valley. Jennifer drove through thick Saturday traffic until she left the Santa Monica Freeway and headed north; by the time she set the Honda climbing out of the Valley, traffic was almost reasonable and moving swiftly. There were fewer cars heading out into Antelope Valley, and once they crossed the pass and came down into desert, there were only a few pickup trucks, an occasional camper.

Robyn had managed the lunch, but Jennifer wasn't sure how; she sat in the passenger seat, eyes closed, and her color wasn't good. *Hung over,* Jennifer thought grimly, but wisely kept her mouth shut. Not that Birdy would lose her temper; she never did. One of her problems, so far as her younger sister was concerned, was that she didn't, which made it all that easier for people to walk all over her. Particularly men. She had other ways of dealing with anger and resentment, though: One word about her drinking and Robyn would make nasty, sarcastic cracks off and on for the rest of the day. On balance, Jennifer would have preferred a nice, clean shouting match. Just once.

"Thought I got to drive today," Chris said, and brought her out of an in-spiral of gloomy thought. She looked in the rear-view mirror. He was spread out across the back seat, side to side, one enormous sneakered foot shoved hard against the driver's seat.

"Not this morning," Jennifer said. "I want to be awake enough to bully you into doing it right." Chris opened his mouth, shut it again, and looked momentarily rebellious. Only momentarily, though. Jennifer cast him a smile over her shoulder, and wondered as she so often did whether he was just a little too agreeable. Whether it was true that mass murderers started out as agreeable little boys, the way all those TV tabloid interviews with neighbors tended to indicate. "Haul that foot out of my back," she added. Chris obediently shifted, sat cross-legged in the middle of the back seat so he could see out the windshield. "If I have to hit the brakes and you aren't belted in, and you go through the window . . ." she began warningly.

Chris laughed. "I'm wedged in back here so tight, where would I go? Besides, I'm insured, right, Mom?"

"Mmmm—much as I am," Robyn mumbled. "Which means County General or the Free Clinic, all like the other poor slobs." She opened one eye, looked out at the bright landscape, moaned and let the eye close. "God. Why'd I say I'd come out here with you two this morning? This is awful, I'm dying."

"Obviously you're a masochist, Mom," Chris assured her cheerfully.

Robyn groaned again. "I must be, keeping a smart-mouth kid like you around. Why don't you go run with the gangs like other guys your age, 'stead of hanging over my shoulder all the time?" She didn't sound even remotely serious and Chris just grinned. "We gonna stop at the fruit stand?"

Jennifer nodded. "Sure, Birdy. Won't be much fresh good stuff in right now, though. Too early."

"Hell with fruit, I'm out of cigarettes."

"Now, Mom," Chris began. He stopped as his mother held up a hand and half-turned in her seat to fix him with a cold eye. "Later, kid. Much later. I can't handle the lecture at this hour, all right?" Chris patted his shoulder. "Don't do that, damnit, you're making my head ache." But Robyn laid her fingers over his hand briefly and managed an almost-smile to take the sting from her words. Chris smiled back and nodded, but his smile vanished and his eyes were darkly concerned as soon as Robyn turned away and let her head fall back against the headrest.

Poor kid, Jennifer thought. Chris had been mothering Robyn for so long, making sure she ate, that she took prescribed pills when she needed them, or got to the doctor when she was sick, that she got some exercise. He fussed over her when her men left, listened when she needed to talk about them before or after they left—he bullied her about her smoking and drinking as much as he dared, saw to it she got out and did things, dragged her off to the movies or an occasional cheap concert at one of the small clubs—to see groups or people who'd been big back in the sixties and still played locally. He hadn't had much chance to be a kid himself, certainly not in the past five years or so.

They bought grapes and two enormous pomegranates; got a jug of sage honey for Robyn, who swore by it for sore throats; bought canned pop and Robyn's cigarettes—three packs. Chris scowled but kept his opinion to himself; Robyn still looked awful. She stuffed two boxes in the bottom of her ancient denim shoulder bag, fumbled out a disposable lighter and expertly peeled clear wrap from the box, had one going before they got back to the car. Robyn looked at her across the car, hand on the passenger door; Jennifer looked back, eyebrows drawn together. "All right, I know. Not in your car."

"Not in my car," Jennifer said firmly. "You smoke, Chris and I will go over there and stare in the windows."

Robyn looked where her sister pointed. "Yah. Antiques. Old coffee cans with rust holes, purple bottles and chipped Depression glass. Have fun, children." She turned away from the car and walked back over to the long porch that ran along two sides of the store, sank down onto the edge and sat there, eyes closed, smoking.

Chris and Jennifer walked across the road. There were several so-called antique stores, mostly unpainted wood, windows that hadn't been washed in a century by the look of them, oddments scattered in the yard out front, dim and cluttered interiors. They walked between rusting claw-foot bathtubs to mount a rickety pair of steps and peer through a window. "Your mother's a witch," Jennifer said.

"What, the coffee cans?" Chris put on a good show, keeping up banter. He didn't look around; neither did Jennifer. "Or the purple glass? Tell her that, though; she'd like it." He bent over and shaded his eyes. "God, there are campaign buttons in there older than *you* are."

"What, Eisenhower?" Jennifer demanded sarcastically, and Chris grinned at her impudently.

"Naw. Stevenson." She aimed an open-handed swing at his ear; he ducked.

"Why?"

"Why—oh, why a witch?" He drove both hands through spiky hair and absently began to pull at the ends, separating them into stiff points. Jennifer had to bite back a laugh; Chris got defensive about getting caught playing with his hair. "I think it's her latest direction; I think she's gone weird since lovely Arnold left."

"What, not cards and all that?"

"I Ching," Chris said briefly. Jennifer cast her eyes up. "I know, don't even say it. The tarots haven't been out of the closet yet—that I know about, anyway. And I bet she doesn't know where the rest of that junk is any more—like the Ouija board and things. She's been talking about Wicca, though." He sighed. "I don't know much about it, except it's a witch-thing, right? I mean, I can just see it now, Mom's going to get hooked up with another bunch of weirdos, until the next Arnie comes along. I mean, witches? Come on! I can see it now, can't you? I mean, the guys at school and stuff: 'Hey, Chris, saw your mother flying over the tops of the palm trees again last night!' "

"I don't think it's *quite* like that," Jennifer replied. "There's a strong mystic side, I think. Feminine mysteries, of course. Other than that, I know someone who did it for a while. She called it a great female support group. Maybe your mother needs that, and we both know the mysticism won't throw her."

Chris was tugging at his hair again. "Naw. She likes all that stuff. God. Feminine mysteries. I can see it now; she gets hooked in with them and kicks me out of her life for being one of the Oppressor Sex, and—hell, I don't know. It just gets hard to live with."

"I know it does."

"Yeah, I guess you would. Look—don't say anything, will you? About this Wicca stuff. I don't want her thinking the wrong thing."

"You know I won't."

"Yeah, I know. One of the best things about you, Aunt Jen." They walked on down the dirt, sand and fine rock that substituted for sidewalk. Chris peered through a double gate and into the back acreage of one of the shops. "God, how can they stand all that clutter? Oh, well. I guess being a witch is no worse than being Buddhist, except when she used to read me to sleep with Alan Watts, for God's sake. Or, when she'd tell the Watchtower people that—you know, that she was a Buddhist, I swear she did it just to push their buttons, because they'd stand on the porch and argue at her for *hours*." He stopped talking abruptly, eyed her sidelong.

"No broken bones," Jennifer assured him. "I wasn't responsible for Mother's choice, after all."

"Sure," he said doubtfully. "Well, anyway. Mom doesn't have any money, so it's not like she's siphoning off my inheritance to keep Reverend Ike in limousines."

Jennifer stopped in front of the next window. "You should move out, Chris. Seriously, you should."

He looked at her, shook his head fiercely. "You know I can't just leave her."

Jennifer sighed. "You know darned well what I mean, Chris. Not tomorrow or next week; but you should plan on your own life; you can't spend all of it watching over your mother. Robyn can take care of herself, even if she doesn't take care of herself the way either of us would like her to. And you need to clear your head, Chris. Do a semester of college down in San Diego or up in the Bay Area. It's not like that's the moon; you can call, drive home weekends. It's not necessarily forever, either." Silence. His mouth was set; stubborn, *like Robyn,* she thought with an inner sigh. "You need to step back from things sometimes, get a chance to see them and yourself with clear vision. Even just for a little while."

"I can't," he said flatly.

"Think about it, will you?" He shrugged; she had to take that for an answer. "Better get back to the car before she lights up again," Jennifer added. Chris closed his eyes momentarily.

"God. I wish she wouldn't." He led the way back across the road. Robyn was waiting for them, sitting in the passenger side, feet on the ground and door open. She let Chris help her up so he could get into the back seat and swatted his jeans as he went in headfirst.

"Talking about me," she said severely. "Teach you, brat." But she was smiling, and her eyes behind the oversized sunglasses were almost properly open.

"Told you she was a witch," Chris said from the back seat. "You called two out of the three on the junk in the window, Mom." Robyn laughed, winced and climbed back into the passenger seat. Jennifer leaned over to pull the seat belt into place.

"County General," she said as Robyn would have protested. "Free Clinic. You'd look like Boris Karloff with stitches all over your face."

"Planning on an accident?"

"Just planning," Jennifer said, clipped her own belt and turned the key.

It was nearly noon by the time they turned off the main highway and onto the narrow road leading south into the backside of the San Gabriel Mountains. Narrow roads ran down through dry washes, around tight curves. Jennifer drove slowly, feeling Robyn tense every time her tires squealed even faintly, every time a car went by the other direction—Chris in the back seat, fairly vibrating with impatience because she was going so slowly. Driving with both of them in the car was invariably a nerve-wracking experience, but it would have been a worse one to bring poor half-awake Robyn—pounding head, morning impatience, queasy stomach and all—up this road with Chris at the wheel.

The park was visible only in brief, tantalizing glimpses until the car was through the gates and over the cattle guard; once in the parking lot, Jennifer could see the vast slabs of sandstone that gave the Punchbowl its name: long, inclined flat slopes of yellowish stone, enormous piles of stone and rubble; the deep, narrow cleft with the stream at its base. The steep wall of rock on the other side that drew free-climbers. Stone ledges and cliffs worked gradually down on that side of the water, but Jennifer had never crossed over, never hiked that side. She came here too seldom and when she did, preferred to sit and watch from places with a view of a vast stretch of valley, others where she could see nothing but brush and more rock.

It wasn't a popular park, not well known, and there was no camping, no major trails. No drinking water for miles. Only two other cars were in the parking lot when Jennifer pulled in. Two white-haired women in corduroy trousers and hiking boots shared a picnic at one of the tables and a family with three small children clustered around the glass case with the tarantula in it. Jennifer and Chris set out down the main trail, clambered up the first long exposed slab and sat on the uppermost edge. Robyn didn't like walking fast, particularly hung over; neither of them could bear to amble the way she did. She'd be several minutes catching up with them.

Jennifer inhaled dry, crisp air—it was a little cooler up here than in town, much cooler than it had been at the store. "Witchcraft aside—how is she holding up?"

"Without Marvelous Arnie? Actually, pretty good, considering. Watching *everything* on TV and smoking too much." Chris drew his knees up to his chin and stared out north. "She was pretty sloshed last night, but, you know, Friday—I guess Arnie was going to take her somewhere, she wouldn't say where, and of course he kept the tickets. So, you know. She hasn't been drinking that much lately. Not really—"

"Really?"

"C'mon, don't look at me like that, last night was . . ." His voice trailed away; he shrugged and shifted his gaze. A glider sailed across the valley floor and vanished to the west. "Hell. I think it was the Civic, the Ventures or somebody like that. Doesn't matter. She'll get over it." Jennifer eyed him from under her lashes. Robyn would; she wondered if Chris would. He never mentioned girlfriends; she never asked, but just now, she found herself wondering.

She cleared her throat, gave the subject a nudge away from the edge where it was heading. "She's taking forever. Do you want to bet she's down there by the nature walk sign still, talking to that woman and fussing over the kids?"

"No bet. Without the kids thinking what a geek she is, too. You know she was the only mom in my seventh-grade class that none of the kids felt uncomfortable around? My friends used to say you could talk to Mom, used to tell me how neat she was." He smiled faintly. "Think *all* those kids are theirs?"

Jennifer laughed. "What, those people we passed? Come on, Chris, three kids?"

Robyn came into sight moments later, walking slowly down the path with the young woman and two of the children. One of them tugged at Robyn's sleeve; Robyn bent down to exclaim over the child's pine cone, or branch, or whatever she held, then straightened and talked to their mother for a moment longer, until the woman was dragged away by her two excited offspring, both now shouting for their father.

Robyn smiled and watched them go, then looked up at the ledge and the two waiting for her. She sighed, shook her head, and—bent nearly double, both hands ready to grab handholds in case her feet should slip—she crawled up to join them. She was panting when she got there.

"Your lungs are full of crud, Ma," Chris said. Robyn sat, well down from the edge, before she tried to clip his ear. He ducked, too late, and yelped. "Child abuse, child abuse, this woman is beating me!"

"Shut up, that poor woman down there might take you seriously." She looked up at Jennifer, nodded her head in Chris's direction. "How'd I wind up with a brat like this?" Chris smirked, cowered in mock terror as Robyn brought her arm up again. "God, all the way to the top? I'm the one who should yell abuse; I hate high places and rock scrambling scares me silly. I suppose you're both going to scream if I light up, aren't you?"

"Fire danger, Birdy."

"Likely excuse. Never mind." She tucked the denim shoulder

bag between her knees, strap wrapped firmly over her knees, and gazed all around. "Why don't I get out of town like this more often? God, I love this place!" And as Chris stood, "Hey, kid, why don't you be useful, go get the lunch. At least one of my orange sodas."

Chris jumped up; Robyn tightened her grip on solid rock and shuddered. "Sure. We can't eat up here, though; picnic area only, remember?" He scrambled down the rock, took the last twenty feet in three giant strides and walked back to the parking lot. Robyn watched him go.

"To answer my own question, I don't know how I got a kid like that. Too damn lucky, I guess. Couldn't be good karma, I'm convinced I'm still working out the last two lives, getting rid of the screw-ups so I don't have to come back next time as a lizard." She ran both hands over her long, straight hair, tucked it behind her ears. "Hell, never mind all that. Job going all right, kid?"

"Not bad. Worked my tail off this last week, doing research."

"So some man can take all the credit for being smart, right?"

"This time, right." Jennifer grinned. "Last time, it was for one of the women partners."

"Hah," Robyn said good-naturedly. "Window dressing."

"Not lately, Robyn. You need to come out of the early seventies."

Robyn tilted her chin back and shifted so she could look up at her sister. "Hah," she said again. "You don't think we've won—you're not that dumb."

"No."

"You're not going to argue it with me either, though, are you?" Robyn laughed. "Don't let them turn you into window dressing, kid. You're too smart for that."

"They haven't shown any tendency to that, we're too busy," Jennifer said. "Working me half to death—that's different. Part of the dues you pay for becoming a lawyer, especially in a good-sized firm. Men, too, before you say anything," she added sweetly.

"Ouch. You do that so well, I would say you and I have had this conversation before. I would also say you probably don't have to worry much about being measured for a pedestal, do you?"

"Not as long as Heydrich needs research done; it's too hard to jump on and off the darned thing with all those books."

Robyn laughed at that. She sighed, then, and turned to look

down the path, out across the desert. "It's so damned crazy. I remember when they said you'd probably go into acting or modeling; you were always the pretty one, the talented one. All that music, all those plays. I was supposed to be the one with the brains."

"You've got brains, Birdy."

"Hah. Sure. Bird-brains, for all I've done with them. I don't know." She shook her head; the heavy blonde hair swayed and Jennifer repressed a dual urge: long-felt jealousy for Robyn's wonderful hair, and a wish that she'd do something—anything!— with it. Not cut it, never that; but she'd worn it just like it was now since 1967—straight, center parted, no bangs, all one length well below her waist. It made her look older than she was. It typecast her, Jennifer realized suddenly. Portrait of an aging hippy, nonproductive member of society, dropout. Doper. Bleeding heart.

"And those labels were Aunt Betty's, remember? Speaking of bird-brains, however well intentioned?"

"Yeah, right." Robyn sounded more depressed, instead of less. "Funny, I was thinking about her last night. Haven't done that in ages. Her and Uncle Hal—God, poor Straights, what did they ever do to get stuck with me? Mom's blood coming out, I guess—"

"Birdy, that's crap. Don't—"

Robyn turned and looked up at her. "Sure, I haven't started hawking Watchtower yet. Skip it, drop it. It's not important. I— it's hard to remember that far back, not what I did, but why. I can't even see what was so damned exciting about it, all I can remember are the bad trips—and that was most of them, getting wiped out on acid or speed and some guy trying to play with my mind, rearrange my head. Stuff like that."

"You can't think about the past when you're in a bad mood. I remember all the stuff from college I'd rather not ever think about again."

"College," Robyn said gloomily. "I never even finished high school. I wanted to go to college, never figured out what I'd take, though."

"Zoology," Jennifer said gravely. Robyn cast her an astonished look.

"Are you nuts? All the animal rights rallies and petitions I've done, and I still don't eat red meat—" She stopped, managed a weak grin. "Nice. I'm not awake enough yet to hassle, girl."

"Sure. No red meat, but you eat chicken and fish. What kind of vegetable do you class them as, carrot or broccoli?"

"We aren't going to get into that today," Robyn said firmly. "No, it was thinking about all that stuff that got me going— Chris told you I was pretty blotto last night, didn't he?"

"No. One look at you this morning did, though."

"God. Disgusting. What am I—ten years older than you are? I'm living in a dump of an apartment, furnished in Goodwill classic—" She held up a hand as Jennifer stirred. "Look, don't say it, you don't get to help me, I don't need a lot of *things*."

"Material possessions are such a drag," Jennifer quoted gravely, but her eyes were alight.

Robyn shrugged; an embarrassed grin crossed her face. "I got out of the habit of owning things years ago, before I had Chris. I wasn't hinting for that kind of help, and we do all right."

"I know. You can squeeze more from a dollar than I can from twenty."

"Practice, kiddo. All the same, I thought a lot last night— while I still could, after a while it got pretty fuzzy. I need to glue myself together, do something with myself before it's too late and I'm a candidate for the old folks home. I hate people who say they should have done things; I don't want to become one of those. Besides, Chris'll be moving out one of these days, going to college. Getting married, I don't know. Did you know he's decided to major in history?"

"He hadn't told me. What can you do with a degree in history?"

"You lawyers," Robyn scoffed easily. "So damned practical. I don't have any idea. Probably teach, though; he just hasn't made up his mind about teaching. But you know how he was a couple years ago, couldn't tell Florida from Italy?" Jennifer nodded; she remembered, because she'd had to coach him for two solid weeks so he could pass World History. "Well, then he got hyped on all those games—Dungeons & Dragons stuff, I don't know what they play any more, I guess it's all different, but suddenly he was *really* into maps. Got books on them, map books of battlefields—" She sighed. "I hated that; he was all the time going on about things like Waterloo. Wars and fighting and killing. It's not real to him, I had to try and remember that. And it's his life; I always swore that even if he wanted to go lifer in the Marines, I wouldn't bitch at him, I went through it and I saw too much of it. Anyway, after that, it was books about the battles, and then what led up to them, and now he's got American history books all over the house and it's the damnedest stuff, not just wars and battles. Who'd have thought?''

"He'd be a good teacher—I think."

Robyn laughed. "Hard to picture, isn't it? Skinny kid with a black leather jacket and a punk haircut standing in front of a class? He's enthusiastic, I always liked that in a teacher.'' She sobered. "God, you know he's a senior already? I worry about the kid, he spends entirely too much of his time taking care of me. I know, you both think I don't know that. I see it. If I could find a way to push him out the door and into some girl's arms— part of the time, anyway—I'd do it. Maybe he'll do it on his own yet. But what I was trying to say: I can't just keep coasting like I have been." She brooded over this. "Where'd he go for that soda pop of mine, back to L.A.?''

"Probably talking to someone; remember last time, the guy with the metal detector?''

"Right. Or somebody with a truck and a good sound system in the parking lot." She fished for her cigarettes; she looked at the pack, sighed again and stuffed them back in the bag. "Fire danger, I remember. I'm thirty-eight years old, Jen, with no job, no man, no way out of L.A., nowhere I want to go, even if I don't want to stay. A kid who's old enough to be in college. I smoke and drink too much, and I haven't done anything worth- while in years.'' She sniffed faintly, surreptitiously rubbed her nose with the back of her hand. "I hope you never have to sit and face a mess like that and realize you did it all yourself. Of course, I can't imagine how you'd ever come close, it's not your style. But it's not fun at all to figure out what a screw-up you are, and realizing you can't go back and fix it.''

"Birdy—"

"Let me, okay? I'm not hitting on you for sympathy. It's just— somehow, I was a kid and then I woke up and I was middle- aged, with a half-grown kid and an old lady's bod. I just can't believe I got from the Sunset Strip to this rock with all that stuff in between. All the good stuff's gone, Jen.''

"Oh, crap," Jennifer said cheerfully. She slid down the ledge and wrapped an arm around Robyn's shoulders, squeezed hard. Robyn wouldn't welcome pity. "Thirty-anything isn't middle- aged, you goop. Listen to you, maybe you should go act.''

"It's not eighteen, either," Robyn mumbled; she leaned into Jennifer's embrace briefly.

"So? Eighteen's a disgusting age; I was all arms and legs at eighteen and I still had zits. Think about it without the rose-colored glasses, why don't you?''

"Yeah, well—here comes Chris, God, do I look like I've been crying?''

Jennifer examined her critically. "A little. Here, look up, let him think you got dust in your eye.''

"Both of them?'' Robyn demanded, but she managed a smile, and by the time Chris got back up the rock with three cold cans of pop, she was near enough her normal self that she could pick on him for taking so long.

THEY climbed—or rather, Chris and Jennifer climbed; Robyn found a depression not far from where she'd been sitting, and watched them. A little later, when the rocks began to sizzle, they slid down to the main path and walked back up to the shaded picnic area. Chris fetched the cooler; Robyn broke out excellent fried chicken and a salad. The air was clear, dry and blazingly hot.

Chris took one last wing and walked down the switchback to sit with his feet in the creek; Jennifer and Robyn moved to another table so they could stay under the trees and still watch him. It was a long way down; by the time he reached the bottom he was a very small, foreshortened figure with brown arms and legs, spiky blond hair. He was standing in the water watching a vulture high overhead.

Robyn was quiet and withdrawn; Jennifer wasn't certain if she was still headachy and hung over or if she was regretting her earlier outburst. Hard to tell. Robyn seldom shared things like that—she thought of it as bleeding all over people. When Chris finally started back up, Jennifer walked partway down the trail to meet him; Robyn sat on the picnic table, feet on the bench, and smoked.

A few other people came and went throughout the afternoon: two hikers with daypacks and binoculars; a young couple with a baby, who followed the marked trails conscientiously and with the air of those who'd fulfilled a duty. They left as soon as they'd finished the marked route, returning the information brochure to the box as they left. A middle-aged man came in as they left; he wore baggy orange Bermudas, a mismatched shirt, and black dress socks, and he ran over the entire picnic area with a loudly beeping metal detector. Chris had to be restrained from overt rudeness. A camper pulled into the parking lot near sunset; a middle-aged man stood on the hard ground and stretched for several minutes, then climbed into the back and drew the curtains. Chris walked down the trail and clambered up his favorite rock to watch the sunset; Robyn took one last trip to the restroom, checked the cooler and stowed it behind the back seat.

Jennifer gathered up loose paper napkins, crumpled foil, paper plates, the paper cup Robyn had faithfully used for not only her cigarette butts, but also the ashes, and tossed them in the trash. When Chris came back to join them, she held out the car keys and indicated the car with a flourish. She had to bite back a grin at the expression on his face—or more correctly, lack of it. He was trying very hard to look as though driving the Honda was an everyday event.

Robyn climbed into the back seat and fastened the seat belt with a nice loud click; Chris cast a dark look over his shoulder, carefully adjusted his mirrors and the seat. Jennifer fastened herself into the passenger seat less ostentatiously and leaned back comfortably. "Got enough leg room back there?"

"Just fine."

Chris backed past the camper and started down the narrow dirt road. He drove carefully, back overly straight, hands gripping the wheel just above the midpoint. The car moved as stiffly, shifting back and forth a little on the downhill side of the road. "Relax, kid," Jennifer said finally, "it's insured. Besides, you're not going to hit anything."

"Don't intend to," Chris said. The words came out cautiously, as though they might interfere with the car's steering or his concentration. But his knuckles no longer showed white against tanned hands and his shoulders were a little less unnaturally squared.

"You won't," Jennifer said calmly, and she turned away to gaze out the passenger window. Chris, more assured by this than by her words, relaxed even more. He drove slowly—probably slower than he'd have liked to. Robyn leaned back in her seat with an almost inaudible sigh; Jennifer heard it, but Chris apparently—or fortunately—didn't. They came onto pavement after a few miles, and he turned on the headlights. Jennifer turned the radio on low, rolled down her window partway and watched sage slide past.

The air was cool, pleasant after the heat of the day. Chris sped up a little on the straightaway. "I forgot, I've got club tonight at eight-thirty. How long d'you think it'll take us to get back?"

Jennifer consulted her watch. "You'll make it. What, more Dungeons and Dragons? Thought you were over that."

"Come on, you know that's ancient stuff, we're well beyond that. What we have now—"

"Never mind," Robyn said firmly from the back seat. "You drive."

"Come on, Mom, I'm not that bad a driver! Besides, you should try it, really. We've got access to two IBM computers now, it's hot." Silence. He slowed to negotiate a tight corner, picked up a little speed on the straightaway again, lost it precipitously as an oncoming car topped the ridge and sped past them.

"I wouldn't know which end of a computer to talk to," Robyn said. "And those games worry me."

"Don't you dare tell me they're devil stuff, Mom," Chris warned. "I hear enough of that crap!"

"Me? Not likely!"

Jennifer laughed. "I don't think you have a lot to worry about that way, not from us. But I thought it was boards and funny dice, not computers. Or are you doing the arcade stuff, too?"

"Not exactly. It's still dice and like that. The computer games have been around forever but they were always just words, or maybe some cheesy graphics tossed in. Good puzzles but dull visually. Some of the new ones, though—Charlie's got access to some rental games and he has an IBM. The games are high-res, a lot better than they used to be. You used to arcade, right, Jen?"

"A little."

"Okay. Difference between Pong and Pac-Man, all right?"

"Got it."

"I like it. It's not a substitute, the IBM, but it lets me try different stuff. Like, I'm a warrior in Saraband, but I get to be a magic wielder on one of the other games, and I actually made it most of the way through before I got killed off."

"I don't think I'd like that," Robyn said. "Getting killed, even in a game."

"They aren't all war games, Mom. Some of your fellow peaceniks are computer wizards these days." Chris laughed; he deftly geared down for a sharp turn and the Honda ran down a steep hill, into thick shade under cottonwoods. It was nearly dark down here, though they could still see blue sky overhead and a brilliant band of yellow and orange to the west, through and under the branches. "But I forget, you don't even like playing checkers, Mom. You just don't like losing."

"She used to hate playing Old Maid for the same reason," Jennifer grinned. She rolled the window up; the air down in this swale was damp and absolutely chill, and Robyn gasped in the back seat as it hit her. "Sorry, Birdy; getting cold out there, isn't it? I just—my God, *what is that?*" Robyn let out an airless little scream; the car skidded and Jennifer gave Chris her full attention. "Foot away from the brake, Chris!" The back wheels broke, the rear of the car came around; gravel flew. Chris swore; his voice cracked. The car slid sideways down the road, heading with what he would have sworn was intent, its goal a pool of absolute night that filled the lowest point of the road. It obscured everything beyond it.

Chris was panting; Jennifer leaned hard against the cross-strap of her seat belt, gripped his biceps and got his attention. "Do not use the brake! Ease the clutch in—that's right, slowly, you're doing fine, Chris! Gear down—slowly; don't try to steer, just hold the wheel steady, concentrate on the shifter, get it slowed down!" She shook his arm, repeated her instructions. Chris was following them but the car was not responding to the wheel, and at first she wasn't certain if it was even slowing; it was entirely too dark where they now were to see. The car took one last sharp turn; the back tires bit into something and the car came to a stop, sideways on the road. Or she thought sideways, it felt that way, but she had no point of reference any more. Whatever caused that unnatural darkness, they were in the midst of it.

Chris had fallen forward over the wheel; Jennifer shook his arm, her own blood thudding so loudly in her ears that at first she couldn't tell if he was breathing. Behind her, Robyn began whimpering; that reached him. "Mom?" He sat up, gripped Jennifer's fingers where they had hold of his arm.

"No. Back seat, don't you remember? Robyn, are you all right?"

"N-n-n-no. God, no! It's—it's all black out there, God, what is it?" Robyn's teeth were chattering. Jennifer heard the click of Chris's seat-belt release, felt the car shift as he slewed around in the bucket seat. Suddenly she could see again, just a little; the headlights were still on, glaring whitely into nothingness. The dash lit the interior, very faintly.

"It's all right, Mom." Chris's voice was too high and it threatened to crack again. "It's nothing, I just got startled. I guess it's some kind of fog? Anyway, sorry." Little noises from the back seat, no real response; Robyn trying hard to gain some kind of control over herself. In the dashboard illumination, Jennifer saw Chris turn the key. Nothing happened.

"Floor it," she said. A faint gleam of eyes as he turned to look at her.

"I am," he said. "There's nothing there."

"The battery's new," Jennifer said. She stopped. The headlights weren't dimming; there was power, the engine simply wasn't responding. "Oh, God," Robyn whispered from the back seat; there were tears in her voice.

"It's all right, Birdy." Jennifer's voice stayed steady; it was something she'd always been able to do, staying calm for others when she had to. Like when Robyn had broken her arm back in Wyoming, or when a friend in swim class had panicked in the deep end of the pool. Collapse later, when it's over, she told herself. After the car starts and we're back on the highway. Chris's fingers trembled on the key, then fell away.

"That was a rough stop," he said. "Maybe something in the wiring came loose, I'll check it—"

"Don't get out of the car!" Robyn threw herself forward in the gap between the front seats and grabbed her son's arm with both hands.

"I'll do it," Jennifer said. "There's nothing out there, Birdy; we'd see it, with the headlights on. And we didn't go far, so if the car won't start, we'll just walk back."

"I—" Robyn was shaking her head frantically. Chris took her hands between his and shifted in the seat to touch his forehead against hers. He was whispering reassuringly, as Jennifer dug her flashlight out of the glove compartment and unfastened her seat belt.

It wasn't as scary as she had feared; she had too much to worry about anyway. It was even darker outside, or so it felt—as though the air was saturated with blackness. But when she tilted her head back and looked up, it seemed there might be stars up there, above thick trees. The car appeared undamaged; there was nothing she could see under the hood that was loose.

Unnatural dark; unnaturally dead car. This was no place to be. They'd have to walk back up the road, find the place where everything had changed on them, find a farm house or a passing car, get help . . . Help for or against what, though? And how were they ever going to get poor Birdy on her feet? Jennifer sighed and walked around the car to the driver's side. Chris let the window down an inch.

"We can't leave your car on the road; someone will hit it. Jen, you and I can push it, can't we? Mom, you come out on this side—no, come on, it's all right, hold onto my hand, you'll be fine.''

"I—I can't—''

"Come on, Mom, you can't stay here." He opened the door, swung his feet out and set them down; his mouth sagged and his eyes went wide in an almost comic expression of surprise as his feet touched down on a cushioned, springy surface. He looked up at Jennifer, who was playing the flashlight on the ground in front of her. "Jen?" he whispered urgently. "Where'd the road go?''

Good question, Jennifer thought grimly. The front wheels had still been on asphalt when the car slid to a stop, the rear ones in sand and gravel. Now, all four sat in thick pine needles, springy grass and fern. Robyn, fortunately, was too shaken to notice anything. At least, until they got back past the rear bumper. They didn't go much farther. Four paces down what had been road, Chris fetched up hard against something solid. Jennifer brought up the flashlight, and in her surprise, nearly dropped it. All around them were trees, an entire forest of enormous fir. The air was heady with the smell of resinous fir. And by the girth of the one directly in front of her, they'd been where they were for a hundred years or more.

5

LIALLA sat hunched over her knees in the dark, just to one side of her door. Her legs were beginning to cramp but she was afraid to move yet, even enough to straighten them out or to massage the calves.

It was late, well past middle night; moonlight had slid across her bed, down over faded rugs and bare floor, had shone briefly against the mirror near her door, spraying the room with shards of light. It was gone now, save the least light on the thick stone wall beyond her windows. She'd sat on that ledge as a child, until her nurse caught her at it; she'd studied then how a deft person could work down from the deep ledge to the narrow, wooden lattice two floors below that shielded most of the balcony.

She hoped it wouldn't come to that tonight; she had all too clear a vision of how such a trip might end, particularly for a young woman who hadn't the strength to pull herself into a saddle without hard effort.

But the hall was a veritable highway this night, or so it seemed to a young woman crouched by her door, using a marketplace charm to tell her where people were—common market charm, she thought in despair, because Thread evaded her sweaty-palmed, racing-hearted, frightened grasp. She glared at the beaten image on the surface of the small coinlike object: too thick for a real coin, of course, a long-eared rabbit on its one side, an owl on the other. A peasant could buy such a charm, if he had the coin for it; any of Lizelle's serving women could own such a charm. She, Lialla, who had wrought Thread for half her life, had bought this and two others a year before, on a whim—she'd never thought she'd have cause to rely on any of them.

One of Jadek's personal men, there—up the hall and down the main stairway, two servants back the other way. Two men not long behind them, two more later, when she'd almost begun to shift her weight and the bar across the door. Those had been regular housemen, sworn to Jadek but not necessarily loyal to him. She hadn't Merrida's ability to read people, though; she wasn't certain Merrida had all the ability she claimed for that particular skill. People were complex, even the simplest of them, and Merrida was notoriously fond of defining them in two directions and one color. *Arrogant*, Lialla thought as yet another set of footsteps came along the corridor—a maid's this time.

Carolan had returned with Jadek from the hunt; he'd unexpectedly remained after the luncheon. Lialla wasn't certain where they'd bedded him. Surely Jadek wouldn't be so brazen as to house the man so near his affianced! Even with Lialla's perceived free consent to the wedding, there were forms to be adhered to—neither man would be so foolish as to attempt to circumvent those, would he? A noblewoman was expected to remain pure until wed; even Shesseran would not—! She tore her thought from an increasingly hysterical path and stared at the carpeting, at her rough boots, until her breathing came back to normal.

That wasn't Jadek's style; he was only crude in words and blows. And he had adhered to the formalities so far; he'd continue to do so—as long as things went his way.

She heard a skittering, a low and throaty growl, a shrilling abruptly cut off. It took her a moment to realize it was distant, a sudden and unexpected response of Thread to an earlier command, now multiplying the strength of the market charm: only one of the cats after mice in the pantry. Outside the door, up and down the hall, there was no sound at all. Someone breathing on the landing of the main stair; a guard, perhaps, or one of the housemen. Nearer, muffled sound that must be Aletto behind his own closed and braced door, since it went nowhere.

How much longer would it take? She could not Wield once the sun rose; unlike Merrida, she couldn't even draw in Threads at night to set working later. The charm would not last the night, if she continued to draw upon it so heavily, and she'd have no access to another this side of Sikkre.

And they had to reach those caves before dawn! The secondary road would be alive with people and beasts by the time the stars faded; there were markets in all the villages and this time of year good weather served as an excuse for holiday, and for a visit to Duke's Fort and the City of Sehfi surrounding it. Women brought fine needlework done over the winter, or wool, young animals and eggs; the men came with worked leather to trade, tools, hides. Only in deep winter or planting and harvest months could they have chanced to travel the roads unseen, or to step from them. The forests held huntsmen and pig-herders, anything not woods was a farm, a herd-holding, and even high country was watched over by hawksmen or shepherds.

She shifted one leg cautiously, kneaded the ankle tendon. Leaving Lizelle still bothered her, and Merrida's assurances meant nothing: Jadek would surely suspect Lizelle's complicity when she and Aletto disappeared. Even if he didn't, that temper— She shivered, rubbed at her other leg, forced herself to stand.

She had to continue to trust in her stepfather's cunning, and his determination to keep Duke's Fort for himself: With Aletto and herself gone, he'd have no member of the immediate family in his control save Lizelle. He'd have to keep her alive. *Until he catches us,* she thought, and shivered again.

There was no one moving in the hall, no one there at all; there hadn't been in some moments. But she was trembling as she pulled the door in enough to let her look out.

One lantern shoved too far back in its niche well down the other way cast ominous shadows across the floor. She gathered up the two bags, pulled the wide leather strap across her arm and pulled the door closed behind her. Setting the bar from outside took only a moment; she'd readied that what must have been hours earlier, leaving Thread tangled around the end. It wouldn't serve to hide the emptiness within for long, of course— by midday, Jadek or Carolan would remark her absence and the door would wind up splintered. At least this way no one would push the door wide with her breakfast at first light.

The packs were awkward and heavy: built for a horse to carry, not an overly thin young woman. She ran down the inventory, suddenly certain she'd left some important item on the floor between her bed and the windows. Silk cloth for sleeping and to layer under her scarves if they encountered rain or cold. Tinder, in case she must start a fire during daylight. Water bags—one full, two empty. As much food as she'd been able to save from her tray, as Merrida had been able to scrounge in the kitchens for her. A knife—but not a woman's fighting knife, which she couldn't have used anyway. The blade was broad at the base, sharp on one side and thick and rough on the other. The cooks used such knives for skinning meat, beating tough cuts, gutting fish.

One spare shirt and a presentable skirt of dark, lightweight fabric. If they somehow went to Cornekka or Dro Pent, she'd not dare show herself in public in breeches, whether Wielder-cut or otherwise. Breeks and women didn't go together in either Duchy, and even a noblewoman could be publicly beaten for flaunting her legs.

Medicines, a small bag of them. She'd had a time of it, getting Merrida to provide her with anything—Merrida had calmly waved aside her concerns about need. Lialla, bitterly aware that her attempt to heal Aletto's cheek was barely successful, had finally gone plundering on her own.

Aletto's door was closed, and no light showed under the lower edge. When she scratched at the wood, he opened it at once, pulled her in and leaned against it. His face was drawn; she thought he might have been standing there for hours, waiting.

"You weren't followed, were you?" he whispered anxiously. She shook her head. "Sure?"

"I can tell," she replied. Aletto frowned and she bit back an angry remark that was at least half anxiety of her own. "You ready? We have to get going, it's a long way where we're going."

"I—" He shrugged, scooped up a length of thick brown wool and slid it over his head, wrapping the front twice around his shoulders and fastening it with a plain black clip. Another piece of the same stuff clipped to the throat of the cloak wrapped over his head, covering his pale hair and face. He paused with a hand on the door latch. "She's promised us armsmen?"

Lialla nodded; anything to get him moving, she thought guiltily. Merrida intended armed protection; what she drew in might be another matter but Aletto would be safely outside the fort and well away from it by that time. Aletto gripped a bag similar to hers in his left hand, balancing it awkwardly atop his second-best stick. In his right, he carried his boots and the sword-harness. The hilt-straps flapped loose.

Lialla pushed past him, stopped him as he started for the main stair, and drew him into Merrida's little room. His eyebrows went up. "Forgot this was here," he whispered. The sound was deadened, even the sound of her boots scraping softly against the stone steps. Lialla stepped into the long corridor, keeping well in shadow, and hurried past the open double doors that led to the kitchens and kitchen gardens.

The door into the courtyard stood mostly closed, and for a moment her heart stopped; Aletto leaned across her shoulder and gave it a shove with his stick. It swung silently out, revealing an expanse of dirt churned by countless hooves and the smell of horsebarns. "Avers said he'd leave it so." Aletto's voice was less than a breath against her ear. He caught hold of her arm, pulled her directly across the open while the two guards high on the outer curtain were at the far end, conversing under the lantern at the corner watch-pedestal. There were normally no guards in the courtyard or the stables, but brother and sister were cautious, waiting against the stable wall for several long, still moments. Aletto slid down the wall to pull his boots on. He shifted the folds of cloak, reached across his shoulder. The least gleam of lantern from high above touched the knife he'd drawn from a neck-sheath. Lialla opened her mouth, shut it again without comment. As Aletto vanished into the stables, she knelt long enough to pull the cook's knife from her bag, then followed him.

Aletto was the least darker motion against a very dark interior. Horses moved, scenting them; subsided as the two moved on, down toward the far entrance and the postern gate. Most of the stalls at this end were empty, but against the far wall were three shapes: two horses and a mule with a bulging pack. Lialla edged past him, pushed the pack across the nearest horse's neck. Fingers and inner sense assured her this was one of the mounts she knew; the trappings were not her usual ones, but had the feel of plain, unmarked ones. But as she leaned forward to detach reins from the wall, Aletto's hand closed over her arm, warningly. Before she could react, he was gone, back out into the open.

Lialla dropped leather straps and coarse mane, fumbled across Thread before finding what she sought. It took longer to get any response. Then: multicolored, dull, black against a darker black, Thread everywhere—and two men coming stealthily toward them. Aletto—he'd moved off to one side, and the dagger was in his left hand now; as she turned her attention to him, he dropped the sword, shifted the dagger to his right. His staff swung out and clattered into a wooden divider. *No, they'll hear!* she thought frantically, and clapped a hand over her mouth to keep the sound in. But the men already knew who was there, and approximately where he stood. They moved too easily for anything else to be true.

"My lord Aletto, abroad at such an hour?" Carolan's silky voice. Carolan, it was rumored, could see like a wolf. The armsman at his elbow was the one who'd mounted guard over the accounting-room door two days before. He towered over the nera-Duke, and there was a look of profound satisfaction on his face. Looking forward to getting even for that door, Lialla realized. "This is an uncivilized hour for a ride, don't you think?"

"But not to come and talk to the horses." Aletto's voice was steady, with just the right touch of impatience. "I often do that when I cannot sleep."

"Ah. Just so. But then, why are the beasts nearest you prepared for travel? And the other—surely that is a pack animal, and laden? Perhaps to sustain a boy in exile?"

"I don't know what you mean," Aletto said evenly. "And I don't need to answer to you."

"No? As the promised of your sister—"

"That has nothing to do with me, Carolan." *Oh, gently,* Lialla thought at him, urgently. Carolan wouldn't appreciate the missing honorific.

"No? Only in theory, young Lord." Carolan took another step forward and his voice went hard. "Where is she? Your sister. She's not in her chamber—"

"Or perhaps she chooses not to answer you when you knock," Aletto snapped. "My sister has an eye to her repute, if you have no concern for it!"

"Perhaps; but I know the sound of empty rooms, as against those where a woman sits silent. Where is she, I say? Does she come here, or has she already gone?"

"The Lady Lialla," Aletto replied coldly, "is not accountable to you. Yet."

"I asked a question you will answer for me, here and now," Carolan said, "or will you have yet another stick broken across your over-proud back?"

"Never by a pig like you!" Aletto hissed, and suddenly launched himself at both men. Carolan, startled, fell back, arms flailing wildly. Aletto's stick caught his temple with a nasty crack; Lialla heard him groaning, swearing furiously, thrashing for balance in deep straw, but her eyes were fixed on her brother and the armsman. And then Carolan lurched back across the open aisle, and threw himself into the fight. Aletto cursed as steel slid along steel with a rasping scree. He pulled away from Carolan's man and fell back, braced his shoulders against a partition and used it to hold to his feet. Carolan came on, dagger up and out; he shoved so hard his own armsman went staggering. Aletto parried Carolan's blade twice but not the third time. Lialla clapped both hands over her mouth; Aletto grabbed at his left biceps but as Carolan relaxed his grip on the hilt, Aletto turned and feinted with his left arm. His right came up and over in a long, fast arc and the knife made a horrid noise as it entered noble flesh. Carolan drew one long, whistling breath, turned away and fell. Aletto swore faintly, and slid down the partition. Lialla hurled herself into the open.

For once this night, Thread readily obeyed her rattled commands: Thread-clarified vision let her see too well for her own peace of mind. Aletto lay unconscious in the dirt, blood running down his arm. A dagger handle wavered back and forth above his shoulder, all that was visible. Carolan lay curled in on himself, curiously delicate, Aletto's knife protruding from between his shoulder blades. Dead, or as good as dead. But his armsman was untouched, and as she stopped, he drew another knife from his boot and took a step toward her.

I can't do this! she thought frantically. *I don't know how, they never taught me!* But she had the cook's knife in her hand, elbow high and out, thumb underneath, the way she'd seen others do it. Carolan's man laughed; the sound was high-pitched, almost a giggle, and the suddenness of the sound nearly made her drop the knife. She tightened her grip, bent her knees slightly.

"Here, girl," he said. "That's no way to be, I'll not hurt you."

"No, you won't." Her voice was breathy, a pant unrecognizable as hers. "Not me or my brother!"

"Certainly not." But he took another step forward and laughed again as she took an involuntary step back. Aletto—she slid her feet sideways, trying to force herself to move, to get between Carolan's man and her unconscious brother. "But you have a problem, haven't you? How to get the nera-Duke on a horse, how to get yourselves past me. How to prevent me giving the alarm." Lialla shook her head. "We might benefit each other—"

"I haven't that kind of coin," she began haltingly. Carolan's man pursed his lips and raised his eyebrows, as though surprised. She didn't think he really was. "Not the kind of coin you'd ask. And I wouldn't trust you."

"No? Well, then, that's not the way to hold a knife. If you intend to kill me, girl, you bring it up so," he demonstrated. "That's the way to gut a man with such a short blade." He was trying to horrify her into dropping it, she suddenly knew; perhaps hoping to anger her so she'd lunge at him and he could grip it. But she was between him and Aletto now; so long as he

thought himself safe playing her and didn't shout an alarm, he
could say anything he wanted. She crouched a little lower, shifted
her grip the way he'd done it.

Straw everywhere, deep drifts of it in the stalls, shreds of it
littering the corridor between stalls. And Lialla, though a far
from competent Wielder, could plait rope under ordinary circumstances without even thinking about it. At a time like this—
but for some reason, now that her need was so great, it again
responded. She reached sideways with her left hand, as though
for balance. Questing fingers closed on Thread, pulled it toward
her, and other Thread went down to the drift of straw behind
Carolan. Thread and straw: She began to plait it, spinning out
a length of near-invisible, extremely strong rope. She fell back
another step as the man brought his knife up. Out of the corner
of her eye, she could see a fine length of straw rope snaking
across the open floor.

Now for the most difficult part: Now to wait until there was
enough of it, strongly woven enough, to bind the man and stop
his mouth.

Carolan shifted the least bit and a bubbling, whispery groan
broke the silence. Lialla nearly shrieked. Carolan's man, supremely sure of himself at this moment, turned to look at his
dying master. Lialla let the knife fall, brought both hands up
and sketched a knot in the dark air before her face. The rope
responded, caught him about ankles and knees, drew around his
thighs and went tight, yanking the legs from under him; he fell
with a heavy thud, air exploding from his lungs in a loud huff.
The knife was under him when he went down. He jerked twice,
brought his head up a little off the floor to look at her. His eyes
were wide, already dead before his head fell back to the dirt.

She was going to be sick; Lialla fought the urge, knelt on the
floor and pounded both fists in the dirt until she was certain she
would not gag. She pulled herself across on hands and knees to
Aletto's side.

He was whimpering faintly, but fell silent when she took hold
of the knife hilt. It was deep in the muscle of his upper arm; it
had missed bone and the large artery, but when she pulled it
out, the wound started bleeding again. Something—anything . . .
She caught Thread, a mess of fine thread like spiderweb, and
used it to staunch and bound it with a length of cloth from
Carolan's cloak. It was all she could do, except get him away;
return to the fort, for Merrida to heal him, and that would be

his death for certain. And if Lialla couldn't heal it, she could at least tend it and make certain he didn't bleed or infect.

She pinched his earlobe, then, hard; he groaned and opened his eyes. "Aletto, hssst! Aletto, let's go!" He mumbled groggily, words she couldn't catch, let his eyes close again. Lialla cast a glance at the horses, back down at him; she couldn't shift that much dead weight. "Aletto, hurry! It's not safe here, they'll find us! You've got to get up on that horse!"

"—protect you," he muttered, and fell back against her. She could have screamed at him, hit him, could have wept. The smell of blood was making the horses nervous; someone would come to check on them to see what the matter was. The smell of blood was going to make her ill any moment. She thought Carolan moved behind her in the dark; she had to fight the urge to turn and watch him lest he be only pretending injury so he could catch her unawares, take hold of her with those soft, deceptively strong hands.

"Aletto!" she implored; something of her urgency and fear got through, finally. She crawled across the floor, came back with Aletto's stick; at his insistent urging, she fought the dagger free of Carolan's back, wiped it on straw and restored it to the sheath at Aletto's neck. She was sick then, and that left her shaking so she wasn't much use getting him to his feet. He was too weak and disoriented to notice her state, and once she got him onto the horse, he passed out.

Lialla found a length of rope—real rope—and ran a length around his chest to bind him to the saddle, two shorter pieces to fasten his ankles to the boot-stalls. The reins went around his wrists under the horse's neck. She dropped the loop in the mule's lead-rope over the knob on the high cantle behind her, gathered up her reins and her brother's, and led both horses and the mule out of the stable, through the unfastened postern and onto the darkened road.

Behind her, Duke's Fort was a gloomy block of building and wall against the torch and lantern light of the city. High on the curtain wall, two men stood close to the lantern. Dicing, perhaps; they were laughing and talking, intent upon something below the level of the wall. They paid no attention whatever to the road that ran past the fort.

"Oh, jeez," Chris whispered; his eyes were all black pupil. He clutched his mother's arm; Robyn sagged alarmingly until he gave her a shake. "Mom, don't you dare conk out, this isn't a

good place for it!" He considered this, stared at the trees picked
out by Jennifer's flashlight and made a strong effort to speak
normally. "You know, that would sound awfully damned funny
under other circumstances. What the hell's happened to us?"

"Don't swear," Robyn whispered automatically. She let her
eyes close, let them turn her around and walk her back to the
car. Chris let out a short, humorless bark of laughter.

"I can see stars," Jennifer said suddenly. "It's not as dark as
it was—I think."

"It was hardly dark at all," Chris began indignantly, but he
subsided as Jennifer cast him a warning look over Robyn's head.
Chris shut his mouth, and when they reached the car he opened
the door so his mother could drop into the passenger seat.

Jennifer slid in on the other side and turned the key; the light
went out of her face as she got absolutely no response. She
sighed heavily, pulled the key out of the ignition, then hit the
light switch. Darkness surrounded them; Robyn huddled in on
herself and whimpered. "Better save the battery," Jennifer said.
She got back out of the car and looked up. There were trees all
around them, visible as blacker shapes against a dark night;
wonderful bright stars overhead, but nothing she recognized.
"Chris?" He stood up and leaned over the roof of the Honda,
then let his head fall back as Jennifer jerked a thumb up. "You're
better at constellations than I am; you recognize anything?"

Silence. He leaned alarmingly back, turned slowly on one
heel. "Jeez. I don't know, I can't tell. You think we're where
we were, somehow? Lost some time or something? I can't see
enough. Shh, Mom; s'all right, okay?"

"It's not, it's not, it's not," Robyn mumbled tearfully.

"Yeah—well, all right, it isn't. But okay, listen, maybe we
got caught in some weird thing, like a Bermuda Triangle thing—
you know, like on the cover of the Enquirer or something? Picked
us up near L.A. and let us out near the Kremlin or down in
Australia or something? Hey!" He clapped his hands together.
"That's all right, we could sell the story, get rich!"

"Mind if we get *out* first?" Jennifer asked him dryly, but she
found his enthusiasm heartening, manufactured or not.

"Yeah, well, maybe getting out is part of figuring out how we
got here and where we are first, you know? Like the games I've
played. We can't drive the car because it won't start and it won't
go through trees, and we can't just leave it and walk off into the
dark; we gotta figure it out, use logic. Now, there has to be a
logical reason for all this, unless we just fell down the rabbit

hole.'' He turned back to look at Jennifer and his young face was briefly drawn and very old indeed. ''Doesn't there?''

''Thinking already. That's good.'' Chris froze; Jennifer let out a startled gasp and spun on her heel, as an elderly, wheezing voice broke over them. ''*It* chose well, even if not what I'd have had.'' Silence then, except branches crackling under Chris's feet and Robyn's frightened, panting breathing. Jennifer swung the flashlight in a circle, but it wasn't illuminating far now, and without warning, it faded to a dull, yellow glow not much better than candlelight. She swore, turned the switch off. Oddly, she could see better without it; see well enough to pick out the figure between trees not far behind the car.

Jennifer felt her seldom-shown temper peak, heating her face. She threw the flashlight into the car and strode back past it. ''What do you mean, chose? Are you responsible for this?''

''I?'' The figure moved, came forward to meet her. A woman, clad in dark swaths of fabric, and if the voice was any clue, very old. She laughed unpleasantly, breathily, and when she walked she swayed slightly. ''Save your anger; there are better directions for it than Merrida. I'd never have asked for such as you, but it chose.''

''You said that already.'' Chris came up to stand next to Jennifer. ''And it doesn't tell us any more this time; stop talking in riddles. Where is this? What kind of name is Merrida? Spanish?''

She shook her head, laughed helplessly. Chris swore furiously and grabbed her arm. Jennifer wasn't certain what happened; the boy was on the ground, the old woman standing where she'd been but no longer laughing. At least, not aloud; her eyes danced with some joke of her own. ''Not Spanish; that's your world and this is mine. They don't touch often, and only when great need drives, and certain conditions are met.'' Teeth gleamed in the dark. ''You, boy—you're virgin, aren't you?'' Chris stared up at her, and though Jennifer couldn't see him clearly she knew he was bright red from his blond hair right down to his throat. Merrida nodded. ''Thought you must be; the drawing had no business going beyond Rhadazi borders for aid but it saw greater need than I, and virgin blood—'' She spread her hands wide and shrugged.

Chris scrambled to his feet, and Jennifer held out a hand to restrain him if need be. But he simply stood where he was, eyes fixed on the old woman. ''Wait,'' he said. ''Your world—our world. Alternate universe. Parallel world? But then, how come you speak English?''

''English,'' Merrida said. ''It's a function of Thread, if one knows how to draw upon it. Picking up foreign speech and making sense of it. Fortunately for you.''

Chris considered this only briefly. ''Magic?'' he said finally, and his voice was a soft, almost reverent whisper. Merrida glared at him, then past him to the dark, silent car.

''It's—ah, call it that, if you wish, it responds, call it anything you choose. If you understand how to make it work, that is. But there's no time for this.''

''Then quit wasting time and tell us,'' Chris said. ''Since we understand each other's words, at least.'' Jennifer blinked, shook her head. The conversation seemed to be taking place on several levels at once, different meanings to everything. But Chris, at least, had no doubts of the situation.

''You'll do, boy,'' Merrida said, and Jennifer heard grudging respect in her voice. ''But this is no game. Death's real, remember that.'' Chris made a noise low in his throat, an impatient gesture. Merrida turned to look searchingly at Jennifer, then to touch her shoulder. Some of the tension went from her. ''*He* brought you through, but it was *you* it chose. Which is it, young woman? Music or dance?''

''I—? I play—I used to play—'' She couldn't remember what she used to play; for the first time she wondered how this strange old woman came to be speaking English. Her accent was extremely guttural, hard to listen to.

''It *was* music, then.'' Merrida folded her arms across her chest in a flurry of black scarves and gazed at Jennifer in satisfaction. ''All right. Listen. Half a league from here, straight through the trees the direction I'll show you, there's a road. Find it, turn left and walk along it until you come to a stream that crosses and recrosses under four bridges. Beyond them, you, young woman, will feel a tug. Like this.'' Jennifer clasped both hands over her breast; there was an extremely odd and not very pleasant sensation under her ribs. ''The nera-Duke Aletto and his sister are down the dell you'll find, in a cave. He's been hurt, he needs your help.''

''I don't know first aid,'' Jennifer managed.

''You'll have access to what I have, at least for the night, by the same kind of means you will all have access to Rhadazi speech. Unlike the language, the healing will not stay with you; I cannot do that for you, or Lialla would not need you to heal her brother. And so I tell you, pay heed to what it does and how it does; there's something in you that will respond. Lialla's a Wielder, she will help you.''

"You're not really explaining," Chris complained. "Where are we?"

"Compared to what?"

"How should I know?" Chris growled. "Why do you think we'll help you? How do we know you're not evil?"

"How do you know that of anyone?" Merrida looked up at the sky, off into the distance. She shrugged. "Words won't prove much, anyone can say anything. But there's a little time." She explained, briefly. Jennifer simply stared at her, caught between utter disbelief and the undeniable circle of trees around her car. Chris, with all his games and books, seemed to have less difficulty.

"You did that to us? Brought us here like this, to fight some-one else's war, to—what are we supposed to do with this Jadek and his what-d'you-call-it? His Triad? Kill them?"

"You do nothing to Jadek and his Triad," Merrida snapped. "Weren't you listening? I asked for those who could help the nera-Duke find his father's loyal housemen, men scattered from one border to another, some possibly across the sea, who knows? It's been years since any of them were seen in Zelharri, and I had my hands full. The boy has need, and the Threads chose. Do you use weapons, any of you? Real weapons, against real men, and to the death?" she added sharply as Chris opened his mouth. His shoulders sagged, he shut his mouth without saying anything. "Or do you use the magic that is in your world?"

"My mother used to read tarots when she was a hippy," Chris said evenly. "And she played with a Ouija board and black candles. I don't think that's quite what you had in mind, though, is it?"

"And music isn't a form of magic," Jennifer added tartly. "You know, I simply cannot believe you *dared* risk our lives like this!"

"I've risked more than mere lives over the past years," Merrida said flatly. "And music—you know better than what you just said. If you don't, you'll learn. I can't return you, not all of you." She gazed over Jennifer's shoulder at the car. "One, per-haps. With the car. But I cannot guarantee her safety."

"She stays with me," Chris said firmly. He turned away and walked over to the passenger side, knelt by the open door and took his mother's hands. When he glanced up, it was Merrida beside him, taking Robyn's fingers away from him. He watched, a faint twinge of anger or jealousy stirring; Robyn drew a deep breath and brought her head up, gazed into Merrida's eyes.

"What are you going to do with us?" she whispered.

"I? Nothing. Save to equip you as best I can and send you to help the young Duke take back what's rightfully his."

Robyn managed the least, shaky smile. "Just like a Dumas novel. I remember when I wanted to live one of them." She swallowed, the smile faded. "Now—"

"I can send you back, you alone, with this automobile—" She stopped talking. Robyn was laughing, leaning back against the car seat and laughing helplessly. Merrida waited her out impatiently.

"Send me back? Without my sister and my boy? With Jen's car that I can't even drive? Isn't that all I need?" She moaned and buried her face in her hands. "Oh, God, I need a drink!"

"I've nothing for drinking save a jug of water. What is your choice? I'm sorry," she added grudgingly as Robyn peered at her over her fingers. "I've no choice myself, and the hour's getting late. The car is creating a hazard, it must go before much longer or it'll reveal all of you, reveal my purpose—perhaps even expose Aletto to his stepfather's Triad." She gazed at Robyn; Robyn gazed back. Robyn held out a hand to Chris then, and let him pull her to her feet. Merrida dragged herself stiffly to her feet. "If there are garments in this car, anything you want or need from it, take it now. I've spring-weight woolen scarves to cover your outlandish clothing; that will see you through to Sikkre. And I have a little coin, enough to dress you for the climate and against odd looks."

"Language—" Chris began uncertainly.

"Understand me, don't you? You'll understand other Rhadazi and you'll speak the language when you leave me—enough of it to get you by. It's similar enough to your own language; at least that will make things easier for me."

"Similar," Chris mumbled. He began tugging his hair. "Then this *is* a parallel world?"

Merrida glared at him. "That's never been a matter of interest to me; find someone else to pester with such fool's questions. You'll understand all but the thickest accents within Rhadaz." She held out a hand to Robyn, took her by the shoulders, and gave her a gentle shake. "You'll be safe enough, woman; these two will see to it. And the boy—the nera-Duke Aletto—he'll protect you. He needs to feel himself useful." Chris stirred at her elbow, eyes narrowed; Merrida ignored him. "If this venture is to succeed, we need his sense of self intact—as much of one as he has." She let go Robyn's shoulders and turned to Jennifer. "Music—you'll have my healing talent for tonight. Mind that you reach that dell before first light; Night-Thread doesn't work except in dark, and it won't stay with you. Pay close attention to what it does; pay attention to Lialla, also. She Wields, if largely by rote and determination, and not by talent. She may resent you, but she'll teach you, if you find the place within you and the desire to expand it. We'll meet again, you and I.''

"What's that, sixth sense?" Jennifer demanded. Merrida smiled faintly.

"A sense of some sort. Perhaps a hunch. Does it matter?"

"It—yes. Damnit, yes, it matters! You just took—reached out and took us away! I have a deposition Monday, I have a career—!''

"You haven't anymore. What you have is here, in Rhadaz. I won't apologize," Merrida said flatly. "If your loss is great, it would be an impertinence. Whatever you left in your world, though, know this: You've an honorable task here, and the future Duke of Zelharri in your debt when you're done.''

"If we don't die first," Jennifer said. But that didn't sound real.

"I may die myself, if that powered wagon of yours isn't gone soon; at Jadek's hands or his Triad's, or simply from the drain on my strength.''

Robyn came around the back of the car, oversized denim handbag slung across her shoulder; Chris called her back, held up the picnic hamper. The two went into a huddle over it and Robyn pulled her purse off her shoulder. Merrida gazed at her back, stroked her chin thoughtfully. "Watch her. Her temper—"

"Temper? Birdy?" Jennifer shook her head. "You're kidding me!''

"She has a temper," Merrida corrected her gently. "In your world, she may have buried it deep, but I can see a disturbing aura around her. It is there, and if it comes out in this world— here there are things that seize on anger and shift it or twist it." Robyn suddenly laughed, swatted at Chris. Jennifer turned and looked at them, a relieved smile on her face.

"What now, you two?"

"Well, I just told Mom that—"

"Jen, tell this brat of mine he's too old to get his picture on a milk carton, will you?" She yanked on Chris's ear, pulled him close and planted a kiss on his cheek. "Besides, who'd want the little monster but me?"

6

⌘

MERRIDA scowled. "What makes you think there's time for jokes?" Chris slipped his mother's grasp and closed the distance between them. The old woman had to tilt her head back to look up at him; he glared down at her and his fingers were twitching.

"I think you've done enough, upsetting my mother, you old bat. It's none of your business if I can make her feel better, so don't you start telling her crap and scaring her again. You got me, lady?" They stared at each other for another long, tense moment; then Merrida turned away as though she'd lost interest, Chris as though he'd scored a point. "C'mon, Mom. Let's make sure we have everything we need; the old bat isn't letting us keep the car." Merrida cast one black look at his back and crooked a finger at Jennifer. The old woman's hand curled around her wrist briefly, then released it. Merrida's skin felt oddly cool, but there was nothing else.

"There, it's done."

"I can't feel anything. Are you certain?"

"Of course I am. It's there, for when you've need. Pay attention; after tonight anything you see or do will be all your own and none of mine. Another warning. Lialla will welcome you for any help you can give her brother; she's got him safe but she can't mend him. I warn you, though, she'll resent that you can do that for him and she can't."

Jennifer rolled her eyes. "Oh, that's just wonderful. Anything else you can do to make this as rough as possible for us?"

"I'm warning you, that's all. Pride and anger interfere with Wielding, and Lialla thinks she wants that above all else. But she doesn't know any world outside Zelharri or any men save

her uncle and his like, that's warped her badly. And the boy—
he's other problems besides that; you'll see for yourself." Merrida gazed at her, eyes narrowed. "You've less knowledge of our
world than either of those children, but you're no fool, I'd say.
Know something of people and how to care for yourself. And
your music—" She sighed faintly, stared across Jennifer's shoulder toward the car; Chris was stuffing something in Robyn's
denim shoulder bag and making her laugh again. "Ever think
about magic, young woman?"

"No. That's Robyn's kind of thing, telling fortunes and the
like. I don't believe in it, quite honestly. Chris reads a lot of
stuff, he plays games. But that's fiction, nothing real."

"He'll think this a game, given the chance. Don't let him."

Jennifer shook her head. "You told him. A boy his age doesn't
accept death as anything personal. And his games are all puzzles, nothing in the real world."

"Well, watch him, and your sister. But you will anyway, I
can see that. Here." She fumbled under fluttering ends of black
cloth and brought out a small, flat wooden box on a leather
strap. "Coin and four precious stones, from the Duchess. You
three will need clothing once you reach Sikkre, you'll all need
food, and there may be a need for bribes. Lialla will know."
She swayed slightly. "Go, hurry then; the fabric's stretched by
that machine of yours and I can't afford to become much more
worn." Jennifer nodded and turned away; Merrida touched her
arm, bringing her back. "I warned you against Hell-Light. You'll
know it when you see it." She managed a brief, drawn smile.
"Anyone of ordinary sense would see it's nothing to approach,
even without knowledge. But now and again, it hides. Be careful." Jennifer merely nodded again and hurried over to the car.

Careful. God. There couldn't be enough caution, in their own
world and this one, for her; Merrida's world sounded as safe as
a snakepit.

She sat in the driver's seat and fumbled through her own leather
bag, checking the contents by feel. Makeup bag—she doubted
she'd call on Max Factor much, but couldn't bring herself to
simply abandon the contents. Her toothbrush and paste were in
there, too, along with hand lotion, vitamins, a small clean-up
kit, and first-aid stuff, a separate mirror, a hairbrush. She pulled
the curling iron out and dropped it on the back seat as useless,
leaned across and fished in the glove compartment for the pair
of leather gloves, a spare pack of tissues, aspirin bottle, her
pocket knife, matches. There wasn't anything else useful. At

least she'd been caught out in jeans and good sneakers, instead of a poly-silk dress and three-inch heels.

She rummaged through the bag again, found the bundle of pens and the small yellow pads on the bottom; together with a few of her loose sugar packets; patted the steering wheel and got out. There was a lump in her throat as she closed the driver's door; her first brand-new car, she'd been so proud of herself.

Robyn and Chris waited by the rear hatch. They were muffled in the long, lightweight woolen scarves. Chris carried Jennifer's old gym bag slung over one elbow. He waggled it at her. "Hope you don't mind, it's the rest of the lunch and the blue ice to keep it fresh." He gripped Robyn's shoulder. "All right, Mom?"

Robyn closed her eyes momentarily, then nodded. "I'm—I think I am. Something—I don't know, I think she did something. I should be shivering and I'm not any more. Maybe it's just so bad, I don't know what to be afraid of."

Merrida came up behind them; she looked even more drawn and her gait wasn't entirely steady. She stopped in front of Chris and held out a long, thin bundle. "Here." Her voice was still rough but not much above a whisper. Chris undid the end and slid a bow partway out. "If you can use one, so much the better; they're weapons in your world, too. If not, learn, one of you." Robyn opened her mouth to protest, shut it again. Chris pulled the cloth back over the end of the bow, tugged the strings tight and slid the case under the strap of the bag he already carried. He managed not to pull back when Merrida took his head between her hands; Robyn flinched visibly when Merrida moved on to her; Jennifer felt an intense wave of dizziness hit her like a blow. The same moment the old woman withdrew her hands and it was gone. "Go," Merrida said finally, and the word was guttural, foreign—Rhadazi, Jennifer realized with an uncomfortable start. "Go, now!" Chris turned, took Robyn's arm and started across the clearing. Jennifer, with one final wistful look at her car, followed.

Merrida leaned against the Honda and watched them go. Worn—Gods of the Warm Silences, she was well beyond worn! But with the vehicle returned now, she'd recover. Perhaps even have enough strength left to tap into the Night and find a bundle of Thread to return herself to the fort. Second Plane travel was considerably easier than the way she'd come; she might even be able to use it to repair her strength, a little. If she found connecting Thread. But first things first. The fabric shifted, swelled briefly, then snapped back into place with a reverberation that shook her teeth; the machine and its contents were gone. As she sank to the ground and let her eyes close, she heard a distant snapping of twigs. It faded.

IT was dangerously dark at first; tree-shadow blending with tree-trunks. At Chris's suggestion they walked in file, hands out to keep from running into anything; he and Jennifer changed places often, keeping Robyn between them, until they reached the road.

The road came into sight about the time they began to think they'd somehow missed it. "Well, at least she didn't lie about that," Chris whispered. "I wish my watch worked."

"It doesn't?" Jennifer fumbled a hand from under the dark swathings of wool, worked her other hand free to press the light button. Nothing happened.

"I checked, back at the car. It's acting all screwy. Which way? She said left, didn't she?"

"Wait a minute." Now that the time had come to leave the woods and step onto that narrow, rutted track, Jennifer felt exposed. But she heard nothing in either direction, not even wind or animals in the leaves. It was silent enough, just now, that they'd hear anyone coming along the road. And anyone using magic, like Merrida, would see them anyway. *Magic*. She looked down at her hands, dubiously. They felt a little cold, nothing else. She tucked them back inside the wool, shoved them into the pockets of her jacket.

"If we're waiting for orcs to come and grab us," Robyn said in a small voice, "I wish we wouldn't. Okay?" Chris laughed very quietly and wrapped a long arm around her shoulder.

"Mom, trust me, this isn't Middle Earth. No orcs, no trolls, nobody to turn you into a pie."

"Don't, it's not funny."

"No? Look, nothing overhead either, no nasties on wings—" He stopped as Robyn giggled and clapped a hand over her mouth.

"You're right," she said finally. "It's silly, and I'm silly."

"Yah," Chris scoffed. "You were afraid of bears and rabid skunks and Bigfoots when we went camping, remember? Jen, I can't see anything out there; let's go."

It wasn't much lighter on the roadway, just easier walking. There was no sound save a very occasional whisper of breeze through high branches and once a high-pitched wail that might have been a bird. For the most part they kept quiet, too, at least until the immediate fear of the comparative open space wore off.

Chris cleared his throat. "Um, listen. What she said, about

not going back—that might not be true, you know. I mean, she's like the guy I took shop from last year, knew *everything*. If he didn't know the right answer, he'd make one up and say it like it was gospel. But she might not know, either. I mean, somebody else might be able to do something to get us home . . ." His voice faded away.

"I—you know, right this minute, I don't really care," Robyn said. "Staying or not. Not that I want to be anywhere right now but on the way home, just like we were. But—well, it could be worse. I have nothing to go back to but an apartment full of junk and a bunch of bills. All I really care about is you two, and you're here."

"Yeah," Chris said. "That's us. And my feeling is, if we *can* get back, I wanna look around here first, see everything I can. Write books when I get home, make a fortune. Aunt Jen?"

Jennifer laughed quietly and without humor. "It reminds me of a college friend of mine, a medieval history major. Said he'd love to visit the middle ages or Troy or something, but only if they'd let him take penicillin with him. But—" She swallowed and walked on in silence. Her job, her apartment, her car: she'd thrown herself headlong into school, only coming up for air after she'd passed the Bar; the apartment, like the job, was a start in the right direction. *My cello,* she thought with an anguished pang. And realized when Chris turned to look at her that she'd spoken aloud. "Sorry," she managed. Robyn dropped back to walk beside her and gave her a quick hug.

"Yeah, well, don't sweat it," Chris said doubtfully. "But let's figure, all right? You saw what that old bat gave me, didn't you? A plain old bow and arrows? That says something about this place, about the people. Because if they had guns, it would make sense that she'd have given us a pistol or a rifle instead of a bow. It's easier to kill someone with one of those than with an arrow. Shh, mom, I'm working something out, I know you don't like the 'K' word. I think this place is pretty primitive, like medieval, and without penicillin, but they have magic. That Merrida must've used some pretty impressive fireworks to drag us here. And she mentioned healing, so I guess that's one plus."

"You can't scare me with primitive," Robyn said, and she sounded almost cheerful. "I spent four years in a commune, remember?"

"Fifteen years ago," Chris reminded her.

"Crap, I can't be that old. But it's like falling off a bicycle," Robyn said. "You don't forget. Jennifer, are you keeping track of distance and markers and stuff? Getting lost would be the absolute end.''

''Yes. Don't distract me, something's—look, over there.'' She stopped in the middle of the road and pointed. ''Do you see that?''

Chris leaned over her shoulder and squinted, sighting over her arm. ''Not really, it's—wait. Wooo, lookit that.'' It was fading again, brightening: a near-circular patch of woods not ten feet from the road. Golden light, like late afternoon sunlight, filtered down through branches, dust motes or the air itself sparkling. For one brief moment they saw grass, brilliantly green grass, and pale flowers nodding in a breeze they could not feel where they stood.

''I don't like that,'' Robyn whispered. ''That's not natural, I don't like it at all.''

''Me, too,'' Chris said. Jennifer stared. Something touched her, tickling her stomach, running along the hairs on her forearms. Something from that Light, but not her own fear. At least, she didn't think so. Either way, nasty.

She turned away. ''Let's go. It's messing up my night vision.''

''No argument,'' Chris replied. Robyn was already several paces ahead of them. Her feet thudded hollow on wood and the air around them suddenly turned chill and damp. ''I just found a bridge, Jen; this must be the creek she told us about.'' They could see white, churning water in the starlight; hear the faint roar of a waterfall in the distance. Jennifer pulled the woolen wrap snug around her throat; it was positively freezing, particularly when they went down a few paces into a depression. By contrast, the night was almost balmy when they climbed to the last of the four bridges, and then up a low slope to open ground.

Robyn stopped. ''Ssst. I hear something.''

''I don't—'' Chris began; Jennifer clapped a hand across his mouth. Robyn had the sharpest ears of anyone she knew. After several moments, she heard it, too. Horses, coming up the road behind them, fast. Chris must have caught the sound when she did; he turned away, grabbed Robyn's shoulders and hurried her off the road, into a cluster of thin-trunked trees. Jennifer sprinted after them and threw herself flat in the shadows. Four horses passed them at a dead run, were gone. She was back on her feet and out on the road almost before they were out of sight.

Chris and Robyn came up behind her. Robyn's face was pale, her mouth set in an angry line. ''What are you *doing*, trying to get caught?''

"Don't be silly, I just wanted to see if they left the road," Jennifer said. "We're near where those two are hiding; I should be able to sense them pretty quickly, if Merrida didn't lie—or overestimate what she says she gave me."

"You can't tell?" Chris demanded. She shrugged. He cast Robyn a sidelong look and squared his shoulders. "Well, look, all right, I don't think we have much to worry about with those four on the horses; they were going much too fast to be looking for anyone nearby. Well, unless they're using magic themselves. But look, logically this stepfather must think they've run for it, gone on to the next town, whatever it is, so they'd be way on ahead somewhere. So they might be on their way there—to the town, I mean, the four guys, to warn someone to watch for the other two, or maybe they'd be looking further up the road, where it's more likely those two might have made it." He glanced back down the road. "That's not to say there aren't others like them out here, of course."

"Thanks, kid," Robyn said dryly. She brushed dirt and dry leaves off her front. "Can we go, please? Before I think about that and either puke or sit down right here in the road?" But as Jennifer started off, Robyn stopped cold and buried her face in her hands. "Oh, *God*. I just realized."

"What?" Jennifer and Chris spoke together.

"I've got one and a half packs of cigarettes left." Chris opened his mouth and she glared him into silence. "One word about this being the perfect time to quit, and I'll—"

"Didn't say anything, Mother." Chris tugged at her scarf-ends and got her moving. "Didn't say a word." But he was smiling complacently as he followed her down the road.

The smile slipped several steps later, and he nearly sat down in the road himself. *Music*. Unless they came through this alive, and got back to L.A., he'd heard his last rock music on the way past Palmdale this morning. His new CD player, all the corners he'd cut getting the coins together for it, the small collection of really good stuff— It settled in his stomach and his throat in a great, sharp-cornered lump.

They walked in silence. The forest was thinning, trees now clumps and bunches, shading into brush. Jennifer held up a hand. "Look, both of you. I feel like a damned fool, but Merrida said I'd be able to sense them from somewhere around here. I suspect I'd better try. Keep watch, will you? I don't know how much concentration this will take." She spread her feet apart for balance and stared off toward the north.

Her ears rang with the silence. But she was faintly aware of small creatures out there; of a large, still bird high above them, watching for the least movement. Chris's misery over his new Paula Abdul CD—she could feel it, almost as keenly as if it were her loss. Robyn, watching her avidly and, so deeply buried even she wasn't aware of it, with envy. Poor Robyn. All those years of tarots and I Ching coins, and it was Jennifer who'd been chosen to bear magic. Jennifer wondered if it would upset her more if she knew how little her sister wanted it.

There was a nagging pain in her left arm; she massaged it, snatched her fingers away as it flared in red-hot agony into her shoulder and down her side. Caught hold of the arm just below the shoulder and squeezed, hard, until the pain ebbed. *His pain.* Aletto's pain. She turned to face up the road; it faded. Increased, throbbingly, as she turned back to the north and walked off the road. ''They're this way.''

''I don't believe it,'' Chris breathed, awed.

''I wish I didn't,'' Jennifer said shortly; it might be Aletto's wound, but it was hurting her terribly, making her breath come short. Merrida hadn't warned her about that. Probably just as well. ''Let's go.''

Brush barred their way; Chris found a way through. The dell was shallow at this point, but it sloped steeply and the ground was boggy in places. It narrowed alarmingly once or twice, but around a bend and then another, opened out once more. Jennifer led, guided by the pain in her arm. Chris put his mother in front of him and rummaged under his woolen wrap, finally bringing out the bow and a long-shafted arrow. It took him only a moment to string it; memories from a summer camp, years before. He'd remembered how to arc the bow, how to attach the string— at least this one was a no-nonsense, no-frills bow like the camp ones. He hoped he'd remember how to shoot it, if he had to.

And that Robyn would forgive him, if he had to kill anything. Or anybody.

He started as movement to his right, beneath rock and over-hanging brush, caught his eye, relaxed as a tethered horse moved partway out and back again. And then Jennifer slowed. ''We're close, very close,'' she whispered. ''Stay with me.'' A black-ness darker than the night, or the overhang sheltering the horses, loomed before them. Before Jennifer could edge through fallen loose stone and shattered boulders to reach the cave opening, a hand came down and gripped her forearm. ''Lialla?'' she gasped.

"Who asks?" came a low, grim reply.

"We—Merrida sent us. We came to help you."

"She—come, you can't stay out here. Hurry, all of you!" The hand stayed on Jennifer's arm, drew her forward. Jennifer sensed rather than saw the flutter of black scarves like Merrida's, a long, pale face. She let herself be led, waved an imperious hand to those behind her. Robyn swallowed, hesitated, but Chris caught her by the shoulders and hurried her after.

"Stay right behind Jen, Mom, we don't want to lose her, right?" Robyn swallowed again, nodded and stumbled across rubble and into the dark. "Cave; watch your head, Mom." Once inside, there was a faint bluish light, just enough to see the ceiling had gone high, vaulting into an unguessed distance. Chris pushed past Robyn, took her hand in his and led her after Jennifer and Lialla, both now distant, dark shadows.

The light grew a little; they passed around a bend and into a small, smooth-walled chamber. A metal box, the source of the light, was wedged between two stones at shoulder level. Another was set on the smooth dirt floor, and by its light, Chris could see Jennifer, kneeling beside a dark-haired man. His face looked terribly pale and drawn; the woman kneeling on his other side— Lialla, he guessed—was nearly as pale. She watched anxiously as Jennifer pushed the cover away from his arms.

Chris dropped the gym bag on smooth dirt. It couldn't be harder than Jennifer's couch, where he had slept a good part of the summer. "Mom, you look done in. That was a long walk for you."

"Yeah. My feet hurt," she whispered. Her eyes were fixed on Aletto's face.

"Well, sit down, then. Who knows, we may be on our way again before dawn." Robyn sighed unhappily, eased herself to the floor and tugged at the grip-tape straps on her sneakers. "Don't take them off, Mom, not unless you've got blisters or something. I didn't see any running water for you to soak your feet in, and if they swell, you're barefoot."

"*I* know. I used to hike a lot, remember?" Robyn dragged her purse up by Chris's gym bag. Her eyes went back to Aletto. "Poor guy. I hope he's going to be all right." She lay down, then, and let her eyes close. Chris cast Aletto a dubious glance before he stretched out next to his mother. He'd seen that look before: Robyn, with her infinite capacity for sympathy, was about to pick up another wounded bird. It was something he admired, really: All the times she'd been stepped on by those she'd tried to help, and it never stopped her from trying once more. All the same . . .

All the same, that was how Robyn had wound up with Arnie, and the one or two before Arnie—and the Mediterranean type who'd *really* been a jerk. Chris levered up onto one elbow and gazed at the limp form between Lialla and Jennifer. All he knew about this Aletto wasn't much, but he didn't sound like such a great deal. "I don't care how blankety-damned noble he is," Chris mumbled under his breath as he punched the gym bag flat under his ear. "A jerk's a jerk. And if this guy's a jerk, he's not going to mess Mom up. Not if I can help it."

"MERRIDA sent *you*?" Lialla stared as Jennifer unpinned and unwrapped the long wool scarf and shook her hair out. There was a visible lack of confidence in both the look and her voice. "You three? That's all?"

"It wasn't our idea," Jennifer said shortly. "It wasn't hers, either—that's what she said, anyway." She bit back a further angry retort. Lialla's gaze had slipped from Jennifer's face; her eyes were dark with worry. Aletto stirred and moaned as she touched his arm. "Look, this Merrida of yours said I could help him. Why don't you let me try?"

Lialla sat back on her heels and studied her in silence for a long moment. She shrugged. "She knew, then—never mind. You're not Rhadazi, you don't have the look of anyone I've ever seen before and your speech is very oddly accented." One hand hovered protectively over her brother. "How, help him? Wait, though. Give me your hand." Jennifer shoved the woolen wrap and her leather satchel aside and held out both hands. Lialla's fingers were icy, her grip hard. "Curious. You're a Wielder? An outland Wielder?"

"No. I'm an American." The proper noun fell oddly in the midst of the implanted speech, and for the first time since Lialla had gripped her wrist, Jennifer *felt* the oddity of speaking this language not her own, when before it had come as naturally as English. "And I'm no—what did you say?—no Wielder; there is no magic where I come from. Anything you sense is Merrida's."

Lialla frowned, finally released her hands. "If you say so." She sat back again. "It doesn't matter. My brother matters. He was hurt when we left Duke's Fort, knifed by Carolan. I—" Her lips twisted. "I can't heal him, I'm not capable of that, all I could do was bind the bleeding, to keep him alive."

"Give me light." Jennifer leaned over the unconscious nera-

Duke and gently pulled the thin blanket from his fingers. It must
have hurt Lialla to admit that, and she clearly loved her brother.
''What you did saved his life; there's nothing wrong with that.''
Lialla looked at her, away again.

It took several minutes for the two women, working together,
to soak the binding from Aletto's biceps. Jennifer could feel the
blood leave her face when she saw the wound, and was glad she
wasn't standing. It was a deep cut, rough-edged and seeping a
little; the skin and muscle gaped. Ugly. The shock of such a
wound alone would account for his present state, even if he
hadn't bled much, and a cut like this would ordinarily bleed.
Should still be bleeding. Jennifer extended a very reluctant hand
and brought it, palm down, over his arm, just above the wound,
not actually touching it. Her own upper arm ached fiercely,
throbbed rhythmically.

Night-Thread? She could sense it, suddenly; she could see it
cluttering the wound, a white wadded mess of it. And unless
she was going mad, she could hear it: There was music, faint
music, in the stuff under her fingers, a distant piccolo or a reed
flute—but it faded when she tried to concentrate on the sound.
Concentrate, she told herself, *on what you're doing*. The sense
of music stayed with her; the nera-Duke's arm was cool under
her fingers. She drew them back when he moaned and shifted
restlessly.

Between her hand and his arm, a network of faint, luminous
lines was becoming visible. Silver, black—all colors. Some ran
straight, others curved, or spiraled, or gathered in rainbow clus-
ters, ran helixlike, binding together and separating. It blurred
before her eyes, separated even more clearly as she blinked.
There was music everywhere, a faint blending of disparate
sounds that was not unpleasant, if not particularly melodic.

There. She knew, all at once, which of them would serve her;
her right hand caught a twist of Thread, four shades of blue; her
left took hold of another, reds shading to purples. ''Lialla—
Lady. Can you remove what you did?'' Lialla, wide-eyed, nodded. ''Do it, now.'' Thread writhed in her hands; blood welled
up and spilled down Aletto's arm. Jennifer swallowed bile and
laid her right hand across the wound, flat. Blood oozed between
her fingers. ''Think what you're doing,'' she whispered. ''Not
what you feel.'' It helped, a little; and then the music caught
her ear and took hold of her. Instruments or voices similar to
flute or violin, all soprano; faint, though. But she had the line
of it, and with that, sudden and profound gut-deep understand-

ing of why those particular Threads were right, what they did. How to seek them out on her own.

It shook her; this was utterly illogical, so unlike anything she'd ever done in her life. The music wavered briefly, resubmitted itself to her ears as she stopped trying to analyze. The Thread itself was cottony and slightly sticky to the touch. It clung to her hands, then to torn and outraged muscle, veins, skin. Aletto's pain, once nearly unbearable, became a mere itch in the back of her mind. And was gone. She blinked. The music faded. When she lifted her hand, there was nothing left of the wound but a faint, pink line. Aletto stirred, mumbled something neither woman could hear, and subsided into a much more natural-looking sleep. Lialla scrubbed a sleeve over her eyes and pulled the cover up to his chin.

"Here, I think your companions are asleep; let's take the light, move away a little. I have wine, you'd better drink some."

Jennifer swayed as she stood, kept one hand on the cave wall as she followed Lialla, and gratefully sat once again. The wine Lialla handed her was over-sweet for her taste but not cloying. She drank, felt the world steady, and handed the leather bag back. "Thank you, Lady; I needed that."

"Lialla to you, Healer. And I am just a sin-Duchess; only my mother is called Lady."

"Lialla. You can't call me Healer, though; that was Merrida's magic."

"Say some of it was."

Jennifer shrugged. She'd have to put some time between herself and what just happened before she'd even think about analyzing it. "Call me Jennifer."

"Jennisar—Jenniser?" Lialla couldn't make it work. "That's no name anywhere, I've never heard it."

"It's a mouthful. Try Jenny, or Jen if that's easier."

"Jenny." Lialla's "j" came out soft, more like a "z." "Your friends—"

"My sister and my nephew. Robyn and Christopher, everyone calls him Chris, though. I—look. I have to know. This Merrida said she couldn't send us home again. Is that so?"

Lialla shrugged, took a swallow of wine and set the leather sack between them. "I don't know. I don't know anything about such things. If she says so, it must be true. But I'm only an initiate; when she said she would find someone, I thought she meant—I don't know what I thought she meant. Men from the Emperor's city, perhaps; or maybe nomad men who carry knives and fight for anyone, for enough coin. We—Aletto expected armed men, Jadek never let him learn to fight, I haven't even the training given Rhadazi women. I can't—'' She shrugged, smiled bleakly and closed her eyes. ''No, I can't say that; I still cannot use a dagger properly, I simply killed a man with one tonight, as much ill luck as anything. And now, Aletto has me, and you—and those two. He won't like this.''

Jennifer let her eyes close and counted to ten. ''He isn't the only one who doesn't like it. And then all this mystery! She said she wanted armed guards for you, but then she said the magic chose us instead. That's a rotten explanation, if you ask me.''

Lialla shook her head. ''That's just how Merrida is. A good Wielder doesn't explain, particularly if she doesn't know.''

''God. Chris was right. But I can't think why this magic would choose *us*! It's ridiculous! I know law, I know music, but I'm not a great lawyer yet and I never was a great musician, and there's nothing useful about either, that I can see, anyway! My sister hasn't killed anything larger than a housefly in her life, she hates violence, and I don't think her so-called ability to read cards is going to be exactly handy. Chris plays games and reads books. People like us—ordinary people where we come from— we don't fight or kill or any of that. That's for TV and spy novels!''

Lialla bit her lip. ''You're using odd words I don't know. But we *have* to trust what Merrida told you. If the magic chose you, then there's nothing more to be said.''

Jennifer shifted. The ground was uncomfortably hard under her hip, and the cold was seeping through her jeans. ''Oh, there's plenty to be said. What you're doing, where you're going. Where we are. Why somebody cut him like that, and who this man is who got killed. Above all, why. Tell me.''

''I can try.'' Lialla turned so she could watch Aletto sleep. ''A long time ago, the Emperor broke Rhadaz into nine individual Dukedomes, and turned them over to his friends. The original Duke of Zelharri was a many-times great-grandfather of our father. Father died nearly twenty years ago, an accident I only recently began to see as convenient; my uncle—his brother— forced our mother to marry him, and took control of the household and the council appointed to oversee Aletto until his twenty-fifth birthday, when he would be named Duke. I just knew Jadek never intended to relinquish control, if he could help it.'' Lialla gazed at her brother; a tear eased out of the corner of one eye and slid down her cheek. ''There's more, but I can't tell it just now. It's enough for you to know that Aletto began to believe only the past few days. He and I left the fort, in hopes we could find men who were loyal to Father. With enough such men at my brother's back, we can return home and Jadek will have to abdicate.''

Right, Jennifer thought sourly. *The way Noriega did. Who is going to run him out, an Emperor with gunboats and Marines?* But she let it pass; Lialla might not be as naive as she sounded on that point, and if not it couldn't hurt to leave her that illusion for the moment. ''Where are we going, and when?''

''Tomorrow night, no sooner, and that's if he can travel.'' Lialla turned away from Aletto. ''It's drylands from here for most of a night's journey, and that slopes down to Sikkre.'' The name was gutteral in the back of her throat. ''There are men there, or so we hear, and the Duke's son—the Thukar's son, Dahven—may be able to help us. We'll need more food, better clothing for you three.'' Jennifer rummaged through her bag and gave Lialla the little wooden coin box. ''That's Mother's.'' She opened it and looked in, shook it experimentally. ''That will help, considerably—at least, if we can find a gemsmith who'll exchange any of these for coin, without uncomfortable questions. In Sikkre, that won't be hard. You'd better keep it, though, in case we're separated. I have money of my own.''

''All right.'' She carefully didn't think about being separated; she wouldn't breathe the least hint of it to Chris or particularly to Robyn.

''Are you hungry?'' Lialla asked. Jennifer shook her head. ''Tired?''

''Not just now. If you are, go ahead and sleep; I'll watch him. I need to think more than I need sleep.''

''I—all right.'' It was hard, admitting to anyone how very tired she was. Lialla hadn't allowed herself to know until just now. It was even harder, trusting a complete stranger like this Jen with her brother's life. A hard woman, this one, but cool and extremely competent—particularly if she'd come into magic for the first time this night. ''I scarcely slept last night, and not at all since.''

Jennifer nodded. ''If I hear anything, I'll wake you. I wouldn't know what to do.'' Lialla wrapped the black scarves around her arms, folded them across her chest and curled up on the hard ground in a tight little ball. She was asleep almost as soon as her eyes closed.

* * *

JENNIFER shoved her bag behind her back as a pillow and leaned against the smoothed stone wall. Robyn was sleeping, Chris next to her, one hand protectively on her elbow. Aletto seemed to be breathing normally and the drawn, white look had left his face.

She wanted to think about it, but she couldn't: too much, too soon, and most of it too painful. Heydrich & Harrison—they'd notice she was gone right away, when she didn't show up for that deposition. "I wanted that, really wanted it," she whispered. Long, red-carpeted halls, Jimmy's cheerful smile, Jan's Xeroxed magazine articles on her chair when she came to work in the morning—even the nasty squeal the copy machine emitted when it first started up and the unpleasant burr of the dot matrix printer just outside the office—she felt their loss like a great, gaping hole inside her. She forced her thoughts away from red-carpeted halls, artificial flower displays on polished conference room tables, the oddball assortment of receptionists who clashed so interestingly with the reception area full of antiques. It no longer mattered; she couldn't afford to let it. Any more than she could entertain Chris's possible return. Dare to think there would be a way back, tonight or any other night, and she'd tear herself to pieces, wanting it.

Three missing Angelenos in a city so large, their car eventually found on a narrow high desert road—they would make a very small ripple indeed. A few people would notice them gone, but not many would and not for long.

And for the rest, everything since Chris—poor virginal Chris, she thought, and nearly laughed aloud—had driven them into Merrida's net. But of all of them, Chris was the only one who'd landed on his feet, thinking almost at once. The only one of the three who'd had any idea what had happened. *I read the wrong things,* she thought wryly, and momentarily felt better.

That faded rapidly. Magic: Merrida's, that unnatural light beside the road—what she had done just now, to that young man's arm. "Why me? Why not Birdy, who's fiddled with all that stuff? Why not Chris?" There was no answer to that. Except, just possibly, the music.

It was there, just outside her hearing, ready for her if she needed it.

Outside the cave a nightbird or some small animal cried out; she jumped, banging her shoulder against rock, and swore. Aletto stirred, pushed himself groggily partway up and rubbed his eyes. "Lialla?" Lialla shifted, mumbled something under her breath. Jennifer crawled past her. "Merrida?" he whispered and blinked furiously. "You're not Merrida."

"She sent us to help you, three of us."

"Oh." He considered this in silence. "You're not a Rhadazi, I can tell."

"No."

"Oh." He rubbed his eyes once more, yawned and lay back down, asleep once more without having been properly awake.

7

ALETTO woke again, hours later; Jennifer gave him water and her name—like his sister, he had difficulty with it. He apparently remembered nothing of the attack in the stables and Jennifer decided to leave it to Lialla to decide what to tell him. Lialla woke not long after Aletto lay down again, and Jennifer curled up where the other woman had slept, leather bag under her ear and Merrida's woolen thing wrapped snugly around her. The cool air drifting along the floor felt refreshing on her face but unpleasant against her arms. But the thin wool seemed more than adequate to deal with the chill, once she managed to get it in place.

She drifted toward sleep, but individual events ran wild through her mind: the way the car had slid on gravel, her first jolting sight of Merrida, standing like a tree in those darkened woods. Hell-Light; Thread-sound—or music, if she dared think it that. Aletto. Poor, handicapped Aletto.

No one had said, except for the vague hints Merrida had dropped. Nothing had prepared her for the hitched-up shoulder, the slightly slurred speech, the mouth mobile only on the left side, the faint acnelike marks running along his right jaw and up under his ear. She had not been certain where to look, coming on his disability so suddenly. She knew Lialla saw her embarrassment, which made it all the worse. Young, noble, handicapped. Probably, judging by what was left, once extremely handsome. And no doubt he was used to looks like hers: surprise, shock, pity, all mixed. Fortunately, he hadn't been conscious when she dealt with his wound, but from the look on his sister's face, she at least wasn't resigned to his condition, and she visibly hated pity.

Illness, then. Illness or accident. If he'd been like this from birth, even a woman like Lialla would have adjusted to it by now. Then again, a woman like Lialla . . .

Lialla was all Merrida had warned her of, though Merrida hadn't used such blunt words as occurred to Jennifer: arrogant, imperious, impatient. The kind of Type A that gave all other Type A personalities a bad name.

Well, she was sorry she'd let so much show; ordinarily, it wouldn't have happened, but the circumstances were scarcely ordinary. Lialla wouldn't see it like that, most likely. Aletto wouldn't either, if Lialla were stupid enough to tell him. Rubbing salt in the wound—no, not likely she'd tell her brother. Not after a night to think about it. Unless Jennifer had badly misread the initiate Wielder. Fortunately, she herself had a little time to think about it; she would just have to go on as though nothing had happened. Let it pass. If she apologized, that could only keep discomfort fresh between herself and Lialla. And she had an uncomfortable feeling there would be enough of that in the days to come. Lialla was pretty obviously a strong-willed woman, and not used to dealing with another of the same ilk.

Jennifer yawned, stretched hard, and curled back on her side. She wished in passing that she could warn Chris and Robyn.

She thought she heard Robyn mumbling, Chris's whispered reply. Poor Chris. Of the three of them, he really had the most to lose, coming here. And he hadn't fully realized it yet, the way Jennifer had. When it hit him—God. At least worry for his mother kept him from worrying about himself. That was the last thing she remembered thinking before sleep took her.

Sun touched the cave floor and momentarily dazzled her; she shut her eyes, moved her head cautiously into shade and squeezed them open the least bit once again. There were gaps in the rock, partway up. Jennifer shifted, edged over flat onto her back, and stretched, cautiously. Sleeping in a wad on hard ground, with a loaded purse for a pillow, had given her bruised hip bones, aching joints and a ferocious headache. That healing of Merrida's would come in useful just now. But the old woman had been right; she couldn't sense anything beyond herself, nothing beyond her normal senses.

Night-Thread, her sleep-fuzzed brain reminded her. Curious; magic that only worked at night. At least, *good* magic that only worked at night. Fortunately it wasn't like some of the ancient earth stuff she seemed to recall reading about, magic that only worked during a full moon, or at seasonal changes or even once a year. Unfortunately, she'd never read much about magic; probably it wouldn't be useful here anyway.

Well, she probably couldn't cure a headache with Merrida's magic anyway. Merrida had certainly tried to imbue it with a massive importance that would raise it beyond such petty concerns. Fortunately, Jennifer had her usual enormous bottle of aspirin in the bottom of her bag. Probably the hard object that had given her the headache in the first place. She sat up, dragged the leather satchel open and rummaged; her eyes misted as her fingers closed over the hard plastic container. Her secretary had given her such a hard time over that bottle—jug, Jan had called it. So had Jimmy when he'd seen it. Well, but it had been so cheap, and easy to find in her bag. She blinked angrily, shook three out and choked them down dry, then eyed the bottle dubiously before she stowed it away again. Suddenly a half-full seven-hundred-count bottle no longer seemed excessive; she'd have to hoard the darned things and use them only in emergencies.

It was quiet in the cave; so quiet she knew even before her eyes adjusted that she had it to herself. She dragged a comb through her hair, considered braiding it and abandoned that when an appraisal of the contents of her bag revealed nothing to tie it with. Not that it braided well: It was thick enough but too fine to stay put, and her hairdresser had cut it in about fourteen different layers the last time. It had looked great with a suit and discreet gold hoops; she didn't want to think how it looked just now. She swore when the tortoise-shell pick snagged in a messy end composed of tangled hair, dirt and two small branches. One of the sticks had thorns, and she swore again as she eased it free, sucked blood from an oozing puncture in her thumb.

There wasn't much a long hike and a nap like that could do to harm her clothes—jeans and a leather jacket and leather hightops were about as hardy as you could get. She'd probably be ready to kill for a chance to wash her shirt by nightfall, though. She groaned as she stood and stretched. "Don't say kill," she told herself in a fierce whisper as she squatted and rummaged through the bag once again and came up with the black nylon padded pouch. "Not here. Not for a smelly shirt." The little bag contained deodorant, hand lotion, all the so-called survival items a young lawyer might need when suddenly scheduled for a one-thirty hearing. She ran a little paste onto her brush and scrubbed it dry over her front teeth, stuffed everything back in the satchel and went outside.

The air was still, clear and slightly damp; the sun's rays nearly level. Still quite early, then. Someone had started a small fire near the entrance. She looked at it, brow creased, then shrugged. Lialla or Aletto surely wouldn't be foolish enough to draw attention to this place with a fire! Then again—*dry wood,* she thought as she studied it, and remembered things from early camping trips in Wyoming. There was very little smoke at shoulder level, just a haze that distorted things when she looked through it. At a height of ten feet, even that couldn't be seen. *Relax,* she told herself sternly, and leaned over to warm her fingers.

There was a pot sitting among the embers, not much bigger than a decent-sized coffee mug; an unfamiliar but not unpleasant herby, sagey smell rose from it. *Not coffee. No coffee,* Jennifer thought with a pang, and then pushed the thought and the accompanying misery aside. She'd have to promise herself, no regrets. She could drive herself crazy, missing things. She wouldn't give in to hope, either; Chris's little series of notions about going home again might make Robyn happier, or make him less unhappy. She couldn't afford to let herself think there might be a way back.

She could see the horses a small distance away—horses and the unmistakable long ears of a mule or a burro. And then Lialla's equally distinctive fluttery black wrappings. The sin-Duchess turned and waved, and came back up the narrow draw with a leather bag in one hand. She settled down on the rocks near the fire and brought out a small loaf of bread. ''Here,'' she said gruffly. ''We'll have to watch the food but this stuff doesn't keep. And here.'' She pulled out a thick, flat bit of dark leather that opened into a sort of cup and dipped it into the steaming liquid. Jennifer set the bread on her knees and took the cup awkwardly. The sides weren't at all stiff and it wasn't easy to keep it from collapsing and spilling hot liquid all over her lap until she got hold of opposite sides with both hands. Lialla rose without another word and walked on into the cave.

''God, another morning person,'' Jennifer mumbled, and swore as she scalded her upper lip. ''We'll kill each other.''

''Nah, she's just generally bitchy.'' Chris had come up unnoticed. Jennifer jumped, managed to balance the sagging cup and steer it away from her knee before it sloshed. She fixed her nephew with a cold eye.

"Warn me next time, damnit."

He grinned cheerfully; Jennifer closed her eyes and began counting. Unlike her—or his mother—Chris was happily on his feet and moving as soon as the sun rose. Most of the time, Jennifer managed not to hold it against him. The look on her face must have warned him, because when she reached ten and opened her eyes, he was gone again. She sipped hot liquid doubtfully and wondered briefly if it was safe for him to wander around. And where was Robyn?

There was entirely too much of the drink for a first taste, and it needed sugar. But even though she had those few paper packets in her bag, she'd have to conserve them even more closely than the aspirin—at least until she found out if there was sugar here. "Or coffee," she whispered, and once again had to remind herself that subject was forbidden.

There didn't seem to be any caffeine in the tea, but the combination of cool, crisp air and the heat of the liquid were helping a little. She was at least able to pay some attention to her surroundings.

She couldn't see far down the ravine; it bent sharply to the right just beyond the horses, she remembered from the night before. From here, the bend wasn't visible; it looked like one solid rock wall. There was water, a narrow and slow-moving stream with a silty, brown bottom. Where the horses and the mule were tethered, there were trees so like cottonwood she couldn't be certain they weren't in fact cottonwood, unfamiliar bushes, thick, brightly green grass that rose to the animals' knees. Beyond them, rock and brush climbed abruptly to a high ledge; the trees there were a mixture, deciduous and piñon pine. Or, she reminded herself, something like that. The resemblance was strong, and the animals were certainly unmistakably horses and a mule.

Just as Lialla and Aletto were unmistakably human—at least, to *her* eye. It unnerved her more than difference would, considering everything. How could it be possible, a completely other place, nowhere on Earth, and yet so many things just like Earth things?

She must have spoken aloud, and Chris, who'd come down from the ledge beside her, heard. "You don't read much, do you, Aunt Jen?"

"I read—" she began defensively. Chris laughed.

"Not the right kinda stuff. Alternate universes? Parallel worlds?" Jennifer scowled at him, finally shook her head.

"Didn't think so. The idea being, something happened and at that point things went one way and wound up being us—you know, L.A., current day, you as a lawyer, all that. But at that same time, maybe it happened differently, too, or should have, and another world went *that* way. And wound up being this place."

Jennifer nodded. "All right, I've heard the theory. The 'what if Hitler won' idea."

Chris applauded silently. "That's one of them. So there would be two worlds, right? One where he did, one where he didn't. Or a bunch of 'em, right? Horses in both, people in both, same kind of trees in both—but some things very different." He sat down close to her, tore a piece from her loaf and stuffed it in his mouth. "Like the bread. Tastes a little weird."

"Any bread that isn't that cellophane special white stuff would taste funny to you," Jennifer told him.

"Well, anyway." Chris swallowed, held out a hand. "You done with that stuff? It's pretty good, compared to some of the herb tea Mom makes, but don't tell her I said so." He drained the leather cup, spilling only a little, and handed it back to her. "Well, with a parallel worlds thingie, the land masses would be the same, too."

"But that's all fiction," Jennifer protested. Chris shrugged.

"Maybe. I mean, how do you *know* it wasn't there first and writers started using the idea?"

"Like the Bermuda Triangle?"

"C'mon, you know what I mean."

"Everything you've said so far reeks of the *National Enquirer* and bad pseudoscience."

"Yeah, I just knew you'd say that. Anyway, I've been talking to Aletto this morning and I can't figure it out. If we're on a parallel world, I don't see where and when we are, in relation to our world."

"You know so much about geography, of course," Jennifer said.

"Not fair! I got better after last year; too much razz from Mr. Edley about not knowing where places were, and besides, you helped me, didn't you? Besides, maps are neat. Well, some maps."

"Game maps, you mean," Jennifer said shrewdly. Chris shrugged. "What's he like?"

"He? Oh. Aletto? All right, I guess. Not like I thought a Duke would be." What he thought, Chris didn't say. Jennifer was relieved and rather pleased to notice he seemed to have taken Aletto's physical problems in stride. But then, Chris would; Robyn would have seen to that. "He's up top, looking around. Said he wanted to talk when he came down, though. You want the rest of that bread? 'Cause if not, I'm starving." Jennifer sighed quietly, shook her head and handed it to him.

ALETTO did come down, moments later. Jennifer glanced up in alarm as she saw rock slithering and bouncing not very far away, then looked down; Aletto's gait was awkward in the extreme on such uneven ground, and she wondered that he would even try it.

Unfortunately, he was at least as observant as Lialla, and just as touchy. "You don't have to pretend I'm not here," he growled as he limped over to the fire. "I don't always walk that funny."

Jennifer drew a deep breath, let it out and tried to send most of her irritation with it. It didn't work. "Look," she said and shielded her eyes so she could look up at him. "I was just as concerned about Chris sliding down there. Don't be so damned sure the world rises and sets on you!" Horror momentarily shut her mouth and guilt opened it again as she shoved herself to her feet. He was no taller than she; his face at the moment was unreadable. "All right, that was harsh. Put it down that I don't have a sense of humor in the morning."

He stood still for just enough longer that she wondered what else she should say; a faint smile creased his mouth, then, and warmed his dark blue eyes. "I'm not fond of this kind of hour myself," he admitted. "Nor to such a bed; one grows soft even in my uncle's loving care. And I seem to have missed my usual helping of late wine." He took hold of her arms at the elbows and squeezed, briefly, "You're Jenni—I can't say it."

"Jen."

"Jen. I remember that now, you told me. You—?" He glanced across her shoulder and Jennifer, turning, saw Robyn down there, talking to the horses. "You and she, and the boy—you're the help that woman brought us?"

Doesn't like Merrida by his tone of voice, or magic either, Jennifer thought, and she remembered Merrida's odd way of referring to Aletto. "Him," "the boy," no name. Apparently she didn't like him much, either. Looking at his face, at the shoulder drawn up under his right ear, his head inclining toward it, remembering that limp—maybe *he* had cause. Had the old woman tried and failed, or simply not tried? "We're what Mer-rida got," she said.

Aletto's smile faded. "We need to talk," he said. "And that most urgently."

IT took her several minutes to round up Chris and send him after Robyn; Aletto was seated by the small fire, Lialla standing be-hind him. Jennifer let Chris help his mother find a half-comfortable place to sit and to drop down next to her; she elected, like Lialla, to stay on her feet.

It was quiet; Aletto looked up at Lialla, across the fire at the others, opened his mouth and closed it again. The silence stretched, and when Jennifer finally broke it, Robyn started ner-vously. "I suppose this is a council of war, to decide what we're doing," she said. Lialla shrugged gloomily.

Aletto stared down at his hands. "Council of war? Five of us, and look at who we are! It's utterly hopeless."

He might have gone on but Lialla's hand closed on his good shoulder; her knuckles stood out white. "You're not going back! I can't—"

"I never said that!" Aletto protested sharply, and began tug-ging at her fingers. "Jadek would kill me right then, or bury me alive in the cellars, and say I'd never returned. And you—" He tore her hand free of his arm, imprisoned the fingers between both of his hands. "I doubt he'd treat you kindly, either."

"No," Lialla said faintly.

"He'd wed you to Carolan before the dirt settled on my grave."

"Stop—" Lialla took a deep breath. Her face had gone an ugly shade of pale green. "Carolan's dead."

Aletto let go of her hand, turned to stare up at her. Lialla nodded. Silence. She closed her eyes momentarily, mumbled to herself. When she opened them again, she looked more herself. Aletto gazed into the fire, then out across the meadow, back into the fire again. Jennifer thought he looked inordinately pleased with himself. "I did that, didn't I?" Lialla nodded, realized he wasn't watching.

"You did that."

"Carolan knifed me? I think I remember that. It hurt and my eyes didn't want to stay open. He's dead? His man—they're both dead?"

"Both dead," Lialla agreed flatly.

"We're not going back," Aletto said after a long silence. "We wouldn't dare."

Lialla stirred. "We don't have to, we can go north. He won't look for us in Holmaddan!"

"No? You think he won't turn Rhadaz inside out until he finds us?" Aletto shook his head.

Chris sat forward. "Look, you two are talking in riddles. Somebody, two somebodies got killed last night after you got out the back door, and you two are responsible, right? And that's going to make the old man—this Jadek that's running the place for you—it's going to make him even madder than he already is, right?" He settled his elbows on his knees, let his hands dangle between his shins. One leg jiggled rapidly, making his hands tremble. Jennifer, who knew his moods fairly well, considered saying something, then decided not to: Better to let her nephew work out his anger at once, it was worse when he chewed on it. "You mind if I ask where we come in?" Lialla glanced down at Aletto, who had gone back to a contemplation of his hands. Chris sighed heavily. "I ask because, you remember, we got dragged here by that old witch, who said you needed us. Us particularly. To go looking for people so you could take back what's yours." Silence. "I can follow that, it's logical. But now you're talking about running off or going home, or hiding out—"

Aletto brought his chin up; his eyes were hard and his mouth set. "My sister said that. I didn't. I intend to go on. But you three—" he gestured, taking them in. "You aren't—aren't—"

"Aren't what?" Chris demanded. "Aren't brutes with broadswords? Heroes in silver armor?"

"I didn't say—!"

"You didn't have to say that, I can tell you mean it."

"Can you even use that bow you're carrying?" Aletto countered hotly.

"I could once, how about you?" Chris snapped. "If we ever get squared away here, I'm sure going to go practice with it. Have I ever killed anybody with one? No! Who'd *you* kill lately, besides this Caro—this whatsis." The two glowered at each other. Lialla touched Aletto's shoulder.

"It's dangerous," she began. Chris laughed and effectively silenced her.

"Oh, sure. Look, where I live there are machines that would eat you for breakfast; there are men on the streets who carry knives and cut people just for fun. Boys and young girls who do that. I'll tell you what I'm scared of here, lady. Not magic, not that old bat who got us here, not even big warriors with shiny swords. I'm scared you'll try to dump us right here, walk off and leave us.'' There was an ugly little silence; Lialla's eyes were mere slits. ''For myself, I don't care nearly as much. But you try to do that to my mother, lady, and you'll be sorry you ever left home.'' Chris drew a deep breath, expelled it in a loud whoosh and sat back. His color was high and a pulse beat rapidly in this side of his neck, but he'd worked out the worst of it.

Or so Jennifer thought until Lialla glared down at him. ''Don't you threaten me, boy! It was Merrida who found you, not me—''

''Give me a break, lady!'' Chris jumped to his feet, waving his arms. Lialla, startled, took a pace backwards, then reclaimed her ground. ''Merrida—why not blame the magic, the way she did? Or my—well, never mind that! I know all about comparative guilt and moral responsibility. You might not have done the work, but you asked for the help, didn't you? You think you don't have any responsibility for us? Think again!''

''I—look,'' Lialla said. She ran a hand through her hair, scattering a handful of fine brass-colored pins. ''I didn't have any choice! Unless I married Carolan and let—let Aletto—'' She spun away on one heel and slammed both hands into the rock wall behind them. ''There's a moral question for you.'' Her voice was muffled by stone. ''The lives of fighting men—Why should I have thought it would choose us anyone else?—or Aletto's life?'' She turned back and leaned into the rock. ''You're right, Aletto, we can't go back; we've got to go on the way we started.''

''I know. I'm dead if we return; he'll hunt us down and he won't quit until we're found, otherwise. If we can reach Sikkre, find men who were loyal to Father— Even if we can't find Gyrdan, or even if Gyr won't help us, there will be someone. Someone to help us plan the next step.'' He drew a deep breath and suddenly looked much less miserable. ''We don't need to plan it in fine detail just now; only the first step. Isn't that right?''

Chris answered him, and his voice was back to normal. ''It doesn't hurt to have a step or two ahead in reserve, but that much should be a good start. Where is this Sikkre?'' He couldn't manage the guttural consonant properly. ''And how far from here? And is this uncle of yours going to suspect that's where you're going?''

Lialla shook her head. "He'll have an eye out in all directions."

"Good. Unless he's got an unlimited number of men, that means he'll be spread pretty thin."

"Just so," Lialla said, and eyed him with a grudging respect. "I *think*, though, he'll suppose Aletto's going to the Emperor down in Podhru, to petition for his rights. It's the logical thing to do, under the circumstances—two unarmed and untrained people out alone, where else would they go, except to hide? Also, I don't think it's common knowledge where Gyrdan is. And Sikkre's not—it's not exactly unsafe. But the Thukar has a coin value on everything and everyone. Sikkre *shouldn't* be where we'd go. The Thukar's not safe, and his eldest son is—"

"Dahven's all right," Aletto said, and he managed a faint smile in her direction. "You don't like him because they wanted you to marry him."

"So." Chris gnawed a knuckle and considered this in silence for some time. "Sikkre—what is it?" Brother and sister looked at him in confusion; both shook their heads. "City, village, open pit mine, forest—what?"

"Dukedom, like Zelharri," Aletto said. "But Sehfi, the town surrounding Duke's Fort, is smaller. Sikkre's main city has the same name as the Dukedom; it's the center of four inland trading routes including the main one from the seaport of Bezjeriad." Chris shaped this silently, closed his eyes and shook his head. "Sikkre's market alone is four times the size of all of Sehfi; people of all kinds come there, outland traders coming from Bez, nomads coming down from Dro Pent—"

"Maps," Chris said. "I need a map. It sounds," he added cautiously, "like a place where even if someone expected you to go there, you might be able to get in and around without being found." Aletto nodded; Chris smiled. "See? You don't need brutes with broadswords after all. We don't look that different from you two that we should stand out very much. Not like hulking swordsmen would."

Lialla sighed. Let her eyes close. Chris would have gone on but Aletto held up a warning finger, shook his head slightly; his expression was as close to friendly as Chris had seen so far. Lialla finally nodded. "Gods. You're right, though. Whatever else comes to pass, we can't leave you here."

"That's settled, then." Chris smiled and held out a hand. Aletto looked at it, puzzled, finally took it in his own. Chris turned to say something to Robyn and stopped short, jaw hanging. Robyn was no longer there. And none of them had seen her go.

CHRIS stared all around but Aletto saw her first. "There, by the horses," he said.

"She doesn't like arguing," Jennifer said. Aletto looked up at her in surprise, as though he'd forgotten her presence entirely. He turned his gaze back down the ravine. Chris started to rise, but Aletto pulled himself upright and skirted the fire. "Wait. I'll apologize." He walked rapidly down the ravine; the limp was painful to watch and Jennifer turned away before he'd gone the distance. Chris cast one black look at the nera-Duke's back but let him go. He'd started the yelling, as he uncomfortably recalled—as Robyn would doubtless remind him if he went after her right now. Not only yelling, but yelling at a nobleman. Not the best way to accumulate points.

Lialla stirred. Her face was utterly expressionless, her eyes chill. "It's apparently been decided for us, Jen; you and I can settle the details, I suppose." Chris squirmed uncomfortably. Jennifer grinned down at him.

"Go get my leather bag," she told him. "It's where I was sleeping. There's paper and a couple pens, for maps."

"A couple pens? A couple dozen pens," Chris said. "If I know you. Never mind, I found some in the back seat and threw them in my bag." He was whistling as he went back out of sight.

Jennifer sighed. "It's temper," she began. Lialla shook her head.

"Don't apologize, he was right. And I have a temper myself." She drew herself up and met Jennifer's eyes. "I doubt this is going to be an easy journey, if only because we're both strong women. Not used to standing aside while someone else decides for us. I haven't dared; Aletto wants to protect me, our mother tried to shield us both. Merrida says she succeeded to an extent; it wasn't enough. I've known what I wanted, and more importantly what I didn't want, and I've known for years what kind of man I was dealing with in my uncle and stepfather. Even if I didn't give him his full due. But I've had to work on my own to achieve everything I have."

Jennifer nodded. "You're right, we're alike. Strong—or hard, depending on the point of view. I had to find my own way, and I'm not good at being protected or coddled. My sister—Robyn needs that; she's never been good at taking care of herself, not in the most basic ways. She had husbands, other men. Now she

has Chris; in some ways, he's the parent, she's the child.''
She considered this a moment, sighed and shook her head. ''She
won't be easy to live with; there are—certain things she craves.
Until she adjusts to their loss, she may be tense, snappish, weepy.
I don't know. This, just now—'' She gestured down the ravine;
Aletto stood in the high grass, leaning across one glossy brown
back, talking earnestly. They couldn't see anything of Robyn but
the gleam of sun on the top of her blonde head. She must have
said something amusing; Aletto laughed, reached across the
horse to touch her shoulder. ''She hates arguing, fighting. Anything like that. Even when she's not part of it; she just fades
out.'' Lialla sighed in turn. Jennifer turned back to her. ''She's
not all wet,'' she added. ''Truly. She's a kind woman, a good-
hearted one. People like her.''

''Aletto seems to,'' Lialla said dryly.

A shy little silence had fallen over the two down in the ravine.
Aletto toyed with the horse's mane; Robyn, who had been picking small wildflowers, stood and held them out. She only just
managed not to jerk her hand back when the strong, white horse
teeth closed over the petals and pulled the plants from her hand.
''They're very placid,'' Aletto assured her.

''They're pretty,'' Robyn said. She dusted her hand on her
jeans, glanced up at him and away again. ''I'm not used to being
close to them; I guess you can tell they make me nervous.''

''Some of them frighten *me*,'' Aletto said. ''The hunting
horses my uncle rides. Of course, I can't manage such horses,
so it doesn't really matter.''

''Oh, but it does,'' Robyn said. ''It's in your voice, don't you
know?'' She came around the horse and gestured at his leg.
''What happened to you?''

He'd steeled himself against the question from one of them,
even though Merrida or Lialla would surely have warned them—
they warned everyone: ''Don't stare, don't ask, it upsets him.''
To his surprise, he didn't mind her question; perhaps it was her
voice—curious, no overtone of pity to it. ''There was marsh
fever, when I was fifteen, just in Sehfi and the fort. Two of my
companions died at once, three more within an eight-day. By
the end of a moon-season, it had run its course.'' He shrugged
gloomily. ''I was lucky, they say; I can use the leg still, and
this''—a gesture took in the raised shoulder, the tilt of his head,
the scars on his face—''this is nothing compared to what it could
have been.'' He managed a faint smile. ''It remains to be seen

whether the disease spared all of me, since I've had no opportunity yet to test whether my seed is good.''

"Oh." Robyn considered this in silence. "That's not right.'' She sounded so indignant—on his behalf?—he felt rather warmed by it.

"I'm used to it,'' he said.

Robyn met his eyes squarely. "No, I don't think you could be. I wouldn't be, I'd hate it.''

He caught his breath. "I'm sorry myself—for what Merrida did to you. My part in it.''

"Your—? Oh.'' Robyn touched his arm, drew her hand back. "All that shouting, that was Chris. I don't feel the same way, not exactly. I agree with him in theory; you can't order something done, or ask someone to do it for you, and then say it wasn't your fault at all when it goes wrong. That's dishonest. For the rest, it's too soon, I don't know how I feel yet, really. About coming here, not going back. But I didn't ever have much where we were, except them: Chris and Jennifer. As long as I have them, I don't need much else.'' She swallowed, let her eyes close momentarily. "I—it probably sounds stupid to you. But I'm scared. I—all my life, I've hated killing, I wouldn't even eat any kind of meat for years because that was killing. I'm—I can see it coming, here; killing. Two men have already died.'' She drew a ragged breath. "More, probably, that I don't know about. If Chris had to kill someone, or if I did, somehow—Oh, God, I'd hate that!''

Aletto caught her hands in his, drew them close to his chest; the fingers were cold and they trembled. He looked down at her long, blonde hair, and something of his own fear left him. "*You* won't,'' he assured her quietly.

"If I could believe that,'' she whispered.

"Believe it,'' he said, and with such confidence that Robyn felt her spirits lift for the first time since Jennifer's car had slid into Merrida's night.

8

JENNIFER had doubts: massive ones. She and Lialla had managed to find common ground but she failed to see how useful it would be to know they were both used to being in charge and doing things their own way. Lialla was a formidable combination of personality and upbringing: stubborn and strong-willed, noble, trained in a form of magic that seemed to require arrogance as part of its working—at least, Merrida was certainly no shrinking violet. Jennifer had no use for class distinctions and Merrida's mysticism heartily bored her. She wasn't going to let Lialla order her around because of rank or because she knew more magic; Jennifer had no intention of letting Aletto take charge either, not because he ranked them by what Jennifer saw as accident of birth, definitely not because she was female. And Lialla, for all her determination to organize the party on her own lines, tended to fold alarmingly when Aletto voiced an opinion, even though he had no more experience than she.

She reminded herself that Lialla might be operating on affection for her brother, rather than deferring to male superiority. But that wasn't going to work either. Not considering the stakes.

They finally managed to agree on a few things: Chris had his map, courtesy of Aletto—he also had Aletto's rather grudging agreement that he could make suggestions based on his study of the map, without brother or sister shouting him down. Jennifer and Lialla had figured their provisions down to the last bit of bread and fruit, from Lialla's bag, and the last chicken wing, from Jennifer's, still cold thanks to the blue ice but not for much longer. They then turned responsibility for feeding the party over to Robyn. "She needs something to steady her," Jennifer told Lialla firmly. "She's no servant, she's my sister, and I hope you'll remember that. But she has a talent for getting the most from a small amount of food and she cooks better than I do." Lialla glared at her briefly, then relaxed and almost managed a smile.

"All right. I'll try and remember not to insult her. That shouldn't be difficult if I'm kept grateful for a full stomach, should it?" The smile widened. "Besides, if she keeps on as she's begun with Aletto—"

"That's her decision, not mine," Jennifer said. "But she's not the sort to hurt anyone."

Aletto had fallen almost at once into a light, chivalrous manner toward Robyn: protective, but different from Chris's protective ways. Chris was too sensitive to his mother's ways with men not to have noticed the budding friendship between her and Aletto, but any resentment he felt he was keeping to himself. It was likely, Jennifer thought, that Chris didn't take it seriously. She could only hope Robyn wouldn't. Because Robyn could never possibly marry a man ten years younger and noble, and of a completely different land. She'd had enough trouble with that Greek a few years before. And if Aletto took back his birthright, he might not want her. Even if he did, he might not be allowed a choice.

She sighed and shoved the matter resolutely from her mind. It was Robyn's problem; she wasn't going to mix in it at all this time. Let Chris, if he wanted to; that, also, wasn't her problem.

Chris had charge of maps, Aletto of the horses and the mule. Robyn the food. That left Lialla largely free to work magic, if needed, or to instruct Jennifer—as much instruction as Jennifer could absorb, or wanted. "I'm barely trained myself," Lialla warned her. "At least, from the standpoint of teaching."

Jennifer shrugged. "It might be better. You aren't as set in your ways as a true instructor, and you'll remember better how you learned things. Some of my best tutors were not long out of school themselves."

"Well—we'll know better tonight, after dark, whether it's any use at all, trying," Lialla said. "I'd get some sleep in the meantime, if I were you. It's a long way to that oasis and we only have the one horse to trade off riding. I doubt we'll be done traveling until dawn, possibly after." She grimaced. "Don't tell Aletto that, and keep Chris quiet about the distances. I've had enough argument for one day."

"Chris isn't any better than Aletto at figuring speed over distance, but I'll watch him." Jennifer looked at the sky. "Nearly midday, isn't it? It's awfully warm here."

"Always cool in the cave," Lialla told her. "And it'll be hotter out in the desert tomorrow. Just so you know." She vanished into the cave.

By the time Jennifer followed her in, she was a still, black shadow well toward the back wall. Jennifer took back the place where she'd spent most of the night, scooped dirt out under her hips and folded the woolen scarf under her head. It was much cooler, particularly since the sun no longer shone through the early morning gaps. She closed her eyes, adjusted the hard, flat pillow and thought her way through the final spats, arguments, to what they actually had decided. It seemed pitifully inadequate, considering.

The road they would take tonight was actually a narrow track, wide enough for one horse, or two afoot. It more or less followed the secondary road out of Zelharri, but wound out through dry and uninhabited lands before heading south once more; it and the road crossed near the Zelharri-Sikkre border. Fortunately it hadn't been necessary to argue out that part of the journey yet; that wouldn't come until late the next night. According to Lialla—who had ridden the track on a hunt—they should only reach the oasis used by caravans traveling between Holmaddan and Dro Pent, and between both to Sikkre. If there were several caravans at the oasis, they would have to skirt it. But that was unlikely just now, Lialla assured them. Jennifer hoped so; they had few water bottles and she'd heard too many horror stories about people dehydrating and going mad in the desert.

She hoped it would be another truly dark night. Lialla had described the country to them, and it sounded like parts of Wyoming: flat and brushy, no real cover. With a good moon, they'd be visible for miles.

Jennifer sighed, sat up and folded the wool into another thickness, then lay back down, shut her eyes and began reciting *Hayes on Torts* in a soundless whisper. It worked; it had worked even in law school before finals, the night before she took the Bar; somewhere between Section 1.4(b)(7) and 1.4(b)(8), she fell asleep.

A distance beyond her, Lialla lay propped against her cloak, eyes wide and unblinking. She couldn't sleep, even knowing how desperately tired she'd be later. Two horses, a mule, five people. And even though he'd already been forced to agree about being sensible, Aletto would give her trouble; he'd hate riding when the women must walk. He'd be touchy all night if Lialla refused to let him walk, he'd be hurting all over and slow them dangerously if she did let him. *She* couldn't heal, and if Jen had got it right, Merrida had given her help for the one night and the one occasion only. But no one had ever been able to do much about Aletto's game leg—or any other leftover damage from the fever.

She wondered about that, at odd intervals, but she wasn't going to let this be one of them. It was scarcely the time or place to worry whether Jadek had had anything to do with it, as Merrida insisted. Or whether that was simply Merrida finding an excuse for her failure to completely cure the nera-Duke—what Merrida, Lialla corrected herself, saw as failure. But it wasn't time to worry about that, either.

At least Merrida had been able to find someone who could help Aletto last night. Lialla had barely been able to stop him bleeding to death. But three of them—three foreign, helpless and likely useless outlanders—Lialla took hold of her hair and tugged, two-handed, blanking the end of that thought.

Unfortunately, her mind turned to gnaw at another. Was Merrida right? "Am I as good a Wielder as I will ever be?" she whispered. Despair filled her and she suddenly wanted nothing more than to roll over and weep. Nothing more, except that silver sash; except to be Zelharri's greatest ever Wielder, if not the greatest in Rhadaz. Maybe her thinking was all wrong: Perhaps Night-Thread eluded her for the very arrogance of her desire. But then, Merrida would never have gone beyond a deep purple, let alone all the way to yellow!

Was it Merrida's arrogance? Unable to exact skill from her pupils, mother and daughter, would she blame them instead of herself? "Would she really discourage me because if she couldn't teach me then I must be unteachable?" It wasn't a pleasant thought, either.

Lialla resolutely forced her eyes to close, and went over her inner lists one more time. Food, water. It might not be safe at the Hushar Oasis, not if a large caravan was in. Aletto's disability was known; he could be recognized. If it was dangerous for them to camp at Hushar, she'd have to go in herself, to draw water and perhaps to bargain for a horse. She was not particularly notable, and everyone knew Wielders were unpredictable;

it wouldn't be so odd for one to appear afoot anywhere in Rhadaz.

Lialla smiled grimly. Jennifer thought she'd convinced her not to try such a thing; well, she either misunderstood, or misinterpreted Lialla's silence for agreement. Jennifer didn't realize how long it might take a party like theirs to reach Sikkre; how much they'd want that horse by the time they got to Hushar Oasis; how unlikely they'd find anyone to trade them coin for meal elsewhere.

Their horses: Aletto's man had chosen well, getting them strong, placid animals. It was a pity they couldn't have had desert-raised horses but then, Jadek would have at once known they were bound for Sikkre. This way—he would have sent a man or two to Sikkre, possibly they'd be searching the Sikkre road together with every other major road. But because of that, they'd be spread thin, easier to avoid.

He didn't have *that* many men to spare from Duke's Fort. She must remember that. And he didn't know everything, however he—like Merrida, really—acted as though he did.

Water was worrying; what if they had to stay out an extra day? She wouldn't let herself think about that: She had done all she could to provide for such emergencies. They had extra water bottles, anyway.

Somehow, somewhere in the middle of gloomy thoughts, she dozed off.

IT was after sunset when Chris and Aletto brought the horses up to the cave so they could be saddled and loaded. It was almost funny, Jennifer thought; watching the poor, patient horses and the temperamental mule bear with five very ignorant humans. By the time the last strap was snugged down, there was little light left in the sky, and the last pack went in place by feel. The mule balked when Chris led it away from grass and water; it took what seemed like forever to get it moving.

Then Aletto wanted to balk once more at riding the entire way. Robyn finally leaned over and said something to him no one else heard; his face was still set in that stubborn expression but he got on the brown and stayed there. Robyn pulled her bag strap over the broad saddlebow and tied it down with one of the seemingly innumerable straps sewed to the colorfully painted leather.

The road was considerably more open than the dell had been; the surface was pale and seemed to shine. It took them several minutes to work up the courage to step onto it—even after Lialla pronounced it deserted for at least a league in both directions.

"How did you do that?" Jennifer asked as they fell in behind the horses. Chris had the mule moving and kept it just ahead of the horses; Robyn rode close to Aletto.

"Do—oh." Lialla launched into an explanation of Thread, almost verbatim the one Merrida had given her years before; she stopped as Jennifer held up a hand.

"I know about Thread—Merrida told me pretty much what you're telling me. Why don't you just tell me which ones tell you if people are about, and how you do it?"

"I—all right." Lialla cast her companion a sideways glance. She couldn't see anything but tall, moving shadows in front of her and Jennifer's dark form pacing her. She had to think a moment, finally nodded. "Can you see Thread? Try—oh, you can? Well, the ones you want are pale, kind of red."

Jennifer found it disconcerting, trying to walk and seeing both the real world and what Merrida had told her was the underlying fabric of it—all at the same time. And hearing—she opened her mouth to ask, closed it again. Merrida hadn't mentioned sound at all; neither had Lialla. If it was important, surely one or both would have told her. Music. Well—Merrida had *mentioned* music.

Now she needed to pay attention to the road, the Thread, Lialla, all three. "Can you touch the Thread?" Jennifer nodded; she was momentarily beyond speech. "Good. Now. when you take hold of them—lightly, just thumb and finger, if you're practiced—and depending how good you are, of course, you should be able to feel the movement along the Thread that tells you if someone's disturbing it. After you've done it a few times, you have a better feel for how many, how far, even how fast they're coming. *Not* those, Jen. Move your hand—*those*."

"Oh." Jennifer felt extremely awkward with Lialla watching her so closely. She took hold of Thread, and found she was also suddenly terrified she might take hold of the wrong ones and create havoc. And it was so far from exact! The ones Lialla called red were actually a light mauve. Touch relieved her of some of her fear; she'd know these again, know how to take hold of them, how to utilize them. They were silent but she thought she could tell how they'd feel if they moved; she could hear the music they'd sing for her. Music—not true music, but nearer music than not. She contemplated Thread, found the ones she'd used to heal Aletto's arm the night before. The music hadn't changed; that took the last of her fear. She was wildly curious now, cautious about revealing her enthusiasm, wary of mentioning sound. Careful to remember the promise she'd made herself not to annoy Lialla. "How do you *not* see Thread?"

Lialla laughed quietly. "Concentrate on what you *do* want to see."

Silence. Then: "It's not working," Jennifer said vexedly. Lialla caught hold of her shoulder and pulled her to a stop in the middle of the road.

"Lean close to me and listen carefully. I can't repeat it." It was an odd sound, the faintest of whispers against Jennifer's ear. "Can you remember that? Don't say it aloud!" she added in alarm as Jennifer cleared her throat.

"I wasn't going to."

"I'm just warning you. Think it and look at the road."

It took several minutes, but eventually it worked; Thread faded from sight, the real world established itself once more. Jennifer realized Lialla was watching her thoughtfully.

"I don't understand how you can just *do* that. It took me the better part of a winter to learn it." There was a grudging respect in her voice, tempered with surprise and a hefty measure of resentment.

Well, Jennifer thought, she had a little resentment of her own, being manipulated by that damned old woman! "I don't know! How should I know? I told you, there is no real magic in my world. I'm a musician, not even what you'd call a good one. For some reason, Merrida thought it made a difference."

"Oh." Lialla considered this, finally shrugged. "Perhaps. It's nothing she ever told *me*, but I'm less a musician than I am a Wielder."

THE road ran level through low trees and aromatic brush for an hour or more, then began to descend, working down a series of long straightaways and sharp-elbowed turns. At the end of one such turn, the road dived steeply down and through a tunnel; Robyn shivered and hunched over the horse's neck, closing her eyes until they came out the other side. Jennifer, who normally didn't mind tunnels, didn't care at all for this one: It had been carved out of the slope, shored with what seemed to her to be an insufficient amount of wood. Loose, dry dirt sifted down onto them all the way through.

As the road leveled out again, a sickle moon came over the crest, casting only a very faint light over them. But they could see how far they'd dropped. Chris whistled faintly. "Wow. It didn't look that steep coming down. No wonder my legs ache."

"We'll stop here," Lialla said. "Not long." Aletto dismounted rather stiffly, then helped Robyn down. After what Chris considered to be a very vague inquiry after his health, Robyn turned her attention back to Aletto.

"You need to walk a little, and so do I," she said. To Lialla's surprise, Aletto accepted this and limped off down the road with her. When they returned, he was walking a little less unevenly; Robyn had both fists dug into the small of her back, kneading sore muscles. Chris fumbled through the novice web of ropes and knots that held the mule's pack in place, finally dragged out a leather water bag. His stomach growled; he ignored it as best he could. Supposedly there would be something to eat once they found this oasis. He'd helped his mother pack the food, though, and he was uncomfortably aware how small a bundle it made.

Something his kind of adventures didn't really get into—hard to take hunger seriously when your supplies were a list on paper and your stomach was comfortably full.

Water helped get him moving again: His legs felt less dead, his mind more alert. He took the bottle over to Lialla, who drank and handed it to Jennifer; Jennifer drank, shuddered as she swallowed warm water that tasted unpleasantly of its bag.

Lialla waited until Robyn and Aletto came back. "All right. Aletto, you did the map, and Chris, you've looked at it enough. I rode this way once, but it's been some time. We leave the road here. The track comes in close to the road nearby. And it's better if we start north from here, where the ground is harder. We'd leave traces further on."

The track wasn't exactly where she'd remembered it; or perhaps looking for it at night made a difference. It took too much time until they found it, miles north of where it was supposed to be. Chris remarked on this, pointedly, and retraced the line on his map. Lialla was fortunately too far ahead to realize he was addressing her, and Jennifer quelled him with a look, before he could start another argument. She had been riding in Robyn's place the past hour; now she slid down and put the reins in his free hand. "You want to play with your map, it's easier riding than walking; the ground's pretty rough here."

"Hey, I can't let you—"

"You can't stop me, I'm not Robyn. Besides, I'm wearing walking shoes. And I have less padding than your mother does." Chris found the arrangement of stirrup and saddle only vaguely

similar to American Western style; he was awkward getting up,
and the saddle, as Jen had said, was extremely hard. Jennifer
looked up at him. "Have fun; he's all yours until Lialla or your
mom wants him. I never was any good on one of the damned
things." Robyn laughed; she was walking next to Aletto's knee,
on the other side of his horse. Nothing of her visible, between
the darkness of the night and Merrida's woolen scarf. "Birdy,
how are your feet?"

"I'm fine," came the answer.

Jennifer and Lialla took turns with the mule and with watching
for other people. When they stopped for a short rest, Chris gave
the horse back over to Robyn and took charge of the pack animal.

The track was not well used this near the western Zelharri
border, and at present utterly deserted. Lialla, whose training
enabled her to differentiate, couldn't even sense animals anywhere near. The trail often vanished in brush or tall, sparse
grass. There was no sign anyone or anything had passed through
since the grass had come to height. Dry as it was now—dry
enough to crackle at their passage—it would be bent over for
days after they reached Sikkre. After an hour of leading and
searching out the safest way for the horses, Jennifer's eyes were
dry and tired. She dropped back to take the mule from Chris
and threw an arm across it. The animal had apparently worked
out its earlier spirit; it paid no attention to her, even when she
leaned more of her weight on it.

The track widened out and became a visibly worn rut around
midnight; by then, the moon had ridden well up behind them,
and two other trails had come in from the flat, arid north to join
theirs. They stopped in the shadow-darkness of a small grove of
trees. There had been drinkable water here, earlier in the season;
the horses pawed through a sandy depression. Chris knelt and
dug down a little ways with his hands. The mule nudged him
aside and shoved its nose into the muddy trickle. He wiped
grubby hands on its flank.

Lialla handed him the water bottle and pushed a chunk of
rather tough bread into his other hand. "Here," she said. "It
won't last if we try to hoard it. Besides, I remember how my
stomach felt the years I was growing. Always empty."

"Uh." He looked at it, nodded finally and took it. "Uh,
thanks." He wouldn't have suspected Lialla of such insight, or
such a kindness. Probably just didn't want to listen to his stom-

ach growling any more. He drank, handed the bottle on, held out the bread. "Anyone else want some of this?"

"Not hungry," Jennifer said briefly. Aletto waved a negating hand.

"My teeth aren't that good," Robyn said. "Eat, kid." He felt a little awkward, being the only one eating, but he didn't let that stop him. It was too dark in this grove to see anyone very clearly anyway. The cramp in his stomach vanished; he sighed happily and tried not to think about the kind of stuff he'd rather have had.

THE air was clear and turning cool, finally. Jennifer pulled the woolen wrap closer around her throat; she was leading, with Robyn and Aletto riding just behind her, Chris leading the mule. Lialla brought up the rear.

The moon was westering, casting enough light that Jennifer could readily make out the trail. The horizon was flat all around them; the slope they'd come down hours earlier no longer visible. Light touched bushes—sparsely leaved, thickly branched, fragrant. They were everywhere, and at first Jennifer had passed them nervously, expecting men to jump from behind them at any moment. Or beasts—lions or something worse. But the night wore slowly on and the worst she saw was either a lizard or a snake: close to the ground, too fast to see clearly. Nothing to worry about, if it ran like that.

Lialla came forward a short while later. "The oasis isn't much farther, if I've gauged distance right. And I think I can feel water."

"How do you do that?"

"Blue, very dark, thick Thread; when you touch it you can just tell."

"Oh." Jennifer bit back a sigh; Lialla's descriptions left something to be desired. "Just tell," indeed.

But it worked. *At least, it did this time,* she thought sourly. It was more nearly purple than blue, and the sound that came with it was so high she lost much of it. It reminded her of that New Age stuff; nice, evocative, but nonmelodic. A repetitive motif rather than a full line of music. Harder to recognize.

Three now: water, movement, medicinal. She wondered how much her mind could keep sorted; how much other stuff she'd have to bury to learn more of this. If—*when*—they got home, she'd have a devil of a time recalling real things, truly important things.

"It's pretty far, still," Lialla said, and Jennifer thought she sounded worried. "We might have to find shelter between where we are now and the oasis, if the sun catches us. It gets hot."

"I can believe that. About this water-Thread; how do you tell distance?"

"Um—" Lialla considered this in silence for a distance. "Thickness, mostly. A little by the color—I don't ordinarily have to track water, it's—let me think about it, try it again a few times."

"Fair enough. I—what's that?" The least sudden light, sharp movement, a faint breeze where there had once been none all evening. Lialla spun around to face north; Aletto, warned by Jennifer's sharp outcry and his sister's sudden stop, drew his horse to a halt and caught hold of Robyn's reins. The mule bumped into them and protested shrilly. Chris cursed it roundly and dragged it back.

"I don't see any—wait. Light? No, it's gone again." The two women stepped off the track to peer into the distance; tall brush defeated them. "Nothing to do with us, it's far enough away. Aletto," she snapped, "don't stop here, keep moving, go!"

The mule, now halted, didn't want to go forward again; Jennifer and Lialla had to take hold of the ropes and pull while Chris shoved. "Stop cussing, Chris," Jennifer said. "It's a dumb animal, and I want to listen. I thought I heard something out there."

Chris glared at her. "Jeez, Aunt Jen, why don't you get *me* as scared as this thing is? Come on, you damned jackass, long-eared—" He went on like that for several minutes, but much more quietly and when Jennifer cleared her throat warningly, he fell altogether silent. The mule suddenly decided the horses were getting away from it and decided to cooperate, so abruptly that the two women were nearly run down.

The brush was lower, barely knee high. Lialla waved an arm at it. "By the time we reach the oasis, there won't be any of this visible anywhere. Just dirt and sand, until we get to the trees."

"And you think we'll find shelter in that?" Jennifer demanded. Lialla shrugged; Jennifer reminded herself of the advice she'd given Chris and kept her mouth prudently closed.

Lialla dropped back a few paces, caught at Jennifer's scarf and tugged. "Look where you thought you saw light, will you? I've been trying to remember what it's like up that way, and as far as I can remember, it's flat. We should be able to see fires from someone's camp for a long distance, but I should be able to sense human presence just as far. And there's no one there.''

"I'll try." Jennifer peered into darkness. Unsuccessfully. She had no luck with Thread either, but she hadn't expected to—not over distance, certainly not the first time. She turned, found Robyn, Chris and Aletto at once; the strands in her fingers vibrated so hard, her fingertips itched when she let go. "If there's anyone out there, I can't see them. It's far enough, it shouldn't worry us.''

"No—you're right." Lialla stepped back onto the track. "They're getting ahead of us, come on.''

But Aletto stopped, dragging his horse back so suddenly and so hard it spun clear around. He wrapped the reins around his good arm and across his palm, held them in place across the saddlebow. "Someone coming!''

"Don't shout!" Lialla implored and ran forward.

"Ambush?" Jennifer called out. Chris had the trail blocked; he had the mule's rope firmly under one heel and he was working hastily to free the bow from its cloth case and string it. Jennifer skirted him, stopped on the track and turned to face north. "How could it be, though? We both searched—'' She clapped both hands across her mouth, muffling a scream, as men on tall white horses, men clad in pale flowing robes, came riding across the open desert, straight for them. Four men, four horses. Four broad-bladed swords. Curved swords. *Scimitars,* Jennifer thought dazedly, and stood watching them come. More men rode behind them, pale faces framed by dark hoods and black flying robes. Their camels were nearly as pale as the horses; they shone an eery blue in the moonlight.

"Jen!" Lialla's outcry roused her; Jennifer turned and ran. Men shouted; she felt the wind of their passing, the hiss of air parted by steel; she smelled the sweat of men and horses, the unfamiliar odor that must be camel. Then nothing. She stopped, spun on one heel. There was no one where the attackers should be, but a vast distance to the south, she saw light again. It faded, grew, faded once more.

"What is that?" she shouted.

"Don't yell!" Lialla implored. Her face was as white as one of the horses.

"Why not?" Jennifer shouted. "They know where we are! Whatever *they* are!''

"You don't want to know what they are!" Lialla said. She

looked down at her hands, stuffed them inside her sleeves. "Just keep your voice down, will you?"

"Why? They're gone!" Jennifer's voice seemed to have a life of its own; her legs didn't want to hold her up.

"Listen to me, carefully." Lialla gripped her shoulders and shook her hard. "They'll cross this track four times. They know we're here, but they can't see us clearly. They can't touch you unless you stand right in front of them. Do that, and you're dead—or one of them, no one knows which."

"Don't let them—" Robyn's voice rose in hysteria; Aletto pulled her off her horse and wrapped both sets of reins around his good arm.

Lialla looked at them and nodded. "Aletto, watch to the south, be ready. Chris, I admire what you're doing but it won't work; you can't touch them with any human weapon. I can't touch them; I don't know if there's anything that can. Watch for them, they don't give you much warning."

"Coming!" Aletto cried out. Jennifer stood still, knees flexed for flight, and watched them come. Magnificent horses, and who would have thought a camel could be so graceful in full gallop? They rode in a close group, horses, camels, across the track, once more gone. A faint gleam of light in the distance. No sound, though a moment ago the air had been heavy with the creak of harness leather and the clink of metal, the harsh breathing of men and beasts, the beat of so many hooves on hard, dry ground.

"Watch," Lialla ordered, and there was a quaver in her voice. "Watch the trail, both ways; watch the north. It's said they sometimes break ranks—" The words were scarcely out of her mouth when the horde came at them, angling across the hard-packed trail. The last time they spread out, practically turned on their own trace, just beyond the small, shivering group.

Robyn screamed; Jennifer started and turned her attention from the oncoming horses for a dangerously long moment. Lialla's wordless cry brought her back around, barely in time: She faked one way, back the other as a horseman separated from the pack and rode straight at her. The muscles in the white chest rippled, silver and red harness gleamed dully; dark, eager eyes tried to meet hers, to catch them. She threw herself down and rolled under a low bush. A small shower of dry leaves and brittle sticks slithered down her back and fell into her eyes; something small wriggled from under her hand. She jumped back, scrubbed her hand down her jeans.

Another scream, this one nonhuman; Jennifer scrambled into the open and onto her knees. Another of the horsemen had broken ranks and rode straight for Aletto and Robyn; two of the camel riders followed close on his heels. Aletto used his horse as a shield, hauled Robyn behind it by mere strength. The reins were torn from her hands. "No, come back—!" Her voice was drowned by the thunder of hooves, her horse's among them. The white horse rode after it and the two remaining horsemen turned to join the hunt. The brown tried to turn, too late; the whites rode it down; the camel-riders rode across where it had been. The white horses wheeled precisely, turned back to the north and were swallowed up by the night. The camel-riders followed. Sight and sound of them was gone entirely, as though they had never been.

Chris took two reluctant steps, a third. Stopped; the mule trailed along behind him, suddenly docile, rope dragging in the dirt. Aletto and Robyn joined him, Aletto leading the remaining horse, Robyn trying not to cry and only just succeeding. Jennifer came up, shaking out her shirt-tails and picking twigs out of her hair. Lialla came back from well up the track. They all stopped and stared down at the narrow track. There was no sign of the second horse anywhere.

9

THE night spun and tilted around her; Jennifer took a step
back along the path, braced herself on wide-set heels and
folded over at the waist, knees bent, forearms pressed against
thighs. Her head flopped and everything went momentarily completely black. The roaring in her ears faded, slowly. Greatly
daring, she opened her eyes, fixed her gaze on the tips of her
sneakers, concentrated on breathing slowly and normally until
they no longer blurred. Even then, she didn't straighten up; she'd
never had a fainting spell before and it frightened her nearly as
much as the cause for it had.

She did raise her head finally. Turned it, carefully. Lialla, a
faint shadow in the gloom, sat right in the middle of the track
not far away, unmoving. Jennifer could hear her harsh breathing.
Behind her, she heard Chris draw a ragged, shuddering breath;
as she turned to look at him, he knelt and carefully began wrapping the mule's lead-rope around his fist, all his concentration
fixed intently on the turns of rope, on keeping them flat. The
mule rubbed its muzzle against his shirt, lipped his spiked hair.

"Lady—Robyn?" Aletto's voice, scarcely recognizable, but
he sounded more worried about her than himself. *God, Birdy,*
Jennifer thought, and pushed against her knees with trembling
hands. Everything swam once more as she got herself properly
upright, finally settled into place. Aletto had turned from the
empty stretch of track, dropped the horse's reins. The animal
pressed close to him, nosing at his neck for reassurance.

Robyn stood a few paces away from him, both hands over her
mouth; tears were spilling down her face and her shoulders
shook. But when Aletto took hold of her arms and tried to pull
her to him, she tore free of him, whirled around and pushed past

Jennifer to kneel by Chris's side. Rope still twisted around his right hand, he turned away from the mule, sat on the hard-packed dirt and wrapped his arms around her. Robyn clutched him fiercely and sobbed against his shoulder.

Aletto gazed down at her, tight-lipped, then turned and limped away. He stopped ten feet or so off the path, just as Jennifer was about to call out to him; the horse followed him anxiously.

Lialla had apparently noticed none of this; she still sat in the middle of the track and was mumbling to herself, words Jennifer couldn't make out until she got closer. "My fault, all my fault. I should have known, I should have—"

Jennifer bit back a sigh, bit back angry words that had to be partly reaction, mostly a strong distaste for people who talked that way. This certainly wasn't the time or place for breast-beating. "Lialla, what was that? Those men?" Lialla stopped muttering, looking up at her blankly. Jennifer flung out an arm to take in the whole desert north of the track. "That, what just happened. Is that Hell-Light, or ghosts, or just what? Are they going to follow us, or come back? Because frankly, I'd rather not meet up with them again, and I don't think I want to go the way that horse did. But I sure don't intend to sit here and wait for them!"

"No, of course not." Lialla got up, rather like a small child reacting to an adult's orders. Jennifer wondered if she was in shock; her eyes weren't focused properly and she was making funny little noises. She wondered how a noblewoman would take to being slapped. Lialla blinked, shook her head. "Hell-Light? That wasn't Hell-Light."

"Are you all right?"

"I—fine, why?" Lialla blinked at her vaguely.

"I'm glad to hear it," Jennifer said dryly. "That—what just attacked us. Is it going to come back?"

"Not—I don't know. They say not, once it's taken life."

Jennifer resisted an even stronger urge than the first one to slap her out of that trancelike calm. "They say. In other words, you don't know. Wonderful. In that case, why don't we get them moving, find that oasis, get away from here, now? Before something else goes wrong? Let's do something, damnit!"

Lialla blinked again, rubbed her eyes hard. "I—look, why are you blaming me? Do you think it's my fault they attacked, or that we lost the horse?"

"I think it's going to be both your fault and mine," Jennifer interrupted her angrily, "if it comes back and catches us a second time. Otherwise, I frankly don't give a damn who's to blame."

Lialla stared at her in stunned surprise and a rising anger; before she could draw breath to reply, Chris was on his feet, staring down at the place where the horse had been.

"That could have been one of us—that could have been my mother. What the hell is wrong with you people, leading us into this kind of disaster?" He was shaking violently, fury and re-action mixed. When Robyn, who still knelt at the mule's head, tugged at his jeans and mutely shook her head, he pulled away from her. "Don't, Mom, you let me handle this! You'd say it's all right, anything to avoid a fight. Well, it's not all right!"

Jennifer stepped between him and Lialla and grabbed his shoulders. "I happen to agree with you, Chris. I resent being dragged out here and getting attacked like that is insult on top of injury. Of course it's not all right, but this isn't the place or the time to discuss it. It certainly isn't time to assign blame before we know what's going on. Now, move." She released his arms and gave him a shove. "Get your mother on her feet; let's get moving." And, as Robyn tried to say something, "Birdy, please, just stow it, unless you see something about to land on us, nothing is that important." Robyn let Chris help her up but then pulled free of his hand and turned her back on all of them.

Lialla broke a rather nasty silence; her voice was too high but she was clearly trying to keep a grip on it. "You're right, of course, this isn't the place to decide anything." She raised her voice a little. "Aletto, where are you? Are you all right?"

"Fine," came a muttered, sullen response from the far side of the remaining horse.

"Get back over here. We can't afford to be spread all over the landscape." He limped back across loose sand, his lame foot sending small stones clattering off the path. His face was pale, set and unreadable. Lialla ignored him; her attention was all for the horse. She felt his chest, his legs, patted his nose and felt the few bags slung around his neck.

"I can't even begin to guess what's left here. What was on the other horse?"

Aletto shrugged. "Not much, I don't think. Don't remem-ber." He wouldn't look at Robyn and apparently didn't intend to talk to her, either. Jennifer's fingers twitched; she stuffed them in her jeans pockets and turned away. There was an unnatural hush all around them, and it was utterly black to the north. She stared into the night until her eyes ached, kept an ear on the conversations behind her, and somehow kept herself from turning around and screaming at them all.

It took everything she had in the way of courage to turn her back on the north and refocus her attention on her companions.

Chris was talking to the mule, making soothing noises against its ear; the beast didn't seem particularly upset but Chris was still too pale and his hands were shaking. He was looking back over the animal's ears, watching his mother, visibly uncertain what to say to her. Robyn was a stiff, unmovable object behind the mule, staring back the way they'd come. Jennifer went to her. "Robyn—Birdy. We're waiting on you, I think. We have to go." Silence. "You don't want to stay here, do you?"

"No." Robyn's voice trembled. She turned around, rubbed her hand under her nose. "I don't want any more of this, Jen, I want to go home. But I'm so scared right now I don't think I can move."

"Sure you can. That oasis isn't much farther."

"Who knows what's waiting for us *there*?" Robyn said wildly.

"Water," Chris said blandly. Robyn looked up at him, stunned, then managed a very faint smile.

"Smart kid," she whispered; her voice broke.

"Mom, your bag wasn't on the horse, was it?"

"Oh, God, that horse." Robyn drew a deep breath and Jennifer held hers, afraid she'd start crying once more. "My bag— oh, God, I didn't, did I? My cigarettes . . ." Her voice trailed away. "No, wait, it's—God, I must be nuts, it's right here on my shoulder under this woolly thing and I didn't even feel it."

"You've got every right," Jennifer said. Robyn managed a watery smile that was no more real than the last one and began fumbling under her wrap. Her hands were shaking so badly it took her several minutes to drag it free and open it. Jennifer opened her mouth, shut it again as Robyn pulled out cigarettes and began fishing for a lighter. She looked up and her eyes went hard, her mouth set.

"Either one of you—*any* of you!—say one word, and that's it," she said flatly. "I'll stay here, and hell with you all. Got it? Not one damned word!" No one did; Aletto and his sister watched in astonishment as Robyn found a cigarette, found her lighter and took a mouthful of smoke. She exhaled and a little of the tension went out of her shoulders. Aletto's nostrils twitched. "God, I needed that. Chris, stop glaring at me, your feelings aren't that hurt. Just go on, I'll bring up the rear with the mule."

"Mom—"

"Don't give me a load of crap, I'm obviously as safe back here as anywhere, go on!" He did, mumbling to himself. Aletto glared at his back, got himself back on the horse and nudged it forward.

It was hard, moving forward across the flat, open ground once more. They felt vulnerable, and it was slow going, walking and watching for lights on all sides. All the same, Jennifer felt no safer once the track plunged into tall brush again. She kept looking over her shoulder to the north, searching for that faint glimmer of light. There was nothing; that failed to reassure her.

Lialla had moved out with Aletto at first, apparently trying to talk to him. Jennifer was far enough back that she couldn't hear any of their conversation—it was all one-sided, anyway. Aletto occasionally turned his head to glare down at her, his mouth set in a tight, lipless line. Lialla finally threw her hands wide, snarled something and turned on her heel. Chris stepped aside for her, his own steps lagging a little to allow additional room between himself and Aletto.

Lialla walked next to Jennifer for several silent minutes. "That back there wasn't Hell-Light," she said finally; her words were clipped, unfriendly. "I don't know much about it, the nomads call it the Spectral Host, I already knew it did—what you saw."

Jennifer stared at her. "Ghosts?"

"Don't laugh," Lialla said sharply.

"Believe me, I wouldn't—not after *that*. It's just—oh, never mind. Spectral Host. Go on."

"There is more than one—supposedly, anyway. But there must be, since some have no horsemen, or the horses are different colors, or all camels. I knew there was one said to be near the caravan way from Holmaddan somewhere along the last furlongs to the oasis; few travel that stretch at night. When we—when I decided on this way, I didn't consider it might have a range that overlapped the track."

"I thought Hell-Light was the bad magic. If this isn't Hell-Light, where does it fit in?"

Lialla shook her head. "Hell-Light *is* bad. You don't know until you've seen it in use."

"Well, I've seen it, along the road two nights ago. I wouldn't have tampered with it; it left me feeling unclean. I'll trust you, it's bad. This other thing, though. Tell me."

"This—what happened tonight—it's older by far."

"The Spectral Host?"

"Yes—no. It's—that's a symptom of other magic, older than Hell-Light, different. No one knows for certain how old it is, but it's tied to the land itself. Hell-Light isn't nearly so ancient; it goes back only five hundred years or so. And it's created magic; does that make sense?"

"Natural versus created? Anything's possible, I suppose." Postulating magic at all, Jennifer thought, but kept that to herself. That much still didn't want to register, even with the reality of Thread jangling in her ears.

"They say Hell-Light was first shaped from the old magic, but I truly know very little about that. Get Aletto to tell you if that interests you; he knows more Rhadazi history than I do. Thread-magic was well established by the time Hell-Light came into existence; it's—" she paused, searching for the right word. Her voice was losing the rough, clipped edge. "The Thread is there, it just took the right people to find it and work out how to use it."

"All right. I can accept that, too. This other, though, this Host. Where else are we going to find one of these things, and how do we avoid them?"

"There aren't any more between here and Sikkre—I don't think."

"You don't—you mean you don't know?"

Lialla sighed, clearly exasperated. "There aren't said to be any! That doesn't mean we're entirely safe, though, does it?"

Jennifer set her jaw and stuffed her hands back in her jeans pockets. "I hardly expected entirely safe, not after our initial introduction to your land. I would just like to know what to watch for!"

"Well," Lialla retorted waspishly, "watch for anything." She turned her head and looked behind them, swore as she stubbed her toe on a half-buried stone and tripped. Jennifer caught her arm and steadied her. "She's still behind us, your sister is. Is she always so easily scared?"

"She doesn't usually have cause to be," Jennifer retorted. "Chris protects her; so do I, when I can."

Lialla scowled, looked over her shoulder again. "What is she *doing*?"

"Calming her nerves," Jennifer said.

Lialla's nose wrinkled. "Smells terrible."

"I happen to agree with you. It's nearly impossible to argue with a smoker, though." The two women looked at each other.

Lialla managed a brief smile that had something of apology to it.

"Well. They say some of the Lasanach raiders breathe smoke, and that certain of the far northern nomads do. Some have said the smoke-breathing was the cause of the plague the Lasanachi brought, but that's foolish. Plague is like the marsh-sickness that took Aletto; people breathe it on each other."

Jennifer shifted her leather bag to her other shoulder; the bones and muscles on the left side of her neck were beginning to ache from the weight. "I didn't know you knew that much about illness."

"We *are* civilized, after all."

"Just so. Marsh-sickness? Is that why he walks with a limp? I didn't like to ask—"

"I wouldn't ask Aletto; it's ten years—more than that, now—and he still won't talk about it. But he was extraordinarily fortunate, though he won't believe it." Lialla glanced at her brother's stiff back a distance ahead, and lowered her voice. "Fortunate, I mean, having two Wielders to care for him. People normally die of it; the paralysis stills the organs and freezes the blood. Merrida and Mother saved his life, but two close friends, boys his age, died. His personal servant lost use of his legs entirely. I think he died, later. Jadek sent him away; I never really knew." She was silent for some minutes, her eyes fixed on the path just ahead of her feet. "Knowing how marsh-sickness comes, I guess Jadek *could* have brought it about himself. It would be like him; hoping Aletto would die with no blame to him. Or go mad, or be paralyzed so he couldn't inherit. And there'd be so little danger to Jadek; the disease does not touch the grown or any female, only boys and young men."

"That's ghastly!"

Lialla nodded. "You say that as if you don't believe it could be true."

"I didn't say that. Men do—*people* where I come from do terrible things, not just men, you know. But the news and the history books are full of them."

"Perhaps. But you don't know Jadek. He's—he looks like Father did, the way I remember him. Tall, handsome. Father—his smile lit up his whole face. But more than that, people loved Father. He was kind; he took care of his people and his Duchy. He was—oh, thoughtful, even in little things. Once, when I was very small, he was called to Podhru for some parley with the

Emperor. He came back with gifts, and mine I remember even now because they were things he knew I liked and wanted.

"Jadek—his smile is something he creates; when he's nice, it's for a specific purpose. People who don't know him think he's like Father, kind, thoughtful. He's thinking all the time, scheming. He's—" She stopped speaking abruptly.

"I know people like that," Jennifer said finally. She could think of two immediately: a woman partner in another firm, and one of the law clerks at her own firm. Power brokers, all of them.

"People." Lialla shuddered. "One of Jadek is enough."

Jennifer cast a thoughtful glance at Aletto's back. The two women walked together a while in silence—an almost companionable silence. "Knowing this Jadek as you do, you can't really think he'll just give up and step down when you come back, do you?"

Lialla contemplated her hands. "He has to," she said finally. "He won't have any choice, he'll have to." Jennifer considered this and decided to leave it; Lialla was obviously fooling only herself if she believed that. But if it made her feel better to believe that, then that, too, was her business.

Robyn had finished her cigarette; she moved forward and handed the mule over to Chris, walked next to him. Chris was unusually silent; Robyn coughed once or twice and even that didn't provoke one of his usual comments about her smoking. But Robyn wasn't in a talkative mood, either, and Lialla had gone gloomily silent. Jennifer left her to mount a rear guard and went up with Aletto.

He looked down at her, face still tight, then turned his attention back to the trail. Jennifer let the silence stretch for a while. Finally, she said, "He's her son, you know."

He didn't bother to pretend he didn't understand her reference. "I know," Aletto said flatly.

"He's all she has, the only one besides me who's ever stuck with her; there've been a lot of men who haven't. Chris has always been there for her, no matter what. You have to expect she'll turn to him when she's that frightened."

"Oh."

Jennifer looked up at him in sudden irritation. "Don't say it like that. She isn't deliberately trying to upset you. Birdy's the way she is, she's always been stubborn and she's set in her ways. She isn't a tough woman. She's a survivor, but it's not the same thing."

"I don't understand—"

"No, I know you don't. That's why I'm telling you, so you'll quit thinking bad thoughts at her and poisoning the air all around you. She's a—I'm not finding the word in your language, she doesn't believe in war and killing. Not even killing animals. As crazy as her life has been, all these years, she's always avoided violence. Any violence—against herself, against other people, animals. So what happened just now was twice as bad for her as it was for me." Silence. Aletto let the horse pick its own way; he was leaning forward, arms resting on the padded saddlebow. "And Chris is very protective of her."

"I noticed," Aletto said dryly. Jennifer laughed, and to her surprise, Aletto chuckled. He sobered at once. "It was my fault."

"You and your sister both. Stop that."

"It was. I should have stayed mounted, I couldn't move fast enough and then Robyn was trying to help me run. When they came at us that last time, her knees buckled she was so frightened. I was trying to hold her up and myself up, and I let go the reins. The horse ran at once. My fault," he concluded gloomily.

Jennifer shook her head. "Your reasoning is as flawed as Lialla's. All right, you let the horse go. Hardly on purpose, did you? And they took it. I have this much in common with Birdy; I wish they hadn't come, and I'm very sorry that poor beast went like it did. But it satisfied them, didn't it? A life. Would you rather have died in its place?"

"Well—"

"Feeling bad is one thing," Jennifer said. "Feeling guilty isn't useful at all. It keeps you from thinking what you should be doing."

He shrugged, embarrassed. "Well, but—"

"Let it go, all right? Tell me about this place we're going instead."

Aletto obediently launched into a description of Sikkre. It was liberally splattered with "they tell me" and "it's said." Aletto had not been to Sikkre since he was very small and remembered only a very few things: the interior of the Thukar's magnificent palace; sneaking out to one of the parts of the market not normally open to children with the Thukar's son Dahven; the small, plain room where he and Dahven had been put for punishment when they got caught—until Dahven got them out again. It kept Jennifer entertained all the way to their next stop.

* * *

THEY rested on the crumbling bank of a dry wash, shared a little water. Lialla rested her chin on her knees and stared blankly into the distance—now very dark indeed since the moon had set. She finally pointed. "We're close, a couple furlongs or so. The animals should smell water soon."

"Anyone already there?" Chris asked. "Or can you tell that?"

"Some people, five or six. Camels and horses. Small trading party probably; maybe a lead group for a caravan, that kind of thing I can't tell. They're well up at the north end, near the spring."

Jennifer's back was beginning to ache, and now that her fear and anger had worn off, she was exhausted. And she couldn't remember how long a furlong was. American furlong, she reminded herself. Here, it could be entirely different. But she could feel the cooler air once they crossed the wash, and then the definite chill of damp-laden air as they went down a long inclined slope. Brush grew more thickly here, shifted from the pungent dry-land stuff.

It was beginning to get light out, and somewhat to her surprise, she saw willow and aspen, white-barked birch clumps. Chris passed her, the mule tugging him along, heading for the water they could all hear. Aletto leaned from the horse and caught its bridle. "Don't let him drink here. Get him down onto the rocks, there!"

He pointed. Chris turned his head and was nearly yanked off his feet. "Let?" he said. But the two got the stubborn beast turned and when Jennifer came limping slowly down to the water's edge, she could see Aletto, Chris and Robyn crouched on a sloping ledge of rock, the mule and the horse between them eagerly drinking.

"Oasis?" Jennifer said aloud. She turned in place, gazing at the surrounding rock, brush and trees.

"Oasis," Aletto said. He sat down to strip off his boots, unwrapped strips of fabric that served for stockings and plunged his feet into the water. "Oh, that feels good. Any washing is done downstream here. Drinking water is up, that way." He pointed.

"Makes sense," Chris said. "Um—we're one short. Where's Lialla?"

Jennifer turned and looked back the way they'd come. "She's not in sight. Wait." She shut her eyes, swayed gently as she tried to concentrate. Word—Thread. It was fading, the sound of it barely audible. "*Night*-Thread," she reminded herself. But she only needed a moment. "I thought as much; she's gone that way." She jabbed a finger upstream.

Aletto dropped his boots and swore. "I—damn her, anyway! I was going to tell her not to—"

"So she's already done it." Jennifer sighed. "No, don't do that," she added as Aletto dropped down and began pulling the boots on again. "She's right, we need things and she's best suited for getting them. Your going after her won't help anything, you're too recognizable, and we three aren't any better. And we're hardly an armed party to go rescue her if she's misjudged them." She fixed Aletto with a hard look. "Is she that stupid, to walk into an encampment that might be dangerous to her?"

"Lialla isn't stupid," Aletto said angrily.

"Then put your feet back in the water and wait. If she hasn't returned before the sun comes up, we'll try something else." He gave her an unfriendly look, but slowly pulled the half-on boot free, threw it across flat rock and went back to soaking his feet. Jennifer rolled her eyes. Her first Duke, and this was how she talked to him? But who expected members of a noble household to act like a couple of headstrong brats? Particularly a pair as old as this pair.

Chris cleared his throat and waded out into the stream. "This is an oasis?"

"Water, trees, shade." Aletto indicated them all with a wave of his hand. "What else should an oasis be?"

"Where I come from, it's palm trees and sand, maybe a well or a spring."

"They're like that if you take the north road into Dro Pent. But this is a spring; it comes out of the ground up near where the caravan is. The water runs down here, drops into rock just past where we are."

"We're safe here?" Jennifer didn't care much for a caravan so near; then again, after their earlier surprise, she didn't like the thought of having the oasis to themselves, either.

"I don't know. I hope so."

"Well." Jennifer ran her hands through her hair. It felt horribly gritty. "At least you're honest."

"I'm also thirsty." Aletto got to his feet and walked slowly up the rock ledge, gingerly across dry sand. "There should be a regular place to drink. Upstream from where the animals are supposed to be."

Above the ledge where the mule still drank, the water was deep, moving fast over a pebbly bottom. Aletto walked north along the shore until he found a pocked granite ledge jutting out into the stream, squatted on its edge and pulled a leather cup from his belt. He drank, filled it again, held it up. Jennifer looked at the stream with misgivings, doubtfully at the cup and its contents, finally shrugged and drank. It couldn't possibly be clean, but what she'd been drinking throughout the night couldn't have been, either.

By the time they got back downstream, Chris had the horse unsaddled and the packs off the mule. Robyn had her shoes off and was sitting cross-legged on the sand, rummaging through the food bags. "No fire, I suppose?" she asked doubtfully.

"I'd rather not," Jennifer said. "I don't like the idea of marking our location, do you?" Robyn shook her head so hard that blonde hair flew. She pulled out the last of the bread, some fruit, the remainder of the chicken.

"Eat it now or forget it," she said gloomily. "The blue ice is just barely cool; the chicken's going to turn gross on us." Jennifer ate fruit, gnawed at hard bread. It wasn't much, barely enough to ease her hunger. Aletto soaked his bread in cold water, squeezed the water out of it and ate it; Robyn followed his example. Chris offered the chicken around, had no takers, and finished it himself. He brought out the map Aletto had done for him, scooted around so they had it between them.

"Where are we on here, and how much farther to this Sikkre?"

Aletto answered his second question. "Half a night if we were all ahorse. Most of one otherwise." He shifted, pulled his feet up and began rubbing his toes. Those on the left foot were too white, oddly jumbled together. "If Lialla—" He stared back the way they'd come, brow puckered, shrugged gloomily and went back to his stale bread. "If she bargains well, there will still only be two horses and the mule. She won't dare get more, if she's pretending to be alone."

"Better than no beasts at all," Jennifer said. "Do your mules carry people?"

"I'd never try to ride one," he said. "But as you choose."

"Not if it hasn't been trained for it." Jennifer moistened the end of her index finger and blotted up crumbs from her lap. "I barely know how to stay on a horse." She sucked the last crumbs from her fingertips and yawned. "Look, I'll do what I can to stay awake until Lialla comes back, just in case. But I absolutely can't sit up another single minute.''

"Sun will come up where you are," Aletto said. He pointed. "Ground's as soft over there and it'll be shaded."

"That's for me, then.'' Jennifer stood, stretched and groaned faintly as her back protested. There was dry sand where Aletto indicated, rather than the grass and fallen leaves she would have preferred. But there were branches overhead, bushes all around. Probably where the scorpions and snakes live, she thought unhappily and dug the knuckles of both hands into the small of her back. She scraped hollows with her foot, edged them out with her hip and shoulder and spread the woolen scarf out. She could hear Chris still talking to Aletto, then Robyn walking nearby.

"Jen?"

"Mmmm? Birdy?" It was almost too much effort to speak; suddenly she was blindly exhausted.

"I'm over here, other side of the bush, all right?''

"Mmmm. Sure, fine."

Tired as she was, she couldn't sleep at such an odd hour, and the sun was barely up when she quit trying. Lialla was back, sitting on the rock ledge with her legs in the water to the knee, the black Wielder breeks discarded and the long overshirt hiked over her thighs. She yanked it down as she heard footsteps, relaxed again as Jennifer came into sight, and grinned at her ruefully. "If my mother could see me like this!" She held up a heavy cloth bag in deep blue. It bulged. And behind her, with her boots over its back, was a small bay. It shied and rolled its eyes at them, but calmed as Lialla tugged on the rope halter and spoke to it in a language Jennifer hadn't heard before. She approached slowly, held out a hand. The pony shook its head; shaggy mane flew wildly. It nosed her fingers tentatively, let her rub its nose. "Not used to kindness," Lialla said. "Most nomad ponies aren't, at least not Holmaddi ones. The foreign nomads north of Dro Pent sleep with their horses, they say. I've seen three; they're the most beautiful things I ever did see. Breathe in his nostrils," she added. "So he knows you."

Jennifer eyed her doubtfully, bent down and blew. It had no effect that she could see, but the horse let her stroke his nose and then his neck. "Poor thing, he looks like he's had a hard life. He's awfully thin. Are you sure he can carry any of us?" His ribs were too visible to her eye, his tail had been hacked short, his nose was scarred.

"They all look that way; they're tough, though. Desert-trained.''

Jennifer gave the horse one last pat and moved away from him to wash her dusty hands in the stream. "You didn't have any trouble?"

Lialla grinned. "Just with Aletto, when I got back. Wasn't that what woke you?"

"You arguing? Never heard it." She shook water from her hands.

"The men up there were an advance for a caravan. The rest of the family will reach the oasis tonight; they'll probably take up the entire area. I know of the clan, they're not likely to gossip with outsiders in Sikkre, but we ought to be gone before they arrive. I got enough to feed myself all the way to Podhru; that's where I told them I was going. There should be enough to last all of us today and tonight. By dawn, we'll be in Sikkre."

"And what then?"

Lialla shrugged, and some of the light went out of her face. "I wish I knew." Jennifer looked down at her; Lialla looked up. She shrugged again. "Oh, within reason: I know of three different inns said to be safe. I know places within the market safe to go to buy food and the like, and others not; I certainly know to avoid the Thukar and any of his men. His son Dahven . . . Dahven is a little mad, but he and I were nearly trothed once. And he genuinely likes Aletto. I think if we cán somehow attract his attention, he can help us plan from there."

Jennifer didn't like the sound of Dahven at all. "If you think you can trust him—"

"We have to," Lialla said earnestly. "We don't have anyone else, until we find Gyrdan." She ran both hands through her hair, tugged at the ends. "Truthfully, I'm not completely certain he *is* in Sikkre. That was never more than rumor, and it's been a while since I first heard it. And he may not want to help Aletto, in which case—"

"I wouldn't worry about that yet. I'd find him first. And as for locating him and all the rest of that, we'll just have to walk carefully and keep our eyes open, won't we?" Jennifer turned to look downstream. It was time to change the subject; Lialla's plan seemed to have more holes every time she heard any of it, and it was beginning to frighten her just how shaky the whole thing was. "There's sun on the water down there, past where the horses were drinking earlier. I'm going to grab it while everyone's still asleep; my hair is disgusting and I'm filthy."

Lialla stood up and shielded her eyes. "I think there's a pool, if I recall from the other time I came through here. Just a shallow one. Wait—" She dug in the small bag hanging from her belt and held out a soft cloth pillow that smelled of lavender and something tangy, citrusy. "There's herb stuff in here and soap." For the first time, Lialla's smile was relaxed and friendly. "Thank you."

"You're welcome. But for what?"

"For not telling me none of it's going to work. I know how bad it looks and I wager you do, too. I appreciate not hearing it."

"It does look bad. That doesn't mean we don't stand a chance," Jennifer said. She took the soap bag and returned Lialla's smile.

10

༄

THE water was icy; her fingers were blue and trembling uncontrollably by the time she was finished, but she was washed and her hair was at least reasonably clean. After Lialla bathed, Jennifer waded to the other side of the stream and sat in the sun on the far bank until the chill baked out of her bones and her hair was dry, then waded back and sought her previous resting place. It was unexpectedly cool down on the sand, even with only dappled shade to cover her. A breeze blew across her face, rustling aspen leaves. It put her in mind of a camping trip, long years before, when her mother and father had still been together—perhaps a picnic, down along a stream bed. Yellow and red leaves everywhere, tall mountains with snow on their peaks. Aspen rustling. She smiled, and fell into a long, heavy sleep.

The shadows faced the other direction when she woke, too warm, disoriented from the nap, and hungry. The shade was still dappled but there was more sun mixed in it now; the breeze was stronger and hot, now; desert-dry. Her eyelids felt gummy, her face and hands horribly dry from sand and wind. "Caffeine," she groaned, and pushed herself up onto her knees. Some attorneys carried packets of instant coffee around with them. "Some attorneys have foresight and brains," she muttered crossly. "And if I ever get home, I'll never be caught out without it again." It occurred to her suddenly there might be something similar here, something in Sikkre. After all, Chris might be right, there might be a crossover point. She sighed. She wouldn't dare let herself hope any such thing. The letdown would be horrible if she was wrong.

She could hear two voices above the noise of the creek—Chris's and Aletto's. Apparently the high feelings of the previous night had been talked out or temporarily forgotten; they had the map between them once more and were at least talking. Chris tapped the paper and ran a finger along it. "So, anyway, this place up here, what'd you call those guys?" He looked up. "Hey, Jen, I think I'm getting a feel for where we branched."

"Huh?"

"Branched," Robyn said with heavy patience from Aletto's other side. She was sitting cross-legged in the sand, wet hair hanging over her shoulders; her eyes were slightly glazed as though she had heard the word entirely too many times this afternoon.

"Branched," Chris echoed. "Look, if you go back far enough, we've got people and place names in common, just like I told you we would."

Jennifer blocked a yawn and pressed her knuckles into the small of her back. "Names. Such as?"

"Rome. Caesar. Moors. Castile. Maya. Cortez." Chris shrugged. "Buncha others. Somewhere around Cortez, it starts falling apart, though. So—"

"Is this actually useful data?"

"Jennifer!" Chris broke into English; it sounded strange, after two days of continuous Rhadazi. "I mean—you know?"

She answered him in kind, sternly: "I-mean-you-know doesn't tell me one damn thing. Try real English."

"I mean—well, yeah!"

"This data helps us get home?"

"Well, not exactly, but—" He shrugged. "It could, you know. Eventually." He shifted back to Rhadazi, and now it sounded even stranger than English had. "Look, I think that old bat doesn't know everything, and besides, he says there are supposed to be other people who've come here. *And* gone." Jennifer, who knew Chris pretty well, eyed him thoughtfully and then transferred the look to the nera-Duke. Not exactly a meeting of minds; more like a temporary truce.

Aletto looked up, shrugged and smiled ruefully. He had moved slightly closer to Robyn while Chris was talking; Robyn apparently wasn't keeping any of Chris's grudges, because unless Jennifer's eyes were blurrier than she thought, Robyn had also edged in Aletto's direction. "Truly, I can't say for certain about Americans." He'd picked up the word from Robyn or Chris but the "c" was almost a guttural, the "s" nearly nonexistent. "There are legends, of course; men or women who suddenly appear— often not knowing any language spoken in Rhadazi or among the Trade Leagues. Dressed oddly. But if I had not met you three—well . . . Certain of those in Sikkre may know. Dahven claims to have met such a foreign.''

"Fascinating," Lialla said dryly. She had come unnoticed from the brush upstream and was trying to adjust her breeches, yawning cavernously. "I have heard stories of that sort myself, though Dahven never said anything to me of meeting Americani. All the same . . ." Her voice trailed away; she nodded in Chris's direction as she stifled another yawn. "Merrida is my instructor in all things to do with Thread. I must defend her if only to say she would not willingly have brought you here. But it is not in her to apologize, either." She tucked the ends of her sash in place.

"We noticed," Chris said sarcastically.

Lialla glared him into silence. "What point to apologize? She could not return you, she hadn't intended *you*—"

Chris shifted; Robyn reached across Aletto's lap to grab Chris's arm, hard, and he subsided. "She intended to ruin someone's life," Robyn said flatly. "An apology wouldn't have made it better, but it would have been nice."

"Nice?" Lialla's eyebrows went up.

"Nice," Robyn said firmly. "I would have preferred to think she was sorry to disrupt our lives." She released Chris's arm, and Aletto slid his hand across his lap to intercept her fingers. Robyn cast him a brief smile. "Look, let's drop it; we already said we'd drop it."

"Fine," Lialla said, before Chris could say anything else. She looked up at the sky, thoughtfully at the creek, now more than half in shade. "I think we should eat now. Refill the water bags, water the horses and that mule. We have to get moving as soon as the heat goes off the sand a little. That caravan is due in here any time."

"We've just been waiting for you," Robyn said. She freed her fingers with an apologetic smile in Aletto's direction, then opened the cloth bag and pulled out unleavened bread that crunched like crackers, flat pieces of dry fruit and some ball-shaped things she stared at doubtfully. Lialla snapped one up, bit an enormous chunk out of it, tucked it in her cheek and spoke around it.

"Oat cake," she mumbled. "Wonderful things, got as many as I could. Grain, honey, fruit—wonderful stuff. Didn't get as many as I wanted, damnit."

"There aren't that many in the whole world," Aletto grinned.

* * *

As soon as they ate, Robyn found two ancient rubber bands in the bottom of her bag; she and Jennifer took turns braiding each other's hair while Lialla filled the water bottles. Chris saddled the horse, Aletto snugged the blanket around the nomad pony, and it took both of them to attach the packs and harness on the mule, though the ropes went on much more quickly than they had the night before, and the animal showed no tendency to balk this time.

There was no sun left on the water, and they could hear men now above the noise of the stream—men, and the high, glad voices of women, the shrill wail of a hungry baby. The pony whickered urgently, sensing familiar voices. Lialla led them swiftly across the sloping stone ledge and through the brush. The running water vanished only a few paces downstream, where it slid between slabs of rock. Almost immediately after, the trees ended. Willow and aspen straggled on a little ways, gave way to dryer things, finally to sage and a gray-and-yellow flowered thing that had a sour smell. It, too, straggled off, ten per small area, then five, then one; all brush vanished at once, then, almost as though a line had been drawn across the sand. Ahead of them was yellow or black rock, sand, and dirt; an occasional scrubby, ground-hugging bush or gray, dry tufts of grass. The sun was an enormous orange ball dipping toward the horizon; a hot wind swirled dirt and tiny shards of rock.

Aletto mounted; Robyn was persuaded onto the nomad pony. Chris dropped behind them, mule in tow. Lialla and Jennifer took the lead. Lialla held them up only long enough to point out their line of travel. "There—between those two hills, can you see?"

"I suppose so," Jennifer said. She squinted. By a stretch of imagination, there might be two knobs out there that could qualify as hills.

Chris came up between them, shaking his head. "Won't be able to see landmarks in an hour. Which direction is that?"

Lialla shrugged. Aletto looked at the sky, thought a moment. "Just south of true west."

"What I thought; hard to tell without watching the sun move, though. We'll need to use the stars. Mom, you're the astronomer, can you figure?"

"God," Robyn sighed. "I don't know, I haven't been watching much. Are they the same, or," she turned to Aletto, "can you point out constellations?"

It was Chris's turn to sigh. "I've been watching, Mom."

"You only know two constellations, kid, the Big Dipper and Orion."

"So? I saw the Dipper last night. You can track us to the west and a little south, can't you?"

"Well, but if they aren't the same, or if they aren't on the same plane, if the direction is off—"

"Mom!" Chris sighed again, exasperated now. "Lookit, all right? The stars *have* to be the same, if they only branched here five hundred years ago. The sun's okay, isn't it?"

"If—" Jennifer began. Chris fortunately didn't hear her and she shut her mouth immediately. No sense breaking his confidence; at least one of them had some.

He was fumbling at his watch band. "Damn. I have that little compass that hooks onto my watch. I usually take it when we do the Punchbowl. I think I lent it to somebody. Damn, anyway."

"Don't swear," Robyn said.

Chris turned to give her an injured, indignant look. "Damn's not swearing, Mom, not really. And look, can we get out of here?"

ONCE the sun went down, it got dark very quickly. The wind let up for some time after sunset but picked up after that and now blew harder than ever. Jennifer snugged the ends of the wool scarf around her hair; it might stay clean but it would be utterly flat when the scarf came off. "Hell," she muttered to herself. "Why do you care? You aren't going from here to court, are you? Who's going to care what you look like?" She turned her head to one side and then the other, blinked furiously to keep her eyes clear; gusts blew sand against her face. It itched.

They found a pile of rock somewhere near middle night; it shielded them from the worst of the head-on wind, though not from the eddies that swirled around and up. They huddled together, ate more of the flat bread and drained one of the water bottles. Robyn leaned back against Chris and gazed up. "You're right, kid. It's the same night sky."

"Don't sound so amazed. I told you it was."

"Yeah, right, smart kid. Shut up, let me concentrate. We still know which way we're going?"

"We were due west when we started out," Chris said. "Right?" Aletto nodded. "So—what do you think?"

"West, but a little south, too? I'd say we're doing all right," Robyn said.

Lialla handed the second water bottle around. "Drink up; if it's still hot here it's going to stay hot most of the rest of the night. Sure about our direction, Robyn?"

"I—sure. Unless your stars shift funny, but it doesn't look like it to me. I've spent a lot of years watching them instead of TV."

"All right." Lialla had apparently given up on trying to make sense of the occasional bit of English thrown into a conversation. "So we should be in good shape."

"I'd prefer the road," Aletto said. "But as long as we don't get lost . . ."

"We won't," Lialla said flatly. The caravan road cut well to the south before heading back in to Sikkre, to take advantage of water and to meet up with the road that went on to Podhru and another that branched off toward Bezjeriad. Lialla had decided they'd do better to avoid any of the roads because Jadek surely had men out looking for them, and so they both could cut off the extra distance, and come into Sikkre from a direction unexpected. Jennifer decided from the conversation that she'd missed quite an argument earlier, when she napped.

Chris nodded. "Besides, if we go too far south, we'll hit the road and know to turn. We're not likely to get so goofed around we head north by mistake."

"Don't even think that," Lialla said. "It would take a sandstorm, and I don't want you calling one down on us."

Chris snorted with suppressed laughter, but he let it go. The wind was still high when they stepped out of shelter, but not as bad as it might have been. Robyn had a clear view of the night sky all the way to the point where they could see the lights of Sikkre.

CHRIS leaned against the mule and shook sand out of his sneakers. "Wow, look at that! All lit up like L.A.!"

"That's the market," Aletto said. "There are houses south and west of the market; you can't see all that from here. Some of the market is dark at night, many of the standard merchants. There's a vast portion of it that goes all the time, other parts that only operate after dark."

"You should know," Lialla said mildly, and Aletto laughed.

"Have a heart, I had maybe six winters when Dahven and I snuck out; I don't remember half of it."

"Just as well." Lialla stretched, hard. "We can take a short rest here—just a few minutes, though. I want to get us in somewhere between the east and north gates well before dawn; there are inns all over that area and most of them more loyal to the market and the caravans than to the Thukar. That's where their money comes from, after all. We can get a little food, a little sleep, before we do any searching. We'll need clothing—most of us. That first, I suppose."

"Weapons," Aletto said.

Lialla cast him a dark look. "Maybe."

"Not maybe; we *need* them. If I hadn't had that knife in the horsebarns—" Lialla held up a hand, silencing him.

"Point made. Protective weaponry, at least. Information. We'll talk about that after we get inside the city and find a place to sleep, all right?" She turned back. "Jennifer?"

"Mmm—ready." Jennifer turned the water bottle over to Chris and started forward. She was tired, and that was making it difficult for her *not* to see Thread. So many people out there—so much activity. Magic, too: And some of what she could sense within Sikkre's walls worried her.

Lialla wasn't as much help as Jennifer needed; she was at least as tired as Jennifer and already thinking ahead to possible conversations with a nosy innkeeper. "I can tell it's all there, of course—the City, anyway," she said. "Specific things, though, I can't really. Not unless I just sat down and concentrated."

Jennifer nodded and backtracked to safer topics; Lialla was still defensive about her own skill level and unreasonably jealous of anything she perceived as a superior talent in this outlander. Jennifer didn't want to break the comfortable truce they'd established this morning; she had a sneaking, unpleasant suspicion they'd need each other over the next few days, just to survive Sikkre.

"Neutral magic," she said finally. "You said the thing last night was neutral."

The tension went out of Lialla's shoulders at once. "In the sense it's not ours or Hell-Light, it's neutral," she said and fell into step with Jennifer ahead of the horses. "True neutral magic is something you'll see plenty of in Sikkre—in Bez, too, they say; the Bez market isn't nearly as vast as Sikkre's, but it's more exotic. More true foreigners, because of the harbor and the roads that come in from Podhru. Sikkre gets a few foreigners, mostly the caravans that ply routes north and west, though; they're largely clans, the routes hereditary. There's magic among them, or so Merrida told me. Neutral, I suppose, they use it only for themselves—medical, now and again love spells. That kind of thing.''

"Love spells," Jennifer echoed, and laughed.

"What's funny about love spells?" Lialla demanded.

"Nothing—except it doesn't sound like it would be neutral to the one affected.''

Lialla thought about this and chuckled. "I suppose not. But if it's a good spell, why would he ever know? They're sold in the market, of course—the spells, not the lovers. At least," she added thoughtfully, "not the parts of the market I ever saw. There are places it's said you can buy anything—which probably includes any*one*. Neutral magic, though. Personal magic like that is neutral, unless it's Thread-worked. Or—fortune-tellers. Some of the caravaners do that for extra coin. Shapeshifters, but they're pretty rare. Well, I've never seen one, but I've only been to Sikkre two times, and both times I was rather carefully escorted.''

"Magic," Aletto muttered behind them. Lialla cast a swift glance over her shoulder and motioned Jennifer forward. They put a little more distance between themselves and the horses.

"I don't know if it's all because of the marsh-sickness," she said in a low voice. "You can see how he feels about it, all of it. But a lot of our people are that way about fortunes, and the shapeshifters are a breed apart. They're most usually women, sometimes men. Some can shift their bodies from human to a dozen or more outward forms of beasts or birds. Others can take only one shape; some are involuntary but some of them can do it at will. Those are the ones I've heard about, in Sikkre. If you see something like that, you'll know.''

"Right," Jennifer said doubtfully. She let her grip on the ordinary night around them relax; Thread shivered and vibrated all around her, moving with their passing, making sound for those who could hear, visual change for those who could see. It made her nervous indeed to think someone in the city before them might now be watching them. If someone *was* watching, though: She had nothing but that odd, uncomfortable sensation. Possibly paranoia. Then again . . .

THERE were no walls around Sikkre; none were needed, since its very isolation counted as its walls. Even during the most recent invasion through Dro Pent, Sikkre had never been in danger of attack. The Emperor permitted no squabbling between the Dukedoms, but regardless, Sikkre was safe from attack: Her marketplace created wealth for those who traded here, and none of them wished to tamper with such sure good fortune.

The Thukar kept a small Outer Guard—largely ceremonial—on the main gates. The Inner Guard was large, heavily armed, composed of well-trained men who walked the city in pairs, for thieves and pickpockets were innumerable, and the Thukar himself made a large percentage of his wealth in levies, taxes and fines. It was very much to *his* advantage to know what went on throughout the city.

The side street Lialla found for them was narrow and pitch black; small, flat houses lined it, doors even with the dirt road, side walls nearly touching. Here and there a light burned, some householder awake, a housewife preparing food or a craftsman readying his goods for transport.

They walked some distance before she found a cross street, and then another. Jennifer, who barely knew the stars at all, was immediately lost, and even Chris looked nervous. A third street opened out almost at once and split around a massive, rectangular brick pool. Beyond it was a long, two-story building, a glass-shielded candle burning before the door. Lialla brought them to a halt. "All right. You wait here; Jen and I will go get a room. Objection? Make it now."

There wasn't any objection, but Aletto stirred. "Where are we?"

"Cap and Feather. Thukar's Tower is that way." She pointed.

"Oh. I don't know anything about it. How far's the Tower?"

"Far enough. Robyn, pull that scarf end over his head. We can't afford anyone recognizing him."

Robyn nodded, dragged the wool forward with trembling hands. Aletto took them between his as Lialla and Jennifer skirted the fountain, stepped over the light and pushed the door open, vanishing into utter darkness. "Lady—Robyn? It's all right, honestly."

"If you say," she whispered. "It looks—people get murdered in places that look like this!"

"No. Not here, trust me." He squeezed her hands, let them go and slid from his horse as Lialla came back out the front door and gestured.

There was a narrow passageway, invisible from the street, that led back into a courtyard and a stable. An oil lamp lit a high wall, an open and empty stall, and across the roughly cobbled yard, a door partway ajar. It led into the inn. There was light along the passage, and faint light spilled out the door. A boy stood there, a small, thin outline of a boy with tousled hair and a long, loose shirt. He came forward to take the horses and unsaddle them; Chris unpacked the mule and let the boy put it next to the horses; he and Robyn split most of the bags, leaving Aletto to gather up the last of them.

Robyn stayed back with him, one anxious eye on the boy, another for Aletto, who was walking slowly and doing his best not to limp. He was reasonably successful, but Robyn didn't draw a full breath until they reached the dark beyond the kitchens and stopped at the foot of the stairs.

Lialla stood at the door, outlined in ruddy firelight, talking to someone inside. "I'd rather we stayed below, if it's possible. We want one room anyway; three beds, if possible."

"Perhaps." A woman's voice, thin and waspish. "Caravaners?"

"Advance. We left part of our clan at water, awaiting the rest. The room would be two, perhaps three days."

Silence. "You have coin?"

"Enough."

"Two ceris and a sef a night," the woman said.

Lialla laughed. "What room do you offer us, the Thukar's?"

"It's busy season," the woman countered flatly. Jennifer shifted nervously, wishing for an end to it. Her eyes met Aletto's a distance down the hallway. He had an arm around Robyn for support and was leaning against a heavy bench. Robyn's face was white, all frightened eyes. Chris sagged against the wall just beyond them.

"Two ceris, for all of us, with wine and a meal," Lialla countered.

The woman came forward, wiping her hands down her breeches. She was tall, gray-haired, bone-thin, and her eyes were hard but not particularly interested in either of the women, or those waiting for them. "Caravaners! Two ceris," she agreed, and held out a hand. "Coin now, though, two nights."

"Sikkreni," Lialla spat in reply, but fished inside her scarves for a pair of many-sided silver coins.

The woman took them, tilted her head and eyed Lialla rather thoughtfully. "A Wielder?"

"Red Hawk Clan," Lialla replied.

"Oh. Descendant of Mioffan?"

"Distant."

The woman lost interest, bit one of the coins and stuffed both in a pocket. She smiled. "Don't be so chill; it's not unheard of for caravaners to stay and leave without paying. After all, you have a world all around to go to and no need to return to this house."

"No one in Red Hawk would do that," Lialla protested.

The woman merely smiled disbelievingly, and came into the hallway to point. "At the end of the corridor, there's a door, left. It lets into my herb plot and the well; your door is opposite. There's a fire laid if you find the night air chill."

"Coming from Genna and Holmaddan? Overly warm, perhaps." Lialla sketched a bow and turned away. "Having ridden the night, we are, however, most tired. Your pardon, and a good night to you."

Jennifer glanced over her shoulder as she came even with Aletto and Robyn; the innkeeper was wiping flour-covered hands down her breeches and gazing after them, head cocked aside. Jennifer turned back and hurried to catch up with Lialla as that worthy was pushing the door to their room open. "I don't think I trust her."

Lialla shrugged that aside. "She's curious; most innkeeps are, I should think." Her voice was brusque, tired; Jennifer eyed her thoughtfully as she conjured a spark of light and lit candles with it to illuminate the room. Lialla's face was an old woman's, all tired, drawn muscle sagging to a down-turned mouth. Not the time to bully her over her choice of inn and keeper, perhaps—better to wait until they'd all slept.

But the room itself did nothing to ease Jennifer's worries: It was small, dirt-floored, and the ceiling was so low she fought not to duck beneath the ugly, smoke-blackened beams. There were no windows, save a pair of brick-sized holes cut high in the wall, near the roof and in the outer wall—smoke egress, most likely. The door was the only way in or out.

The beds were wide and long, but on close examination nothing more than thick cloth stuffed with not entirely clean straw. This was covered with even thicker woolen blankets; a handful of cushions and pillows were scattered across the surface. As Chris and Jennifer exchanged stunned looks, Lialla brushed her hands together briskly. "Well! Not precisely the style in which I was kept my last journey here, but certainly above what we might expect!"

Chris found his voice, with effort. "Might expect—wait, let me figure it. One large room, everyone bundled together in a

reeking pile—?'' He sniffed, cautiously. "How many would ordinarily bed down here?''

"Fifteen, twenty—who knows?'' Lialla shrugged. "They
would be of a single party, however; that's the best of private
rooms—no sharing with strangers who might be murderers.''

Chris sniffed again, louder this time. "It's a little close in
here. Unpleasant, actually.''

Lialla glared at him. "You noticed, how clever of you! If
you're truly clever, though, reason that one out as well, why
don't you?'' She moved away, stopped short of the widest bed.
"We women can share this; the men may shift as they please.''

"Not having windows,'' Chris said stiffly, "keeps out thieves
and other riffraff. Second floor I think there were a few windows, but since people sleep all together, who cares what comes
in from the streets?'' Lialla turned and gave him silent applause.
Chris executed a sweeping bow, but nearly fell when he over-
balanced. "For my reward, I'm taking this lump right here.''
He pulled wool around his shoulders, sat down gingerly, untied
his high-tops and eased them off, sighing loudly and happily as
he got himself flat and shut his eyes.

Aletto looked down at him a long moment, then nodded decisively and limped over to the other small bed. But on the way,
he stopped, thought, and went up to the door instead. There was
a bar; Lialla had dropped it into place. But he couldn't be certain
the wood was solid, and there was no other fastening, not even
a latch on the door handle. He looked around the room thoughtfully, finally tested the table near the fireplace. It was awkward,
moving it, but it seemed heavy enough. Chris edged back up
onto one elbow; the women fell silent. Lialla alone glanced up,
saw what he was doing, and turned her attention back to the
bedding. Aletto edged the table under the cross-pieces that held
the door bar, wedged it in as firmly as he could. He turned away;
Lialla, who was on her knees on the far side of the wide bed,
tossing pillows and cushions over to Robyn, looked up. She met
his eyes, finally gave him a curt nod. Aletto turned away, edged
himself down onto the bed and got his feet out of the heavy
boots. He sniffed the blankets cautiously, finally wrapped himself in them and pulled pillows under his head and shoulders.

Robyn already had her sneakers off and was prowling all
around the bed barefoot. Jennifer stood watching her, arms were
full of cushions that smelled of a mix of herb, very faint mildew,
woodfire and an even fainter hint of wine. Her back ached again,
and she was beginning to have an unpleasant feeling she knew

why. *All I need,* she thought despairingly, and let her eyes close. She was swaying gently, half asleep on her feet, when Lialla and Robyn relieved her of her burden and shoved her down in the middle of them.

Robyn's hair tickled her nose; she freed a hand, pushed it away, and tucked the hand back under blankets once more, rolled onto her side and curled into a ball. Tired as she was, though, sleep wouldn't come, no matter how she wooed it. She lay finally, curled the other way, and watched light grow in the two vents near the ceiling.

Magic. And in particular, Night-Thread Magic. How had someone stumbled onto that, made it work? Harnessed it? And how, magic here and none in her own world? None, of course, verified. And why only at night? She considered this last, finally shut her eyes, and thought about Thread.

It was there, lines going in all directions, all colors, all thicknesses of strand—multicolored strand, and strand doubling back on itself, or twining around other strands. Healing strand, some of that last, and yet not all of it was. The music—odd, she could hear that, too: perhaps not quite as loudly as the previous night, but then, the thread was almost a pastel of itself in daylight.

So little she knew how to do yet: Suddenly, she wanted to know, all of it. The names of each kind, and its use, and where it went and what it did, how it connected to itself and to the world, and how one simply walked through it unnoticing, until one found it in need or after training. The sound of it—why that reached her and why Lialla made no mention of it.

Perhaps Merrida could sense it at all hours; perhaps Lialla could. They hadn't said anything about that, merely that it was only workable at night. But—was that true, either? Because. . . .

She reached, feeling her way across Thread cautiously, gingerly seeking out known substance, until she found the familiar ones. People there—above them but not directly above, and many people. People down, straight—back in the kitchens. The horses, beyond the kitchens. How curious; did she recognize the substance of their own horses or was that wishful thinking? But there was no mistaking the mule. Jennifer let out a pleased sigh and glanced around the room again. She let Thread fade from sight, then, and turned to another, more immediate consideration: this marketplace. What would they absolutely need, apart from any considerations of Lialla's for them? She was deep in thought, running up a mental list, when she suddenly fell asleep.

II

NOISE in the courtyard roused her: poultry nearby, someone trudging down the hall, heavy-footed and grumbling loudly, to feed them. There was a thin gray light coming through the vents, a little stealthy noise overhead—as though some of those who woke early wished to avoid waking others sleeping in the large room. Jennifer sniffed cautiously; there was an off smell coming from somewhere. The bedding? No; at least, the blanket she was wrapped in, fully clad, and the straw-filled cushion that prickled the back of her neck were a little musty but nothing worse. Probably the food. Correction: It had to be the food; it smelled just like her Aunt Bet's stroganoff. She stifled a groan, lay back and closed her eyes. Inedible, awful stuff. How long, she wondered, can a woman live on oat cakes and flat bread—even with a medium-sized bottle of vitamins in the bottom of her leather bag?

And at the moment—how long could she hold her breath? Somehow, she slid back into sleep. When Lialla wakened her a while later, there was a little sun coming through the vents and a great deal of noise coming from the street beyond—men shouting, women shouting in particularly shrill voices, horses and the high-pitched noise made by camels and mules. And what sounded like someone walking slowly past the inn and banging on an immense gong. Lialla gave her another shake. "Get up, we need to hurry."

Why? Jennifer thought irritably, but kept quiet while she found her hairbrush, picked Robyn's rubber band out of the ends and unsnarled her hair. She dabbed a little paste on the tip of a finger, ran it over her teeth. "Water?"

Lialla handed her one of the leather bottles. Jennifer made a face at it, ran a little into her mouth and swooshed it around, spat it into the fireplace. The taste of leather nearly overcame peppermint. "Ready?" Lialla was practically trembling in her hurry to be out and gone.

"Nearly." Jennifer's socks were stiff along the soles, sagging at the tops, and the length stretched. The heels rode up to the top of her sneakers when she pulled them on. Wash water, when they got back. She wasn't about to put up with those long, narrow wraps people used here until she had to. *Nurse those socks along,* she thought, tucked the ends of her laces in the tops of the sneakers and stood up. Lialla tugged at the woolen shawl and disposed its ends over her feet.

"Shoes stand out," she said. "Try to keep them out of sight, will you?" She didn't wait for an answer; at the door, she turned back and looked around the room. "Aletto, promise me you'll wait for us." Aletto, still half-asleep, hair nearly as spiky as Chris's, yawned cavernously. Jennifer turned away to stifle a yawn of her own. "Aletto," Lialla repeated insistently. He nodded.

"Promise. No good my going out until dark, remember?"

"Just *stay* here, we'll be back soon after the market closes for midday. Maybe before that." She looked at Chris, who was still sound asleep, then across to Robyn, who was sitting cross-legged on the wide bed, rebraiding her hair.

"Don't worry about me," Robyn said. "I'm not going anywhere except maybe back to sleep. I'm certainly not going out there!"

"Good." Lialla pulled the door open, turned back again after she shooed Jennifer through. "Eat whatever you like; we'll bring food."

It was still very early, already quite warm. Jennifer let Lialla tug the woolen scarf ends over her forehead without protest but she shuddered as the sin-Duchess turned away and began walking swiftly up the wide street. Wool in such heat! She knew Saharan nomads did it—the very thought had made her itch then, too. She threaded her way through heavy foot traffic, behind a line of young camels, around a wagon and three carts drawn up across from the inn. Lialla waited for her just beyond them.

"Look," she said. "You'd better let me do the talking this morning. Your accent, your lack of experience in trading, they both would mark you. I haven't much marketing experience but it's enough to get us by."

"I don't mind," Jennifer said easily, and Lialla looked less anxious. "Let's go, before one of us gets run over."

The market itself was all Lialla had said: Jennifer, who had spent any number of Sundays at the larger swap meets, found herself astonished by the physical vastness as much as by the variety of things for sale. Those would seem to include anything and everything—clothing, new and used; fine work, jewelry, prosaic cooking pots and hammered silver dishes. Rugs, boots, armor and weaponry. Food—any kind of cooked food, sweets, fresh grown, bread still warm from hive-shaped clay ovens; meat fresh, dried, roasted, stewed. Meat and poultry killed to order—that she fortunately only saw, and heard and smelled, from a goodly distance.

She let Lialla lead her for some distance down wide aisles, then succeedingly narrower ones, before she caught up to her and gripped her sleeve to pull her to a halt. "Food first," she said firmly. Lialla considered this blankly, finally nodded.

"You're right. I—Merrida tells me I get this way, all pointed in one direction to the exclusion of others. I forget to eat."

Jennifer grinned. "I do that, too, but not this morning. My stomach's growling something awful, and something around here smells wonderful."

Lialla tested the air, pulled Jennifer out of the middle of the aisle and back the way they had just come, then down an extremely narrow corridor between permanent wooden stalls. "Honey and spice cakes," she said over her shoulder. "You obviously have excellent taste."

"Smells better than what was cooking at the inn this morning," Jennifer replied.

"Mutton," Lialla said. "They eat a good deal of it in this part of Rhadaz, or so I hear. One thing I considered when the Thukar's son asked Jadek for my hand." She grinned and shrugged. Jennifer laughed. "Well," Lialla temporized, "I would have, if I'd intended to marry anyone."

They bought two cakes apiece, a mug of cool herb tea to wash them down with. Jennifer handed the empty cup back to the stall owner and sighed. "I'd kill for coffee."

Lialla shook her head. "Coffee? Another of those words of yours! *I* don't know it. But that doesn't mean it doesn't exist, just that it's not a Zelharri thing." Jennifer sighed again and followed her back into the wider—and now considerably more crowded—aisles.

They left hours later, both laden with bundles. Lialla had found a money changer and, leaving the gemstones in Jennifer's bag for later, had turned her coins and Jennifer's into readily nego-tiable silver and brass coins—the standard fare for all but highly expensive items. "And we're not buying rare oversea furs, or racing camels anyway," Lialla said. She found black garments for Jennifer—breeches similar to her own, a pair of loose shirts, a plain black sash that would pass for an initiate Healer's sash. A long, charcoal gray cloak to replace Merrida's scarf. "Since you won't be parted from those shoes," Lialla said.

"I paid a fortune for them, and if I have to walk all the time I'm certainly not giving them up," Jennifer retorted vigorously. "Besides, if Merrida's right, if your brother's stories are, there are other people from our world around here. Sneakers can't be common, but surely they aren't that outlandish!"

Lialla scowled. "I wish you'd quit sprinkling your conversa-tion with these foreign words. Sneakers," she spat. But she didn't argue the matter further, merely paid the stallholder for the black garments, wrapped them in the scarf and tossed the cloak around Jennifer's shoulders, and stalked off.

Robyn and Chris, then: Cloaks for both, a loose, long dress for Robyn, thick brown breeches and an overshirt for Chris, a hardened leather vest that laced under the arms. "Aletto will just have to make do, same as I will," Lialla said. "We're cov-ered and we won't freeze; it should be enough."

Food next: They went from stall to shop to stall, checking, bargaining, purchasing fresh fruit, net bags of dried meat, and tightly woven cloth bags of thin-sliced, cured meat—*not* sheep of any age, Lialla assured Jennifer. Jennifer, after a cautious sniff and a gingerly tasted sample offered by the standkeeper, decided she could live with the stuff; Chris wouldn't care so long as he had enough to eat. And Robyn, as a legacy of her years in a commune and more of them on welfare, would eat abso-lutely anything—well, anything that wasn't red meat, at least. Most of what they had didn't encompass red meat, except the dried meat; she could simply avoid that.

Lialla bought more bags of caravaner's supplies: oat cakes and thin, crisp bread like crackers, boxes of fine-cut and dried veg-etables for soup or stew, two strings of onions and another of assorted peppers, a woven ring of fresh herbs, a bag that smelled of lavender. "Soap," Lialla said.

Jennifer ran a hand through her hair. "Great. Get a couple more of those; I'm used to washing more often than you are."

"I noticed," Lialla said. "I don't think it's good for you, all that water."

"Yah, Louis XIV said that, too," Jennifer said cheerfully. Lialla made an uncouth noise.

The sun was nearing zenith, the morning becoming unbearably warm, but the pack of bodies was thinning out as more people left the main thoroughfares of the market to seek shade, a noon meal, a long nap. Lialla, already burdened with bundles and bags, wanted one more stop, for a pair of lightweight pots and a knife or two. Jennifer, who was now in the lead, stopped so abruptly Lialla cannoned into her. That smell—that wonderful smell. "Coffee," she breathed. Lialla bit back an angry remark, adjusted her bags, picked up the bundle she'd dropped. She doubted Jennifer would have heard her anyway. Jennifer inhaled deeply, turned and began walking down the alley between two poultry sellers. Lialla followed.

Jennifer stopped two stands on. Lialla came up behind her, sniffed dubiously and looked at the pale blue awning, the darker blue carpet spread under it. "You can't go in there. That place is for men, caravaner men!"

Jennifer turned and scowled at her. "Want to bet it is? You smell that? Know what it is? It's coffee. The stuff I said I'd kill for. You only *think* I didn't mean it."

The look on her face was certainly formidable enough. "You can't go in there; women aren't allowed, and besides we don't have that much coin left."

"Oh? Remember three pairs of boots we didn't have to buy?" Jennifer glared at her so fiercely Lialla retreated a pace. "We have money. Think of something—and get me some of that stuff!"

Lialla glowered down at her hand, loosened her grip on Jennifer's sleeve only slightly. "All right—wait. Let me think a minute." She gazed at the carpet, scarcely seeing it, thought furiously. "Right. I think it might work, wait here, hold these things. And keep your mouth shut! I'll do what I can for you."

It cost; Lialla clearly thought it an exorbitant cost to purchase the stuff, ostensibly as part bribe, part dowry to one of the caravan masters for a younger sister. "The gods will have my tongue for a string of lies like that; this coffee of yours had better be worth it, Jen!" she growled. Jennifer scarcely heard her. She was contemplating certain of the items she carried, adding up a value that had nothing whatever to do with coin value. A flat pan for roasting, a grinder, a pot capable of brewing two large cups of what her father would've called "cowboy coffee," grounds and water all together until a dose of cold water sent most of the grounds to the bottom. And her left forearm was rapidly growing numb under the weight of a large bag of green coffee beans. Coffee, she thought happily. Genuine, honest coffee. This wretched world could throw whatever it liked at her now; she was ready for it.

ALETTO was prowling the room when they returned. Chris lay on his bed, feet propped on the wall, watching him upside down. Robyn had shifted to the room's one chair. "Good thing you got back," Chris said.

Jennifer grinned. "Why, kid, you hungry again?"

"Well, that too, of course."

Lialla dumped her bundles on the bed the three women had shared and went back out. "I'll get something for us. Wait here."

"Wait here," Aletto mumbled sourly. He turned, met Robyn's anxious eye, and walked over to touch her hair.

"Christmas time, folks," Jennifer said, and began rummaging through the piled bundles. "Birdy, here, clothes for you and Chris. Hope you can handle the skirts on this thing—wait, that's mine—here. It should go over your jeans and it'll pretty much cover your sneakers."

"What, no boots?" Chris demanded.

"They don't make them with good insoles; you'd be crippled in no time," Jennifer said. She caught her breath, tried to let it out normally, made herself not turn and look at Aletto, not apologize. *Damn,* she thought angrily.

There was a flat little silence behind her, but when she turned around, Robyn was shaking out her dress, holding it up to her shoulders. "What do you think? Personally, I've never liked me in black."

Aletto gazed at her appraisingly before replying, "You look pale." Jennifer opened her mouth, closed it again without saying anything. Maybe he hadn't heard her faux pas.

CHRIS and Aletto went out later, to tend the horses and the mule and to get wash water, to let the women change and clean up. When they came back, Robyn, Jennifer and Lialla went out into the road, across to the fountain. There was a bare trickle of water running from a clay pipe in one corner of it, and the water bore a thin film of dust from the road.

Robyn hitched up her skirts and sat on the edge of the stone wall and gazed around her. "I feel like a raven, or somebody's Italian grandmother," she said. Jennifer laughed.

"Try wearing these pants with the funny crotch," she replied. "They feel like a pair of tights two sizes too small, except for all the material bunched up above the knees."

"Pass," Robyn grinned. She turned her attention back to the road. "Camels—I don't know why, I find the camels hardest to accept."

"I know, they're odd-looking beasts, aren't they? Like something made up."

"No, not that. Just that—if Chris is right, and this would have been our world except for something changing, say, five hundred years ago, then it seems right there'd be desert, and horses, and—well, I guess, all this. But camels—"

Jennifer considered this in turn as Robyn's voice faded. "Well. If you want to believe what Chris gets from Aletto's bad maps, and all. There *were* camels in Arizona and Texas, that end of the country anyway, in the 1800s. Probably got brought over from Africa in *this* history line, too." Lialla looked from one of them to the other, her face reflecting lack of understanding and a growing irritation at the fact. "But since they also seem to have imported coffee, I don't really care what else got brought in."

"And you pick on me for my cigarettes," Robyn said, but she was smiling. The smile faded; she was watching people passing, gazing at the visible faces of the nearest. "The other thing—what Merrida said. About other people. Be funny, wouldn't it, if you saw someone here you actually knew?"

Jennifer shrugged. "She wasn't very specific. I think it might just be rumor; Aletto's stories and all that. But I can't think of anyone *I* personally know who's gone missing—unless this is where Amelia Earhart and Judge Crater came." Robyn laughed; Lialla cleared her throat and Jennifer looked at her. "Sorry. Just—family joke."

"You should be a little careful," Lialla said sharply. "Your accents aren't enough to cause a problem in Sikkre but all these words you use just might be."

CHRIS found the leather vest uncomfortable but agreed to wear it while he and Aletto prowled the market that evening. Jennifer, who was becoming increasingly sensitive to mood, was uncomfortably aware of Aletto's impatience to be gone. And Lialla, now seated in shadow on the wide bed, back against the wall and feet tucked under her, biting her lip to keep herself from blurting out her worries—Aletto of all of them could be recognized, Aletto alone was worth taking, he must not risk himself. . . . But Lialla also knew only Aletto and Chris could go in search of Gyrdan, at night and in the less wholesome corners of the market when and where women weren't permitted. And Aletto would not forgive her for coddling him.

Chris *was* going with him. To Aletto, that seemed to be all the argument necessary to silence his sister. The market, after all, was a place he and Dahven had explored when very young, and they'd come from it unscathed. Chris seemed to have no more concern than Aletto for what might await them; Robyn had apparently given up trying to warn him, and Jennifer saw no point in alienating either young man. Since they were going to go anyway . . . And Chris had Angeleno street smarts; he knew better than to get caught in dark corners. It would simply have to do.

But Jennifer had waited until Robyn was deep in conversation with Aletto before she fished in the pack of kitchen goods and brought out one of the knives. She wrapped Chris's hand around it and pushed the hand back under his cloak. "Don't let your mother see it; you know it'll just upset her. You told me once you thought you could use a knife, if you had to. Did you mean it?" Startled, he nodded. "All right, remember we both need you, and so does Aletto. Doesn't that vest thing have a place to put a knife?"

"Think it does," Chris said cautiously, and felt around the waist. "Yeah, at the back; tight fit, though."

"Don't get it in too tight, then," Jennifer said evenly. "And buy yourself one that fits, why don't you?" She wrapped his hand around four coins. "It goes pretty far out there. Let him do the bargaining, though."

"Right." Chris stuffed the coins into a pocket and gripped her arm. "Hey, I think we're finally ready."

"Be careful." Jennifer gripped his shoulder in turn. Aletto was at the door, looking down the hall. He gestured imperiously; Chris settled the black cloak over his shoulders rather self-consciously, and followed. Robyn gazed after them anxiously, long after Lialla closed the door behind them.

ALETTO walked down the long hallway, stopped just short of the common room. It was busy at this hour, two past sunset, but

most of the traffic was over near the fire and the bar. Only two
men sat at the nearest long bench, and neither noticed the two
young men who walked behind them, skirted the ends of three
more benches, and went out the open doors into the night.

The road was comparatively quiet but still far from empty: A
few horsemen rode together, stopped at the fountain to let their
horses drink. A pair of caravaner wagons passed them; a boy
with two dogs and another herding ducks came after. Two horsemen going the other direction, at a canter. An old woman leading a laden camel, another wagon and an empty cart. Aletto
eased into the stream of traffic, Chris right behind him and then
at his side. In the midst of so many, and in the evening gloom,
the nera-Duke's limp was scarcely noticeable, with the way Robyn had adjusted his cloak and the throat and shoulders of his
leather jerkin, his imbalanced shoulders were even less visible.

Chris felt a warm, satisfied glow spreading through him as
they slid through the crowd: the thick and exotic mix of smells,
the look of people, the buildings—it was wonderful! And here
he was, part of it all. All the books he'd read, all the movies,
the games—never in his most ridiculous and embarrassing
dreams had he ever reckoned himself in such a situation! He'd
never felt so alive, so aware of things. The people around them—
now and again someone would glance at them, but no one paid
any real attention to them. Partly the dark, he decided; partly
that people who were strangers in such a crowded place as this
market—like people back home—tended to mind their own business fairly strictly.

His fingers slid across the knife hilt that lay sideways along
the small of his back. The person for whom this leather armor
had been made no doubt knew how to draw and use a knife from
such a position—or draw and throw it. Chris wondered if he'd
be able to get the blade free; he'd jammed it in pretty tightly to
make certain it didn't fall out, or slide around and somehow cut
him. He wondered if he'd be able to use it, if he had to.

Get mad enough—that was all it ought to take. He hoped he
wouldn't need to find out tonight, though.

It took time; Aletto had difficulty finding the right area of the
market, and then finding the right kinds of shops. And then more
time still, finding the right style and class of blades, the right
degree of ornamentation, or lack of it. It took what seemed
forever for him to bargain down prices. Eventually, Aletto had
two swords—short, wide-bladed, double-edged weapons which
Chris found to be uncomfortably heavy. There were unadorned

leather shoulder straps for them, a hardened leather buckler that looked woefully inadequate to protect anything, not even the forearm it was strapped to. A fine-bladed dagger fastened to the upper arm strap of the buckler, another on the inside of the shield-curve. More arrows for Chris's bow.

Another part of the market, a dizzying number of aisles down and across. Chris no longer had any idea in which direction the inn lay, and the thought of being separated from Aletto made him nervous. Aletto seemed unconcerned by anything. He went to a seller of maces, then to an alesman, seeking information—this mostly, bafflingly to Chris, dealing with caravans and the northern and western roads from Sikkre.

Chris's attention wandered, his eyes fixed on the men and women walking past them. The women were very few, and for the most part richly dressed. The men, on the other hand, were a wildly contrasting group: Men in dark, dusty leathers, carrying enormous swords or pikes, rubbed elbows with men in richly colored, flowing fabrics covered in embroidery, beads, jewels. Everything and anything.

He was getting hungry again. *Hollow leg,* he thought ruefully. Dinner—bread and a funny-tasting but thick and filling soup—had been all right but it seemed hours ago. Aletto was leaning across the alesman's counter, talking to two men, deeply absorbed in his conversation—he'd be forever. Chris stepped out into the open, glanced one way and then the other. They were near a corner—two stands down. And this place had torches and banners both, he couldn't possibly lose sight of it, particularly if he only went around the corner to look . . .

Aletto, deep in his conversation, didn't even notice as Chris cast him another appraising glance, and eased away.

He sniffed. Nothing but a mixed smell of leather, horses and sweat. Garlic on almost everyone's breath. No vampires here, he thought with a grin. The smell of dust coated everything.

The corner stand was given over to pottery: blackware, or so it looked in the light of a cluster of lanterns on the counter. Jugs, bowls and cups, anyway. Practical stuff. Beyond it, leather and wood, a rope holding fifty or more of the flat leather cups like the one Lialla carried. More pottery cups and some jugs beneath the curved rope. Chris glanced over his shoulder, was reassured to see light striking the familiar banners. One more stall, then he'd try the other direction.

But just past the leather cups, there was an opening, a narrow way he at first took for an alley between stalls. There was light back there, though: dim light of a guttering lantern, high above a woven box, perhaps six feet on a side. The lantern cast long shadows out across Chris's feet. It was so dim back there, below the light, that it took him several moments to realize someone inside the cage was staring back at him.

His heart stopped, then thudded heavily; his knees threatened to give as he backed two steps away.

"Sssst! Boy!" A whisper floated out between the branches that formed the weave of the cage; a long, thin hand edged between them to beckon. Chris stayed right where he was. A flush of anger buried the terror that had nearly dropped him.

"You scared me half to death! Come out of there and I'll teach you to scare people like that!"

"Can't!" came the urgent, whispered reply. "Locked in, both of us." Chris took one cautious step forward, squinted. There might be two of them; the light was snapping and fading erratically, making it nearly impossible to tell. "Let us out, eh?"

"Why?"

"Why what? We were put in here for theft, but we didn't this time. Wasting time; let us out."

"Why should I?" But Chris could think of several reasons—all those horror stories about one-handed Iranians. "What will they do to you?"

"I'd rather not think about that," the voice replied shortly. "What's the matter, you afraid?"

Chris glanced over his shoulder. There was no one around; the shops on both sides apparently closed for the night. Three men stood talking across the narrow aisle to the proprietor of another shop, but none of them paid the least attention to him. "I'm not afraid; I might be sensible."

"Look," the voice said persuasively. "Semeden's gone for the guard—the leather goods next to you. Freoda has the other stand, but she's half deaf anyway. Unlatch the door; we'll wait until you're gone before we come out, no one will blame you." Chris took another reluctant step forward.

"Someone will have seen me—"

"Why would anyone bother? You don't stand out until you open your mouth. Now, pay attention, the latch is in the center of the wall, there's a loop—look, just come over here, pay heed, will you?" Before he knew it, almost, he was standing in the shadow created by the woven cage, fumbling with the unfamiliar lock while the calm, rather resonant voice inside talked him through it. "That's done it. Thank you. Wait, don't go just yet. You're the boy with the spiky hair, aren't you? Gold hair?"

"I—" Chris stared. He could make out general shapes: a long, thin face, an angular body; someone a little shorter behind, gathering up something, practically vibrating with the need to leave. "How did you know that?"

"Because we saw you earlier, of course. But word's already getting around. The one you're with—no names, please!—tell him there are folk here who'd help him, ones he knows and others, friends of the true line, not the Usurper's. Tell him, be cautious; give his identity to no one, there are plenty in Sikkre who'd betray him for fear or for coin—or both. Tell him—never mind. You'd better go. We'll find you later."

"But—" Chris swallowed. What had he done?

The voice was urgent; it pressed him back into action. "Go, quickly, we'll give you time to get away. No—not back out that way! That way"—a hand came out to point—"and along the far side of Freoda's place. There's an eatery, just across; buy something. Walk back the way you came, then, as though that had been your only intent, coming this way."

"It *was* all I intended," Chris retorted waspishly. 'But if you try and pull anything—"

"Go!" the voice pleaded. He turned on his heel, and went.

12

PART of one of the brass coins went for a round sweet bread and two soft oranges; he got back a pile of oddly shaped copper coins in return. Aletto was standing at the corner when he came back up the narrow aisle, clasping and unclasping his hands and trying to look as though he were merely considering the next place to spend his own coin. But his eyes were black and wide, his jaw wabbled. "Where were you?" he demanded.

"Hungry," Chris mumbled, and offered him part of the bread. Fortunately neither his own jaw nor his voice gave him away; he'd had enough time to think the past few moments and he was terrified of what he'd done. Aletto shook his head, cast his eyes heavenward, finally took one of the oranges.

"Warn me next time," he growled. "I thought the guard had you."

"Sorry. Didn't want to interrupt you back there. Where next?"

"Tavern," Aletto said rather indistinctly around a mouthful of orange. He swallowed. "Called the Dancing Ram."

Chris chewed and swallowed hastily. "Tavern?"

Aletto scowled at him. "Tavern," he growled. "So?"

So I'm nearly five years under age for taverns back home, Chris thought, and shrugged. "Nothing. Why?"

"Nothing," Aletto said, before he turned and stalked off. Chris watched him rather anxiously. But Aletto was still walking fairly normally, if a little slowly. Chris took another bite of his orange, spat pips into his palm and tossed them onto the ground, then followed. Aletto wasn't even bothering to see if he was there.

They passed the cage; it was silent, dark, the door closed, but

Chris could tell the difference at once. What had possessed him? he wondered angrily. He'd given in to an impulse based on irrational emotion; for all he knew those two could be axe murderers. He gazed at Aletto's stiff back, just in front of him, and debated whether to tell him about it. He finished the orange, rubbed his hand down the harsh trouser leg, and decided to leave well enough alone. So long as one of them knew to keep watch for anyone who might be following them.

They walked for some distance: The market crowd grew, changed, thinned out and grew more dense. There were fewer women, then none—at least, not walking around. Chris closed his sagging mouth tightly and kept it shut as they walked through an area devoted to entertainment. "Jeez, look like a geek, why don't you?" he mumbled to himself. Many of the buildings here were low, one-story and not very tall at that. Many were open all across the front, some closed off with sheer fabric one could almost see through—enough to see dancers. Music everywhere. Most of the traffic here was wealthy, and all of it male. Now and again there might be a woman or two, discreetly veiled, before one of the stalls, or perhaps a sedan chair or an enclosed, curtain-covered lounge waiting outside. Nothing so obvious as money changing hands, but once he saw a girl who must have been years younger than he was, being led from the interior of one of the stalls to such a chair. She was veiled to her cheek-bones; he caught only a glimpse of dulled eyes: drugged or lost to hope.

He'd read enough to have an idea of what was going on here: slave trade. The idea of it had been amusing, or rather exciting, depending on the content of the book or the story; in person, it sobered him and it made him a little ill. He set his jaw, reminded himself of his various promises to his mother and his aunt, told himself sternly that one upset kid wasn't going to change anything, and followed Zelharri's would-be Duke.

Moments later, he came to a sudden halt, practically cannoning into Aletto's back. The nera-Duke was staring with narrowed eyes and a tight mouth at a half-clad woman who stood on a low platform at the entrance to a wood and brick building. Woman—no. Her form rippled and she shifted shape as Chris stared at her, glassy-eyed. Woman—now there was more cat to her than human female. But—cat? A faint music played softly, somewhere; she did not actually dance to it, simply swayed in time. Cat/woman became wolf/woman; she raised long, black-haired arms, arched her back; hair became feathers. . . .

"Were," Aletto hissed the word; Chris blinked and turned away. Aletto caught hold of his forearm and yanked, pulling him off balance. "Were! Get away from it!"

"Were?" Chris let himself be dragged off, unprotesting; the music followed him, mocking, taunting—tugging at a part of him Aletto's hand could not reach. "She's a—what is she?"

"Shapeshifter," Aletto mumbled. "She does that for coin, to amuse people!" He looked and sounded utterly disgusted.

Chris sighed and dug his heels in; Aletto stopped perforce, since his only alternative was to let go Chris's arm. "Right. I've heard that kind of talk most of my life. You don't look that dumb, so you must just not know any better. Maybe she doesn't have any other way of earning enough to eat, ever think of that?" Aletto just looked at him; his mouth twisted. "All right," Chris added wearily. "Don't think about it, don't worry about it, you have a way to live, who cares about her, right?"

Aletto glared at him until someone passing stumbled into his shoulder and swore. "It's disgusting," he said flatly, turned and stalked off.

It was darker here, past the shapeshifter's platform. A few more anonymous stands crowded into ancient buildings, stands where, apparently, women could be purchased. A scryer's tent, wedged between two buildings, as readily marked with signs as any palmist's Chris had seen in L.A. Weapon dealers, then—a clutter of them on both sides, then all around an open square, two-story buildings here, with dark balconies overlooking the square. In the square itself, a bonfire, torches, a double pair of jugglers entertaining a large number of men, a few heavily veiled women.

Heat, on the far side: heat and a hellish noise. Aletto was waiting when Chris came up. "Smithy," he shouted over the racket. "I wonder—the man I just spoke with said a man named Gyrdan had a forge, somewhere."

Chris's eyes went wide. "You asked about him, by *name*?"

"And gave him mine," Aletto snapped angrily. "Of course I didn't! Stupid! I used care. But I did learn that much, and maybe I can learn more here, if someone doesn't keep raising idiotic objections!"

Gloves off, Chris thought as heat flooded his face, and not my fault, either. "Oh, right," he sneered. "You're supposed to be a caravaner, and you just go and ask all these stupid questions they'd know the answers to? Besides, who else would want to know about the old Zelharri Duke's General, who'd ask for him by name—who just *happens* to be missing from home—?''

"I'm not going to raise any suspicions," Aletto interrupted.

"Sure you're not," Chris said. "Because you probably already have! Look, anything you ask anybody in this market could be suspicious!"

"Anything I don't ask, *boy*, might keep us in that inn another night or two and get us taken in!" Aletto hissed.

Chris glared back at him, finally shrugged. "All right, whatever you want. Go ask questions, get us killed." And, under his breath, "Jerk."

"He's not a Zelharri man in there," a voice murmured behind Aletto's ear. He started to turn. Chris, who started forward as Aletto shifted stance, found a hand gripping his arm, a familiar voice against his ear. "Hold," was all it said. "Don't call attention to yourself, sir," the other voice said to Aletto. "The market's wide open at this hour but a drawn blade causes comment. You shouldn't want that, and we don't either."

Aletto let the dagger slide back into place and removed his right hand from behind the leather buckler. His shoulders were still tense, and his eyes locked on Chris's briefly; Chris could read the thought in them as clearly as if they'd been friends or arms-mates for years: Wait for my signal, attack when I do. *Attack with what?* Chris thought unhappily. Aletto was as green as he was. "Who are you?" was all he said.

"Friends." The man who held Chris's arm stepped briefly into a patch of light, revealing himself to be the tall and overly thin fellow from the thieves' cage. Chris eyed him in surprise: A boy, really; he was Chris's age, or even younger. "Sikkreni," he added, with a courteous nod in Aletto's direction, "but a friend all the same."

Chris opened his mouth, closed it again. Somehow, he was certain the other wasn't going to mention that cage, and Chris's part in freeing him and his companion. Well, that was fine with him; he had no intention of mentioning that impetuous act either. Not that he was going to trust the fellow just because he saved them both another argument with Aletto.

He turned and looked the other guy over: He wasn't very tall, either; just thin enough to make his height look excessive. His face was all bones and hollows, his eyes dark and expressionless. Even so, he was so average in appearance, size and shape that Chris wasn't certain he'd recognize him again. Perhaps he was a thief after all, like he'd said.

"Whose friend?" Aletto demanded; but he'd lowered his voice.

The thief smiled faintly. "Would you mind if we walked as we discuss this? Since that will draw far less attention than if we continue to stand here like two dogs, sniffing and growling at each other?" Aletto eyed him warily, glanced at the surrounding market. "I think you are intelligent enough to remain in the open and the light, where no harm can come to you; I am certainly intelligent enough not to try and lure you into the dark and away from people."

In spite of himself, Chris laughed. When Aletto glared at him, he bit the corners of his mouth and thrust his hands in his belt, to keep them from shaking. "You could be taking us to someone, here in the market, who'd harm us," he said, and promptly wished he hadn't thought of that.

"Anything is possible, of course," the thief agreed genially. "But if the direction we walk is your choice, then again, what harm?"

For answer, Aletto turned and walked back across the square, skirted the jugglers and the crowd watching them, took three rapid turns in succession and wound up walking down a broad thoroughfare leading into the main part of the city. "Now," he said as the others drew even with him. "Tell me what your intentions, and why you spoke to us back there. And no more riddles, so please you," he added. "I seldom walk so far as this, and I am growing weary."

"If your leg hurts, we know a place nearby you can sit and drink a cup of decent wine. I agree, no riddles, there's little time for that, and no purpose served by them. My name is Edrith, I'm Sikkreni by vocation if not birth. My friend who speaks so seldom is Vey." Edrith gestured; his silent companion inclined his head the least amount. "You, if rumor has it right, are Aletto, the true heir to Zelharri's Ducal seat, and you occupy rooms at the Cap and Feather with three women—one said to be the sin-Duchess, two others to be outlanders like this boy with you tonight." Chris opened his mouth, shut it again as Edrith looked at him curiously and Aletto glared at both of them.

"Say I am Aletto," he said finally. "What then?"

"Then?" Edrith spread his hands wide, shrugged, drew his arms in hastily as an older man ran into him and swore furiously. "Well. Sikkre is not the best place for you to be, but of course Duke's Fort was worse. Here, at least, there are those who would aid you, if only to collect on the various wagers circulating the city—''

"Wagers?''

''Well, of course! As to which of you will rule Zelharri, you or Jadek. And, if Jadek, what tale he will post to Shesseran to convince the Emperor that he had nothing to do with your demise." Silence; an uncomfortable silence as they waded through thick crowds and turned down a narrow alley between market stalls. "The Thukar is of course his own man, not Jadek's ally. But he appreciates coin and the things one trades for coin; by that, you must surely see that unless you bring wealth with you, and a promise of more when you assume your father's seat, the Thukar will either back Jadek outright, or he will play you, one against the other, so long as it pleases or profits him. Then he will sell one of you to the other." Chris cast Aletto a black look; Aletto, concentrating on his footing, on Edrith's words, and on following the pace Vey set, didn't see it.

"Father's men—if you know so much, do you know where any of Father's men are?''

''Certain of them I know personally. After all, it is my business to know people, and things. Otherwise one such as myself tends to vanish from a marketplace quite young, and not be seen again. A very few went into the Thukar's forces, when your uncle took Zelharri. Most went on—a few to Dro Pent, some to Holmaddan. Most who remained guardsmen passed through Sikkre and took the road to Bezjeriad, and thence went to sea or took service overseas. Those who stayed behind buried their swords under mattresses or gardens. Or, like Gyrdan, hung them as signs to lure custom, and made others.''

''Can you take me to him—Gyrdan?'' Aletto demanded. Edrith shook his head.

''Not directly, no. It's not safe, for you *or* for him. He kept his sword in plain sight but buried his name, safer all around. The Thukar knows him, of course; and after Jadek's men came to Sikkre, warning of your escape, such places as his are being watched.''

Chris drew a deep breath, made himself let it out slowly and without any of the words he wanted to say. But he thought them, furiously, at Aletto's back: *All your fault,* he thought. *If my mother is harmed at all, even scared again like she was by that old bat Merrida, I'll—!* He didn't finish the thought; he was trembling again, but this time he was angry, so furious he couldn't think coherently. That wasn't useful; the most useful

thing he could do would be to get Aletto back to the inn and out
of sight. If he could. If not, the second most useful would be to
get him simply out of sight, and the tavern Aletto had mentioned, the Dancing Ram, would do as well as anything else.
Jadek's men—well, of course they had already come to Sikkre!
Well horsed, riding hell-for-leather while the five of them fought
that lousy mule and drank stale water, and ran from ghost camels—!

"There are others who can help you," Edrith said; Chris tried
to set aside everything else and concentrate on what the fellow
was saying. Thief, he thought, and therefore not really completely trustworthy. But if anyone would know how to stay alive
in a dicey situation, a thief would. "A few, anyway. There's a
tavern, the Dancing Ram. It's nearby."

Aletto turned to eye him; Chris thought he looked a little
nervous, all at once. Maybe it was simple exhaustion; they'd
been on their feet for hours now. "The others you speak of—
they'll be at this inn?"

"Perhaps. If not, there is another inn, perhaps a third after
that. The folk you seek are cautious, which cannot be of much
surprise to you, can it? We'll find those who can find those you
want to see." Edrith spread his hands in that broad shrug again.
"Roundabout, but necessary. One uses the Thukar's methods
against him, and so lives. We can take you to a man you know.
My cousin's gone to leave messages for him."

"For who?" Chris demanded roughly. Edrith grinned at him,
rather challengingly.

"Forward, aren't you? You know, I might have thought you a
servant of his, but the accent gives you away. You're an outlander, obviously, and your kind brags of being no man's lesser,
don't you?"

"Outlander?" Chris fastened on that eagerly. "You mean,
there's more people like me around here?"

"Later," Aletto growled. "Not here!" Edrith nodded.

"We'll talk, and about that at least, I'll answer any questions
you ask, if I can. Better we were all inside for the time being,
however."

Aletto considered this, then turned away and started walking.
Edrith touched his arm, directed him down a narrow and nearly
deserted alley to his left. Vey had vanished, gone on his errand
before Chris noticed. "If—" Aletto ran a hand through his hair.
"If you recognized me, if you know so much about me, then
the Thukar—"

"You're still safe," Edrith assured him. "But we'll get your party moved tomorrow morning, first thing. Don't fret that just now; concentrate on walking, on making no move to call attention to us."

Chris's feet were starting to ache; one of his socks was bunched up against the outside of his left foot, rubbing against his small toe. Raising a blister, probably, he thought gloomily. He wondered how much longer he'd be able to stay awake, and hoped this Edrith wasn't planning on walking them all the rest of the way across the city.

Somehow he'd pictured a different kind of building entirely for the Dancing Ram—certainly *not* this grubby, windowless, squat building. It was much smaller than the Cap and Feather—only a single room for drinking and eating, if anyone were fool enough to eat here—and a space on the flat roof where men could sleep for a copper the night. The entry had no door; a mingled odor of stale, unwashed bodies and flat ale, and heat from many lanterns hit him like a blow. Aletto wrinkled his nose, but kept moving, following Edrith who pushed his way into the room and found them space at the end of a trestle bench against the far wall.

The room was jammed, the noise level almost painful. Chris forced himself not to stare, tried to look as though none of this were new, or odd—certainly not frightening. The men here were not the kind he'd normally run across; even his mother, among all the odd types she'd brought home, had never found anyone quite on the scale of these men. They looked like bikers: the same kind of swaggery-tough, loudly, obnoxiously macho trouble. He slid back on the bench until his spine touched the wall, and kept his hands firmly tucked in his belt so they wouldn't shake and give him away.

Edrith stood and waved a hand, shouted something over Chris's head. Some time later, an older man pushed through the crowd carrying a small bucket and a handful of dull metal mugs. He shoved bucket and mugs into Chris's lap, took coin from Edrith with an evil grin that showed a three-tooth gap, and went back the way he'd come. Edrith dipped a deep red liquid into cups, shared them out and lifted his. "To easy takings and deep shadows," he said. Aletto took a deep draught of his, made a face and choked. He contented himself with short sips after that. Chris sniffed suspiciously. Wine. Sweet wine, the kind that made for hellish headaches, and he didn't like wine much anyway. He held the cup to his lip and barely wet it, then began looking for a place he could dump the stuff.

Edrith gave him a shove to move him over closer to Aletto and squeezed in between Chris and an extremely overweight man whose greasy shirt smelled like camels. Chris cleared his throat; Edrith laid a finger across his lips, gestured faintly with his head. Vey was quietly and suddenly there.

"He's here, Edrith. The potsman's daughter caught up with him just inside the doorway, though." Vey was shorter than Edrith, extremely small—lack of decent food, Chris thought, rather than build—and hatchet-faced. His only memorable features were a wide, mobile mouth and very blue eyes that at the moment gleamed with malicious amusement. "It may take him time to assure Kosilla he had business last night that wasn't another innkeeper's daughter."

Edrith sighed and closed his eyes momentarily. "By all the little brown sand-gods at once, if he gets us killed for a bit of soft flesh—well, never mind," he added, and jumped to his feet. Before Chris could move or react, someone else took his place, a young man who dropped onto the bench with enough force to rattle the man on the other side. The camel-scented man scowled; his eyes widened suddenly and a moment after, he was on his feet and gone. Edrith took the place he'd vacated before anyone else could. "Dahven, did Kossi forgive you?"

The new arrival nodded. "For the moment, silly woman. Jealousy's so irritating, doesn't she know that?" He leaned back against the wall, rolled his head and fixed very dark and intense eyes on Chris. He smiled then. "I know your companions, you I don't, but I've heard about you from Vey, and market rumor—not necessarily true, the latter." He held out both hands, palm up, then clapped Chris's arms with them. "I'm Dahven."

"Dahven," Chris echoed. "I'm Chris." *Title?* he wondered. *Do I call him Lord, or something?* But Aletto didn't use one—and this Dahven seemed even less likely to. Dahven grinned at him and turned away to talk to Aletto, who had greeted his arrival with visible pleasure and excitement he was clearly having trouble holding in.

This Dahven wasn't particularly tall; and unlike most of the men and boys Chris had met or seen so far, he had good, visible arm and shoulder muscle. Brownish hair that looked sun-bleached fell just over the neck of his shift and curled a little at the ends. A dark face—suntanned, Chris thought, even though his eyes were nearly black. They darted from one to another of his new companions, around the room, never quite still, and there was something about him overall—wild, Chris decided. Like Lialla had said. He tried to picture stiff, proper, arrogant Lialla married to this Dahven and failed utterly. But the man seemed genuinely glad to see Aletto, even if he was not as effusive about it.

Aletto was babbling like a kid, Chris thought critically. *Poor guy, his home life must really be dull.*

Dahven gripped his hand finally. "Careful," he said and cast his eyes at the men nearest them. Aletto colored, nodded. Dahven turned to look at Chris. "This isn't the place to talk, I was just reminding Aletto. So we'll slip out as soon as the wine's gone, if you don't mind. That's if I can evade Kosilla. You know," he added appraisingly as he looked at Chris again, "she might find *you* interesting. Maybe you'd distract her for me? I could make it worth your while." To his annoyance, Chris felt the color heating his face; he shook his head. Dahven grinned at him. "It wasn't a good idea anyway; I might want her back." Chris nearly laughed; as though anyone could take a girl from someone who *looked* like that and was royal to boot! Dahven leaned over, ostensibly to top off Chris's cup, and murmured against his ear: "Vey told me what you did tonight; most folk wouldn't have."

"I—Frankly, I don't know why *I* did," Chris said.

"No?" Dahven's eyebrow went up. "I should wager you let trapped things go, rather than the other way about. You have that look. I'm surprised Aletto would back you in such an act, however. He's not unfeeling but he has too much riding on his decisions to dare operate from the heart just now."

Chris cast a glance at Aletto, who was deep in conversation with Vey, and shook his head. "He—uh—doesn't know."

Dahven's other eyebrow joined the first. "Mmmm. And you don't want him to know, that it? Don't want—wait, let me finish, will you? You don't want him thinking you're impulsive and so not particularly trustworthy to watch his back. Never mind, I won't give you away."

"Thanks." Chris wet his lip with wine a second time; it tasted terrible. He was tired, suddenly; too much stale air, stale bodies, not enough sleep. He stifled a yawn. "It probably wasn't the brightest thing I've done, turning them loose. They could have been anything."

"True enough. You aren't going to worry about it now, are

you? After all, they're all right and so are you. Drink up, have another.''

Chris shook his head. "I don't, usually." Dahven laughed, took the cup out of his fingers and eased the contents onto the floor under the bench. He leaned across and got Vey's attention then.

"Go ahead, we'll be only a few moments behind you. The Purple Fingers, an hour from now, get a room and tell Halydd it's for me and a—well, for me. You know what to say. But tell him to keep his mouth shut! Father's got the guard out for me—but between us, the guard isn't looking only for me. Understand?''

"You, a—hem—a lady, room," Vey enumerated on stubby fingers. Chris noticed with a painful dropping sensation of his stomach that one finger was missing, severed at the first joint. He looked away. "Ground-level room?''

Dahven snorted. "Certainly not! Circumspect, that means the corner room one up. Halydd knows which I want. It's easy to find, easy to get in.''

Vey nodded; he went back to his conversation with Aletto, moments later setting aside his empty winecup and wandering away. Chris watched the door but never actually saw him go. Edrith somehow got hold of Aletto shortly after and the two of them walked off; Dahven took Chris's sleeve and held him back when he would have followed. "Wait. Watch to see if anyone's interested.''

Chris cast him an irritated look. "I can barely see anything in here! And who d'you think I am, James Bond?''

"You said you were Chris," Dahven replied mildly. This struck Chris as extremely funny; he had to clap a hand across his mouth to keep from spluttering all over both of them. By the time he got his mirth under control, Dahven was on his feet and ready to go. "Look," he directed, "over there. Young woman, red hair, lots of it loose down her back?'' Chris squinted, saw what looked like red hair between and just beyond two bulky men in indeterminately gray, sloppily loose robes, and nodded. "That is Kosilla. I love her dearly—well, so as to speak of course. She's in rather a temper tonight, and we truly haven't time to deal with one of her longer and louder fits. So if you see her eye on us, warn me, will you? And be prepared to run.''

It must be because he was so tired; Chris found this funny, too. If Robyn could see him now, sneaking out of the local equivalent of a biker bar with a lunatic young nobleman who looked like that adventure guy on TV with the Swiss Army knife and the duct tape, slithering away from some blousy barmaid who was—now he could see her clearly—literally half out of her dress . . . *that* thought sobered him, rather abruptly. Robyn would *not* see the humor.

Outside, Dahven pulled him into a darkened doorway and kept him there for several long, silent breaths. "No one following us, good." *No,* Chris thought in some despair, *I'm certainly not James Bond.* He hadn't even considered the possibility of some-one following them, and now that he had, he didn't care for it. It took everything he had, for the rest of the night, not to keep peering nervously over one shoulder.

"Where we going?" he asked finally; he kept his voice at a whisper, easier to disguise the wobble in it. Dahven didn't seem in the least concerned; he looked like a fellow out on the town, a guy out for a good time. Of course, it was *his* town, and he knew where he was and who people were. Who knew, maybe he did this kind of thing all the time.

"Purple Fingers Inn," Dahven replied promptly. "Weren't you listening?"

"Sure—for all that tells me. Where is it—like, how far?"

"Oh. Not very." It wasn't; at least, it couldn't have been as far as it seemed. Chris's watch—it had decided to work again, somewhere during the previous night—showed it had been barely a half hour since they'd left the other inn. He was definitely growing a blister on that little toe, though, by the time they moved into the edges of the market. Two streets further on, there was a pool—round, instead of rectangular, but otherwise much like the one in front of the Cap and Feather. Beyond it, a width of deserted, cobbled street, and directly across from the pool, a sign, illuminated by twin hurricane lanterns. It was garish, dreadfully proportioned, a hand with six fingers and an outsized thumb; Chris couldn't make out color but it certainly seemed to him purple would be right. He didn't have much time to look at it; Edrith and Aletto were sitting on the edge of the fountain, waiting; as the other two came up, they stood and Edrith swept them all across the street and into a gated alley that ran down one side of the inn.

It reeked of goat or sheep—something much stronger than mere horse, less immediately recognizable than camel. They came out into a courtyard not much wider than the alley—no stables back here that Chris could see. But he could hear animals, and the stench was at least as strong. He pinched his nostrils, hard, to fight a sneeze, and breathed through his mouth. Dahven had hold of his sleeve now, and pulled him along, behind the darkened inn. Someone sleeping in the room above them let out an explosive snort; the two young men stopped cold and Chris leaned into the wall for support. Silence, then a loud, rumbling snore. Dahven looked up, shook his head, and caught hold of Chris's sleeve once more.

It was a full ten feet or more up to that corner room, and at first Chris wasn't certain he could manage it. His knees were still weak from the sudden noise that had startled him. But after Dahven pointed out the first uneven bricks in a very roughly laid wall and got Aletto started up it behind him, it was easy: Chris pulled himself up behind Aletto, and Edrith came last.

The air was smoky from several oil lamps; chill and rather dusty, as though the room hadn't been used in some time. There were cushions all along three walls, a bench and the narrow balcony on the fourth. A table in the middle of the room, with lamps clustered on one end, Dahven perched on the other. One of its two benches was occupied by a broad-shouldered man of middle years; two others standing behind him looked older, but that might have been their stoop-shouldered stance, the long beards that were heavily grayed. Aletto ignored the two older men, however; his attention was all for the third. And that man pushed the bench back to stand, to close the distance between them. He momentarily loomed over the nera-Duke, then went stiffly down onto one knee.

"Gyrdan? Is it you?" Aletto's voice wasn't entirely steady; nor was the hand that gripped the man's shoulder.

"My Duke." Gyrdan looked up at him and held out both hands. "They said you'd come to Sikkre; I wasn't certain I believed the rumor. How do I serve you?"

You had to give him credit, Chris thought. Aletto was at least ten years older than he, but one would hardly know it—the guy wasn't any bigger, no more muscled, and he was hardly worldly and sophisticated, the way a naive twentieth-century American might expect a nobleman to be. But it must have been there despite his uncle, despite his upbringing. Something in the blood. Aletto squared his shoulders and brought his chin up and somehow, in that moment, he was all the Duke anyone could want. Not chilly and distant, though, the way Chris might have expected Aletto to be under the circumstances. The smile that turned his lips warmed his entire face, and his hand stayed on the older man's shoulder.

"Gyrdan, I'd not have known you in the street. You've changed—as much as I, likely."

"You've the build of your father," Gyrdan said simply. "And his mouth."

"Not enough else of his," Aletto said ruefully, "or else I'd have had his seat the past three years. It's for that cause I've left Duke's Fort and come in search—of you, and men like you." He drew Gyrdan to his feet, indicated one of the benches and sat next to the man.

Gyrdan nodded. "We get gossip and rumor, now and again letters or messages from friends still there. And two days ago, word spread across the market that you and the Lady Lialla had vanished entirely, with rumor wild as to the cause." He listened while Aletto made him a succinct tale of matters. "You might go to the Emperor, but I personally would not recommend it. Jadek surely expects that, and he certainly has ears of his own at Court. Or men there, to put forth his own version of matters." He set his elbows against his knees, buried his chin in his hands and thought, hard. "Direct force of arms would not be advisable, either."

"No," Aletto said soberly; his eyes were nervous when he turned away and Chris could almost read the thought there: Was Gyrdan refusing to help him? If the man had been so many years in Sikkre—if he had family and a trade, could anyone blame him for not wanting to put himself in the position of a traitor to one side because he supported the other? "I don't want any man dead, not even my uncle. But I am scarcely a man to lead such an expedition, even if I wanted it."

Gyrdan cast him a sharp glance. "No," he said. "And thank the gods you've the intelligence to realize it. I've seen too many men sacrificed to such lack of ability to countenance it in my age. Besides, the Emperor would surely take exception to in-fighting. He has not interfered in Ducal matters in the past but that does not mean he would not now—whether to back the rightful heir against a usurper or the other way about. Shesseran is in ill health and very old; there is no certainty and logic to his decisions these days.

"But Jadek has only a standard-size household; if anything, he has decreased the number of armsmen he holds—they say this is so no one thinks he keeps you from your rights by physical threat."

"Well, that is to Aletto's advantage, isn't it?" Dahven asked. "He can return home with a company of his father's men—not as armsmen threatening the gates, not as an overt threat to Jadek, rather an honor guard of those who served his father and who look to the privilege of serving Aletto once the confirmation ceremonies are finally held. Jadek would be forced to act as though he of course intended to confirm Aletto. And, of course, Aletto, there you would be, surrounded by your armsmen—your father's householdmen, pardon me!—returned from across Rhadaz to serve you now that you are Zelharri's Duke. Of course they would never be men armed to depose Jadek, would they?"

"Why, of course not," Aletto said dryly, and they both laughed.

Gyrdan spread his hands wide, shrugged massively. "Shesseran in such an event—no violence on your part because you intend none, no violence on Jadek's part because there are more men supporting you—Shesseran would accept your version of events. Particularly if you were named Duke, or about to be. And since it is your proper place, after all. Jadek surely knows that."

Dahven stirred. "He's kept Aletto close-quartered all these years for that reason, hasn't he? Any fighting would reflect badly on the man who claims to be only serving as regent until Aletto is able to take his rightful place. But Aletto, you'll need those men, and you'll need money. And he'll find little of one here and less of the other, Gyrdan." Silence, a momentary one. "Except if you help him, of course, Gyrdan," Dahven finished, and smiled.

Gyrdan shook his head but the smile he offered Aletto was a friendly one. "Pay no heed to him, young Duke, he's a wheedler born." Dahven laughed. "All these young women purring in his ear, that's what does it. No, he's right, though: There's little in Sikkre for you, but there are Zelharri merchant families in Bez. Fedthyr, whose grandsire grew plants and made dyes, and who now presides over an empire of weavers and cloth-traders in Bez, with strong connections in Sikkre. He owes that empire to Duke Amarni, and he can afford to be generous. And he will certainly see that others like him subscribe to your efforts. I know men who can ask on my behalf and yours among the merchant-ships and locate men I once led."

He rose to his feet, paced back and forth. "There are not many of us in Sikkre; the Thukar is suspicious of us and keeps us under close scrutiny."

"Speak of whom," Dahven said, and pulled a small, dark ornament out of some inner pocket. He studied it for a moment; Chris came over and stared as it pulsed a dull red. Dahven folded his fingers around it, shrugged, returned it to its hiding place. "Just checking," he said. And, to Chris, "Father's always been mad for magicians, and of late he has one or more of them trying to keep an eye on me. I doubt any of us want his friendly eye on us tonight! But I always have at least one token about me to ward off interference with my private comings and goings; no one is at this hour interested in us." He grinned at Chris. "I think, myself, because at this hour I'm too often in Kossi's room—or someone else's. Magicians can be such prudes." Chris managed a nod; he could feel the blood hot in his cheeks and throat. It wasn't what he *said*, damnit, more the way he said it.

Aletto was back on his feet, hands clasping both of Gyrdan's. "I am reminded by this; we should not stay together long. I had no real plans beyond finding you. I am grateful for any aid you feel prepared to give me. But I don't feel safe in Sikkre; the Thukar has no reason to support me over my uncle and I have no means to persuade him. I think it would be best if I went to Bez as soon as possible." But he sounded and looked rather doubtful. Gyrdan nodded firmly.

"I agree. Remember these names—Fedthyr in the Street of Weavers, Kamahl at the wharves, on or near the ship *Gull*." Aletto repeated the names, the locations. Gyrdan nodded again. "They'll help, and they'll find others, or direct you to them. I'll do all I can here. I'll send my own messages through to Bez; with luck, they'll precede you." He sighed. "My family—aye, better they were out of this city as well, whatever the future holds. I'll send them to Bez and myself go to Podhru. We can meet there. Lord Evany has taken a house within Podhru's walls, near the port. I know Evany; he and I grew up together."

"Evany," Aletto mumbled. He brightened momentarily. "I remember him; he was on Father's council, he did magic at the supper table with pigeons in his sleeves."

"I'd forgotten that," Gyrdan said. "But I do know he'd return to Zelharri tomorrow if his estates were given back to him. And he'd be properly grateful to you. Also, he has access to the Emperor's Court and other important places in Podhru. He knows where certain of your father's magicians have gone, and unless what he tells me is wildly amiss, you could still persuade many of those men and women to return.

"But we're overstaying our time here, I'd be tucked up in my blankets behind my forge before daylight takes me, and I'd rather you were back at that inn, my Duke. I'll send word with Dahven if I must speak with you again before you depart; any other messages I'll send on to Bez.'' He inclined his head briefly, gripped the hands Aletto held out to him. "I had given up; even tonight, coming here, I wasn't certain I'd care to leave the life I've built up here. But you're my Duke's son. We'll win through.'' He and his men left. Aletto stood where Gyrdan had left him, face pale and unnaturally solemn.

Dahven led them out the door this time, into an absolutely dark hall, down a dozen or more deep stone steps and back into the narrow courtyard. There was no light from the chamber they'd just left, no sound. Nothing but that snore, muted now, broken by a fit of thick coughing as they slipped silently into the side passage, and into the street. Once on the street, they made better time. Chris looked around for the two thieves, but saw no sign of them. He couldn't, now that he thought about it, remember when they'd faded from that room.

It wasn't important, though. Keeping his footing on streets that were unevenly and damply paved or thick in dust and rock occupied all his attention. Fortunately, it wasn't that far from the Purple Fingers to the Cap and Feather; almost at once he recognized a few landmarks. But it was starting to get light; people were moving around and Chris could hear increased activity in the market, some distance off to their left. And he was uncomfortable; there was an itch in the back of his neck, or somewhere in his mind—as though someone were thinking about him, the way his mother used to say that worked. Here, with magic thick on the ground, maybe it really did. *God.* He hunched his head down between his shoulders and caught up closer to Aletto, who was right behind Dahven.

A corner, a second, and then that familiar rectangular fountain, a blue-gray shape in the false dawn. Chris tensed and relaxed his shoulders a few times to ease the muscles, let out a sigh, and moved into the shadow between the inn and the passageway back to the stables. Dahven came to a halt abruptly, caught hold of the edge of his cloak and shook his head. "Wait," he mouthed silently, and his eyes were urgent, compelling—every bit of humor drained out of them.

Chris waited nervously, shifting from foot to foot until an irritated shake of Aletto's head stopped him. Dahven drew out one ornament, another that was a complex figure of multicolored pale string. He squatted on his heels and bent over these for

several moments, then gestured urgently. Aletto dropped awkwardly to one knee beside him; Chris squatted, nearly overbal-
anced, caught himself on both hands, stingingly against the stone
wall of the inn. Both waited impatiently, nervously. Dahven
clutched his odd assortment of baubles in one hand, motioned
them close and mouthed: "Something's gone wrong in there."
Aletto tried to stand, subsided as Dahven wrapped his hand in
Aletto's sleeve and yanked him back down. "I can't tell who,
but I can smell what's waiting in there." He held up his fistful
of charms; they and his grimly set face were all too visible in
the increasing morning light. "It's a trap."

13

AT the Cap and Feather, in the last room across from the garden door, the night crawled; the room itself was stuffy, even with occasional puffs of breeze coming down the smoke hole and in the two vents. Lialla opened the door for several minutes, late in the evening, but even though she'd been standing there the entire time, watching, Robyn was nervous, and had said so, loudly. More to silence her than anything else, Lialla had finally shut the door. But she was impressed when Robyn dragged one of the knives out of a food pack and wedged it firmly in the door.

"Learned that trick years ago, living in Hollywood," she said. "Great way to make sure you finished a night alone, if that was what you wanted." The momentary lift in her voice faded; she looked at Lialla anxiously, at Jennifer unhappily. "Um—look, you two don't need me, I'm going to try and get some sleep. Wake me when they get back, will you?"

"Sure, Birdy," Jennifer said, and hoped her face looked as reassuring as she made her voice sound. Sleep was the last thing on her mind just now; she frankly doubted Robyn would sleep, either, from the look on her face. Jennifer shifted the new black trousers, tugged at the loose waistband, dropped onto the edge of the bed Aletto'd used and patted the edge. "Sit down here, why don't you, Lialla? Save your feet for later. Come on, tell me things."

"Things," Lialla said distractedly. She perched on the edge of the bed where she could keep both eyes on the door. Most of her weight was still on her feet. "I shouldn't have let him go," she muttered.

Jennifer sighed, loudly and deliberately. "Look, you did that hours ago, you let him go. He's gone. It's *done*. Tearing your hair and wailing won't change that, and it won't alter anything that's happening right now. Tell me things, teach me things! I'm probably not much use to you but I won't be any use to you or anyone else if I don't know a damned thing, don't you think?''

"What makes you think you'll be any use even if you know things?'' Lialla demanded.

"How should I know? Maybe I won't! I've done all right so far, though, haven't I?'' Silence. Lialla took her eyes off the door long enough to glare at Jennifer. Jennifer folded her arms and waited. Lialla's shoulders sagged the least bit; her gaze slipped. "Tell me things,'' Jennifer said again, mildly.

"Things.'' Lialla sighed tiredly and went back to her study of the door. "All right. Things like what?'' And as Jennifer cleared her throat, Lialla rounded on her. "Keeping in mind I don't know everything you're going to ask.''

"So? Tell me what you know.''

"Like what?'' Lialla was brooding on the door once again.

"Magic,'' Jennifer said. "What else?''

"That's a broad subject; even *you* must know that by now,'' Lialla said flatly. "Specify.''

"Well—all right. They've been gone long enough that you're worried. So why don't you just check on them, or can't you do that with Thread?'' Lialla turned to gaze at her blankly. Jennifer shrugged broadly. "I don't pretend to have read the right kind of books—I don't have time for that kind of fiction and the occult stuff bores me half to death. But Chris reads books with magic, so I hear about it, some. It seems to me one of the favorite devices is an ability to see or sense particular people at a distance. Talk with them—communicate that way. Can't you use Thread for that?''

Lialla shook her head. "I don't know. I can sense people, animals, tell them apart. Not—I can't just pick out a person. I never have, I've never heard of doing that. Merrida's never said anything about it.''

"But that doesn't mean it's impossible,'' Jennifer said persuasively. "Just that she never mentioned it. Maybe if it's something particularly advanced, she wouldn't have. Of course, if your books don't mention it, either—?'' She paused; Lialla was shaking her head again.

"I never saw any books on Night-Threads. At least, Merrida has books but not—there aren't teaching books, nothing like that.''

"No books to tell you how? No—spell books?"

"No!" Lialla said firmly. "You don't use spells with Night-Threads, not the way you mean. And books to tell you how—that's stupid, why would there be?"

"Why? Because what one person could remember everything?" Jennifer was keeping her voice relaxed, the way she'd learned when questioning difficult witnesses or eliciting testimony from hostile ones. Lialla seemed to take any lack of knowledge personally, and any remarks against Merrida's teaching set her off even worse. Maybe Chris was right, maybe the old woman wasn't half as good as she thought, massive drawing spell across worlds or no. She certainly had Lialla convinced she was among the immortals, though.

Lialla did have additional reason for her shaky temper, of course; Jennifer could see her fingers drumming the prickly straw mattress. Well, Jennifer thought, she's not alone in that, my nephew is out there too, and with even less to gain by it than her brother has.

Lialla sighed. "Thread-magic is handed down the way it is, teacher to initiate, because there are only certain ways to do things. If you had books, if just anyone could open a book and begin Wielding—" She hesitated, frowned, began chewing on her lower lip.

"What?" Jennifer prodded her finally. "I thought you said it couldn't be misused."

"It can't!"

"Well then—?"

"You have to have someone teach you the right way to do it because that's how it is, that's all!" Lialla got the words out in a rush, plumped herself further back on the bed and drew her feet up.

"Terrific logic," Jennifer said dryly.

"What do you know about it? Coming from a world with no magic?"

"We have enough other dangerous learning experiences—all right, forget that. But tell me this: You showed me how to find people, out in the desert. Now, I was able to do that, at least with real people. So, using that same Thread, I can right now reach out into that hall, or in the street, or even further away—as far as my grip on the Thread will hold, and I will be able to locate people. Isn't that right?" Lialla nodded, one sharp dip of her chin. There was a mulish set to her mouth. "Now, is there anything else to that particular Thread—I mean, another way to hold it, another way to look at what you find, or is it only that much knowledge? What I mean is, can you only recognize life—people or horses or camels but who knows which it is?—or people as a general type separate from the animals? Is there a way to tell men from women?''

Lialla nodded unwillingly. ''All right. People from animals, you usually can, unless there's a real pack, like the market was in places today. Then you can only tell there's a lot of living things there.''

''That makes sense,'' Jennifer said; Lialla's shoulders relaxed slightly, and when she went on she sounded slightly less defensive.

''Ordinarily you can tell people from horses and camels, anywhere like the desert—could you tell on the trail?''

Jennifer shook her head. ''There was a little excitement just about then; I don't remember, frankly.''

A faint smile moved Lialla's mouth. It faded as her eyes were drawn back to the door. ''Even in Sehfi, you can usually tell. Here, though . . . You couldn't do that here in Sikkre, it would be impossible, there are too many people—''

Jennifer held up a finger and cut off the increasingly rapid flow of words. ''But! No, wait a minute, let me finish, will you? There aren't very many people walking around Sikkre at night, are there? Not in the areas where people live, or around the inns like this one? There certainly weren't last night, when we first got here, after all. So—except in certain parts of the market and in the ale houses. Am I right?'' Lialla nodded. Jennifer shifted her visual focus, found Thread and took gentle hold of it. ''And—correct me if I'm wrong, please—it's *those* particular Threads, isn't it?''

''That, and those,'' Lialla corrected her quickly. ''And—not like that, that way!'' She held up her own hand, then folded her arms across her chest and watched in narrow-eyed silence. Jennifer wriggled back on the bedding and stared blankly across the room, eyes falling on the door but not seeing it except as a thickening of certain Thread. She blinked finally and found her way back to the normal world.

''All right. It's harder than it was in the desert, that's for certain. But I can tell there are people in the big room out there. Several people, not exact numbers or anything else about them. In the street, though, there's the fountain—I remembered how to find water—and on the far side of the fountain, there are five men.'' She paused doubtfully. ''I'm only fairly certain of men,

but I know there are five of them and beasts—horses, I think."
She brought her chin up a little. "Go ahead, check me, why
don't you?"

Lialla's mouth twisted but her own chin came up and her attention left the door. She mumbled to herself, finally swore
under her breath and closed her eyes, both hands moving
shoulder-high in front of her. Thread jangled against Jennifer's
senses, and she filed another question to ask—later. She'd probably done all the asking she'd dare tonight. Lialla finally opened
her eyes and nodded. "You can't tell who they are, though. Can
you?"

"Well, of course not!" Jennifer replied irritably. "Who do I
know here, besides you and Birdy—and Chris, who's got no
business prowling dark, unfamiliar streets or being in a tavern
at his age—and your brother?"

"Who's got no business being—" Lialla sighed and shook her
head. "I *wish* he had no business. Aletto's only been here as a
child. He's hardly been out of Duke's Fort at all, he only knows
the world through the kinds of books his tutors gave him." She
sighed again. "Ancient, out of date, foolish books, I can't think
why anyone would want to open them. Heroes, and quests, and
the women are all fair and to be protected—" She stopped in
sudden surprise; Jennifer was laughing quietly and shaking her
head.

"Heroes and quests and magic swords, and helpless dam-
sels—but the women in Chris's books and games are just as
likely to wear the swords as the men are."

"I was supposed to have been taught to fight," Lialla said
gloomily. "Dagger and kick-fighting, mostly, it's expected for
women to be able to protect themselves. My uncle—Jadek
wouldn't permit it." She drove both hands through her hair.
"Jadek. Gods. If Jadek's men found Aletto, or if the Thukar's
men did!" She got off the bed and began prowling the room. "I
cannot believe they've had business out there all these hours.
And it's fading."

"What is?" Jennifer watched her pace.

"Thread," Lialla said impatiently. "Can't you tell? It's almost dawn. If they don't come—! But we can't do anything now
until after sundown."

"Fading?" Jennifer shook her head. "But it's not, I can still
see it—" Her voice faded as Lialla stopped and stared at her,
much as though she'd said something utterly obscene. "Look,

Lialla, it's paler than it was, and not quite as loud, but it's right there, I can still touch it, I can still differentiate between—"

"You can't!" Lialla said sharply. "No one can!"

Jennifer stared at her in bewilderment. "But I can! It's right—"

"Don't say things like that! You can't, no one can do that, not with Thread!" Her voice was almost a howl; she clapped a hand over her mouth as Robyn moaned and sat up, blinking sleepily. "You can*not* see Thread in day," Lialla insisted in a fierce whisper. "What kind of—of *thing* are you? Oh, gods, Merrida, what have you done to us?" She turned away to lean her head against the wall. Jennifer stared at her in astonishment. As though she'd accused a Christian saint of being the Antichrist. She opened her mouth, closed it again. There wasn't anything she could say and none of the questions she wanted to ask seemed to be a good idea. But if she couldn't ask Lialla about such things, then who?

"Jennifer?" Robyn yawned. "Everything all right?"

"Shhh, go back to sleep, Birdy," Jennifer said automatically; all her attention was on Lialla. Silence. Robyn yawned again, pulled the harsh blanket around her shoulders and lay back down. Jennifer glanced at her, then turned back to Lialla, and sighed soundlessly. Good intentions would have to go to the wall; this wasn't going to be the place for them, and there wasn't time. "Lialla," she said gently. "Lialla, listen to me. Please."

Silence. Then: "I'm listening," Lialla mumbled against the wall.

"Do that. This is all new to me, remember? Your world, your language, your magic. Maybe my grip on the words isn't right. But we're misunderstanding each other and we can't afford that."

Silence. "No."

"I'm not trying to break the rules or do something deliberately wrong, if that's what's got you upset. I'm just telling you what I see. If it's a problem, I'm sorry. I have no intention of doing anything to hurt you or Aletto, and I certainly will never intentionally hurt Robyn or Chris—or myself, as a matter of fact. So why don't you explain it to me? If I'm breaking some law or some moral matter, tell me what it is. Tell me what I'm doing wrong."

Lialla raised her head, braced herself with both hands flat on the wall. "Wrong?" As Jennifer shifted and straw rustled under her, Lialla turned on her. Her face was terribly pale against the black scarves, and her chin trembled. "I don't think I want to hear this."

"Why?" Jennifer demanded. "Give me a reason why, Lialla! Is it because utilizing Thread during the daytime is wrong, because it doesn't work the same way as at night? Because it does bad things? Because you've never heard it can be done, so that means it can't? Or maybe it's because *you* can't do it—or your precious Merrida can't—and *that* makes it wrong?"

"You can't talk to me like that!" Lialla shouted.

"Oh, can't I?" Jennifer pushed herself off the bed and closed the distance between them. "Look here, woman, what do you want? Respect for noble blood and rank to the point where I stay totally ignorant and get us killed? Is it more important to you that I kiss your feet than that I help you? As an equal?"

"It's not—"

"Not what? Not that simple? Welcome to the real world, honey! Look, you've got me, and by God, I'm going to get pretty damned mad if you don't use me! I had a good life going where I was, and it's bad enough to lose all that without losing it for nothing! Or because someone else was stubborn and stupid!" Lialla stared at her blankly. "You think about that, and you think hard," Jennifer finished evenly. "And if you have something useful to say, come talk to me, all right?" She turned away and walked over to sit down next to Robyn. Robyn rolled over, let out a genteel little snore and subsided into her wrappings.

Jennifer looked down at her sister for some time, then up at the vents near the ceiling. Odd. She could see the first light against the wall. It was still too faint to illuminate anything inside the room, too early for the sun, but she *could* see Thread! She could still hear it very clearly. Wonderful, she thought sourly, as Lialla threw herself into the room's one chair. Neither one of us knows a damned thing about this stuff, and she's about as useful as a paper umbrella. Except paper umbrellas don't sulk, and they don't throw screaming fits when someone suggests a different way around a problem.

Well, let her sulk, then. Jennifer turned away from her and experimentally, cautiously, shifted her vision once more and took hold of Thread. The main room of the inn was now empty, save for two people asleep on benches against the far wall. Two definitely, and human. Somewhere beyond them, perhaps another room away, someone walking back and forth across a small space with definite purpose in the stride—the innkeeper, preparing her bread, no doubt. Jennifer cast Lialla a dark look—the look went right through the collection of shifting, varicolored Thread—and altered her grasp on what she held. Female? Was it a different feel, a different sound?—thickness, actually, she thought. The two sleepers were both the same sex, surely male. Different from the one. The five she'd found earlier, out by the fountain. . . .

But they weren't there any longer. The beasts were, however. Jennifer's brows drew together. Horses, she thought. Not—chickens or goats, at least. Surely they could not be the same horses from an hour or so earlier, could they?

No, surely not the same. Because then, where were the men who'd been with them?

A puzzle. Thread jangled discordantly nearby, dragging her attention from the feel of water and—surely!—horses; she shifted her grip, feeling wildly all around her, and sensed the men only one brief moment before she heard the sound of a door opening nearby. It was the door leading into the herb garden. Men—five men coming straight toward them, so near her hands were numbed by quivering Thread.

She couldn't regain her place in the real world entirely, and doubled vision made her dizzy. Stealthy, slow movements now, then no movement at all. They stood just beyond that door. *Their* door. Jennifer reeled to her feet, conscious of Lialla staring at her in sudden alarm, halfway to her feet. Jennifer fought shifting vision and light-headedness, trying to find the inner word that would clear Thread from her sight; it evaded her. Her mouth wouldn't work, words wouldn't form, her hands moved with nightmare slowness, to join and shakily point at the door—at Robyn's knife, the handle protruding above the latch. It was moving up and down, the door nudging in a little at a time as someone tried to quietly shove it open. She found her voice finally, began to shout out a warning; the door slammed into the wall, the knife flew across the room to clatter at her feet.

Five men stood there, four in dark leather and darker metal armor. Two of those held drawn swords. They fanned into the room, watchful, making way for the fifth. He wore plain black, trousers, boots, long-sleeved shirt, long cloak. Jennifer, still badly disoriented from doubled vision, had to fight an urge to laugh. The swords hardly looked real at all, and the men holding them were dressed like opera extras. The fifth man resembled something out of a very badly costumed fantasy movie; or someone trying to create an aura. If that was his intention, he certainly wasn't frightening her.

She fought her way out of Thread-vision, back into the "real" world. Poor creature, he needed all the aura he could get, she thought, but without sympathy. He was tall, over six feet, but too thin. His shoulders were narrower than hers, his Adam's apple prominent, his face all hollows, even with all the hair—mustache blending into beard into sideburns, into long, dark hair that tangled wildly over his shoulders and looked as though he hadn't combed it in days, and hadn't washed it in weeks. The black shirt was open further than it should have been, revealing a thin white chest and ribs instead of muscle or hair. He carried a long staff with some kind of silver device on top of it, wore another silver object on a long chain—she couldn't see what either was. Probably, she thought in amusement, something that says "I am a wizard" in the local patois.

Robyn was struggling to come awake; shivering in the sudden influx of cool air, blinking muzzily at the strange men. It suddenly wasn't as amusing; Jennifer eased a step or two sideways to place herself between the bed and the door.

The wizard wasn't even looking at her, though. Lialla had crossed the room to confront him angrily. "Who are you and what outrage is this?"

"There are three of you; there were said to be five," he replied indirectly. "Where are the other two?"

"Not here," Lialla said crisply.

He smiled; not a nice smile. "I see as much. Where are they now?"

Lialla bared her teeth at him in turn. "They've gone on to join with our family. Gray Fisher's Carts, Red Hawk Clan, coming down out of Holmaddan—"

"A lie, every word of it. That is unimportant, however; we'll have the truth."

Lialla let her lip curl and took a step back. "You sorcerers! You think by such a show of confidence to frighten the untutored?"

"We'll have the truth," he repeated, and stepped around her as though he'd lost interest. He cast one brief glance in Jennifer's direction, then walked past her to nudge their packs and bags with one booted foot. Several more aimless paces brought him to the foot of the bed the three women had shared. Robyn, now thoroughly awake, shoved hair back across her shoulders and stared up at him glassily. The color left her face. "Bring them. And their belongings, all of them. Sin-Duchess Lialla, His Serene Honor Dahmec asks your company. A certain matter to do with your brother.'' He stared down at Robyn, began to turn away, then stopped. For a very long moment, he looked at her; there was no expression on his face or in his eyes. Suddenly he spun on one heel and walked out of the room.

The armsmen were thorough and swift; the bags were bundled together and piled beside the door. Jennifer had to help Robyn on with her shoes and her cloak; Robyn trembled violently but was otherwise either in shock or too frightened to move. Lialla stood by the door; she was still trying to argue them free, now with one of the swordsmen, a squarely built man with a small silver token on one shoulder. ''You'll make no friends of our family, doing this.''

''Give it over, sin-Duchess,'' the man replied shortly. ''Better, tell us where the other two are, save us the trouble of looking for them.''

''Look all you like,'' Lialla snapped. ''You won't find them!''

''We may not,'' the armsman said; a nod of his head indicated the man in the hall. ''*He* will, though; the Thukar puts trust in that particular of his magicians and wizards. And with good reason. But you'll see.''

''I doubt it.'' Lialla turned away and caught up her cloak. Her eyes met Jennifer's, rested a brief moment on Robyn. The thought was as clear as if she'd spoken, and Jennifer shook her head minutely; there was no way Robyn would be able to stay on her feet just now. Fear and some other emotion Jennifer couldn't fathom had her helpless. Lialla let her eyes close briefly, then pushed past the armsman to take hold of one of Robyn's elbows. The woman rose unresisting between her and Jennifer, her breath coming in little faint whimpers. ''Come,'' Lialla said loudly. ''Let's get this done with. One can only hope their master has the brains to see the stupidity of what they've done.''

Brave words, Jennifer thought, and schooled her face to indifference as they half-carried Robyn out between them, surrounded by armed men. She fought a shiver as they came into the street, fought an urge to let go of her sister's arm and run madly. The men hadn't drawn any weapons, but they were watching her very closely—waiting, she thought, for just such a reaction. She wouldn't give them the satisfaction of dragging her down the street, kicking and screaming. And Robyn needed her. God knew how Chris and Aletto would find them.

The horses were piled with their bags; they and their guard walked behind the horses, through a deserted market, down a welter of streets, alleys, narrow walkways, until she and Robyn both were completely lost. As they came into a vast open area, all hard-packed dirt, Lialla hissed, "Thukar's palace." One of the men shoved her so hard she momentarily lost her grip on Robyn, who staggered and in turn nearly fell.

"Keep silent," he ordered. Lialla glared at him, shut her mouth with a visible effort, and kept walking.

"What are they going to do to us?" Robyn gulped. Jennifer patted her shoulder and drew up a reassuring smile from somewhere. She didn't feel particularly confident, and Robyn didn't look reassured.

Three locked gates separated them from the outside world: one at each end of a long, damp stone tunnel, a courtyard with a third that led into the main building. The horses were left behind, the bags taken up by two of the armed men.

There was a vast, echoing hall, empty except for a fountain in its center, gloomy despite the openings to the outside. A series of painted arches beyond that. They were led beneath the arches, down a dark corridor, up stairs. Two—three floors. Perhaps four; Jennifer couldn't keep count. A heavy, iron-bound and barred door, then. One of the men undid the bars; the room beyond was very dark and smelled musty. The three women were shoved into it, their bags tossed in behind them, the door shut solidly, and a series of rattles and slams followed. The clatter of retreating boots.

"Was that all of them?" Jennifer asked. She sensed rather than saw the look Lialla cast her.

"You said *you* could still see Thread in daylight, you tell me!"

"How do you think I saw *them*—?" Jennifer began hotly. She stopped as Robyn sagged against her arm and sat hard on the floor, sobbing heavily. She knelt, wrapped both arms around her sister. "Shhh, Birdy, don't, pull yourself together, don't—Lialla, are there any windows, or candles, or lights, or *anything* in here? I don't think you need Thread to find that, do you?"

Silence. Then Lialla's feet scraping across the floor as she shuffled and felt her way to the nearest wall and along it. "I think—no, damn, that's the door—wait." More furtive noises, then the rustle of cloth, the scent of ancient dust, and a thin line of light. "Here—I think—that's got it." The room was flooded with daylight, blinding after even a few minutes in total dark. Jennifer looked over Robyn's head.

Lialla leaned across a deep windowsill flanked by thick gray curtains of some heavy fabric that were held back by wooden shutters; dust motes danced in the near level rays of morning

sun. It shone on a dull, filthy wooden floor. Lialla's footprints
showed clearly. Beyond those, two padded benches against the
opposite wall, a door leading into another room, as dark as theirs
had been. Nothing else. Lialla turned away from the window
and leaned back against the sill. The outer wall was at least two
feet thick.

"It's far enough down that you'd break your neck, if you
jumped."

"We knew that from the climb up," Jennifer said impatiently.

Lialla cast her a dark look, pushed away from the sill and
walked past the benches. "It's filthy enough to have been the
apartments of the Thukar's last wife; she died four years ago and
it can't have been used since. There's stuff all over the floors
and it's filthy. Gods, I hate dust, makes me sneeze." She did
sneeze, resoundingly, rubbed her nose on her sleeve and peered
through the doorway into the dark. "There must be a bedcham-
ber in here, maybe a privy. I'll see if I can't find more shutters."
She vanished into the room; swore loudly as something went
clattering across the floor. "Ow! Who'd leave—oh, damn!"
Something fell; moments later there was light, dimmer this time.
"We must be in one of the corner towers; I'm looking out toward
sunset from this side. I think I can see our inn from here."

"Robyn—Birdy, will you wait here for me?" Jennifer whispered. Robyn's fingers tightened on her forearm, and Robyn
shook her head fiercely. "Well then, get up, will you? Come on,
let's go look, get out of this hallway, all right?" But she froze
where she was as the outer door opened once again, and three
men came into the room.

They wore uniforms—the Thukar's housemen, Jennifer later
learned—and though none of them was visibly armed, they were
large and solid-looking enough. She had no urge to challenge
them—even when one of the three crossed to the pile that was
their goods, squatted down, and began emptying bags onto the
floor. A second went in search of Lialla and brought her back
with him, the third stood by the tantalizingly open door they'd
just come in by.

The searcher took knives, Chris's spare arrows. He seemed
puzzled by most of the items in Jennifer's and Robyn's bags, but
he asked no questions, made no comments, and took nothing
but the weapons. The third man held the door for the other two,
paused in the opening. "The Thukar asks you to dine with him
at midday—himself and his family. A discussion between those

of equal rank, he said to tell you.'' The door closed heavily, and
the three women heard the faint rattle of chain on the far side.

Jennifer got to her feet, tested the latch, tugged at the door.
Shook her head. ''No chance; it's solid. That leaves us a few
hours and the windows, doesn't it?'' The other two looked at
her blankly. ''Unless you're looking forward to this lunch,'' she
added flatly. Her eyes locked on Lialla's, challengingly. ''It's up
to you.''

Lialla glared back at her. ''I can't do anything; you know that.
I *told* you.''

''All right.'' Jennifer came back into the room and patted
Robyn's shoulder. Robyn still sat mid-floor, now gazing discon-
solately at the wild disarray all around her. ''Birdy, why don't
you get everything put back where it belongs, so we're ready to
get out of here if there's a chance?''

''All right,'' Robyn whispered. She cleared her throat and
spoke in English. ''You gonna kill me if I smoke?''

Jennifer let her eyes close, finally shook her head and replied
in the same language. ''You earned it, lady; you've been a real
trooper.''

Robyn fumbled through the tangle of things at her feet, finally
came up with her battered cigarette packet and matches. She
thinned her lips, finally broke one of the remaining two tubes in
half and lit the end. ''You don't know the half of it,'' she mumbled around a cloud of acrid smoke. ''I know that guy.'' She
glanced up as Lialla shifted her weight impatiently, and switched
to Rhadazi. ''I know the guy. The wizard. I can't remember
where right now. I will, something about the eyes— Look, Lialla,
you'd go crazy sorting out the words that don't translate, let me
work this in my own language first, will you?'' She pointed to
the door with the stub of cigarette, brought it back and drew on
it. ''God,'' she mumbled in English. ''What a helluva way to
quit smoking!'' She took another drag, pulled a hairpin out of
her bag and used it to grip the tiny remaining bit of burning
tobacco for one last puff.

''You know the Thukar's pet wizard?'' Lialla stared down at
her. ''He's supposed to be one of the Thukar's favorites, he's
called Snake—'' She stopped abruptly; Robyn was rocking back
and forth among the contents of her bag and laughing.

Jennifer eyed her dubiously and brought up a hand; Robyn
caught hold of it and shook her head. ''Don't—I'm all right, oh,
God, Snake! I can't believe it—'' She thought about it briefly,
and something set her laughing again. ''All right,'' she said in

Rhadazi. "I was right, I know him. Give me a minute, it's complex." She tugged on Jennifer's black breeks and brought her down into the rubble of their goods.

"All right. Snake," she shifted to English, and her cadence changed. It was, Jennifer realized after a moment's confusion, nearer the way Robyn had talked in the late sixties than the way she did now. "I used to, like, hang out at the Whiskey, remember it?"

"Club," Jennifer nodded.

"Yeah, right. Whenever I could cadge enough cash on Hollywood Boulevard, or when someone would take me. Saw a lot of really good groups there, too. And some you've never heard of, of course. Anyway, I can't remember exactly when it was—before the big earthquake, I think, but after Manson. I wasn't hitching rides on the Strip any more and I still lived close in. The Doors were way too big for the local clubs—maybe this was after Morrison bought it, I don't know, too much shit went down, too long ago, and I was pretty stoned most of the time. Whatever. There was this one group, called Blue Borealis, played funky stuff, cross between Kaleidoscope and Blues Connection—electric fiddle, all that. The kid on fiddle—Ray, I remember, because I had a terrible thing for him for the longest time—anyway, it was his group. They weren't going anywhere, though—too much like everyone else, and most of the guys spent too much time inside their heads instead of writing and playing.

"Then this guy comes along—tall, skinny, dark guy, really intense black eyes and this way of looking at people that a lot of the chickies really dug. Called himself Vincente de Balboa, and there were all these rumors about how he was half Mayan, or full-blooded Maya. Well, next thing you know, he's taken over Ray's group and now they're calling themselves Quetzal and he's El Serpente—and there's all this *really* weird shit they're doing now, strange sounds and these lyrics—" Robyn shook her head. "Wow. Myself, I was never so far gone on Morrison, but this guy was filling a gap for a lot of chickies—so to speak. Word was, though, he'd picked off most of the girls on the Strip. Buncha guys, too, supposedly liked everything that moved and wasn't picky about how he got it.

"So they cut an album, did really good with it—I mean, it comes out the guy's really plain old Vinnie Harris, he was working on a psych degree before he dropped out, his old man was filthy rich and a friend of the governor—Reagan, right? All that went around and no one even *cared*, that's how good these guys were. Anyway, his old man was a Central American anthropologist, so that's where he got names and stuff. And later I could see he'd obviously read all the Carlos Castaneda books, all his Mexican witchcraft stuff was too pat. Real weird stuff, not satanic but definitely dark. Not my kinda stuff—Central American myths and that are too damned violent—but it was going down big with other people.

"So Vinnie and Ray were coming down from Mulholland one night to join the rest of the guys, they were working on the second album—and poof! they just vanished." Robyn cocked her head to one side and watched Jennifer in silence for a moment. "And then, the cops and everybody, they're looking, right? And there's the bike, the Harley the guys were riding, it's parked on the side of the road, not a scratch on it, but it hadn't been there before. And no one saw either of those guys again." She shrugged. "Well, people did just take off back then. Some of us figured it was the guy's way of dropping out and going back to the straight world again but he had to make a production out of it. Odd about Ray, of course—anyway, it got talked about for a while, then something else took over. No big deal. And then he shows up here." She sighed. "There ain't no justice."

Jennifer let her head fall back, closed her eyes. "Vinnie Harris." She laughed faintly. "Yeah, I can see it. Poor geek."

"Wasn't much geeky about him on a stage," Robyn said soberly. "He had presence like you wouldn't believe. He wasn't a real sorcerer, of course. But he liked having people think he was—more of that Mexican witchcraft and Mayan religion jazz. Of course," she added thoughtfully, "you weren't a magician before, either. But—music?"

"Music," Jennifer agreed somberly. "Maybe it's a key to more than Thread. It's not important just now. Is he going to recognize you?"

"Doubt it. I only met him once, and he spent most of his time coming on to another chick. I got bored with him trying to play with my mind and let him know it. Besides, it's been twenty-something years." She considered this. "There really *ain't* no justice. He doesn't look it, does he?"

Jennifer shrugged. "He doesn't look any forty-odd, no. Maybe he's got a fountain of youth in his closet."

Robyn managed a weak smile. "Yeah, right." She sobered again. "Look, magic or not, he wasn't anyone to cross back then. He liked mind games and sex—I don't know in what order—and he really used to get pissed when things didn't go his way. He'd blow on stage, and I knew a couple chicks he blew on. Not a nice guy. And people like that don't change. You warn Miss High Horse there, I'm gonna get stuff put back where it belongs. And please—'' She caught Jennifer's hand as her sister got to her feet. ''*Please* don't get her screaming again, will you? You *know* I hate that!''

''That's so easy, of course,'' Jennifer retorted sourly. ''But I'll do what I can.''

14

⌘

IT was dark where the four crouched: dark and extremely dirty.
Aletto peered toward the faint line of light, shifted impatiently, subsided again as Dahven caught hold of his forearm.
He more sensed than saw his friend shake his head. He knew
Dahven's face was uncommonly grim; it had been since they'd
huddled along the side of the inn, just inside the passageway that
led to the stables, and watched the rest of their party being led
away. It had remained that way the entire time they followed
Edrith through a maze of narrow market alleys and narrower
paths.

It was a little lighter now, perhaps. Aletto stifled a sneeze
against his sleeve, pinched his nose until the urge subsided. They
were in what remained of an ancient mud-brick structure in the
very midst of the market: fallen roof timbers and crackly, ancient palms, woven branches and the rubble of brick returning
to its primary form. A faint breeze blew across the floor, stirring
dust that was definitely mud-flavored. Aletto sniffed hard, and
tensed as something snapped not far away. It was Vey, sliding
under what looked to be an impassable, tilted doorway and into
the open area. He and Edrith had led the other three here—they'd
practically had to threaten Aletto to get him to come, and then
nearly had to gag Chris to keep unwelcome attention off them.

Aletto had scrapes down his back, under his shirt and cloak,
from working his way into the small sanctuary, since he was not
limber enough to easily fit the opening. Inside, it was surprisingly large, considering the state of the outside; there was an
aged carpet or two for sitting, a pair of ancient and tattered
cushions, a little food. A large covered jug of cool water, a cup
tied to its cracked handle.

And now there was the least light; Vey had fixed the maximum shielding around a candle, but there was still enough flickering, yellow light to see faces, the nearest wall. "Keep your voices low, we can talk," he said. His own voice barely reached Aletto.

Dahven shifted. "I can't stay here much longer; Father becomes difficult when I'm not at morning table and tends to restrict my movements. And of course, I can learn where they are and what Father thinks he's up to."

"Selling them back to Jadek," Aletto hissed.

Dahven raised one eyebrow. "Well, of course *that*. But those weren't Father's personal men, those were Snake's. Anyone else, and I might say he'd merely been sent to bring them in for the old man, but with Snake—he has motives of his own, and at least one scheme going at all times." Dahven cast Chris a glance. "He's one of those said to be from your world, but not one I'd suggest you question about it." Chris merely nodded; he was afraid to use his voice, afraid they'd all see how frightened he was. His lips moved continuously as he whispered over and over what was becoming a litany: "Mom, it'll be all right, you hang on, I'll come get you, I swear I will. Mom—" He started as Dahven gripped his arm.

"We have to get them back," Aletto said. He didn't sound very hopeful; his shoulders had sagged and he was biting his lip, blinking furiously.

"Oh, we'll get them back," Dahven said flatly. "You know, I've never really wanted to succeed Father—such a horrid, *boring* life he leads!—but I do resent the way he's given Sikkre a reputation I'll find it hard to live down, once I do succeed him. There's such a thing as honor, after all." He considered this briefly, then shrugged. "It's growing late and I can't go directly back to my apartments from here, of course. Aletto, swear to me you won't act without me!" Aletto hesitated. Dahven caught him by both shoulders and gave him a hard shake. "Swear it!" Aletto nodded reluctantly. "Not good enough, tell me."

"I—all right. I swear I won't act without you."

"Good." Dahven let go of him. "I know I can trust your sworn word. You won't regret it. Chris—" He stood, looked down at the boy. Chris looked up at him, his face carefully blank. "We'll get her back for you. Whatever Father and his sorcerers think. Whatever Jadek thinks." Chris nodded once, abruptly, let his eyes drop to the candle. When he looked up again, Dahven and Vey were gone, and there was only the faintest of noises to tell which way they'd gone.

* * *

JENNIFER did what she could to condense Robyn's story and make sense out of it in Rhadazi for Lialla. Fortunately, Lialla had heard about this particular of the Thukar's wizards before, or she probably would have found the story harder to believe. She gazed over Jennifer's shoulder for some moments, watching Robyn restore the last of the food to one of the new bags, then looked out the window behind her. "Nearly midday. What do we do?"

Jennifer considered this briefly, then nodded. "Several things. But for a start, you'll have to trust me."

Lialla hesitated. "I—well, why not? My thought processes have been reduced to mush. All I could think of was to keep up the pretense—" She shook her head. "But they must know."

"Never mind," Jennifer said. "Just trust me." She turned away and went over to collect her leather bag from Robyn, beat the worst of the dust off one of the benches and sat down facing the sun. Lialla watched with puzzled curiosity as Jennifer broke out a brush and her makeup bag. She turned to grin at her companions briefly, then went back to applying liner and shadow. "One of the tricks of confidence—having to do with how good you feel about how you look. Robyn." She wiped her fingers on a tattered tissue and broke out blush and gloss. "Both of you, just let me talk, will you? No matter what, let me talk."

Lialla opened her mouth, closed it again as Robyn touched her forearm. "She went through a lot of years of training for this very sort of thing, Lialla."

"You're a negotiator? I thought you were a musician?"

"A better negotiator than I am a musician," Jennifer mumbled as she spread gloss over her lower lip and studied her reflection in the small mirror. "Or we'd better all hope so, hadn't we?"

She got her hair brushed out more or less the way it was supposed to look, the brush returned to her bag, the Initiate Wielder's blacks brushed and pulled neat before the three housemen came for them. Back down the stairs, but not all the way— this time they turned partway down and followed a long corridor that on its right side was lathe and vines for shade against a miserably hot sun, with dark openings or closed, heavy doors on the left. Around a corner, stairs mounting another tower like theirs. And then an open doorway into an exquisitely tiled room. Water spilled down the wall on both sides of the door, immediately cooling the air; water ran from the wall through a series of pipes and ducts, down and away from the door, into low-walled ponds that flanked a low table. The melodic sound of water falling on hard stone, on pottery pipes, on ceramic tile, was all around them. There was no other sound except their own feet and Robyn's discreet cough.

There were several persons around the table, but at first it was difficult to see them: Lighting was subdued and most of it daylight through latticework high on the walls. As they came nearer, the three men escorting them—guarding them—moved away and vanished into shadow beyond the left-hand pond. A man seated near the middle of the table rose to his feet and inclined his upper body, extending his hands to either side.

He was tall, slender except for the stomach that tugged at his light-colored shirt that he wore loose and unsashed over wide-legged britches of a slightly darker shade, a faint line of embroidered leaves running down the outside of one leg. The fabric might have been silk; it was undoubtedly expensive.

He was otherwise a very medium man: brown hair and eyes, skin not very dark but not pale—nothing to mark him as important save his taste in garb and his bearing. "Ladies," he said, and Robyn fought not to smile. His voice was reedy, thin and petulant-sounding—not at all what she'd expect of a ruler's. "Welcome to my household; eat and drink with me and my sons." He resumed his seat, indicated places for them across from him.

Dahven? Lialla didn't see him—only the twins; nearly impossible to tell apart, dark-haired and olive-skinned like their mother, black-eyed. Very much heavier than the last time she'd seen them. Not surprising, considering the way they were eating.

They look like chubby little baby tax attorneys, Jennifer thought irreverently. Or accountants. The kinds who didn't wear white socks with their suits or pocket protectors for their pens, but fit that classic niche every bit as well as their less classily clad brethren. Quite obviously, neither of these young men could be Dahven, even if they hadn't been mirror images of each other.

There was a cool soup waiting for the women, deep bowls but no spoons. Jennifer, watching Lialla pick hers up and use it like a cup, took a cautious sniff. Fruit. It had an odd but not entirely unpleasant taste. She met Robyn's eye, nodded briefly. Robyn eyed the bowl with misgivings, picked it up, and drank. The Thukar waited until they had finished and a servant had removed the crockery before he spoke again.

"It is a very great pleasure to welcome the sin-Duchess Lialla and her companions to my household," he said smoothly, "and to tell her that her uncle and her mother will be most glad to hear she is safe under these ceilings." There was a chill little silence. Lialla opened her mouth, shut it as Jennifer jabbed her, hard, in the hip.

"If I may suggest," Jennifer said, her voice as smooth as the Thukar's, "that I speak for all of us?" The man's eyebrows joined over his long and very thin nose. "It is our position that a—call it a mistake, shall we?—a mistake has been made. May I finish, please?" He stared across the table at her, rather glassily; Jennifer thought it unlikely anyone had interrupted him in such a fashion in all his life. Then again, she'd been polite about it, hadn't she?

It felt damned odd trying to conduct a settlement in Rhadazi.

"Also, I believe the Thukar is unlikely to prefer that three women speak at the same time," she finished, and sat back to await his reply.

He blinked at her, twice, fiddled with one of his numerous rings, finally grinned. "A—mistake."

"Her mistake," one of the twins mumbled around his food.

The Thukar shook his head. "No—this is not what I expected, let us hear her out, shall we?"

Treacherous, Jennifer thought. Even without everything Lialla and Aletto had told her about the man, she knew the type. So sharp he'd cut himself, given the chance—or meet himself coming and going. So long as he didn't cut *them,* she thought with a sudden nervous pang, and took a sip of the wine someone had just set by her elbow. "You think this woman is Lialla, the sin-Duchess of Zelharri, if I understand correctly. As I say, a mistake, but an honest one, given my companion's years and that she, like the sin-Duchess, is a Black-Sash Wielder."

"Say, rather," the Thukar said, with a rather unpleasant smile, "that we are quite willing to sell all three of you to the uncle of the sin-Duchess. Oh," he added as Jennifer would have spoken once more, "perhaps there is a chance in a thousand that she is who you say and who the innkeep at the Cap and Feather says: a Wielder from Red Hawk come early to Sikkre. Say the chance becomes less, considering one of her companions is a young man with the mark of marsh fever clearly on him—a young man who searches the night markets for word of a Zelharri Smith who *may* be named Gyrdan?" He paused; just as Jennifer opened her mouth and drew a deep breath, he smiled and went on. "Such coincidences; the fortune-tellers might dote upon them, but I find them difficult to believe in, don't you?'' He shrugged. ''All the same, it might be true—but I might still collect a sum from my neighbor for delivering all of you to his householdmen. Jadek is so tight with his coin, it would be a veritable pleasure to take his reward and then watch him fight for its return when he found the goods rendered not exactly what he wanted.''

Lialla reached under the table to grip her leg; her face remained expressionless and she was applying herself to bread and a poultry broth with the other hand. Robyn was visibly nervous, swallowing frequently. Jennifer hoped she wasn't about to be sick. She sopped up broth with her bread, caught Robyn's eye and nodded. No red meat in it. Robyn's face bore the sheen of sweat as she bent over her plate.

''Yes,'' Jennifer said finally, pleasantly. ''I can see your point. However, I would suggest you consider two things: If my companion is Red Hawk, if we are, then surely their goodwill is worth more than a tightfisted usurper's? And the same would certainly hold true if she is who *you* say she is? More, though. In either case, you may find us worth more in solid coin, now, than Jadek could offer.'' The Thukar considered this. As he began shaking his head, Jennifer let her fingernail ping against the winecup. ''No, think! A tightfisted man such as Jadek might have unsuspected ways of retrieving coin, if he finds himself cheated.''

''So might the nomads,'' the Thukar grumbled, but there was a faint light in the narrowed eyes now.

''They'd be harder to manage if they found their honor breached. They are not only allies, but they contribute great amounts of coin to the operations of your market, they bring in trade goods from outside, and take Sikkreni goods away. Is that not worth more than a single portion of coin from a man not even legally Duke? But there is another consideration,'' she added sweetly. ''You have only the three of us. Surely the Zelharrian would demand five, in return for his payment?''

''All five.'' The wizard Snake stood just behind the Thukar; Jennifer would have sworn she'd seen no sign of movement. The wizard looked down at her and smiled. ''We have all five; we found the others just a short while since, and brought them in.''

Robyn started to rise to her feet; Jennifer caught her elbow and held her down, and cast Lialla one sharp glare, a desperate thought she hoped the woman could somehow catch. *He's lying to us! Can't you see that? That's one of the oldest tricks—!* Robyn went limp under her grasp, buried her face in her hands.

Jennifer watched the wizard watch Robyn, and she didn't care
at all for the look on the man's face. Lialla drew herself up and
tipped her head back to eye the man down the full length of her
nose.

"Why should we believe you? Anyone can say anything! Let
me see them!"

Snake shook his head; a lazy smirk touched his face. "Not
just yet. One of the Thukar's men is questioning them." Jennifer
got a new grip on Robyn's arm; fortunately, Robyn didn't seem
to hear what he said.

"Lies," Lialla said flatly.

"He is the nera-Duke Aletto," the wizard said, as flatly.
"That, and your brother. Even if he had not told us so, the limp
would have given him away."

"Ah." Jennifer smiled. She sounded supremely unconcerned.
"And his companion—the name of the fifth person?" It gave
her a good deal of pleasure to see the faint uncertainty in the
man's eyes.

"He—he hadn't said when I left. An outlander—" Now it was
Lialla's turn to look uncertain, and her eyes were definitely
frightened. Jennifer felt her stomach drop, even as most of her
mind was assuring her the man was lying.

"You do not have possession of the nera-Duke," she said
evenly, and her voice sounded pleasant, belying her hard eyes.
"Or of the young man who is our companion. He twisted his
ankle at Hushar Oasis; we brought him with us as a protector
and to heal his injury." Silence. "Marsh-sickness is a dreadful
thing, but none of us have it." Another silence, this one rather
unpleasant. Thukar and wizard eyed each other, then turned as
one to gaze at their unwilling guests. But before either could
speak, Jennifer heard rapid footsteps behind her; Snake colored
noticeably and stepped back a pace.

The Thukar's eyes left her face for the first time in a long
time. The footsteps came close behind her, then went around,
skirting the far edge of the table. "Father, so sorry to be late,
it seems I overslept." She couldn't see him clearly yet, he was
still all shadow, but his voice was dryly, lightly sarcastic.

The Thukar's color was ruddier than it had been. "Overslept!" he snorted. "You were again not in your rooms this past
night! The heir has no business—!"

"Now, Father, I did oversleep, truly. Unfortunately, you have
caught me again, I fear; I was *not* in my rooms until quite late—

or early, if you prefer. But why not? I'm simply trying to learn my future holdings a street at a time.''

"And a woman at a time," someone mumbled—the twin nearest the approaching man. Jennifer could see him a little better now; a tall man with pale, wildly tousled hair and excellent shoulders under a shirt like the Thukar's. Unlike the Thukar's shirt, this one fit snugly against a flat stomach and was neatly tucked into bright blue breeks under an ornate sash.

Dahven—it could only be Dahven, Jennifer thought blankly—stopped to clap his brother resoundingly on the back. He laughed as the young man choked on his bread. "Well, dear Deehar, since no woman of Sikkre—none of them with taste, that is—would look at you or Dayher, *some*one certainly must take over the task. Think of it," he added tenderly, "that I remove an onerous burden from your—hmmm—*ample* shoulders, to let you concentrate on those things you love best. And since you aren't heir, who cares how many children you breed to back me for the succession?''

"Father," Dayher began in a plaintively high voice. Dahven laughed, silencing him, and dropped into the place next to—but not quite within reach of—Deehar, who glared at him, coughed one last time, and went back to his food.

"No, truly, I did oversleep; it's most unkind of you to make me out a liar before these young women. Am I to know who they are?''

"Fool," the wizard growled. Dahven ignored him.

"You know perfectly well who that woman is," the Thukar said peevishly and pointed at Lialla. *Easy to see where the twins got the whiny voice,* Jennifer thought. "That is your once-affianced.''

"Oh?" Dahven leaned forward and planted his elbows on the table so he could look down the table. Jennifer got her first good look at him.

She felt suddenly light-headed, too warm; she must be blushing, her cheekbones burned, he certainly would see her gawping at him like a teen-aged girl. But she couldn't move, could only watch him, dumbfounded, until he leaned back again and picked up his cup. She sat back herself then, heart thudding against her ribs, face afire and the blood bubbling in her veins.

Why? He wasn't that handsome; his mouth wasn't her idea of good, his cheeks were too hollow; she didn't even like blond men! And this—she'd never gone silly over a man at first sight before; had the Thukar drugged her food or wine? She couldn't tell; with Snake standing right there, she was afraid to probe Thread. She didn't *feel* particularly different, except for this— this strangeness. Stupid, she assured herself tartly. But she didn't dare look at him again, not when so much depended on what was left of her wildly scattered wits.

"It might be the sin-Duchess," Dahven said carelessly. Long-fingered hands deftly tore flat bread into strips, which he dipped into his winecup. His brother eyed him with disgust. "I haven't seen her in some time, and I confess I paid little attention to her at the time; she clearly did not want to marry me and life isn't long enough to waste on lost causes, is it? Really, Father, there are so many women who would meet such a description. But I'm curious, where did you find these women? Lialla never leaves Duke's Fort." The Thukar muttered something under his breath; Jennifer couldn't catch words but it sounded ominous. Dahven began tearing more bread into strips. "Well, I admit there are rumors all over the City; but I heard the nera-Duke was with her. If this is Lialla, I don't see my friend Aletto. I think I'd know *him*."

Before the Thukar could swallow, Robyn leaned forward. Her eyes were wet and her voice a mere whisper. "He says they took them, too. That they have them here, Aletto and—" Jennifer's hand tightened on her elbow; Robyn cast her sister a frightened, reproachful glance and bit her lip.

The wizard shifted his weight. Dahven laughed, interrupting whatever he was about to say. "What nonsense! Father, have you been letting your Lizard frighten these poor ladies? How very unkind of you—"

"Snake," the wizard gritted through clenched teeth.

"Of course, I'm so sorry," Dahven replied smoothly. "But they aren't here, of course; no prisoners have been brought here save you three." A doubled roar broke over whatever else he said. The Thukar was positively purple; the wizard's eyes glittered unpleasantly and his hands clenched as though he'd like a certain throat between them. Dahven came partway up onto his knees so he could look at his father over his startled brother's head. He looked quite hurt. "I—well! How was I to know you didn't want them told? But that isn't a nice way to treat ladies; how can you seriously expect I'd have known that was what you intended?" Another roar; the Thukar had fought free of surrounding cushions; Deehar ducked as a wineglass, still mostly full, sailed over his head. Dahven avoided it easily, then brushed at the few mauve drops on his shirt, apparently aware of nothing else. But he tilted his head up just the least bit, just enough to meet Jennifer's eyes, and let one of his lids droop shut. She could only stare back. There was nothing playful in that wink; there was a solemn intensity in his dark eyes that left her hands suddenly cold and her fingers trembling.

The Thukar roused her; he was swearing furiously, viciously, and in several different languages. Dahven stood, inclined his head, tentatively held out his hand; the Thukar slapped it away. "Father, your heart. Get the poor man another cup of wine, someone, and give him his special liquid, all this fuss isn't good for him. Deehar, Dayher, one would think that you long for the day I take his place, for all the care you take of our father. And Snake, you must know your future in Sikkre depends upon keeping the *present* Thukar in very good health indeed?" The smile was suddenly an extremely chill one; his eyes had gone hard. The wizard shifted his weight onto his toes, fists closed. There was a brief, tense silence. The wizard suddenly turned away.

"Someone get the Thukar's man, have him bring the Digitalis." Robyn jumped as the English word hit her. "And return these women to their rooms." He looked at each of the three in turn, black eyes brooding on them. Robyn wouldn't even look at him; Jennifer did, without expression—Lialla's eyes and the set of her jaw were challenging.

Dahven was nowhere in sight. The way back to the upper rooms was extremely hushed after the echoing scene in the family dining room.

DAHVEN had taken a shortcut—via halls created for the servants—to his rooms. He was high in an east-facing tower, one of seven. The height of the tower never kept him from coming and going, whatever his father's desires on the subject, though occasionally he had to wait longer than he wanted, and to take chances he'd rather not. But to tamely accept the old man's querulous and meaningless orders! "After all," Dahven murmured to his small reception hall as he barred the outer door and leaned momentarily against it, "it isn't as if he didn't have at least as much fun when *he* was a lad! Now he's beyond it, no one else must enjoy himself, apparently." He made a half-turn and sketched a mocking bow in what might have been the Thukar's direction, finished it with a very rude flipping of fingers past his smooth-shaven chin.

He crossed the room quickly, divesting himself of formal sash and the heir's ruby, tossed them in the direction of the bed—they

both missed by a wide margin—and leaned across the deep windowsill to study the wall and the courtyard below him. He twisted
around to pull himself up onto the sill, sat momentarily with his
back to the view, then gripped stone on both sides and leaned
back to gaze up. No sign of anyone there; and no one below
him in the courtyard at this hour—particularly in such unseason-
able heat—was bothering to look up. It took him a moment of
hard blinking, one brief release of his left hand on stable stone
to shade his eyes. No Vey, but the slender, tan rope was there,
dangling to his left. Not far. He braced both legs against the
sides of the sill and leaned, flailed himself back to upright, and
slid back into the room with a gusty sigh of relief. "Dear and
Beloved Hosath—and all the other sand gods, too!—I used to
climb that wall? Must have been mad!"

He laid the rope across the sill, secured it there with the heavy
cloak he'd worn the night before, and went back across the room
to find ink and pens, either a bit of paper or something else—
anything else!—to convey his message. Before Aletto lost what
little patience he could have left, and came out of hiding.

Fortunately his servants were more organized than he, Dahven
thought; the inlaid box that matched his table contained three
pens, recently pointed, ink that was still liquid—barely, anyway—
and there were two full sheets of thick cloth pulp paper and one
cut half-skin that someone had salvaged from a draft document.
He used that; easier to roll and tie, smaller and so less likely to
draw attention. And the pulp stuff was so expensive, even in the
market, that it made him nervous to set pen to it.

Too bad he'd never managed to get on with that outland wizard
of his father's, like the twins had. Both had wooden writing
sticks with the flexible ends for taking writing away. Snake's gift.
Yes, well; Dahven thought sourly. As well covet that paper Snake
had for music and the system for writing it down, *there* was a
thing to covet! The twins couldn't care less about such a trea-
sure, and Snake would never offer it to him. "Cannot think why
he doesn't like me better," Dahven said to the inlaid box, and
laughed aloud.

He sobered as he gazed at the thin parchment, considered,
began writing, and when he was done, rolled the skin into a thin
tube and eyed it critically. It wouldn't be much more visible than
the rope, though, and no one had noticed that. And it was the
heat of the afternoon. He crossed the room, wrapped the tube
in coils of rope, tied the end securely and tugged gently on the
end. Several moments—nerve-wracking moments indeed—

passed before he felt the answering tug, and then watched as the tube was jerked up through the open window, and on toward the flat roof some distance above his head. Vey had it now; Vey would find his way unseen from the Thukar's palace—as he often did—and would see that Aletto got the message.

Until sunset, then, Dahven had little to do except think. He dropped onto his bed, stretched out on his back, and stared up at the ornately patterned ceiling. Think. He wasn't certain he wanted to think, knowing what—who, actually—he would think about.

After so many women over so many years, how was it possible this astonishing, glorious outlander should so capture his heart?

VEY crossed the tower roof and two narrow ledges, dropped down a long, thin incline of crumbling brickwork, crossed two more flat roofs and entered a hole broken in the next: There were old rooms here, rooms built by the Thukar's many-times great-grandsire, when the market was new and small, and if tales were true, all colored tents grouped around the blue well near Genhali's cloth shop. No one used these rooms now; they were pulled down a wall or a room at a time, when brick became necessary elsewhere, or when walls or timbers grew dangerously old and unstable. He hurried through a long corridor, out a window and down a leafless vine that grew long spines in summer. Just now it was sticky and prickled a little in places, nothing more. He rubbed his hands in dust when he reached the ground, to counter the sap, skirted the base of the deserted hall. There was a tunnel, its inner opening lost under mounds of rubble. Like the hiding place where Aletto now paced and fretted, the opening was hard to find, narrow; the inner area was opened out and shored up, the tunnel a sudden drop into utter blackness. Vey counted fifteen steps down, seventy-nine paces on packed, damp sand. This came out into the city's underground water cisterns, or would, if he went left. At eighty paces, his hand groped air; he turned to the right and began counting again. Seventy-nine paces; another turn, this time to the left; there was dust underfoot now, and then, ten paces on, a little gray light and steps leading up.

The escape end of the palace tunnel had originally come out inside the curtain wall surrounding the palace. That original wall had fallen long since, little of it remaining save here and there, including the mound of rubble certain nearby merchants had planted in small citrus bushes and trees. They and their shade

neatly masked the sod-covered block of stone that covered the
stairs, and the nearest merchant owed Edrith certain favors. He
paid absolutely no attention as Vey slid from shadow to shadow,
past the fruit-piled counter, and into the dark shop and living
space behind.

The rest of his journey was uneventful; no one had seen him
or followed him. Vey took two more detours to make certain,
then cut back across the market and pressed himself between
fallen stones, back through the narrow tunnel, into the open
area. He was there before Aletto saw him—almost, Vey realized
smugly, before Edrith did. He put the thin tube of hide in Aletto's hands and turned away. "I'd like water," he said to Edrith.
"It was hot work, waiting on that roof."

Chris was hanging over Aletto's shoulder, scowling at Dahven's message. He couldn't read it; apparently Merrida hadn't
thought of reading when she gave them the language. Another
one he owed her, that. "Read it aloud," he said.

" 'Aletto, all three women safe for now, let Vey bring you to
the palace at first dark, I think I have a way to get them out.
Remember your word.' " Aletto stared at the writing, shook his
head. "He *thinks* he does? That's the best he can do?"

"Better than what we had five minutes ago," Chris urged.
"Go on, that can't be all of it."

"No, there's more. Get Edrith or Vey to purchase a blurring-
stone before then." Aletto's lip curled. "Magic!"

"Magic?" Chris echoed blankly.

"Blurring-stone," Edrith said helpfully. "It's a charm, keeps
people from noticing you're where you are."

Chris scowled at his hands. Funny: Once he would have been
thrilled at the very thought of such casual use of magic. Now all
he could think was, How good was it? "Invisibility?"

Edrith shook his head. "Don't I wish they'd sell a charm for
that! I'd be rich tomorrow!" He laughed. "The look on your
face, boy!"

"That's dishonest," Chris growled.

Edrith laughed again. "Of course it is! Merely dishonest, it's
not murder." Chris waved a hand, shook his head and turned
away in disgust. "A blurring-stone just makes you hard to see.
Better than nothing." He looked around the ruin of fallen stone,
crumbling brick and wood that housed them. "They're hard to
find, too—very few places sell blurring-stones. Vey, we'd better
both go." He held up a hand for silence as Aletto crushed the
message in one fist and opened his mouth to argue. "You stay

here; you're a little too obvious, particularly in daylight. Besides, you promised Dahven, I heard you. You stay with him,''
he said to Chris.

Chris glared at him. ''I wouldn't go out with you two; we
could all wind up in one of those boxes, and who'd get us out
then?'' He glowered at the dust in front of his feet, on his grubby
high-tops. ''God, I don't believe this. Bring something to eat,
will you? I'm starved.''

15

꒩

JENNIFER moved across to the nearest window as soon as she heard the door bolt slide into place behind them. She leaned out across the sill, looked down. Shook her head. "It's a long way down there. Lialla, isn't there anything we can do?" And as Lialla made an impatient, wordless sound, she added testily, "After it gets dark, all right, I understand that! Can we *do* anything? Anything at all?"

"Not to the door; at least, I don't think so. I could bolt my door at home from the other side, but I had to set that from inside, before I went through it. The window, though . . ." She contemplated it, finally shrugged. "It's a matter of how badly you want out, and whether the thought of hanging your feet over all that space makes you ill. I don't like any of that very much; I can do it if there isn't any other way. Just now, I don't see one." Momentary silence. "Besides, there was Dahven."

"Dahven." Hard, even getting his name out, and Jennifer could feel the blood in her face. She turned to look out the window.

"You couldn't have seen it, I don't think. He—somehow, he knows Wielder hand sign. He passed me a message before he sat down: Second hour dark, grove. Blur. Rescue."

"Rescue?" Robyn's voice rose to a squeak.

Lialla shrugged. "We're doing most of our own rescue, the way I see it, if I understood him correctly. Being Dahven, he might have simply been moving his hands, not knowing what he—no, that can't be right. But we have to get down to the grove—one of those groves of trees out there!—at or about second knell after sunset. Then he—or they, his signing is *not* very clear—he'll come get us out of the palace grounds, and to safety.''

"God," Robyn whispered. "Out *that* window?" Lialla nodded reluctantly. "I hate heights. But if I have to—" Robyn was pale, her eyes closed, but her jaw was set. "Just get me out of here, will you? Get us down to that grove. I don't care what it takes to do that.''

"I really don't care," Jennifer said. "Height doesn't bother me."

Lialla nodded. "Good. One of us should have enough nerve left to take charge, then. So let me explain to you about Thread and rope. And about using Thread to make your presence less obvious." She glanced at Robyn. "Why don't you see what you can find in that bedroom? We'll need—oh, I don't know. String, straw, ties from the bedding, old cloth that will tear into strips— anything like that. It doesn't have to be in good shape, or strong, it doesn't have to be very thick. It's just to reinforce Thread." Robyn pushed herself heavily to her feet, poked briefly around the entry room, tested the curtains, sneezed at the cloud of resulting dust. She backed away, went on into the next room. Something solid hit the floor, followed by the sound of cloth tearing.

"I hope you're right about the condition of the reinforcement," Jennifer said mildly. "Whatever she's got sounds utterly rotten."

"Rope." Lialla managed to pull her scattered wits back to the moment. "You braid Thread with something real, how much or how little depends upon your skill, but the resulting rope is as strong as Lasanachi rigging rope, or so I'm told. I know it will hold to get us out of here and down to the ground.''

"That's enough," Jennifer said. "Braid? Just—like hair?"

"Like hair. Three-strand—four if you're using it for a longer time, three-strand won't hold above a couple hours. Five, according to legend, can only be made by a White or Silver Sash. That, they say, stays woven until it's unmade, deliberately." She sighed faintly. "I can't show you the Thread yet; I'll do that later. It's twisted, easy to find and use. *I* can do it, after all," she added bitterly. "Even under pressure."

Jennifer folded her arms and leaned back against the wall. "I simply don't understand you. Why are you doing this to yourself?''

"Doing what?" Lialla demanded.

"Fighting so hard for something that eludes you. Look, I can

understand wanting something badly; I wanted music that way
for *years*. But I compromised, I kept the music to myself and
went in another direction to earn my keep. Why can't you do
that?''

"Do what?''

"I—hell, I don't know! Compromise! Find another kind of
magic, something that isn't so hard on you! Or a better teacher!
Or something else entirely, there must be something else you
like or want, or—''

"What business is that of yours?'' Lialla snapped. Her eyes
were black and narrowed.

"I'd say none,'' Jennifer replied evenly. "Except that I think
you can be a pretty enjoyable person to be around; I've seen a
little of that when you aren't so knotted up over your damned
Threads. It's got to be hard on everyone around you; did you
ever think of that?'' She paused. Lialla just looked at her. "And
it's eating you alive. Why do you have to be the best ever? To
prove something to yourself, or to Merrida, or your uncle?''

Another silence. Lialla bared her teeth. "How dare you say
such things?'' She wrapped her arms across her ribs and held
onto herself; she wouldn't give this outland woman the pleasure
of seeing her tremble! But somehow, it was just as though Jennifer had read all her uncertainties of the past days and put them
into words, as though she'd deliberately found the pain and
pressed as hard as she could. "You have no right!''

"Oh, yes, I do! Because every time I try to get information
out of you, we wind up fighting. I hate these shouting matches,
Lialla. They aren't productive, they waste time, and they upset
my sister.'' Lialla glared at her; Jennifer shifted her shoulders
against the hard stone wall. "Look, how many times do I have
to say this? It wasn't my idea to come here! It was *not* my idea
to have this magic; we can wring Merrida's neck together when
this is all over, if you like! And I'm *sorry* it bothers you so
damned much that I can use the wretched stuff!'' She straightened up; Lialla's breath went in on a hiss. "That's the real problem, isn't it? That I just came in and picked it up, like it was
natural? That you still fight it, and I haven't had to do that yet?''

"It's not—!'' Lialla's voice went up a notch; Jennifer sighed
inwardly and strove to keep her own voice reasonable.

"Look, I don't know. Maybe that's the answer; have you
thought of that? Maybe if *you* try what I'm doing, just go at it
a different way, see what works, put your preconceptions and
Merrida's out of mind, quit saying it doesn't or you can't.''

"You can't—!"

"Or," Jennifer overrode her loudly, "why not supplement what skill you have? You keep telling me there is so much different magic; it's not like saying you should incorporate Hell-Light with Night-Thread Magic! Maybe—maybe flesh out your talent with some neutral magic! Use charms, you might not have to forever! There can't be anything wrong with that, can there?"

"Charms?" Lialla laughed breathily. *"Charms?"* Her voice went up another notch. "How do you think I got us out of Duke's Fort in the first place?" Her laugh gained in volume and trembled on the edge of hysteria. "But after you came! Oh, no, I couldn't use them then, could I? A year short of my first Color and here Merrida sends me a novice, an Initiate all my own! My first big chance to show how great a Wielder I am; a great Wielder would *never* stoop to supplementing Thread, would she? And *you* didn't need charms and neutral magic; how could I think I was better than you if I used them? I never even *saw* the Host out there on the trail, or those men at the Cap and Feather, I *told* you out there it was all my fault, and you wouldn't listen! I guess you don't know everything after all, do you?"

She was practically screaming. "Stop that," Jennifer said, her voice cutting through Lialla's with hard authority. Lialla shook her head and tears flew. Hysteria. Jennifer reluctantly grabbed for her shoulders.

Lialla flinched away from her, averted her face sharply. Jennifer snatched her hands back. Lialla looked at her, face drained of color and eyes all black pupil; she spun around abruptly and ran into the next room.

Jennifer stood still, uncertain what to do next. "God," she whispered. "Her uncle! Why didn't I see it before, it was all there—!" But even if she'd realized, what good would that knowledge have done either of them, besides serving as a reminder to Jennifer to keep her hands off Lialla? "She thought I was going to hit her, going to hurt her—" It made her faintly ill. She turned away and planted her elbows on the windowsill so she could gaze out across city and the desert beyond it.

There was nothing she could say, this was Aletto's handicap and worse—a hands-off situation. And she had never known what to say to Robyn, even after Robyn's old man put her in County General. Robyn had never welcomed any intrusion into that part of her life. The way Lialla felt about Jennifer, she'd want it even less. Jennifer let her head fall forward and drove her hands through her hair. "I can't handle this. Damn. Why do people have to be so damn complex?"

LIALLA leaned her forehead against cool stone near the west window and closed her eyes. A faint sound brought her around; she'd forgotten about Robyn, who sat on the floor next to the bed, a ruined mattress cover rapidly becoming a pile of grayish cloth strips, a pile of musty-smelling straw that had been mattress behind her.

Robyn cleared her throat again, tentatively. Lialla turned away and let her forehead rest on the stones again. They were cool, smoothed and felt pleasant at the moment. "Lialla," Robyn said quietly. "It was your stepfather. Wasn't it?"

"What was?" Her voice sounded rusty.

"Aletto told me a little about him, you know. When we were riding together, out in the desert that first night."

"Told you—what?"

"Not much. He never came out and said Jadek hit either of you. I didn't know that until just now. I understand—"

Lialla shook her head, rubbing skin against stone. "No. You can't."

"I can. Your stepfather isn't the only man like that. They aren't nearly rare enough—men who hit people who can't or won't hit them back." Lialla turned her head just enough to look at Robyn in disbelief. Robyn nodded. "I've been there, Lialla. That's how I know. The little your brother told me—about Jadek. How he always managed to sound like he really loved you, except the way he said things left you feeling like you weren't worth it." Silence. It somehow wasn't an uncomfortable silence. "I know that kind of man," Robyn continued; her voice was soft, soothing. "I was wed to one, I lived with another. They—after a while, you know you can't do anything, that you aren't good enough, or pretty or clever enough. Some of them come right out and tell you how stupid you are, how worthless, but they all make certain you know it."

"Jadek never really—" Lialla bit her lip, shook her head. Robyn waited, and when Lialla shook her head again, went on.

"No, he's one of the other ones, isn't he? I think they're worse, myself. Because you can't lay a finger on it, they never say anything right out, so you can't tell yourself, 'It's not me, it's him.' But after a while, there isn't enough brain left in you to do that." She fell silent; there was a sound of ripping cloth as she went back to tearing mattress cover into strips. She focused her gaze on the work, as though it was the only thing important, but she was watching the window out of the corner of her eye, too. "He hit you, too, didn't he?" Lialla opened her mouth twice; sound wouldn't move past her tight throat. She nodded once, abruptly. "All right, don't. I won't push you. But if it helps you to know, I had one of those, too. Unlike you, I didn't get mine when my mother married him; I chose him myself. I don't know if that makes it worse, I can't compare. It's bad enough, however it happens."

"He—" Lialla shook her head, swallowed. Robyn was somehow on her feet, near enough that Lialla could smell the tobacco smoke that clung to her clothes.

"Don't." Robyn touched her shoulder. "Don't try to talk about it if you don't want to. I understand that, too. But remember this: You're away from him now, you don't have to hear that ever again. He won't hit you again. Or Aletto." There was grim promise in her voice at the end. Lialla blinked and looked at her through wet lashes. "No, he didn't say. I told you, I know what it's like, I could see it. He won't learn from me that I know. Remember something else, too: If you ever want to talk about it, I'm here, all right? I've been there, and I'll listen. There isn't anything you can say to shock me, I know what it's like." Lialla nodded. Robyn touched her arm again and turned back to her pile. "I think I have most of this done; is it safe to just leave it here?"

Lialla shook her head. "Covering—was there once a blanket or anything over the mattress? I don't remember." It was hard to talk, but not as hard as it had been. She looked up as movement in the other room caught her eye. "Jennifer—I'm sorry. It's—"

Jennifer came into the room, sliding sideways through the doorway, their bags an enormous burden between her arms. "Let's not worry about it right now, we can talk about anything once we're out of here. No emotionally charged subjects for the rest of the day, if no one minds."

"I don't mind," Lialla whispered.

"Good." Jennifer cast her a faint smile. "So the only acceptable topic is Out, and its major parts How and When." She dumped the bags on the floor. "Here, pile the stuff back on the mattress and strew these over everything, that should camouflage pretty well." She dropped onto the edge of the bed and looked up. "Lialla, you said the Thukar has no Wielder. Is it likely any of his magicians understand Wielding? I ask because of this," she added hastily, indicating the pile of cloth strips and straw with a wave of her hand. "Is it going to be immediately apparent we're making rope once we start? Or even that we intend to make it later? Is there a way for one Wielder to read another's mind—whether the second wants it or not?"

"I—" Lialla managed the faintest of smiles, more a peace offering than anything else. "I don't know. I doubt anyone in this palace understands Wielding, not if they aren't Wielders. Wielders don't ordinarily spread their knowledge about. It's rare that a Wielder will go on," she added with an even fainter shrug, "to another form of magic, once he's been a Wielder. Or that someone who isn't attuned to Thread *as* a Wielder could utilize it—I don't believe it would be that simple to see someone making rope anyway, unless you were doing nothing but watching that person closely. We're already imprisoned, so why would they?"

"The Thukar has a lot of kinds of magicians," Jennifer said doubtfully. "Using Thread doesn't touch off another kind of magic?"

"The questions you ask! I've never heard of it. I guess that doesn't mean much. Charms—perhaps. Again, I think they would have to be watching us closely, through that charm, doing nothing else. Unless the Thukar or one of his magicians thought I might somehow contact Aletto using Thread—but he's never made any attempt to learn any form of magic, and I think his aversion to it is fairly well known. The Thukar must know, because Dahven does."

"So, chances are we're reasonable safe—but we work as quickly as we can, as soon as we can." Jennifer considered the view she'd had of the courtyard below the window and the Thread itself: Even if she'd wanted to chance another of Lialla's fits of hysteria by trying to Wield during the day, she couldn't be a hundred percent certain the result of daytime Wielding would be the same. She couldn't chance anything less than total certainty. Besides, there were men below, horses—guards on the walls, walking the stones. They'd be seen as soon as they touched ground, if not sooner.

And there were trees, small, tight groves of them, within fifty feet of the base of their tower. They would be pools of deep shadow after nightfall. She considered that and felt a certain degree of relief. After dark, it would not be as easy to *see* ground from the tower window. Jennifer did not like heights at all when they were man-made ones. She twisted around so she could look out the west-facing window. "How many more hours until dark?"

"Too many," Robyn replied gloomily. She studied the pile of stuff at her feet and wrinkled her nose. "Is this enough? The material is hard to rip and the straw is making my nose run."

THE thick stub of candle was burning down, flickering occasionally. Chris sat on a frayed, ancient and dusty rug, knees drawn up to his chin, and scowled at it. Edrith and Vey had gone out what seemed hours before and Aletto was no decent company at all. He mumbled to himself and seemed unaware there was anyone else in this miserable hole. Chris's scowl deepened as his stomach snarled at him.

He heard the footsteps only a moment before he smelled that smoky, incenselike odor that he identified with Edrith. A long hand reached over his shoulder to dangle a cloth bag close to his nose. Chris caught it as Edrith let go the strings. "All yours," the thief assured him. "I brought another for the rest of us, and Vey is arranging both food for tonight and transport from Sikkre."

Aletto came around at that; his face was drawn and his jaw set. "I'm not leaving—"

"Transport for *everyone*," Edrith overrode him somehow without even raising his voice. "We're retrieving your missing women after dark, remember?" He opened a second bag, pulled out bread and tore it in half, stuffing one piece in Aletto's unwilling fingers. "Eat, or I'll sit on you and force it down. You can't help your sister or anyone else if you're light-headed, and you'll call down the Thukar's guard if your belly's howling." He ripped a piece from his bread, stuffed it in one cheek and squatted down to pull other things from the bag—a wide-mouthed pot with a heavy wax seal; a tall, corked jug that smelled of sweet red wine, even closed. Aletto's nostrils quivered; he closed his eyes and waved the wine bottle aside. He concentrated on opening the pot, dipped his bread in the contents and chewed. "It's two hours until sunset," Edrith went on around his mouthful. He tore off another bite and dipped it in the pot. "There's another of these in your bag, Chris; it's a meat broth."

"Let me try it, first," Chris rather gingerly tested the stuff: The meat could have been anything, its flavor was so buried in an eye-watering chili powder. "Wow," he gasped, and went digging in his own bag. There was water and wine both; the bread did a better job of putting out the fire, though. His own pot of stuff wasn't quite as fiercely hot, and he was only certain the meat wasn't beef. Possibly sheep?

"All right?" Edrith inquired.

Chris nodded. "Mom wouldn't eat it, she only eats chicken and fish. I'm not nearly as hard to please, especially when I'm hungry. Long as it goes down, fills the hole and stays put is all I care about." Edrith laughed. Chris looked at the bread, at Edrith. "Damn. I suppose you paid for this?"

Edrith clapped him on the shoulder. "You know, I like you despite myself! I've never heard outlanders were so narrow in their interpretations of ownership—particularly hungry ones!"

Chris glared at him. "All right, big joke, really funny. I don't usually make it so easy for people but you looked like you needed a laugh. I just—" He looked at the bread, back at the still smiling but obviously puzzled Edrith. "I'm sorry, I just never could see it. It's dishonest."

"It also feeds some people who wouldn't otherwise eat," Edrith said lightly.

"Oh, right. Look, I know the arguments, okay? You think I haven't heard them from my friends and kids in school and even the guys running *our* country? It's still stealing and it's still wrong! How about the people you take from? How about maybe what you took was the difference between their family eating and not eating?"

Edrith shook his head; the smile was gone but he didn't look unfriendly. "I don't take from people as poor as myself. Or anywhere near as poor. That *would* be dishonest." He tore more bread from his portion and dipped it in the pot he and Aletto shared. "Eat. If I took food merely to have it wasted, that is also wrong, isn't it?"

Chris rolled his eyes, but obediently went back to his meal.

THE setting sun was an uncomfortable presence in the tower bedroom, level rays coming across the city and over the sill, making the room stuffily hot, making it impossible to see anything for the glare of sun on floating dust. The women moved back into the entry alcove.

"Not long now," Lialla murmured as she stretched out on one of the benches and brought up her knees so she could flatten her spine out on the hard surface. It was the first thing she'd said in hours. Jennifer nodded absently. She was rubbing lotion into the backs of her chapped knuckles. She eyed the bottle with resignation—it was nearly empty—and returned it to her leather bag, pulled the zipper closed with finality. She was dithering, out of nerves and boredom in equal mixture; she hated women who played with their purses when they were bored.

Robyn was running a brush through her hair, a rubber band and four bobby pins clenched between her lips. Lialla absently watched as she pulled the golden stuff over one shoulder to braid it, flipped the colored band around the end and crossed the pins over the loose ends above her ears. She looked younger with it off her face; her eyes were too wide and frightened. She swallowed. "Um. This thing, this rope-thing. It's safe, right?"

"Won't unravel," Lialla assured her firmly. "I'll go first, to prove it." Robyn looked only partly assured. But she turned then, held up a hand.

"Someone's coming."

"No, they're not," Lialla began, but then she could hear it too: boots, at least two sets of them. And men's voices. She sat up, glanced anxiously toward the doorway leading into the bedroom, at the destroyed mattress and its piled bags and parcels. At Jennifer's hissed warning, she brought her eyes back to the door. The bar clattered, wood against wood, a scrape of metal. Jennifer stood as the wizard Snake came into the room. The man behind him, one of those who'd been at the inn, stepped back into the hall at the wizard's gesture and pulled the door closed. He didn't look particularly pleased about it, Jennifer thought. She doubted this Vinnie-person would be very pleased himself, if he knew his man didn't think him safe in a locked tower with "merely" three women.

He leaned back against the door, crossed one booted ankle over the other and folded his arms across his chest. Metal glimmered down his sleeves—tiny silver buttons running all the way from shoulder to cuffs—and there were a few discreet gems on the high collar.

Silence, a long one: He was clearly trying to score some sort of point by making them speak first. But Robyn was too nervous to trust her voice, and Jennifer was serenely confident she could outwait him. His stance was slightly off-balance, she thought with amusement. But by his measure, he'd lose points if he moved, or if he let them see him wobble. Lialla leaned back against the bench and managed to somehow make herself scarcely noticed. But then, Snake's full attention was directed toward the outlanders. And, after the first moment, when he cast Jennifer a confident grin, he focused his intense gaze on Robyn. "You know, you look so damned familiar," he began easily, and in English. Robyn started, looked up at him and back down at the floor. She shook her head. "No, really. It could be just, like, the hair, the no makeup. You're not local, either one of you, I knew that right away. Not only that, you're American—they always used to say you could tell, wherever you were. Guess so, huh?" Silence. "That's not it, though. Blonde—there was this little blonde, spent a week with me up in Santa Barbara—"

"I've never been to Santa Barbara," Robyn said softly.

"Right. Tell you what it is, chickie baby. You used to hang out on the Strip back when it was happening, din'cha?" Robyn cast a desperate sideways glance at Jennifer, who shrugged minutely. She didn't know what to do either.

Robyn brought her chin up finally, tilted her head thoughtfully to one side. "Maybe," she said finally. "Maybe I did. So? There were a lot of people hung out on the Strip—Sunset Strip, right? Lot of people in a lot of places. America's a big country, remember?"

"Don't try mind games, babe. Not with me. So, maybe it was the Haight instead, huh? Maybe we got stoned together someplace?"

"I doubt it." There was a little color in her face, a little challenge in her voice. "Why?"

"Wait." He finally shifted his feet when it seemed to Jennifer he must fall over if he didn't move. "Naw, it wasn't the Bay, you don't have the look. Besides, I didn't do much Frisco." He snapped his fingers. "Spent most of my time out on the west end by Doheney—and yeah, right. You were one of the chickies from the Whiskey, wasn't it?"

"Come on," Robyn protested. "It's years since all that. You remember all the people you ever saw, let alone the ones you knew, from way back then? I sure don't."

"Cool it, I'm thinking—right. It throws me, it's the time thing, runs funny here. Little skinny blonde chickie, real head, used to wear a thing in your hair with beads and a couple peacock feathers?" Robyn stared at him, then shook her head. He laughed. "Right, I got you now, it was those feathers. And you were always right up there by the stage, used to come drool over funky little Ray and that damned squawky fiddle of his, right?"

"You're out of it, man," Robyn said flatly. "All those years, you don't remember all that suff."

"Only five years since *I* left," he said. "And I remember the broads that turned me down, you know?"

"What," Robyn asked with heavy sarcasm, "all both of us? Come on, Vinnie-babe, you weren't *that* cool!"

Jennifer blinked to try to pull herself out of this oddly synched conversation. Lialla, of course, wasn't following any of it, except perhaps by the tone of voice. Jennifer caught her eye, cast a swift glance toward the west window; the sun had left the window except for the uppermost corner of the recessed sill, and the sky was a dusky purply blue.

She turned back to watch the wizard; he hadn't moved but he looked considerably less casually relaxed—and would-be more satisfied—than he had. He nodded. "Right, I knew it!" But he seemed at a loss for something else to say.

Robyn watched him in silence for some moments. "Where is Ray?" she asked finally. He shrugged.

"Who knows? Didn't stay with me, but we didn't like each other much. Could be dead, for all I know; this Rhadaz is a rough place, chickie." He scratched his neck thoughtfully, looked at his fingernails. "You know, like, maybe you could use a little protection."

"Got all I need," Robyn said flatly.

"Oh, right! Me, too," he chuckled. "You mean the young Duke with the game leg or that kid that's with you? You balling 'em young these days, or is he yours?" He straightened abruptly, pushing himself away from the door with a twist of his shoulders. The air around him went briefly very dark indeed, coalesced in shifting patterns about his hair. "Protection, babe. A gimp and a green kid and a couple snotty broads ain't gonna keep the sky from falling on ya. I got pulled through by one of the Thukar's best wizards. I can protect you from everything but a full Triad."

"Thanks, no," Robyn said. She edged back though, scooting on her backside. The wizard chuckled. "That's a nice light show," she added politely. "You could really clean up back home with that kind of act."

He turned his head and spat. "That was all such bullshit, all of it. All the good shit's illegal, the people in power are pigs, guys like me don't stand a chance." He grinned at her unpleasantly, cast Jennifer a black, warning glance as she shifted her own weight. "Pigs like you, lady. Arrogant ball-busting broads in fancy clothes, talking big words, swaggering around like you think you're tough, pushing guys like me around. You wish, lady, not here. Not a chance. You sit down over there next to the Duchess, got it? You don't even think about moving, not until I say it's all right, you got me?'' The air between them crackled with tension. Jennifer finally moved, before he could. Let him finish his ranting, she only wanted him *out* of this room, gone so they could go themselves! In the meantime, she was right where she wanted to be, next to Lialla and out of direct sight-line. Lialla looked at her sidelong, cast a cautious glance in the direction of the window and the fading light beyond it. Her hand moved, touched Jennifer's leg, and as Snake turned away from them, her lips moved, shaping the words: ''Get ready!''

Robyn broke a long silence. ''Look, Vinnie, I can't see where we have a lot to talk about,'' she said carefully. ''I don't plan on staying here, anyway. And you and I never did have anything to share, that I remember.''

''Don't jump to conclusions, babe. The Thukar's gonna send you home all right. With *her* and her brother. And Jadek'll off the lot of you, you got that?''

''He may decide not to.''

''Guess you haven't met him yet.'' He grinned. ''He's not a nice dude, not like me. Guess you'll see, though, babe. Last chance, all right?'' Robyn shook her head. ''Well, if you're gonna be like that.'' He took hold of her arm and brought her to her feet. Jennifer's muscles tensed; she forced herself to remain where she was as Lialla tugged at her sash; her eyes were wide, full of warning. ''So, how about one for the road? You and I never did get it together before.'' Robyn looked at him blankly. ''Look, you're gonna find it's not easy for a chick here, you can't just go cruisin' around and find something pretty to ball. Myself, I can have what I want, but the local broads just don't smell and act right.''

Robyn managed a faint smile. ''Thanks all the same, I'd really rather not.''

''I wasn't *asking*,'' he overrode her sharply. ''Look, chickie baby, we can do this two ways, my way or the hard way, got that? Nothing against us having a little fun, the local girls don't do me, and what's my odds of finding another sixties free spirit, huh?''

''Nothing, except I'd rather not,'' Robyn said firmly.

His grip on her arm tightened. ''You know, you had a nasty tongue back then, too! All right, you want a different set of rules, huh? That it, huh?'' He was leaning over her now; his voice had gone up a notch and the hand that gripped her arm trembled. Obviously not pleased with rejection, Jennifer thought, however nicely phrased. "Maybe I just get the guy outside the door to carry you off; he ain't gonna care what *you* say. Or maybe I should just find a decent pry bar, huh? That what you want, a better reason to say yes? Don't want *them* to think you're loose, that it? That kid of yours, the little square with the basketball sneakers and the weirdo hair?"

"What about him?" Robyn said faintly.

"Right, we'll get him up here, too, then you and I can talk some more, huh? Or not talk, maybe, you get me?"

"You don't have him—!"

"Bull*shit* I don't! All I gotta do is pound on the door; that dude I left outside knows right where to go. Come on, baby," he murmured against her hair, "let's have some fun."

Stop him—Jennifer was halfway to her feet. She hesitated, but Snake had forgotten them both—everything, apparently, but the trembling Robyn. The room was noticeably darker, Thread ready to her fingers, but she stopped short of touching it. Which? Thread vibrated all around her, the room tilted. Jennifer tore her gaze from the far side of the room, forced her vision back to normal. Lialla was bent forward over her knees, eyes closed in fierce concentration. Thread moved, vibrating the air all around them, and movement on the bed in the next room caught Jennifer's stunned eyes. She wrenched her gaze from the rope forming under their bags, slithering down from the bed frame, braced herself hard against the wall and reached for Thread. Lialla's hand clamped down on hers. Hard. "Make us a long piece," she muttered. "To get out with. I'll get *him*."

"Get your hands off me!" Robyn hissed. She flailed out wildly; the wizard swore and grabbed for her. A little blood ran down his temple and ear where her nails had caught him. "You lay one hand on me and I'll—"

"What, yell for the cops? Don't like nice, is that it? Want it rough, huh, baby? All right, you got it—you and that skinny blond kid of yours both." Robyn let out a wordless squawk of fury and lunged for him, this time deliberately and with clear, murderous intent. The air shimmered between them and stopped her as though she'd run into the wall. Snake laughed nastily and beckoned with one hand; the other was dabbing his cut cheek. "Well, hey, tiger, come on! You want to stop me getting that kid of yours up here? Come on, let's see it." He deliberately turned his back on her, slowly started toward the door, brought up his fist to hit the thick wood. Robyn's scream rose, shifted to a much higher note. The wizard ignored her until Lialla's sudden, startled curse and Jennifer's frightened shout warned him.

Robyn's body shimmered, like fog or ink in water and for one terrified moment, Jennifer thought the wizard's spell had somehow taken her. Rope, wizard—everything was forgotten: Robyn seemed briefly to tower over them all, her body formed and reformed like a shadow under moving lights. Jennifer heard the distinctive *fwump* of large wings unfurling and felt air move through the room. The scream that filled the chamber was no longer human.

Vinnie Harris stood with his back against the door, staring open-mouthed; he brought his hands up to shield his eyes, dodged reflexively. Jennifer saw a flurry of dark wings, the outline in failing light of what might have been an eagle or a condor—if such birds grew to human size. Her vision blurred. She stuffed a finger between her teeth and bit down on it to keep from fainting; this was not the time or place for it. She heard vast wings; the hair lifted from her forehead in their wind. The sound she heard then she only later realized was a human neck snapping. She found herself staring down at the fallen wizard's body; his head was at an odd angle. He looked ineffective, rather pathetic—a child in costume, seeking to frighten grown-ups.

But that bird. Bird . . . "Robyn?" she whispered. "Birdy?" A cold, black eye fell on her; the creature that had been her sister furled its wings and was somehow on the sill, out the window. Jennifer turned to follow its progress, but lost it almost immediately in the gloom.

"Jen! Rope!" Lialla bellowed. The door slammed open, bounced off the wizard's body and nearly slammed shut again. Jennifer fell back against the opposite wall, finger still gripped tightly between her teeth, and somehow found the correct Thread once more. Rope: Thread and straw and cloth, and Thread and straw and cloth. She could feel it working; she couldn't see it. She didn't have to see it, so long as the braid came together smoothly. Three-part, over and in, over and in—she hadn't the mind left for anything more complex.

But she couldn't take her eyes off the three men standing just inside the doorway; the original guard stared down at the dead man, a second at Lialla, who at casual glance might have been ill or mad, hunched over her knees, muttering insanely and rocking back and forth. The third man forced his way past them and drew his sword. Lialla bared her teeth at him and abruptly sat up, hair a wild aureole around her face, partly over her eyes.

The man slowed uncertainly; Lialla sketched the tying of a knot in the air before her. She yanked; the rope which had slipped unnoticed across the shadowed floor wrapped around his ankles, hard. A second strand caught the man standing just behind him. The last was blinking dazedly as he bent over the body of his wizard-master. Jennifer threw herself across the small room, grabbed his arm, spun into him and pulled his feet out from under him with a yank of her leg. His head hit the stone wall with a nasty crack and he fell soddenly.

Lialla kept her distance from the first two men until they were tightly bound; she skirted them cautiously, knelt to check the other for pulse. She shrugged, reached behind her for rope. Jennifer giggled weakly, clapped a hand across her mouth to keep the sound inside. It did no good; after a moment she gave it up. There *was* no sense or sanity here: The rope end Lialla had plaited was following her across the floor like a pet four-strand snake. Jennifer looked toward the bedroom and giggled again; a long strand of rope, her own three-part braided rope, was slithering down off the bed and heading straight for her feet.

"That was a good wrestling trick, you must teach it to me," Lialla said flatly. Jennifer's laughter faded.

"It was dumb," she said. "Getting that close to him."

Lialla eyed her with a rising irritation; somehow, she kept her voice level. "No, it wasn't stupid; he was off-balance and not prepared. And it worked. Stop making that noise!" she added irritably.

Jennifer swallowed. The giggle was trapped just below her Adam's apple, threatening to resurface. "My sister just flew out the window!"

"Your sister just flew out the window," Lialla agreed evenly. "You want to be down there when she shifts back, don't you? You want out of here, don't you?" Jennifer found herself suddenly and appallingly unamused.

"Did I—is he dead?"

"Why would I waste rope and time on a dead man? No, of course you didn't kill him, not with such a kick, or such a blow to the head. A man like that has a skull harder than mere stone, wouldn't you suppose? But he won't come after us himself. Not tonight or tomorrow, either." Silence. "Can we go, Jen? Before—as Robyn would say—before someone else comes? Wait—have you got your bag? I'll throw the others, once you're down. Remember what Dahven said—remember to try to blur; can you manage all that?"

"I think I can. But—but Birdy—!"

"She'll find us, Jen! At least, if we get out of here alive, she'll stand a chance of finding us! Where's that rope of yours?" For answer, Jennifer felt around the bench for her shoulder bag, hoisted it high onto her arm, and crawled up onto the sill, one end of the rope in hand. She felt the movement as Lialla carried off the other end and tied it somewhere, tugged at it uncertainly.

She looked down cautiously. It had taken her weeks to get used to seventeen floors of sheer drop at her office. This, fortunately, wasn't anywhere near that high and there were no lights around them; in the growing dusk, it was impossible to see very far below her feet. There was no bird in sight—there was absolutely nothing to see, except, possibly, the darker shade that was the nearest of the groves of trees. Where Dahven—no. She absolutely would not think of Dahven.

She worked her feet determinedly over the edge of the deep window sill, caught hold of the rope in both hands and began to slide down it. It wasn't comfortable wrapped as it was across the back of her right ankle, but her sneakers held her firmly in place and that let her take some of the strain from her shoulders and forearms. "Lialla?" She tilted her head back and hissed into the darkened opening. "Lialla! What if someone comes?"

Lialla was leaning across the window ledge, staring down. She glanced over her shoulder toward the open door. "Hurry and they won't. Get down and wait for me. Remember how I told you to blur?" Jennifer nodded.

"I think so."

"Good. It's not perfect, but it might help. Speed will help more. I'll throw the other things down once you're below. Give a tug on the rope if it's safe, two if I should wait. I'll bring your sister's bag. *Go!*"

Jennifer slid most of the way; rope burning her palms and her calves. One of her feet cramped, eased only a little as she flexed it cautiously. Her forearms and her shoulders burned with the extreme overuse. "I'll pay for this one tomorrow," she whispered. Her feet fortunately touched ground a bare moment later. She listened to dead silence, then yanked gingerly on the rope, felt Lialla's answering tug, limped back against the wall and worked her cramped foot between two numbed and rope-burned hands until she could stand on it again.

Blur. For the first time, she felt unequal to the task; the Thread she needed was slippery and made no sound she could identify. And she could still see herself so clearly—how could she tell if it was working or not? Bags fell all around her, one with a muted clatter—the cooking pots must be in that one—how, possibly, could no one have heard it? And then the rope jerked madly back and forth, and Lialla was down, Robyn's enormous denim bag pulling down one thin shoulder. She shook blood back into her hands, grimaced as she stretched the muscles across her shoulders, and gathered up several of the fallen bundles. Jennifer grabbed up the rest. And then Jennifer waited, increasingly nervous, as Lialla walked several paces to either side and peered into the by now near complete darkness. She sensed rather than saw the woman's gloomy shrug.

"Doesn't matter, I suppose," she whispered. "There's two groves of trees close by; either could be right. I can't sense anyone in either, could you?" Jennifer shook her head. "May not have arrived yet. I think the one right in front of us is maybe closer. Trees are taller, anyway, that makes it a better choice; let's go." She started off directly, confidently, across the open. Jennifer wasn't certain she could convince her shaking legs to carry her that way. She caught up with Lialla just as the other woman reached deeper shadow. Very chill shade confronted them. *Trees*, Jennifer realized. Lialla stopped, dropped her bags, and sat abruptly on the hard ground. Jennifer eased down cautiously beside her. Lialla put her head close, tugged on Jennifer's arm and whispered against her ear, "I hate to keep saying I don't know. I *really* don't know much about shapeshifting. Except your Robyn certainly did an impressive first shift, didn't she? She's extremely sensitive to people in her present form."

"The size of her—she could be anywhere by now!"

"No. That is still Robyn; unless she's a lot stronger than she looks, she'll be ready to come down and roost if she hasn't already done so. You think descending that rope was hard—imagine pulling yourself through the air with those wings! But she will want you, Jen, I'd wager on it, she'll want someone familiar and close to her. Knowing that—she'll find you."

"She'll—how does she shift back?" Jennifer's voice cracked; she clapped a hand over her mouth, let her eyelids close. She was suddenly so terribly tired.

"They do. They always do." Lialla sounded so reassuring. For a moment, it eased the inner tension. But a breath later, Jennifer was doing her best not to remember how little Lialla actually knew about the real world—and about her own magic, let alone any other variety.

16

※

WHAT could she do? Jennifer wrapped her arms around her chest and paced back and forth until she sensed Lialla's dark eyes on her; sensed Lialla's tension. And became aware of the silence all around them. If there were men anywhere around them—men watching the Thukar's palace, waiting for the least movement where no movement should be . . .

But Lialla was using Thread now, taking over from Jennifer, blurring not the entire grove but the area nearest them. Now that she was not responsible for manipulating that Thread, she could see how it was being moved, how it worked. For the moment, unless a very powerful magician was searching for a Wielder or for them, personally, they would be safe. They'd certainly be safe from accidental discovery by any of the Thukar's house-holdmen.

She looked up, all around her, finally moved across the darkened glade and stopped just short of an immense tree. Its bark was rough, thick like that of a fir; it wasn't fir. *That for Chris,* she thought dryly. How would he fit this into his latest scenario for where and when they were, in relation to their own world? She settled her back against the bark, eased herself down until she was squatting on the ground, and prepared to wait for Robyn.

How to tell?

She knew so little! In truth, nothing. Even though there were books—intentional fiction and the other kind, books written in supposed sober truth or at least sober belief about worlds no one could have visited—books that told about such shifts in body shape and kind. Jennifer had read so few of them, and even now she couldn't believe there was the least amount of truth to any of them. There *was* no Atlantis, no Mu, no hollow earth, no ancient aliens come to teach feebleminded cavemen how to become human! How would people who made up such wild fantasies have any clue to a *real* shift of human shape? But there was a tale, something Robyn had read her once, long ago: a Celtic tale wonderfully retold—a boy killed and fed to pigs, his soul transmuted into a vast hunting bird. And the brother or the father, she couldn't recall which, who'd sung him back into his human body. She let her head fall back, hair catching in coarse bark, and began to sing.

Lialla cast her one horrified look, then turned away and began desperately weaving Thread around them, blurring as heavily as she could—or dared. If another magician sensed the spell, if Dahven could not find them because of it!

The song had very little melody—not to Lialla, who seldom found pleasure in music. But the words caught at her heart, foreign though they were. And Jennifer, she realized with knee-weakening relief, could sing quietly and could pitch her voice the direction she wished it to go: 'O, Mio Babbino Caro'' scarcely reached Lialla's ears but it rose straight up the tall trunk behind her, seeking the sky beyond.

And it found what it sought.

An enormous black-winged bird paused in its slow, awkward flight, tilted its head consideringly, circled the grove. There was water down there—there was something else. Something—there was protection down there. With what might have been a sigh of relief, the bird brought vast wings in partway and began to descend. Some distance above the singer, it found a branch and folded the wings, sat listening. Singer—something of that voice, something that said warmth, safety. The bird came down a few feet, a few more, head turned aside to catch the least sound, the faintest nuance of that disturbing voice. By the time Jennifer had finished, the bird was balanced on a narrow, broken end of long-dead branch not far above her head. Jennifer looked up at her without blinking.

''Robyn? Robyn, come down, I need you,'' she said quietly.

Can't, the bird thought in sudden panic, but she had already partly furled the great wings, and somehow they were changing, shifting, feathers fading . . . and then she knew, the remainder of the shift went as *she* decreed it. She fell forward onto trembling hands and knees that would no longer hold her upright, felt Jennifer's strong, young hands on her arms and then around her shoulders, heard Jennifer's voice murmuring simple, reassuring nothings against her ear. For several minutes she buried her face in Jennifer's shoulder and let the past hour wash over her, and shook uncontrollably.

"Shhh, Birdy, it's all right, don't worry about it." Jennifer smoothed her wildly ruffled hair. "We're out of there, it's all right."

"Vinnie's dead," Robyn whispered. She *saw* his death with two sets of eyes; somehow, that knowledge brought her an unexpected calm. She pulled a little away from Jennifer's protective embrace and looked at her sister. "He's dead, and I killed him." And as Jennifer hesitated, then began to shake her head: "Don't! I remember—oh, God, I couldn't ever forget that!" Jennifer looked at her helplessly, shook her head again. "I thought—when they turn into werewolves in the movies, they don't remember."

"I know. It's different, Birdy. Don't worry about it, it isn't your fault."

"Don't," Robyn said quietly, and for the first time in this particular world, she felt calm, somehow in control. Perhaps because the worst had happened—or at least one kind of worst: A woman who had sworn all her grown life to prevent death—human or animal—had sought another human's death. Worse still: She wasn't sorry. "I killed him," she said.

"Yes. You broke his neck," Jennifer agreed soberly. "He never felt a thing. But if you hadn't done that, Birdy, I hate to think what he'd have done."

"I know. But don't, Jen, it's all right. I'm not sorry, truly. He—what he would have done to Chris. Or to me. To anyone, a woman out of that market, sold to him for a handful of coin. He deserved it." Silence. Jennifer pulled herself together with an effort, patted Robyn's arm. "What was that you were singing? It sounded familiar, kind of."

"No, it didn't," Jennifer said with an embarrassed grin. "It's opera. Puccini." With lyrics that translate roughly, as "If I can't marry that young man, I'll simply *die*." God. Her subconscious was having a great time with her. Sensible women in the real world, sensible women nearing thirty, didn't act like that! "Birdy, you never listen to opera."

"Hah," Robyn grinned weakly in reply. "They used that on TV for a champagne commercial, I *knew* it was familiar. Lovely melody. Oh, God," she added in sudden despair, "I'd kill for a drink!"

"Nothing here but pond water," Jennifer said mildly. "Let's get you on your feet, shall we? And truly, I'm sorry this hap-

pened, Birdy; I'm only glad you're taking it so well. If you want
to talk, you'll tell me, won't you? Promise you will.''

"I promise.''

"Not around Aletto, though,'' Lialla said quietly; there was
an urgency in her low voice. Robyn shook her head; Jennifer
looked up at her uncertainly. "I told you how he feels about
magic. This—he *mustn't* know this happened. There aren't any
witnesses but us; he won't find out otherwise.''

Robyn nodded. "I know, he's said. How he feels about—
shapeshifters.'' Robyn felt her voice come from a vast distance;
her vision was suddenly tunneling at an alarming speed. "I don't
feel very well,'' she added faintly. She was barely aware of
Jennifer's arms around her, Lialla's worried exclamation. The
little light around them faded and she went limp in Jennifer's
grasp.

She could only have been unconscious for moments; the light
from various windows and from the city beyond the Thukar's
palace hadn't changed; the grove itself was still extremely dark,
only a little light from overhead stars and the reflection of city
light on a few clouds reaching them. Jennifer's damp fingers
lingered on her throat; Robyn pushed them away. "Don't—that's
cold,'' she whispered.

"You're awake, good.'' Lialla's voice. "I haven't seen any
sign of the boys, and we can't stay here long; even if the Thukar
wasn't likely to want us tonight, someone might miss Snake. I
must have misread Dahven's sign. It doesn't matter; we're out,
that's the hard part.''

Robyn let her eyes close again briefly. She didn't really want
to sit up, ever again. Aletto—he'd find out; he'd change from a
friendly—if shy and young for his years—man to a slit-eyed
stranger. The thought was terribly depressing. But mention of
Snake reminded her of Chris; thought of Chris was enough to
get her moving. Lialla handed over her shoulder bag, two small
bags of food, and the container of cooking pots. Robyn arranged
the too-thin straps so they wouldn't cut her shoulders. The three
women crept across the glade, stopped just short of the sound
of falling water.

It was another of the walls of water: This one was no taller
than Jennifer's shoulder, and water slid in a thin sheet down its
tilted surface to fall into a circular pool. As they came up, she
heard a large fish splashing in deep water some distance away.
She held up a hand for silence, gripped Robyn's arm when the
latter tried to speak, shook her head.

"It's Father's favorite pool." Dahven's voice sent a chill down her back and threatened to weaken her knees. She hadn't sensed him; his presence neither surprised nor alarmed her, somehow. "He had fish brought from Podhru years ago, tiny things; I remember they were scarce the size of my thumb, all gold and black and white." He materialized from the darkness, took Jennifer's fingers from Robyn's arm and transferred them to his own; she could feel his heart beating rapidly through thick cloth. "They're quite large now. Perhaps some day you can come and see them in daylight." He turned as Chris caught Robyn's shoulders and hugged her fiercely, as Aletto took hold of his sister.

"Li—you're all right?"

"We're fine now, thanks to you," Lialla whispered. Jennifer opened her mouth to protest—all that work with rope, everything else they had done themselves! Lialla's warning look in her direction kept her silent. "Let's go, before they become aware of us."

For answer, Aletto led her around the edge of the pool. "Dahven? Can we?"

"Waiting on you only," Dahven murmured cheerfully. He pulled something that glittered red from a pocket, held it up and turned slowly from side to side. "All clear, at least in our direction. You and Chris go ahead, we'll bring up the rear." Aletto was already gone, a faint shadow against the outermost trees, Lialla's hand clenched tightly in his. A count of five later, Chris, arm around his mother's shoulder and most of her bundles making him a lumpy, top-heavy looking shadow, followed. Dahven counted down on his fingers, held up a closed fist and turned a carefully expressionless countenance in Jennifer's direction. "Blurring-stone." He held it out so she could touch it. "I know very little about Thread, and anyway, it seemed prudent for us to bring our own safety with us." He laughed quietly as he stowed it away. "Besides, I like magic—particularly this kind; one buys it and uses it, and there's no other effort to it." Jennifer couldn't think of anything to say; she nodded. Dahven led her after the others. "Chris says you don't care for enclosed places. Can you bear them?"

Jennifer laughed breathily. Dahven's presence was bubbling her blood like champagne; she was keenly aware of the warm touch of his fingers through the Wielder blacks. She was glad he couldn't read the thought behind her eyes. "After tonight, there isn't much I couldn't bear! Lead me to it."

Dahven laughed quietly in turn and touched her hair. "There's my lady,'' he whispered, and with one hand on her wrist to guide her, he started out, skirting the pool and going back the other way through the Thukar's favorite glade.

There was a young man—tall and angular in an ill-fitting dark robe that was too short in the sleeves—waiting where the trees ended. Waiting, Jennifer realized with a breath-stopping pang, next to an opening half-hidden behind a thick wall of scented, flowering vine, hand on an enormous slab of carefully balanced stone. It led down into darkness. She stifled a sneeze, fought another, braced a finger hard under her septum until the thick odor was behind them. A flight of broken stairs lit by one of those odd blue lights Lialla had used their first night—she swallowed dread and picked her way down. At the bottom, Dahven pulled her to a halt and waited himself, listening. Silence. And then a deep, hollow thump; the ground under her feet vibrated briefly. And the young man caught up with them, blue light balanced on one open palm.

He glanced up; Dahven's eyes followed his. ''Closed the entry. Not for good, of course; it's too useful.''

''Well, of course,'' Dahven said mildly. ''Edrith, this is a kinswoman of Chris, the Lady Jennifer.'' He managed her name with a soft ''J,'' and the last syllable definitely rhymed with ''air''—almost Frenchified.

''Go on, I'll bring up the end,'' Edrith said. Dahven took Jennifer's hand in his and turned her away from the stairs.

The others were already out of sight. Jennifer swallowed hard and began walking. She wouldn't think about the stone that now covered the way they had come down. She wouldn't let herself think about the size of the tunnel she could barely see stretching before them. The passageway was narrow, barely wide enough for two if they walked very close; the ceiling was a full foot over her head but still too low, and the floor was unpaved, damp-smelling and littered with fallen stone and loose dirt. Somewhere she heard a constant, slow drip of water. *Robyn*, she told herself firmly. Robyn needed her; Chris did. Her fingers tightened instinctively on Dahven's; his held hers reassuringly. Just before the tunnel became oppressive beyond bearing, it started to slope upward. It was enough. She drew a deep, easy breath when the steps appeared, leading up into darkness. Edrith went ahead here, Jennifer following, Dahven a warm, reassuring presence at her back. And then she was scrambling over flat slabs of tilted stone and mounds of loose rubble, into fresh, warm night air. There were lights before them, sooty night behind, a

few stars overhead. Someone pulled her back against a low wall.
Edrith's voice was a hissing collection of sibilants against her
ear and nothing else at first. "New outer walls here," she finally
understood. "Behind us. Old walls over there—" A hand pointed
at the rubble they'd just left. "Civic improvement," Edrith
grinned.

"Go." Dahven was on her other side; his single word and
gesture for Edrith. He turned to Jennifer as their companion
vanished with only the faintest click of overturned stone to mark
his passage. "Ready?" She nodded. The tunnel had taken almost all her reserves of strength and nerve. Thoughts of Robyn,
Chris—they were confused, muddled thoughts; nothing at the
moment was real except the warm, long-fingered hand that lay
across her fingers. "There's a place to hide for a while, it's rough
but safe. I'll get you there." She nodded again, let him take her
arm, and followed blindly where he led.

SHE vaguely expected an alarm of some kind; it never came
while they were in the open, not until the Thukar sent for his
pet outlander magician at sunrise and discovered his bed undis-
turbed, his laboratory and plant rooms empty, three of his
personal guard missing.

She followed Dahven through parts of the market she recognized, more of them she didn't, some she would have sworn
she'd seen at least twice since they escaped the Thukar's walls.
She saw the backs of buildings, the insides of buildings—
wrinkled her nose at curious and downright horrid odors. Her
legs ached and were beginning to tremble, one of her high-tops
was rubbing against an irritated tendon; shoulder muscles and
mid-back muscles ached steadily from that rapid rope descent.
And her stomach ached from lack of food. All at once, there
was a particularly dark and dusty area, two- and three-story
buildings that leaned alarmingly toward each other over a narrow, muddy street; a pile of rubble where one had fallen in on
itself. Somehow, Dahven had her on her knees, was guiding her
under thick wooden beams, past piles of brick and over shifting
mounds of junk. There was the least light before her; then suddenly enough—two candle lanterns and two of the blue lights—
to make out everyone.

The tall young man and his companion—Chris reluctantly
turned his attention away from Robyn long enough to introduce
Jennifer, Lialla and Robyn to Edrith and Vey—had food and
water for them. Robyn ate a handful of dried fruit, took a bite

of bread and chewed exhaustedly, eyes closed. Chris hovered anxiously next to her, Aletto—once he was reassured Lialla was all right—at her other elbow. "Mom?"

"Chris?" Robyn dropped the chunk of tough bread to her lap and shook her head miserably. "Chris, I've had it. I need wine."

He shifted uneasily, looked across her bent head. "Mom, we're leaving tonight, I don't think—"

"I don't care," she whispered intensely. "I *need* wine! You don't know!"

"No." It was Aletto who answered from her other side. "I do, though." He gestured; Vey came over and squatted next to him. "Wine—do we have anything but that red?" Vey shrugged. "I'd appreciate it, greatly, if you could find a bottle for the lady, preferably one which isn't sweet." Chris looked at Robyn unhappily, cast Aletto a very hard look, and turned away. Aletto ignored him; Robyn was mumbling into her hands. "Lady? Robyn? I can't understand what you're saying."

"You'll think I'm awful," she said miserably.

Aletto touched her shoulder and when she looked up from under wet lashes, he smiled. "You're not awful," he said. "Some people can cope with anything. They have all the answers, or at least, the answers that satisfy them. The rest of us—" He shrugged. "The rest of us are still looking. I looked in enough winecups before I left Duke's Fort."

"It's no answer," Robyn whispered. "I know that." She shuddered, let her eyes close. "But tonight—"

"You don't need to find excuses," he said. "It's all right. Whatever you do, whatever you need."

"For tonight, anyway," Robyn whispered; this time, Aletto didn't hear her. Vey came back a short while later with an extremely tart, pale yellow wine. It was also extremely potent: Robyn washed down her bread and fruit and something similar to smoked halibut with two cups of the stuff and fell asleep in Aletto's arms moments later. Chris cast him one black look but his heart wasn't in it: Robyn had visibly relaxed with that first cupful. And the look on Aletto's face as he gazed down at her—how could he hate a guy who looked at his mother like that?

He turned back to Edrith and Vey, who were sitting and eating with him and playing some kind of complicated dicing game at the same time. "I think he likes her," he said. Edrith glanced over Chris's shoulder, watched Aletto measuringly for some moments. He nodded.

"You care for her a good deal yourself, don't you?"

Chris considered this in mild surprise. "She's my mother—"

"Everyone has a mother," Edrith said. "Vey—how much longer have we?"

"Third hour hasn't rung yet. We'll need to be gone by fourth, to meet Red Hawk Clan near the north gates."

"Good. Plenty of time." Edrith tossed dice, picked up several bits of stick he'd culled initially from the rubble around them, pulled several out and tossed the rest into the oval he'd inscribed on the ground between them. "Vey, it's going to be strange, not having you at my elbow."

The younger boy shrugged, tugged at one ear. His dark face showed red across the high cheekbones. "Edrith, I admire you, going with them. I would be useless outside Sikkre. It's all I know, all I'm good at."

"I know. I'll still miss you."

"Going with us?" Chris fastened on that. "Who says?"

"Aletto," Edrith said promptly. "And Gyrdan. I *have* been to Bez, I can find the Street of Weavers and get all of you out of sight before there is comment and gossip all up and down to the very wharves. Besides," he added. "I have a piece of information—written evidence against Jadek. Aletto knows; I told him earlier when you slept."

"What evidence?"

Edrith shrugged. "My mother owns a stand close by, in the old market; she sells fruit and—well, other things. She is Sikkreni by blood, but Zelharri because she was married to one of the old Duke's housemen. When Duke Amarni died, there was a good deal of upset, of course; hardly anyone noticed that my father vanished a few days after the funeral. My mother never knew what came of him; she was given a sum of coin—Father's pension—and came back here. By then, her own family was scattered but she had no use for them anyway; she used the money to buy her place in the market." Edrith sighed. "I see her seldom any more; she doesn't like me much because I remind her of Father and all she lost when he died. And she always has one man or another; *they* like me around even less."

"I spent the entire last summer at Jen's house, when Mom had one of her men living in," Chris said sympathetically, and reached out to grip Edrith's shoulder. "I've been lucky with Mom, but some of her men—"

"Yeah." Edrith gripped his fingers. "Anyway, I went by her stand this afternoon, when I was getting food. Told her I was going away, something to do with Zelharri and all the rumors about the nera-Duke. She gave me something Father had Duke Amarni's scribe write down for him. She's had it ever since—afraid to keep it, afraid to throw it out even though she'd never use it. She's probably regretting she gave it to me, now. It says he was not far from the Duke's side when the pool of Hell-Light opened up. He said the Duke's brother did it himself, that he forced the Duke's horse into it.''

Chris stared at him in a blank lack of comprehension, then rising excitement. ''But—then all Aletto needs to do is take that to the Emperor!'' Silence. ''Isn't it?''

''Proof.'' Aletto shrugged; Robyn murmured something in her sleep, shifted, and slid down in his arms a little. Aletto pushed damp strands of hair off her forehead. ''It was sworn to, of course. But Elar—Edrith's father, you know—and the scribe are both dead.''

''Insufficient evidence, then,'' Chris said flatly. ''Damn. All the same, it's something to know—isn't it?''

''I suppose,'' Aletto said. He was stroking Robyn's hair, gazing down at her thoughtfully. ''It doesn't change much. We still go to Bezjeriad, once we get free of the Thukar and his city. But now, Edrith goes with us, and we try to make better speed and cut less of a wide path as we go.'' He looked up at Chris; Chris merely nodded.

''Is it you, Chris?'' Robyn's whisper barely moved the air in front of her. Her forehead puckered; that was wrong. The scent, the shape of him . . . ''Aletto?'' His arm tightened briefly around her shoulders.

''It's all right, you're safe and there's still time. Sleep if you like.''

She shook her head faintly, pulled herself up into a more comfortable position and leaned her cheek against his chest. ''I'm not really sleepy just now. I think—we need to talk.''

''We?'' He liked the sound of that; his voice showed it, the smile he turned in her direction did. Robyn smiled back at him, rather helplessly.

''Aletto, I—you're a wonderful person. I'm just—I don't think I'm suitable—''

''I say you are,'' he interrupted her firmly.

''Aletto, you're a nobleman! Surely you can't just marry anyone you want.'' He shook his head reluctantly. ''Well then—Aletto, please, before you get past being able to think, I've been wed before—''

"That's no barrier—"

"I have a son—"

"It's always good to know a Duke's wife can bear heirs." His mouth quirked and despite herself, Robyn laughed.

"Silly! I'm—God, I'm thirty-eight, I must be ten years older than you!"

"That's right. But it's not so many, not compared to some."

"People will laugh at you!"

"They won't."

"They will! Look at me," she overrode him. "I smoke—I used to smoke," she said bitterly, "until I came here and ran out of tobacco. I'm going to ache for the stuff for*ever* until I get it out of my system, it's going to make me bitchy. I drink too much. I've never yet chosen a decent man, all the men I've had—there's another thing to consider—"

"Hush," he said, and laid a hand over her mouth. "I'm twenty-eight, and three years past my majority; my left leg doesn't work quite right nor half my face, and I've never dared speak to any woman not my mother, my sister or a servant because of my face—and all the rest. I drink too much. I may not be able to father children. My temper isn't stable, I'm arrogant and the next moment uncertain whether I have the right to breathe, even. There—is that match enough for you?" Silence. Robyn looked up at him, sighed, and reached up to take hold of the fingers he was using to stroke her hair.

"I don't know," she said simply. "I like you, Aletto. But it's not fair to you, and I can't trust myself."

"I'll worry about fair to me," he assured her. "I can trust you. I do, you must see that. But it's all right. And we have a long way to go to reach Duke's Fort. Don't worry, it will sort itself out."

Did she see him with doubled vision—her own and the bird's? She pushed that thought aside fiercely, tightened her grip on his hand. She wouldn't think about that, not until she must. She wouldn't think about Snake, about that tower, about throwing herself from the deep windowledge and sailing on black wings, out over a darkened courtyard. She blinked, looked up at him, and brought up a smile from somewhere. "It just might."

VEY had disappeared again. Jennifer sipped at a pottery cup of Robyn's tart white wine, nibbled the last of her bread to wash down the aftertaste. She looked up to find Dahven's dark, appraising eyes on her; felt color wash her face and throat. His own color was rather high, and he looked away at once. "I wish I could go the entire way with you," he said abruptly. "But it wouldn't be sensible, Father would make a fuss. I don't care for myself, you understand," he added with an engaging smile and one swift glance at her face. "But his tempers become worse all the time; I fear one of these days he'll fall down dead in the midst of one and I'll be stuck with Sikkre. I really don't want it yet. And he turns increasingly petty in his rages; they never do the city any good." He sighed. "Fortunately, no one ever expects me to be in my own bed at night. So I shall ride out with you."

"If you were caught . . ." Jennifer said hesitantly.

"I shouldn't worry about that," Dahven said. "At least, not in the sense you mean it." He shook his head. "I know twenty songs or more that describe such a thing, and yet, had anyone asked me if it were possible to see a woman's face, one particular woman's face of all the faces in the world—" He shrugged helplessly.

Jennifer laughed. "I know plenty of the same kinds of songs, and I'd have said it wasn't likely. Not for me, at least; I'm far too sensible."

"I'm much too practical," Dahven said and grinned impudently.

"It's not the word I've heard most used of you," Jennifer replied with a grin of her own; the off-balance feeling she'd had since her first full look at him moved somewhere into the background, still very much there and likely to catch her at odd moments but now hidden behind a much safer certainty that here was someone who could be a very good friend.

"Oh?" Dahven laughed. "You've spoken to Lialla," he accused.

"Among others. But you said songs. Do you—are you a musician?"

"Not the musician I would like to be; unfortunately, it takes time and care, and long hours with the a'lud, longer ones learning the words to songs. There are too many things competing for that time."

"A'lud?"

"I forget, you're outlander." He smoothed the dirt between them and drew something vaguely guitar-shaped, seven-stringed, then held his hands apart to measure a length something less than guitar, more than violin. Jennifer sighed.

"I had a—something like that. It's larger, played so, between the knees.'' She did her best to convey cello playing from a cross-legged posture on the floor. ''I miss it.''

''I'm sorry I don't have my a'lud with me tonight.'' He leaned over and touched her hand. ''There's nothing like you describe here, but there are other things, other instruments. I'd like to hear these songs.''

Jennifer smiled. ''Cultural exchange?'' she said.

''Everyone trades songs,'' Dahven said. He glanced around the untidy, ill-lit chamber thoughtfully. ''Once we're on our way tonight. I can borrow an a'lud, I daresay. From one of the Red Hawk.''

''You're certain it's safe to go—''

''Safer than letting you all leave without me,'' he said with certainty. ''None of you know which way you go once you've left the caravan. There's a route that winds through rough back country and into Bezjeriad from the north and west. Much safer for you than the Bez road. I can get you started in the right direction; that's surely worth some risk.'' Jennifer still looked so doubtful he smiled and took her near hand between both of his. ''Keep in mind also,'' he added soothingly, ''that I'm the Thukar's heir. Only Father has any right to beat me—and he never has, it's not his way.'' He brought her fingers up and looked at them, turned them over and kissed her thumb. ''It gives me several extra hours with you; don't you want them?''

Jennifer shook her head. ''If I said no, would you believe me?''

17

THERE had been a shift in the weather, a least breeze coming from the north and west that shifted again to north. The air was chill for the first time and Jennifer shivered inside the Wielder blacks. The line of Red Hawk carts and caravans was a variety of darker shadows in the dark hour before dawn. Here and there she heard muted voices, a clink of pans, now and again the squeal of some foul-tempered beast objecting to harness.

She wanted to object when Dahven draped his own cloak over her shoulders, but somehow didn't. He gripped her shoulder briefly, leaned over to speak against her ear. "I won't be long; one last talk with the Grandmother and the caravan master. I can't think why there's been no search anywhere yet."

"I wish you hadn't reminded me," Jennifer whispered back, but Dahven was already gone. Robyn came up beside her, Chris hovering nervously behind her.

"Reminded you of what?"

"Hmmm? Oh. Nothing, Birdy."

"Nothing, Birdy," Robyn said, but she showed no real inclination to argue. "Are we leaving soon?"

"I hope so." Jennifer looked at the east horizon—could she see anything there yet, the least shift in color? Robyn let Chris lead her back to the horses Vey had bargained for them, the small horse-drawn covered caravan that would carry them out of Sikkre and bear their goods until they left Red Hawk. Jennifer peered after them. Odd that Aletto would let Robyn out of sight *or* reach. She thought she saw him two carts down, arguing with Edrith. *If we could go, now—* She sighed and let the thought go; it sounded too much like a very frightened Robyn.

"Don't look so down." Dahven's whisper tickled her neck.

"I'm only coming with you partway, you know." She turned to smile at him; the smile widened as he held up his right hand and something jangled rather sweetly. "The old woman's a'lud; there's trust for you!"

Jennifer laughed quietly. "Trust—or the thing's so old it's beyond tuning."

"Well now, that had not occurred to me," Dahven admitted. He held it up close to his face and peered at it thoughtfully, then turned and held out an arm. "They're ready to go, any moment now. It only remains for the city guard to give them passage—"

"City guard—"

"Don't look so unnerved; it doesn't seem at all fitting to you. It's a mere formality, probably dating back to the days when they had to bribe the guard or submit to search in order to escape. Of course, the caravans—Red Hawk in particular—keep Father in gold to pay his magicians and fund their experiments, so it's in his best interests to indulge them."

"Don't," Jennifer replied, her light, bantering tone matching his, "sound so blasé; it doesn't fit *you*." Dahven laughed and let his hand slide down her forearm to take hold of her fingers.

"I hope you've thought," he warned her. "I fully expect to hear every one of those songs."

"You're under a matching obligation, remember." Jennifer clambered up the two steps that led into the back of the covered caravan—gypsy wagon, she decided as she looked approvingly at the interior. One blue light showed it to advantage: walls lined with stretched canvas, painted or stenciled in flowers and signs she could not decipher, pots and other oddments hanging from the corners. There was no window, only another hanging length of quilted canvas blocking the way to the front seat. She could hear Chris, Robyn and Edrith out there, Aletto off to one side—mounted, apparently. And then Lialla, somewhere to the other side. She was laughing at something Chris had said; it sounded very odd.

A creak of leather and wood, the sound of hooves and metal-bound wheels against stone. Their own cart started with a sharp jerk; Dahven, thrown off-balance, fell back into the wall, making the caravan sway. Robyn's voice came back through the curtain. "Sorry!"

"Both alive," Jennifer replied dryly. "Don't press your luck, though." Robyn giggled; Jennifer held out her hand and righted Dahven.

"Novice drivers," he said and rubbed his hip. "Fortunately the Grandmother's a'lud isn't damaged; she'd have my ears for that!"

"You'd look odd without them," Jennifer said gravely. Dahven laughed.

It was quiet for some time, save the various, continuous noises made by the carts as they moved slowly through deserted Sikkreni streets and into the open country north of the city. After a time, there was only the steady creak of unoiled wood and leather harness. An occasional, distant growl of thunder.

She felt twenty pounds lighter, as though someone had taken weights off her shoulders. "We escaped," Jennifer whispered. Dahven laughed quietly and nodded toward the front of the caravan. Beyond the quilted curtain, she could hear Robyn and Chris bantering, Edrith's occasional remark. Aletto's laugh. Even Lialla's. They sounded light-headed, every one of them. And little wonder.

"Another hour," Dahven said, "and we'll cross the Sikkreni border. Father knows better than to come after a Red Hawk caravan anyway, but he'd *never* bother one in Dro Pent lands—even if Jadek offered him an Emperor's ransom for you." He brought up the a'lud to his ear and began tuning it. Jennifer slid down off her perch on the narrow bed so she could watch his hands and hear what he was doing.

She'd seldom played a guitar; this looked similar but enough different that it would probably confuse anyone who *had* played guitar. And Dahven, despite his earlier disclaimers, was an excellent player. His singing voice was thin and flatted a little in the mid-range, but it was pleasant enough, particularly for the rather sweet love songs he sang to her.

He broke off, partway through one. "I feel quite foolish, singing these things to you," he said.

Jennifer drew her knees up to her chin and shook her head. "Why?"

He bent his head over the strings, began fiddling with a complex picking pattern. "Because—oh, I think of the last time I played this one, in particular—"

"Dahven." Jennifer leaned forward to touch his hand. He glanced up at her, colored oddly and went back to a study of his picking hand. "Dahven, I'm twenty-eight years old. I'm not the kind of young girl who expects a boy in virginal whites to match her own." Silence, except for a burst of laughter outside and the faint sound of a'lud within. She set her fingers under his chin and raised it. "Please. Whatever this thing is—it doesn't need to make us totally foolish, does it?"

"Well—" He tilted his head to one side and grinned. "You make me feel very foolish at this moment. You're right, though. I'm not the boy in that last song—"

"I'm not the girl," Jennifer finished for him, and added, "Thank God." She held out a hand. "Here, let me see that instrument. I may not get another chance to touch one for some time to come."

It wasn't easy; she finally sorted out three basic chords with Dahven's help and sang him the few Child and folk ballads she knew that utilized only three chords.

"Curious language," he said finally. "I almost begin to think I understand it, or a word here and there, and then I'm no longer certain. You'd better stop, though; your fingers will hurt if you don't."

"I know." They already did hurt; she shook them out, used Thread to staunch one small broken and bleeding blister on her index finger. "Let's see if they want a change of driver out there; I'm falling asleep and I'd like to see the countryside."

"There isn't much to see just yet," Dahven said. But he set the a'lud carefully aside and held the curtain for her.

Robyn moved into the back to rest; Lialla went with her and handed the horse over to Chris, who went around the back of the caravan and came up on Aletto's other side. The two moved off a short distance and for some moments Jennifer could hear them talking—inevitably—about local history, language, the odd time shift Snake had mentioned and his mother had passed on.

Jennifer huddled down in Dahven's cape and folded her hands up snugly under her armpits, letting Dahven take the reins. "I don't know the first thing about this; I'll watch."

"Sensible woman," he said. He held the leather straps easily, in one hand. "Though admittedly, in the middle of a string like this, there isn't much to do. The beasts are all very well trained, and it's unheard of for anything to come and spook them. I did warn you," he added, "that there wasn't much to see."

"You warned me," Jennifer agreed. She could see the outlines of tall, scrubby poplar along one side of the dirt road, and beyond them, open land that might have been grain fields or pasture or simply desert. Here and there she saw narrow waterways—irrigation canals—and once they passed right by a flooded rice field. The air was suddenly quite cool and there were mosquitoes everywhere.

The change was subtle; there was little water, and then small, flat streams everywhere: The road dipped through wide, dry beds or crossed clattery wooden bridges over others.

The Red Hawk clan stopped for a short while just before the road began to climb toward foothills that flanked the Holmad River most of its way down to the sea. When they went on again, Jennifer and Dahven had taken horse, leaving the interior of the caravan to a deeply sleeping Robyn and Lialla. Aletto, Chris and Edrith sat on the driving seat now and joked back and forth.

"Tell me about yourself." Jennifer started; it was the first thing Dahven had said in what seemed hours.

"There isn't much to tell, really."

"How can you say that, coming from an entire other world? And such a world! When Snake first came—bless old Fiddkro for finding him, poor old idiot—I think he hoped to win my approval, perhaps thinking it would be useful in getting Father's eye. Poor stupid Lizard—but then, he didn't know. But when he first came, he told me such wonderful things."

"Well—" Jennifer considered this.

"Some quite odd ones too, of course. But they say outlanders are not all alike, and of course I can see *that* for myself now." He leaned over and touched her knee. "Tell me about yourself."

She did; told him about her office, her music.

"Then you also know about the special paper for writing down music."

"I—? Oh. Of course."

"I'd dearly like to learn how to do that," he said wistfully. "If things sort themselves out, after this night—" He looked at her sidelong, and his face was troubled. "If they do, I'll make you a bargain. An a'lud, and the teaching of my old music master, in exchange for which you will teach me how to write down music."

"It's a bargain," Jennifer said. She looked over his shoulder into heavy brush, back across the road to a shelving bank and scrubby, dry trees. "We haven't much longer, have we? And you haven't told me anything about yourself."

"I—"

"I can always ask Lialla," Jennifer added gravely. Dahven laughed.

"Don't, please! Poor lady, I wonder how well she slept when my father first sent messages to Jadek proposing to merge our

houses! But as to myself—what can I tell you? I'm Father's eldest, two years above Aletto but since Father still enjoys breath
if not true good health, I am still an heir, not a Thukar. My
beloved brothers you met at Father's table; they're a trifle short-
sighted, caring for little if it isn't a column of figures, or food
prepared and within reach—or one of Father's innumerable nasty
little schemes which he calls hard bargaining. It's certainly un-
fortunate for him that either Deehar or Dayher isn't eldest; they
might have sprung three seeds from the same pod. However!

"I have all the usual education expected of a man of my class
and station—at least, as much of it as they could force into me.
I frankly have no use for figures or the intricacies of geometry.
I learned the nomad language quite rapidly, and took well to
music and dance. I read passably, depending on what it is I read,
and absorbed almost nothing of the history they held me to—"

"Hold, please!" Jennifer was laughing. "I didn't ask for a
list of accomplishments, you know!"

"Oh." He considered this blankly, then rallied with an im-
pudent grin. "I am also considered very good at selling myself
to attractive women—"

"You're hopeless."

"I know." He sighed heavily, but the grin hadn't shifted. "Do
you know anything about the country you will be crossing?"

It was a change of subject; maybe, Jennifer thought, he didn't
want to open up to her. Again, maybe he simply didn't know
how. And that wild crash of feeling aside, they scarcely knew
each other. She let it go; they could talk another time. *Whenever
I see him again,* she thought and realized with a sudden pang
that it might be a very long time indeed. *Don't think,* she told
herself fiercely. "I don't know anything about the country around
here." She managed normal-sounding words through a very tight
throat. "Tell me."

SOMEWHERE around midnight, there was a longer stop. Edrith
broke out water, a small, leather-wrapped pottery bottle of
brandy, hard sausage and bread. As they finished eating, Jennifer
became aware of the two women standing just behind them.
Caravaner women, come to take the wagon. "Oh, no, not yet,"
she whispered. Robyn looked at her as though she hadn't quite
heard. Jennifer shook her head, turned away to catch the back
of her hand in her teeth, blinking hard. When she turned back,
Chris and Aletto were distributing bags on the pack horse's
back, Edrith was strapping riding pads on the last two riding

horses. Lialla was deep in conversation with an older woman under a blue-light lantern hanging from the caravan just in front of theirs. Robyn made a face at the smell of brandy, sipped a little water and went when Chris called her. Jennifer stood alone, still blinking by the front seat of the caravan; Dahven was suddenly at her side, peering at her uncertainly.

"It's all right," he said, and wrapped an arm around her shoulder. She leaned into him momentarily. Nodded once.

"I'm being foolish. I'm not like this, honestly."

"It's all right, I know. I'd far rather stay, but I think there would be more trouble for you if I did. The gadgets I carry and the magic you and Lialla use are no match for a Triad. Father has access to two of those, and I fear he'd use them. If I stayed, he might find you through me."

"I—you take care of yourself," she said finally, and pulled back to look at him. Dahven nodded once, abruptly, and brushed her hair with his lips.

"I'm quite good at that, you know," he said mildly. "But you—"

"Oh, I'm a survivor," Jennifer said. "If nothing else, I intend to reach Duke's Fort so I can murder Merrida for bringing us here and ruining my life—you know," she added thoughtfully, "maybe I won't, after all."

"Keep the thought," Dahven grinned. "It's good to have something to look forward to." He reached back behind his neck, fumbled under the collar of his outer shirt, finally pulled a slender chain over his head and held it out. "I got this a while back, just because I liked the look of it. But it's also a charm; a small one. It's said to bring fortune to the wearer."

"I can't—"

"Please." He somehow had it over her head, settled around her throat before she could push it away. "Think how much better I'll sleep."

She laughed shakily, held up the pendant. It was lost wax formed, silver by the look and feel of it—a sign made of crossed lines and a spiral. There was a small unfaceted stone set in the center of the spiral; she couldn't tell what. "Think how awful I'll feel if you don't have it and something happens to you," she said.

"Something," Dahven scoffed gently. "I'm the Thukar's eldest son and his heir; things don't happen to a collection of titles like that."

"Pray you're right," she said somberly. He gazed at her fo

a long moment, then bent down and kissed the fingers holding
the pendant.

"I'd best go," he said decisively. But it took him a visible
effort to take his eyes away from hers, to let go her fingers. He
turned, walked away with a firm step and did not look back.

By first light, the six riders and their spare horse were miles
from the caravaner's road, back in the hills up a trail that ran
through a series of draws and out onto a high, crumbling ledge.
Edrith and Chris argued over the map here while the others
rested; finally they turned the horses right. It was another hour
before they reached the base of a massive oval bluff, almost an
hour after that until they came up the last steep portion of rain
gully and onto the windswept, flat and nearly treeless surface.
The sun was above the horizon, now; the air warm.

Edrith, Chris and Aletto found heavy brush and a fallen tree
to secure the horses—they were carrying on like a pack of goofy
teenage boys, all three of them. Robyn sighed, stretched and
began foraging through the food bags—Chris would be hungry,
even if no one else was, though Edrith showed symptoms of the
same hollow leg. Lialla wandered around the plateau; her face
was drawn and wan and she seemed to be avoiding them all.
Jennifer hesitated only briefly, then turned away. She'd raised
enough bruises on the poor woman's psyche; let Lialla come to
her if she wanted to talk.

The talisman was warm against her throat. She smiled, shook
her head in mild wonder at two grown fools acting like lovesick
adolescents, and walked back the way they'd come to shade her
eyes and look toward Sikkre. He'd be home by now—home, and
safely abed and asleep. She sighed happily and turned away.

The market was beginning to wake when Dahven rode through
the north gates. He left the horse at Gyrdan's smithy, left a
message with the man's apprentice for when he should come in,
and hurried across the market. It was later than he'd intended,
still not overly late. Not that it really mattered. He skirted the
main gates, worked his way across a low and seldom occupied
portion of wall—more decorative than anything else—passed the
great pond with its enormous fish, and slid from shadow to
shadow until he fought his way through strangling lengths of
vine to get into a long, deserted hallway. There was a new fall
of stone on the floor; the whole thing would be down around

their ears one day soon, he thought, and hurried toward the occupied end of the building.

He missed his charms, and wondered briefly if it had been necessary to give them *all* away last night.

The door to his room was ajar. One of the servants come early to wake him, he thought impatiently as he walked in. They should know better, after all these years.

He stood still, staring; his heart must have stopped momentarily, because he was horribly aware when it began pounding wildly. His mouth was dry; it hurt to swallow, but he managed a genuine smile, and his voice sounded almost normal. "Father! Isn't the hour a little early for you?" The Thukar was seated in his best chair, the contents of both his desk boxes strewn across the surface. His brothers sat side by side on his bed and he realized with a sinking feeling that they were both smiling. This could not possibly bode well. Not for him, at least.

But there was someone else, too. As his eyes adjusted to the light pouring through open shutters, he made out the three men standing behind his father.

The Thukar pushed heavily to his feet and gestured; the men came forward and took hold of Dahven's arms. He fought them, automatically and uselessly; they were half again his size. Massive, callused hands dug into muscle until he forced himself to stand still. "Lasanachi," he whispered. One of his brothers giggled; he'd spoken aloud. "Father, you can't do this—"

The Thukar looked at him coldly. "I can do whatever I choose. It's a pity you've never bothered to understand that." He stood, arms folded across his chest, watching; a third Lasanachi seaman came forward with black metal leg-clamps and thick rope.

"You can't do this, Father! I'm your heir!"

One of the twins giggled again. "You were. It's a pity, isn't it, Deehar? Our elder brother was always a little thoughtless, and now he's simply vanished. Rumor has him halfway to Dro Pent, with an outlander girl, a caravaner's earring and purple slippers on his feet."

The Lasanachi bound his wrists behind him, brought the rope around his chest and put a loop in the free end; another knelt and dragged the boots and cloth wraps from his feet, fastened the manacles around his ankles. Cold chain lay in a short loop between them. Somehow he stayed on his feet, held onto what was left of his dignity. Somehow managed to force air into an agonizingly tight chest, out again. Pray Jennifer never knows of this, he thought miserably. But he didn't dare think of Jennifer.

One of the Lasanachi turned away from him and groped at his belt; he held out a small, clinking coin bag, which the Thukar took. Dahven felt heat in his face as he watched himself bought and sold, and he looked away from them all.

"You'll regret this," he said finally. The voice no longer sounded like his.

"I greatly doubt it," the Thukar said. "Consider that you brought it about yourself, meddling in my affairs when you had no right."

"Sikkre *is* my right, Father."

"No more. The heir is gone, rumor says to Dro Pent."

"In purple shoes. I heard," Dahven said sarcastically. He stumbled as one of the seamen yanked on the rope, pulling him off-balance; he twisted and caught himself against the edge of the table.

"Such a dreadful thing," the Thukar said evenly. "He was captured by a Lasanachi ship off the coast of Dro Pent, and since he had no coin to redeem himself, he was sold into ship's service—for three years, I believe."

Dahven could think of nothing to say to this remarkably indifferent speech: Even a strong man in Lasanachi ship's service might never live half that long, unless his luck was phenomenal.

"Where did they go?" the Thukar demanded abruptly. "Tell me now, and I'll see they keep you a year only."

Dahven brought his chin up and gazed at the older man. There was a long, chill silence. He finally laughed. "I have such trust in you, Father, of course! Only a year, why, that is most generous. Shall I kiss your feet?"

"Buffoon!" the Thukar roared. "Tell me where they have gone, or you'll live to regret it!"

Dahven bared his teeth. "What regret can surpass having had such kindred as I once did? But tell me, will you search for Aletto personally? He's gone to hell, then!" He had one last, blurred glimpse of that familiarly suffused face; his father's open hand and a huge seaman's fist slammed into his jaw at the same moment. Everything was gone but Deehar's high, excited voice, a low growl of sea-slang high above him, the rattle of chain. And then, that, too, was gone.